I0724755

Premise of Innocence

The Innocence Trilogy

Proof of Innocence
Price of Innocence
Premise of Innocence

Other mystery by Patricia McLinn

Caught Dead in Wyoming series
Sign Off
Left Hanging
Shoot First
Last Ditch
Look Live
Back Story
Cold Open
Hot Roll
Reaction Shot
Body Brace
Cross Talk
Air Ready
Holiday Bullets
Cue Up

"While the mystery itself is twisty-turny and thoroughly engaging, it's the smart and witty writing that I loved the best."
—*Diane Chamberlain, New York Times bestselling author*

Secret Sleuth series

Death on the Diversion

Death on Torrid Avenue

Death on Beguiling Way

Death on Covert Circle

Death on Shady Bridge

Death on Carrion Lane

Death on ZigZag Trail

Death on Puzzle Place

"Great series. McLinn's Secret Sleuth series has the same winning components of her Caught Dead in Wyoming series: a likable central character, well developed setting, fun supporting cast, and a great story. McLinn writes intelligent cozies that are a level (or two) above the typical offerings for the genre." —*5-star review*

PREMISE OF INNOCENCE

Book 3, The Innocence Trilogy

Patricia McLinn

Copyright © 2022 by Patricia McLinn
Paperback ISBN: 978-1-944126-89-6
Ebook ISBN: 978-1-944126-88-9
Print Edition
www.PatriciaMcLinn.com

All rights reserved. No part of this book may be reproduced in any form or by any electronic or mechanical means, including information storage and retrieval systems, without permission in writing from the publisher, except by a reviewer, who may quote brief passages in a review.

Cover design: Art by Karri

PROLOGUE

OVER. IT WAS over.

The case finished. The news conference finished, the questions asked and answered.

Yes, a half dozen people with cameras walked backward in front of them, snapping and videoing, as her family crossed the plaza, leaving the Fairlington County, Virginia, Courthouse. But this counted as barely a trickle compared to the height of the attention.

In a while even this interest would wane. It always did. No matter how notorious. No matter how intriguing. No matter how dramatic. Wasn't she the proof of that?

Ally Lindell Northcutt allowed herself a small smile. Something she never did in public.

It was all over.

She tightened her hold where she had her left arm hooked through Jamie's right, as Maggie did on the other side with J.D. Carson. Jamie's parents and their family lawyer were behind them.

By rights Ford Belichek should have been with Jamie.

But *by rights* wouldn't preserve his career. Jamie had been adamant about that.

Ally watched her sweet cousin overrule the detective and make it stick. Though she suspected the dozen officers split to either side of them well out of camera range had been Bel's doing.

She and her two cousins paused in the May sunshine, just an instant, getting their rhythm for the three steps down to sidewalk level so they wouldn't jostle each other in their locked-arm hold. Before that next step forward—

Sound.

A single sharp burst.

It swallowed the hearing in her right ear. Reverberated distantly in her left.

Before she could absorb that, she felt her hold on Jamie being torn away. She turned that way. Saw J.D. encompassing Maggie and Jamie in a flying tackle, his body between them and the street. From the corner of her eye, she saw Jamie's parents huddle together, dropping low, even as they reached toward the three cousins.

They'd be okay.

With that thought, she released her hold on Jamie.

The same instant, she felt herself being brought down. Half turned toward her cousins, she couldn't see by what.

"East. Shot came from the east."

Somehow, she knew that was roared near her right ear by whoever had taken her to the ground, yet it came muffled to her.

"Are you hit? Ally. Are you hit?"

"No. I'm fine. Everyone else—?"

"She's not hit. Anybody hit?" the same voice demanded.

From a great distance, she heard what sounded like Maggie, then Jamie's father.

"Everyone's okay. Stay down." She'd started to try to rise, but felt herself firmly shoved down.

Then the covering body lifted before a new one draped over her.

How did she know it was a different body? She hadn't seen—

"Stay there. All of you. Don't move. Got them, Bel?"

"Got them."

Jamie's Detective Belichek was here. He gave orders equally muffled.

The officers who'd been along the sides, now stood between them and the street. They hustled the family backward to the courthouse doors, and inside.

They hugged each other and surreptitiously—or not so surreptitiously—checked for injuries.

Jamie's dad said to the lawyer, "Thank you for protecting Ally. We couldn't reach her."

"It wasn't—" Ally bit off her correction.

Smell.

She *knew* that first protector. And knew it wasn't the lawyer.

But—

"That wasn't me." Behind her, the lawyer spoke at a speed powered by fear and adrenaline. "The guy came from the police line. Wasn't in uniform. He—There he is. That guy."

Ally turned, first glimpsing a pair of trousers marred by ground-in grit at the knee, a streak of something on the thigh. The streak continued up the front of a suit jacket to…

"Tanner."

That first protector's smell. She *did* know it.

Had known it.

But her brain rebelled at her senses. It wasn't possible…

"Tanner Landis?"

—DAY 1—

TUESDAY

CHAPTER ONE

DETECTIVE TANNER LANDIS didn't blame her for vocalizing her shock.

She hadn't seen him in something like a decade. He'd made sure of that, though he'd seen her, even before today.

Maybe he shouldn't have—The hell with that.

He wasn't going to stand around with someone shooting at Allison Lindell Northcutt. At anyone. That was his job.

After the question she'd made of his name, Ally didn't say more.

Landis hoped for maybe thirty seconds that amid the chaos and stress her using his name was missed.

Thirty seconds of delusion.

Absolute minimum, four people picked it up.

His partner, Ford Belichek, plus Ally's cousins Jamie Chancellor and Maggie Frye, and Maggie's significant other, J.D. Carson.

Any one of them would have been a major headache. Taken together, they were a nightmare.

Then throw in his boss, Chief of Detectives Wilson Palery, who'd taken charge in the lobby. Because Landis was seventy percent sure he'd picked it up, too.

"Landis. Get with Belichek. Stay on the family. Keep them from talking to each other until we can question them. Take somebody to help."

Seventy percent went to one hundred percent. Otherwise, Palery would have split them.

He thought Landis had a connection and also would pick up inside info. But, while Belichek might keep it to himself because he was head over heels for Jamie, Landis would spill.

The case first. Always.

This situation, though, lined up like the opposite of inside info. Allison Lindell Northcutt wasn't about to confide in him, no matter what.

"Yes, sir."

His boss had already moved on to the next task. Palery was on the scene because today's hearing wrapped up one of the county's biggest cases, one of the most attention-grabbing in the Washington, D.C., metro area. He'd been with the Commonwealth's Attorney, talking to the media when the shots were fired.

That was a piece of luck.

Most of the media gathered in one place let the police corral them on the spot, temporarily.

"Schmidt," Landis said, both naming his choice of *someone* to Palery and calling over the young patrol officer. He'd done well on the investigation into who'd tried to kill Jamie, the case just wrapped up with a plea deal that would keep that nutjob in prison for the rest of his life.

Bel preferred a sentence of drawing and quartering, but Jamie worked her magic on him, persuading him this was a better way to move on with their lives.

"Sir?" the uniform asked.

"Find us an empty courtroom with deputies still on duty to man the doors."

"Sir."

"Landis," Maggie started. "What the hell? You and Ally—?"

"Mags, you know the drill." He raised his voice slightly to take in Jamie's parents and the lawyer. "No talking. No questions. No answers. Not until each of you has been questioned individually. We don't want anyone's evidence influenced by anyone else." Schmidt gestured from a courtroom door, third down the hallway. Good. Not too near the entrance. Just in case.

"If you'll all come this way."

✧ ✧ ✧ ✧

JUST INSIDE THE doorway of the courtroom, Maggie Frye took her cousin's arm in a firm grip and addressed her, while watching Landis, "You know him?"

Maggie was his favorite Assistant Commonwealth's Attorney to work with. He considered her a friend. Right now, he wished she'd shut up.

Ally's face went blank.

But he'd been preparing for this since Ally said his name. Maybe longer.

From when he'd brought her down to the ground and covered her body with his.

"Sure, she knows me." He grinned. He knew how to produce the right grin. It had gotten him in places and out of situations. "How could she help it with Bel and me so wrapped up with the Maggie Frye family tree these past months?"

Maggie immediately shook her head.

That was bad enough. But he didn't get help from anyone else, either. Including his partner.

Instead, Ford Belichek leveled a look at him, then swung his attention to Ally with a check-in on Jamie on the way. None of that was a good thing considering Bel not only was one hell of a detective but knew him better than was always comfortable. Or, in this case, safe.

Good thing Ally had withdrawn. Like trying to get a read on a turtle after its head disappeared inside the shell.

Wouldn't stop Bel's questions, but would hold the answers at bay for a while.

Ally licked her lips.

The motion drew his gaze immediately. Thank God, he wasn't the only one. They all turned toward her.

"The academy." That's all she said.

They put it together.

"Tanner was at the police academy with Chad?" Jamie asked. "I never knew that."

She made it sound so innocent.

Maggie wasn't having it.

"*You* never knew it? *I* didn't know it. Bel?" The other detective shook his head before Maggie turned her prosecuting attorney stare on Tanner. "Because you never told me—us. You *knew* Ally is my cousin and she's married to Chad Northcutt. You've known that practically as long as I've known you, including the day Chad was shot, and the hell we went through getting there, and you never said a word about knowing her—*them*. Not a word."

Even Bel, who'd kept his own share of secrets from both Maggie and him, had the gall to look accusing.

But what he said was, "Palery said we shouldn't talk."

"It's not about what just happened," Maggie argued, which was her profession.

"Too early to know connections. Even tangential can muddy witnesses. Not talking's best."

Unsatisfied, Maggie still conceded by sitting next to Carson. Their hands touched, held, and Maggie's shoulders eased.

Jamie drew Ally to a first-row bench and clasped Ally's hands in both of hers, apparently trying to warm Ally's hands. Dana Chancellor sat beside her daughter, resting one hand on her arm without interfering with her connection to Ally. Wes Chancellor sat next, his arm across his wife's shoulders and his hand touching Jamie's closer shoulder.

The lawyer sat apart, his head down, his hands not steady.

Bel remained standing in the main aisle, between the others and the door.

Landis took a position in the side aisle, one hip hitched on the top corner of a bench back. He, too, would immediately see what came through the door, but without being in the direct line of sight of the others.

The greatest danger he faced would not come through that door.

It was already in the room.

He'd almost told Bel and Maggie of the connection the day four and a half years ago when news came of Chad Northcutt being shot in the head by an unknown assailant, in the driveway of the house where he and Ally lived.

Almost told Bel and Maggie, even though he'd only worked with them for a few months at that point.

The moment passed amid the rush of the immediate emergency. Fighting their way through heavy security to find out where Northcutt was taken, getting Maggie to her cousin's side, learning what they could as outsiders about what happened.

And his additional mission—desperately digging to find out if Ally was a suspect, without ever appearing to be concerned.

It was clear early that nobody thought she was the shooter.

A neighbor four houses down saw it happen. Saw a car with heavily tinted windows pull sedately into Chad Northcutt's next-door neighbor's drive, then, at the last second, scream across the Northcutts' front lawn to knock Northcutt down, giving the driver time to open his window and shoot twice to the head. The car then peeled out across the next yard's lawn, bumped over the curb and sped in the opposite direction from the witness.

Still, she'd gotten a partial plate, as well as a good description of the car.

They knew within an hour that a car matching the description and the partial plate had been reported stolen thirty minutes before the shooting, from an owner with a doctor's exception to have deeper tint than Maryland's standard.

It took five days to find the burnt skeletal remains of the car in an isolated spot behind a deserted warehouse that backed up to a forested area.

The forlorn hope of forensics came to nothing. The fire destroyed what might have been there. If that shooter left any evidence to start with.

That shooter.

Now there was another one.

Who'd taken aim at Ally Northcutt.

Twice.

His brain wanted to wrestle with the issue of the immediate shooter, even as his sense and experience told him lack of information made it futile.

He belonged out there, gathering that information. Damn, Palery.

The void of information about what just happened sent him back to the shooting four and a half years ago.

The delay provided by getting Maggie to the hospital to be with Ally was what he'd needed for his habit of keeping things to himself to reassert itself.

In the days that followed, the habit solidified to rock.

He never told Bel and, having not told Bel, there was no chance he'd tell anyone else.

Especially as it eventually became clear Chad Northcutt wasn't likely to die immediately. There was even a rumor he might wake up at any time.

But now, with someone shooting at Ally…

He stopped, considering that thought.

How sure was he of his instinctual reaction that the shot was aimed at Ally?

He played through the events in his mind.

Then again.

Midway through the third time, Palery entered, making brief eye contact with Bel, then him, recognizing their positioning and telling them to stand down. He kept a hold on the knob of the open door as two other Fairlington detectives passed him to enter the room.

"Detectives Belichek and Landis, come with me," Palery said. "Detectives Terrington and Ewer will wait with the rest of you until you're questioned individually. We'll do this as expeditiously as we can," he said to the family and the lawyer, "but thoroughness is vital. This isn't going to be fast."

For a moment, Belichek studied Terrington, not the brightest color in the department's crayon box, then turned to Jamie. "Don't talk. Not to anyone. Understand?" He widened it to the rest of her family and Carson. "At all."

Satisfied by what he saw in the faces looking back at him, Bel pushed at Landis' shoulder to get him started out of the room.

Maggie and Carson would make sure none of the rest said anything Terrington could misinterpret, which he surely would. Yet Landis' gaze went to Ally.

Her gaze bounced away, as if she might have been looking at him. And didn't want to make visual contact.

✧ ✧ ✧ ✧

TANNER LANDIS.

Her brain couldn't get past those two words.

She frequently found silence the safest realm over these past years and with the reinforcement of Bel's instruction, she could remain there with impunity—for now—from the questions all of her family members wanted to ask and Maggie would.

What was *he* doing here?

She wanted to shake her head at the inanity of her mental question. She didn't, because that would raise even more questions among those watching her. They all were, she knew, even though she kept her gaze straight ahead and unfocused.

He was Bel's partner. That was clear from their few words and interactions, as well as those of Captain Palery. That made him a detective with the Fairlington County Police Department. On the Virginia side of the Potomac River now, when she'd known him in Maryland, when—

No, better not to stir the mud of memories into this water.

She needed her wits as clear and focused as possible.

Tanner Landis.

CHAPTER TWO

IN THE OUTER office of a judge's chambers Landis hadn't been in before, Palery took the command chair behind the desk. He told Bel to sit on the visitors' side of it.

"Go into the judge's chambers until I call you," he ordered Landis. "Close the door behind you."

In the bigger office, he found Detective Danolin putting items from the desktop into a drawer.

The veteran detective didn't look up to identify who'd come into the room, before saying, "Move that screen from that corner to over here, behind the desk." He meant a fabric-covered folding screen that came to Landis' shoulder. "Good. Now, turn that cushy desk chair around and put it in front of the TV. Okay. Now, I want the two wing chairs from the corner over here, angled at the desk."

When Landis finished, the portly Danolin sat in the wing chair closer to the door. After a moment, he got up, moved a trash can to deep under the desk, then adjusted the blinds. Within the packed office, he'd created a calm visual oasis for the person who sat in that wing chair. His own view, from the other wing chair, didn't matter, because he'd be focused solely on the witness.

"Recording them?" Landis asked.

Danolin grunted affirmatively.

A civilian aide came in with a tray. "One pitcher with ice, one without, a dozen glasses. Not easy to find."

"Not all the glasses at once. One glass at a time for each witness. Take the extras back out."

Another small touch to avoid distracting the witness' thoughts of others coming before or after.

Landis was willing to bet Danolin's soothing tactics got more from Jamie's mom than she'd ever given him during their previous investigation. She'd vehemently resented his viewing Jamie as a suspect.

She'd be eager to help clear this up, with her niece the target. Mr. Chancellor would be reasonable and reasoned.

Jamie Chancellor's observations would be accurate and helpful. Her conclusions, though, could be skewed by her too charitable interpretations. Though Bel balanced some of that.

From temperament and training, J.D. Carson would keep a lot to himself. What he did reveal would be accurate.

Maggie would be a great witness—observant, prioritizing what mattered most, and concise—when she wasn't fighting any attempt to relegate her strictly to the role of witness.

"Landis!" Palery's bellow came through from the outer office.

Bel was still there and showed no sign of moving, so he took another chair from against the wall and pulled it up next to Bel's.

His partner didn't react as Palery took Landis through the events.

There wasn't much to tell about today that Palery didn't already know.

"We stayed out of the courtroom for the formalities on the plea deal as Vic requested." That was Vic Upton, the Commonwealth's Attorney for Fairlington County and Maggie's boss. It had been more than a request. "Checked the security was set up as we'd agreed, then Bel went in the north wing and I went in the south wing. Watched the proceedings on the inhouse stream. When the family finished their short news conference and Upton took over, I checked that the security detail knew they were coming out.

"We'd agreed Bel would go along the north wing's corridor and I'd take the south, checking each room one last time as we went."

The corridors formed arms in front of the main block of the courthouse. Inside those arms sat a paved plaza, divided by a series of rectangular planting beds, big enough for trees. They divided the plaza into the main promenade in the center and narrow side pathways close to each arm. The planting areas were interrupted at regular intervals for cross-paths.

"When there was a shot, I ran toward the party, reached Mrs. Northcutt and covered her." He didn't stutter over her name. He'd been reminding himself what to call her. "The rest were taking cover."

"What direction?"

He didn't need to specify he meant which direction the shot came from.

"East. I'd say the Edisto Building across the street, next one north from directly across. Doubt the roof. But well above street level."

Firing at street level risked too many other things getting in the way. People, sure, but also cars, trucks, buses. Shooter would want to be high enough to avoid those obstacles.

Palery grunted.

Landis translated that as meaning Bel told him the same thing.

"How'd you get there so fast?" his boss asked abruptly.

Landis frowned, remembering. "I'd been staying even or a bit ahead of the Chancellor party, checking through the windows of offices with their doors open. One office was completely empty, no furniture, so it was faster. I pushed on ahead to where that emergency exit comes out. Disabled the alarm and opened the door to see where they were. They were ten, twelve feet short of being even with that door and nearly in the middle between the two wings. Saw Bel coming out the emergency exit on the other side. Just before the shot."

"Then what?" Palery demanded.

Seeing it all again, the backs of the security detail members, the family group with the three cousins linked in solidarity.

"First shot. Kicked up dirt. Pretty much tackled the lady. Second shot. Grabbed the closest person to stay on her—"

"The lawyer."

"Found that out after. As I went past, I yelled to the security detail to get them all out of there. I ran toward where the shot came from. As if I had a hope of seeing anything." His mouth twisted. "Realized that soon enough and circled back into the courthouse. Anything from forensics yet? Bullets? Trajectory?"

"Not even going to start until we clear those buildings. Probably long gone, but not risking having our people on the steps as sitting ducks. And clearing's going to take a long time with all the offices to go through across the street. How many shots?"

"A second one hit the concrete. In line with the planter, but in front of it—closer to the street."

"Yeah," Bel agreed before Palery asked him.

The three of them sat for a moment, each knowing the others' brains were following different paths but assessing the same information.

"The plea deal," Bel said.

He didn't need more words. They'd all recognized the possibility of someone who hadn't liked the plea deal—too harsh? too lenient? no telling—choosing this way to express an opinion.

"Doesn't have to be anyone personally connected," Landis added.

Palery snorted. "That would be too easy. We'll pursue that line. You two are going to have plenty to do with the family."

"Thanks." Bel's single word expressed appreciation that the chief of detectives' plan let him stay close to Jamie, while also demonstrating confidence in his detective's ability to keep his head on straight.

"If anything points to any connection to the family—" Palery warned.

"It won't. But I will."

Landis said, "I can be of better use on the main investigation of the shooting—"

"No. It's going to follow a lot of routine to start. Want you two on the family. That's it. For now."

"Outside—" Bel started.

He wanted to get out to the crime scene, to assess it, read it, get to know it. He maintained that the crime scene, the home of the victim, the home of the murderer, each told its story. And even though this scene was a public space in front of a courthouse, he'd find import in details. Gathering them one by one, like the pebbles he so often likened them to.

Rutherford Belichek was the best he'd ever encountered at it.

And he'd recognized early in their partnership that it gave Bel a kind of peace. Occupied his mind, relieved some of what they saw, heard, experienced.

Would it work for Belichek now, with his emotions irrevocably tangled with Jamie Chancellor?

He'd already been connected to Maggie as her best friend and the ACA they worked with the most. Now that his involvement with the Frye cousins had widened and deepened would it affect Bel's investigative ability, tying up his partner with emotions?

Him? He'd be better at following the ordinary routine, as he'd told Palery. That way he knew the facts to contribute when he and Bel cross-referenced their knowledge.

"No." Palery quashed Belichek's request, too. "Stretching it to have you two with the family. No way out there."

"Where's Upton?" Landis asked.

"Security detail hustled Vic out the back as soon as we heard the shot."

That was good. Harder for the Fairlington County Commonwealth's Attorney to follow his first instinct to grandstand. That would give his second instinct—to avoid being the face of the investigation, in case it went south—to take hold. And that would mean he'd leave Palery to run this. Plenty of time to swoop in later for glory.

Landis asked, "You sending us to Danolin's tender mercies next?"

"No. I'm satisfied. We'll start with the members of the security detail. You two go back to the family."

"Captain, I'd be more useful—"

Palery cut off his second try. "They're not supposed to be talking, but they might. And even if they don't, you might pick up something useful."

CHAPTER THREE

PARTWAY BACK TO the courtroom where they'd left the family group, Landis asked, "Did you have anything I didn't?"

Bel cut him an assessing look.

He shouldn't have asked. He should have known Bel would tell him if he had.

"No."

He said nothing as they turned into a new hallway.

Bel spoke again. "He took me through our coming outside."

They'd scoped it out carefully. "Made sense. To check that door, get outside for a moment to check the scene. Then go back to the corridor, continue checking the rest of the rooms on each side."

"That's what I said."

Landis tipped his head, acknowledging the deputy outside the courtroom door where they'd left the others. He reached for the doorknob.

Bel's voice stopped him. "Anything you want to tell me?"

"No."

He opened the door.

$\diamond \quad \diamond \quad \diamond \quad \diamond$

THE FAMILY AND the lawyer said nothing when they entered the room and sent Terrington and Ewer out.

They'd moved. Someone had gathered chairs from the well of the courtroom, grouping them around the prosecution table. It let them see each other's faces instead of being strung out along rows of gallery benches.

Each of them had a paper coffee cup from a machine. Ally's was untouched. Maggie's was gone. The rest fell in between.

"Coffee?" Schmidt asked the newcomers.

The uniform must have noted him inventorying the coffee cups. That kind of observant was mostly good in an officer helping out. But not always.

When Schmidt left to fill his and Bel's requests, Maggie waited for the door to close, but not a second more.

"What do they know? What did you find out? Where—?"

"On duty, Mags," Bel said.

She swore.

"Margaret," Dana Chancellor murmured.

"I don't care if you're on duty. My family—"

"Maggie. You want this to go by the book."

J.D. Carson's low voice brought her head around to face him. Her urgent worry didn't leave, but the man's words clearly triggered her prosecutor mode, too. She wouldn't let up on wanting the investigation done yesterday. But she'd also be more cognizant of preserving the best case for prosecution.

Sometimes that drove Landis nuts, but in this case, it might gain them a bit more breathing room on the investigation.

"Then tell me what's with you and Ally, Landis. You met when you and Chad were at the academy together. Then what?"

So much for breathing room.

Ally made a faint sound of protest.

He didn't look at her.

"Large group that graduated together, with a few people from the year before and year after, all got together for a while. Whole big group played sports, shot the—" He deliberately sent a look toward Dana Chancellor as he sanitized the saying, hoping it might distract Maggie. "—breeze, compared notes as we started our careers. I was there now and then. All before I came over to Fairlington."

"I figured *that*. But with you the lead on Jamie's case, you must have seen Ally—"

"Case kept me damned busy. Our paths didn't cross. Obviously."

The door opened to Schmidt entering with a cafeteria tray with more paper cups, a coffee pot, and various additives. The kid was resourceful.

Beyond mutters and murmurs about coffee, silence returned.

A phone going off ripped across the stillness.

Ally's, he realized.

It took her two beats to come to the same conclusion.

She fumbled in a pocket and pulled it out, intensifying the noise.

"Sorry. After we left the courtroom—the other courtroom—I turned it back on because of…" She looked at the screen, then up at Bel. "It's the long-term care facility where Chad…"

"Go ahead," he said.

"Allison Lindell Northcutt," she answered. Crisp. Assured. "Yes. Hello, Doctor… Oh." It was more a breath than a word.

He couldn't say her expression was blank this time. But it wasn't… her. At least the woman he remembered.

Her face used to reflect her emotions in quicksilver runs of responses. This was like an avatar of that person, instead of flesh and blood.

Or was that a flaw in his memory?

"His family—?" she said into the phone, then listened. "Yes. But his mother….? I understand. As soon as I can."

She clicked off. Her gaze went to Jamie, then Maggie, skidded past him, touched on her aunt and uncle, paused at Bel, then went to Schmidt. "Officer, you need to get your commanding officer to come here immediately. Or take me to him. My husband has taken a serious turn for the worse."

Unexpectedly, she jerked her head in a single terse negation.

To her own words? To the fact?

She used to shake or nod her head emphatically, making her hair swing. That was one of the first things he'd noticed about her. Okay, not the first thing. But one of the individual things about her.

This gesture was contained. More than that, it was restricted. No hair-swinging.

Before anyone else reacted, she added baldly, "My husband is dying. I have to go to him. Now."

CHAPTER FOUR

SCHMIDT SENT A slightly wild-eyed look toward him. Bel said, "Go get Captain Palery."

The younger man moved quickly.

Dana Chancellor leaned across her daughter. "Ally, dear. I'm so sorry."

Jamie tightened her hold, but said nothing.

"You can't leave," Maggie protested. "Someone shot at you. As long as Chad's been in that condition—"

"I have to. Doctor Sala was quite clear. He's led Chad's care—" For the first time she hesitated slightly. "—recently. He's a top expert in the region. In the country. He wouldn't say to get there now if it wasn't… necessary."

She slid her phone back in her pocket and gathered her purse from the bench without looking up.

"I know you'll need statements and things, and of course I'll come back, but I didn't see anything. Nothing useful. And right now—"

"It's dangerous."

The faces coming around to stare at him confirmed he'd spoken aloud.

Ally dropped her gaze to her hands, resting on her purse. She closed, then opened the fastener.

The door opened and Palery strode in.

"Mrs. Northcutt, you've had a call from the hospital?"

"The Chate Long-Term Care Facility, where my husband is. Dr. Frederick Sala heads his care team. If you want his phone number to confirm that he called and said my husband has taken a turn for the worse, which the doctor expects to lead to his death as soon as an hour, possibly several hours, I will give that to you."

"That's not necessary, Mrs. Northcutt."

"I have to go. Immediately."

"But, Ally," Jamie's mother protested. "As Detective Landis said, with someone shooting at you, it's dangerous for you to—"

"I have to, Aunt Dana." She never took her gaze off Captain Palery.

He knew the backstory. He didn't hesitate.

"Lights and sirens. Bel, Landis, you take her with—"

"All of us," Maggie inserted.

"—a marked car to lead and follow. I'll put out the call for us to facilitate. I'll let Piscattoway County know the status." That was Chad Northcutt's department in Maryland. Palery's call would send department members streaming toward the facility.

"And Rock Creek County. That's where the long-term care facility is," Maggie said. "We'll have to pass through there, too. Rush hour."

Palery nodded. "I'll call both Maryland jurisdictions." And explain that it was a law enforcement officer about to die. Accommodations would be made. "We'll get you there, Mrs. Northcutt."

"Before we go—" Landis spoke with deliberation, stopping the small movements of preparation. "—did anyone see or hear anything before or after the shots? Something that could indicate location or the identity of the shooter?"

Bel added another layer. "Or have any knowledge or suspicion. Anything odd or off-kilter that's happened lately."

Ally's eyelids fluttered, as if she were going to look up, but she didn't. Instead, she shook her head.

The others followed suit or said "No."

The difference was he believed the others. He wasn't so sure about Allison Lindell Northcutt.

A patrol car led them. Landis thought he'd gotten lucky when Bel took Ally and Jamie in his car … until Maggie climbed into his vehicle, along with J.D. Carson. He would have preferred Jamie's mother and stepfather as passengers, even if a hint of tension remained from their feeling that he'd treated Jamie too much like a murder suspect a while back.

Didn't bother him. She *was* a suspect. And it likely would have made for a quiet trip.

But Schmidt was the lucky one who drew them as passengers, in a marked department vehicle, with one more at the end of their compact motorcade.

They were barely on the George Washington Parkway, headed north with clouds closing in now, when Maggie started. "You knew Ally from when you and Chad were in the police academy."

"Already covered that, Mags."

She didn't relent with his use of the nickname. "And you never mentioned it."

"Never came up."

"Bullshit. With the investigation around Jamie and the legal—"

"As you say, it was about Jamie. No reason—"

"Bullshit, again. Ally's been around a lot from the start of it and for all these months getting to the plea deal. Must have taken considerable effort for you to avoid running into her. But Bel had all the contact with Ally." The recognition of that fact slid right into accusation. "You made sure of that, didn't you? You were actively trying to avoid Ally. Why? What happened between you two that—?"

"Nothing."

He might have snapped that off because a driver in a blue BMW with Maryland plates chose that moment to try to cut into the middle of a line of vehicles running lights and sirens.

Odds were high it was another self-important idiot who thought laws, rules, and basic manners didn't apply to him, but no way in hell was Landis letting any other vehicle get in behind the one carrying Ally.

He closed the gap, squeezing the guy back into his own lane.

As Landis drew even with the BMW, the guy had the nerve to glare over at them. Landis spoke a command to his phone, then rattled off the tag number he'd automatically memorized.

"Jerk." Presumably Maggie meant that for the driver. The next part, though was not. "Don't think I missed all that cuteness."

"Cuteness?"

From the passenger seat, she looked directly at him. He looked straight ahead.

"The feint that you were going to swear and upset Aunt Dana. The emphasis on the *whole big group* playing sports and talking *career*. I know a misdirect when I hear one. A first-year law student could've spotted distraction after distraction in that speech. Besides, I know *you*, Landis."

He'd rather it didn't but his peripheral vision automatically caught the familiar narrowing of her eyes as her considerable brain processed information.

"My first thought was that Ally was another woman who got the Landis treatment. Except your reactions are off for that. Both of you. She'd be either trying to get you back—and thank God she has too much sense for *that*—or embarrassed she ever fell for you. And you'd be truly smooth and above it all instead of pretending to be."

"I've told you. Met her through Chad when they were engaged, part of a big group. You're way off on this, Mags. You're reading something else into it when it's the weirdness of these circumstances."

Her narrowed eyes didn't change.

"You do know what I'd do to you if you hurt my cousin."

"No worries, Mags."

Because it had been the reverse.

She didn't let it go. "You must have worked hard to avoid her, so there must have been a reason and I intend—"

"Maggie. Let the man drive." J.D. Carson kept rising in Landis' estimation. "Grill him after we get to our destination alive."

His view of the other man dipped a bit at the invitation to pick this up later. Still, it did divert Maggie. For now.

She spent the time calling her assistant, Nancy Quinn, updating her on where they were—Nancy would already know what happened—and tapping into Nancy's sources for any information outside and/or faster-moving than the official.

✧   ✧   ✧   ✧

IT WASN'T THE fastest trip. But considering the traffic, what with rush hour in the D.C. area basically going from six a.m. to 10 p.m., they made good time. Some people even pulled over for their lights and sirens.

Landis saw Ally being whisked inside by Jamie, as Bel's vehicle pulled away. He took his turn to drive under a portico to drop off his passengers.

"Come inside after you've parked," Maggie ordered.

"I have to check in and—"

"Come inside after you've parked," she repeated.

J.D. Carson added a look that reinforced the order before he closed the back door.

Landis pulled his vehicle forward, out of the protected area so Schmidt could drive in and take his place to discharge his passengers, then considered the choices. His top choice—if he'd had a real choice—would be to leave, but that was out of the question.

A knock on the passenger window jerked his head around. That wasn't good. Not noticing someone coming up on his vehicle.

Even if it was Bel.

He unlocked the door.

His partner slid in, letting in the smell of mist consolidating toward rain.

"Why're you sitting here?"

"Strategizing about looking for a spot to park. No reason for you to stick around—"

"Staying. Owe you. Took the last good one."

Committed to a course of action by his own words, Landis put the vehicle in gear and looked for a place to park.

Someplace they wouldn't get blocked in, someplace with a fast exit, someplace not too far from the building. He'd picked out four possibilities with the first circuit of the lot.

Instead of going immediately to join Jamie, Belichek sat silently beside him.

He was accustomed to his silences.

Silences while his partner processed what they'd seen, heard, discovered. Those silences both comforted him and challenged him.

Comforted because the silence meant Rutherford Belichek was on the job, working hard, as always. Bel would come up with angles and insights he wouldn't.

Challenged because his job was to come up with angles and insights Belichek wouldn't.

He usually did, though he seldom recognized them before the words came out. Another difference between him and Belichek, who examined each facet and every long-range implication before he spoke. Or acted.

But this silence… Not the same at all.

This silence challenged without comfort.

Its only similarity to their usual silences was he knew that during it Belichek's brain churned through the raw material of what he'd seen, heard, and discovered.

Landis' second-choice parking spot came open when a gray-haired man with the slow, shoulder-slumped walk of grief came out and got in a sedan. The man sat there a full minute before he turned on the car. He backed out slowly.

Landis waited for the man to clear the spot and start away, so if the circumstances pierced the man's preoccupation, it didn't look like Landis had been tapping his fingers impatiently waiting for the man to be gone.

He backed into the spot, turned off the engine, reached for the door handle.

"You know her."

The words caught Landis off guard despite knowing it was coming eventually. "Told you all at the courthouse that I knew her. Barely. Knew of her, more like. Way back."

"Bullshit."

Landis looked at him. But his amused indifference wasn't the genuine article. "It's not. Chad was a guy who'd been at the academy the same time as me. They were engaged."

"Is she the reason?"

His mistake had been not getting out of the vehicle without answering Bel's first words.

Though that probably wouldn't have made a difference.

When his partner intended to say something, he said it.

With that thought barely formed in Landis' mind, Belichek continued, talking as if Landis had said *what* or *who* or some other lame response, when he hadn't said a word, hadn't even acknowledged the words with a glance. "Is she the reason for accumulating all the unavailable women. The commitment phobia on steroids. Why you are how you are with women."

None of what Belichek said constituted real questions. He wouldn't have answered anyway. Sure wasn't going to say *I have no idea what you're talking about* the way so many stupid arrestees did when anyone could see they were trussed up and done for, each futile struggle only tightening the bonds.

"You fell for a married woman—"

"She wasn't married."

If he couldn't manage to keep his mouth shut, he shouldn't have said it fast, like it mattered. Or like he had anything to feel guilty about.

To feel *anything* about.

All of it was water that was never going to see that bridge again. Ever.

"—and after that you went for ones just like her."

He'd given too much away with that *She wasn't married*, but did Belichek think he'd blurt out something like *There wasn't anyone else like her. All the others have been—*

No, he wouldn't dismiss them or himself that way. Even in his own head.

Belichek didn't let his lack of response stop him. "Because you couldn't have what you wanted."

The phrase gave Landis the toehold he needed. "That's exactly it. Turned down by a woman—years ago, so a girl, really—and decided right then and there I'd revenge myself on the rest of the sex forevermore."

Bel nodded, as if the sarcasm dripping from Landis' words didn't leave them both wading in a flash flood of the stuff. "That fits."

"Christ, Belichek—"

"Except the revenge was on yourself."

"Hah. You know how many guys in the squad envy my life? Sword master, that's what Terrington called me." He chuckled. "Some revenge."

"You've been miserable."

"You're crazy. And deluded, Belichek. Don't be a dumb f—"

"You've got that position filled, Landis."

Another silence. No better than the previous one.

"You know the history. The three girls, all cousins—"

"Do you think I missed the genealogy during Jamie's case, Bel? There were four Frye siblings. Two brothers—Maggie's father and Jamie's father, who died young and then his widow married Wes Chancellor. Two sisters—Ally's mother and Vivian, the aunt the three girls spent summers with."

"Right. Until she fell for a master manipulator and pedophile, who courted Vivian but wanted Jamie. Tried to snatch her. Except Maggie, with help from Ally and others, foiled that and got him caught. But the trial… He got off."

Landis cut him a look. "And Mags blamed herself. She doesn't confide in me the way she does in you, but I've known Mags for years, too, and I am a detective for God's sake. And yet you're surprised I know."

Bel's silence confirmed it.

Landis produced a grin. "Guess your detective instincts aren't half bad, either. Your grandmother told me."

Bel snorted knowingly. "Of course she did."

"Don't worry, Bel, she still loved you, even if she did confide all your deepest secrets to me the first time we met."

His partner didn't rise to that lure to be amused. "Putting aside my grandmother's soft spot for you, at least tell me you stayed away from Allison, no contact after she married." Not waiting for Landis to obey that order, Bel pushed open the passenger door and got out, but immediately leaned back in, halfway across the seat to glare at him. "Maggie and Jamie's cousin. That's bad enough. But the wife of a cop in a coma? God, Landis. That's as bad as it gets."

She hadn't been his wife.

Not yet.

That had been the real kick in the gut. She could have broken it off. Walked away.

She chose Chad.

✧ ✧ ✧ ✧

THEY WALKED TOWARD the entry. At the last second, he peeled off.

"Calling in," he said.

Bel's laser look called bullshit on that. But he kept walking and went inside. That worked for Landis.

He made good on his words, pacing to the edge of the portico, where he wouldn't block traffic, although the rain could get him if it put some effort into it.

When Palery answered, he said, "We got them here to the long-term facility without incident. Bel and Schmidt are inside. I stayed out to call you, Captain. I need to talk to you. Alone. Not on the phone."

"When and where?" His boss didn't ask anything else. He knew Landis would have already said more if he could.

"As soon as possible. I could come back—"

"No." Palery confirmed what Landis had expected ... and hoped against. "Stay with them."

"I'll call when I shake free."

Palery grunted acceptance of that, then moved on. "See anything on the way?"

"No. The others?" Anything major he'd have known about from radio traffic, but there could have been something Bel or Schmidt spotted that didn't warrant the radio.

"No. Northcutt's department knows the status, including what happened here. There'll be plenty of law enforcement there shortly. But if you or Bel think someone from Rock Creek County needs to be there officially, here's the contact."

He rattled off name, rank, and phone number, both of them knowing it might be the second call if 911 would get people on scene faster.

Even without a 911-level situation, this had potential to be dicey.

If whoever shot at Ally—he was going with her being the target unless something proved to him otherwise—followed them over here and was stupid enough to try again amid the influx of law enforcement about to start, there'd be three jurisdictions involved.

First, the Rock Creek County, Maryland, locals whose turf this was.

Second, Northcutt's Piscattoway County Police Department from a smaller, neighboring county with a chip on its collective shoulder toward the home guys at the best of times. This wasn't the best of times, so add in emotions heightened by the imminent death of one of their own. Particularly this one of their own.

Third, Bel, him, and Schmidt from across the river. The three of them would hardly be factored in at all by the other two groups except for one fact. They were essentially in possession of the almost-widow and intended shooting victim, as well as her family, including an Assistant Commonwealth's Attorney.

That status was borne out when he checked in at the desk and was taken to a waiting room filled with the contingent from Virginia, while a handful of Piscattoway County uniforms remained in the hallway just inside the main door.

Actually, the room held the contingent from Virginia, with the exception of Ally, he saw immediately.

He took an empty seat between Bel and Schmidt. Bel had taken the chair where he would be the first to see who came in the door. Now Landis would be second.

After a moment, Landis realized Jamie wasn't in the room, either.

Schmidt tapped away at his phone, then said in a low voice, "That document's to you, sir."

Bel switched from reading one document to another on his screen.

"Copies to you, too, sir," Schmidt said to him.

Landis got busy on his own phone, reading the earliest of the prelim accounts from other officers on the courthouse scene. Those were followed by initial witness accounts, focusing on the direction the shots came from.

A lot would follow.

This was the first trickle of what would become a flood. With that many witnesses in a public place, with multiple cameras on them, definitely a flood.

The trick would be to pick out the relevant pieces and do it fast enough that nobody drowned in the flood. Not the investigators. And not Ally.

CHAPTER FIVE

WITH THOSE FEW early reports long read, re-read, and digested, Landis had also drained his cup from another round of coffees Schmidt brought in a while back.

The opening of the door when Schmidt left, then returned, allowed a low, subdued sound to reach them.

Landis had heard that sound before.

A waiting crowd saying little, but shifting their weight frequently, sending their shoes on short, overlapping *shushes* of slides.

"Piscattoway County?" Bel asked Schmidt, clearly also identifying the sound. They'd both been at hospital vigils for fellow law enforcement before.

"Mostly. A few from Rock Creek, too. Piscattoway brass is in a room next door."

The rest of them drank their coffee without comment.

The door opened, a nurse stepping in first to hold it open. Ally came in, with Jamie beside her, one hand wrapped around her arm.

"Come, sit here," Maggie said, putting Ally between her and Jamie.

Maggie was the oldest of the cousins, with Ally next, and Jamie the youngest. Maybe from that, certainly from her job, she had a habit of command. Her cousins often went along … on the small things.

Bel got up and sat on the other side of Jamie.

"If you need anything, Ally, come get one of us," the nurse offered. "I'll check back in a bit."

"Thank you, Judith."

Schmidt was up and out the door before the nurse pulled it closed behind her.

"You do not need to be brave, Ally. Not for us," Maggie said fiercely. "Tell us to shut up or talk if you want or—"

"It's okay, Maggie." Her voice held steady, but she didn't make eye contact. "Really, you don't all need to stay—"

Her older cousin emitted a harsh *huh*. "Forget it. You're not getting rid of us to sit here by yourself."

Ally's shoulders slumped, though whether in surrender that she wouldn't get any of them to leave or in relief, Landis didn't know.

As if she were a hostess who needed to make the others comfortable, Ally said, "This isn't unexpected. It's a shock, I suppose, that it's happening now, but we've known for a while…"

"A while? How about from the start?" Jamie said. "That first week after he was shot, they said the damage was too severe. Then that article a month later said he'd never come out of a coma."

"And Mrs. Northcutt wanted the editor's head on a platter," Maggie muttered.

"Yes. But he hasn't been in a coma. He's in a vegetative state. A permanent vegetative state." For a second, Ally seemed to sway in the chair.

"How do they define the difference?" J.D. asked.

Landis flicked the man a look. Because those few words righted Ally.

"In a coma, the person appears to be asleep. There is neither wakefulness nor awareness. Vegetative, the person has waking and sleeping cycles. Their eyes are often open, sometimes giving a sense that … but there is no awareness.

"Immediately after the shooting, Chad was in a coma. When he opened his eyes… His mother never let go of the hope from that moment. But they did every test—no, not every. She wouldn't allow anything that might have shown he was brain dead. She insisted he would come out of this. We tried every way to reach him. Talking, singing, touch, scent, everything…"

She closed her eyes. The lids looking transparent with an exhaustion beyond the repair of sleep.

Yet she seemed to draw some relief from talking.

"Iris would read about someone waking from a vegetative state and insist that whatever therapies they'd used, we use it. Full-bore. Even if we'd tried them before. No matter how many times we'd tried before. No matter that those people came out of persistent vegetative states, not permanent."

"The kind people don't come out of," Jamie murmured.

"The doctors said from the start that he had essentially no chance of coming out of this. Each day made it even less likely. Most people with that kind of damage die within the first six months. Of the others, they can live two, three, even five years. But then…"

Schmidt came in, letting in louder sighing of position-shifting from a growing number of feet in the hallway, and handed Ally and Jamie each a cup of coffee. Both thanked him, but only Jamie drank any.

"The doctors have been saying for the past six weeks that Chad was losing ground. The cause of…"

She didn't say the word they all mentally filled in: *death*.

She started another sentence that wouldn't include the word. "Most often the dangers are from respiratory or urinary tract infections. Chad had those early on, but got past them. Lately, however, his organs have been declining—multiple organs. The doctors have been clear there's not a way back from that."

"They said that to his mother?" Maggie asked.

"They did. She wouldn't listen. She's been trying to find someone else to lead his care, to replace Dr. Sala. She always said he'd recover. She fought the medical staff using *permanent*.

"She was so angry. Ready to fight them with her bare hands, to try to make them take back what they were saying, as if their words were what was killing Chad. That has been her fuel. The anger. I don't know what she'll do now that…"

"What about Chad's partner?" Tanner didn't ask it to distract her. He didn't mind that it did, but it was an investigative question.

Even when a partner wasn't dearest, they were almost always nearest, offering a view on a law enforcement victim no one else could. If they would share.

She responded, still focused on her hands. "What about him?"

"Does he visit Chad?"

"He's come a few times. He wasn't Chad's partner when—at the time of the shooting. He'd already left PCPD and gone to the FBI's uniformed division. After a year or so they realized what a gem they have in Shindell and they've had him traveling for special events ever since."

Landis, still on this side of the Potomac River then, remembered the word on Chad's original partner. Shindell Ortiz was smart, well-liked, good at deescalating. A potential star who'd left for the FBI.

"Except now he's being transferred to something hush-hush. Can't get here a lot, but he checks in regularly. Phone, email—Oh. I have to let him know. And Chad's sister-in-law, too. I have to call and tell—"

"No, you don't. Department will take care of that," Maggie said. "They'll contact the sister-in-law officially and if Chad's former partner's stayed in touch with anybody—"

"He has."

"—he'll hear from them."

"How long were Shindell and Chad partners?" Bel asked, as if making conversation rather than following up on the same line of logic as Landis' that the partner was the cop version of a spouse or significant other. Always of interest.

"Almost three years. Chad's very first partner retired quickly. Then he and Shindell were partnered."

"What about after Ortiz left for the FBI? Who was Chad's partner then?"

"He had a few. That was just before the department moved away from official partners for patrol. More flexible staffing."

"Remember their names?" Bel asked.

That drew three distinct looks from the cousins. Ally thought he was being kind by trying to distract her. Maggie's attention focused, thinking he asked because he was on to something. Jamie concluded he was doing both and showed her approval.

She was right.

"Some of those early ones came and went pretty quickly. I never met any of them in person. There was a Brent, though I'm not sure if that was his first name or his last. A Ted, I'm pretty sure. Susanna… Susanna Wuertl. In between the other two, I think."

"Any issues there?" High partner turnover could be a sign of trouble. Though it could have been with the partners, while Northcutt was viewed as a stabilizing force.

"Issues? No. He seemed to like each of them okay." She paused. "He thought Ted might be a regular partner, but then they changed the system."

"He must have had other people he was close to in the department," Landis said.

She answered without looking at him. "Oh, yes. His cousins, Rachel and Mark."

He'd heard there were a lot of Northcutts in that department. All related.

"Brother and sister?"

"No. Mark's father and Chad's father were brothers. I suppose Rachel is more distant than a cousin, because her father was a cousin of those two brothers, although she's always been close."

"Chad close to anybody who wasn't a Northcutt?" Bel asked.

The firm line of Ally's mouth eased at his light question. "Dewey Selton and Ethan Paulz. The four of them—those two and Mark and Chad—played cards, watched sports, went fishing, and stayed in a cabin on the Eastern Shore."

"So they've come around a—"

The door swung open sharply.

A neatly dressed woman of about sixty, with a dramatic sweep of white through the bangs of her otherwise more pepper than salt hair, strode in. The bangs did not hide that two pillars of wrinkles rose, one from the inside corner of each brow, disrupting the horizontal furrows in her forehead.

She glared around at the occupants of the room.

A female uniformed Piscattoway County Police Department sergeant entered behind her. The nametag on the uniform explained her presence: R. Northcutt.

If Landis had doubt about the newcomer being Iris Northcutt, Chad's mother, the presence of what had to be Sergeant Rachel Northcutt trimmed it to zero.

"Ally, I'm so sorry," Rachel started. "If I'd known, I would have been here right away."

"It's okay, Rachel. I'm glad you're both here now."

"We're here, all right," Iris snapped. "You weren't. Where were *you*? My boy dying and you weren't here with him." The force of the woman's words jutted her jaw forward and strained the cords of her neck. "They told me he was all alone."

"Dawn—"

"His *aunt* here. Not his *wife*. How could you not be with him? That is your *job*. Your only job. The only thing you're good for. The *only* thing. Never gave him a child. Selfish and barren on top of it and—"

Maggie surged up.

J.D. caught her around the waist at the same time Bel and Tanner stepped in front of Ally and faced her mother-in-law. But before they could close shoulders, Jamie slid between them and stood in front of the older woman.

"Ally was with me today. In court, Mrs. Northcutt."

"*You?*"

"I'm her cousin, Jamie. Jamison Chancellor."

The woman swung back to Ally, trying to jab a finger at her, but blocked by Landis and Bel. She might have made contact with Bel. She was lucky she didn't with him.

"You chose to be with a *cousin* for some court formality instead of with your husband when he was dying."

"That's not fair," Jamie said. "She came here as soon as she was notified that he'd taken a turn for the worse. How could she possibly know before that?"

Maggie went for the jugular. "Where have *you* been while your son's dying?"

The woman's lips drew back from her teeth. Maggie didn't flinch.

"Iris." Ally came around his left side and reached out to touch the older woman's arm.

"No," Maggie snapped. "She has no right to talk to you like that. Never has."

"Maggie." Jamie put a hand to her shoulder.

Only the opening of the door eased the standoff.

A doctor with thinning hair, tired eyes, and red marks beside his nose that said he usually wore glasses, stopped inside the door, followed by the same nurse who'd accompanied Ally. His gaze acknowledged Iris, but he addressed Ally.

"Mrs. Northcutt, we've stabilized Chad again. If you'd like to come back in now… I'm afraid, though, that it won't be long."

"I'm coming, but if you'd done your job, this wouldn't be happening," Iris spat at him. "There wouldn't be any need to stabilize—"

"I meant Ally Northcutt could come in. His wife."

"I'm his *mother*. I'm—"

"Let her go in and see him, Doctor Sala. I've had the chance to say my good-byes if there's no other opportunity. She hasn't."

The doctor and nurse gave her sympathetic glances. The doctor turned and left. The nurse gestured to Iris and said in a neutral voice, "This way, Mrs. Northcutt."

"I know the way," she snapped. "I've been here every day, in case you didn't notice."

As she turned toward the door, her large handbag swung wide and clipped Ally's hip.

She didn't turn or acknowledge the contact.

Rachel shot Ally a look mixed with apology and fatalism as she followed the older woman, then pulled the door closed behind them.

"Those Northcutts need to—"

Ally cut across Maggie's vigilante intent. "Don't lump Rachel in with … others. She was terrific—*is* terrific. She was always friendly to me and from the day Chad was shot she's been great. Couldn't have been easy at the time. She'd just gotten promoted—even before she made sergeant—and that was barely noticed with everything that was going on. She never complained. She pitched in, trying to face the reality of Chad's condition although it caused her trouble with Iris. She had to back off that. But by keeping Iris on more of an even keel, she's helped smooth the sometimes very rough seas.

"Plus, she tried several times to help me—No. Not to help. It was more than that, because I wasn't doing it on my own. She *initiated* the efforts to sort and clean out Chad's things. But…"

Maggie filled in, "Iris wouldn't allow the dismantling of the shrine."

She grimaced. "She wanted everything left the same. Even when we tried to straighten out the garage or clear out things from the medicine cabinet he couldn't possibly use even if… Iris would not have it."

"We offered to help with that," Maggie said.

Ally chuckled, both fond and dry enough to ignite a fire. "You would have gone head-to-head with Iris. I didn't want that. You don't know what she's like."

"I have a pretty good idea. And it wouldn't have bothered me in the least. I could take her."

"I wasn't ready to deal with the aftermath." She sucked in a long breath. "I didn't want to lose that family."

Landis turned away to resume his seat. Also to keep from saying it looked like she had now lost whatever passed for family in Iris Northcutt's world… and it was no great loss.

AFTER ALMOST HALF an hour, the nurse who had escorted Iris away returned. Judith, Ally had called her. She looked only at Ally.

"You should come now."

Jamie rose with her, their hands clasped. Ally half turned and held out her other hand to Maggie. She immediately took it and stood, too.

Without a word, the three cousins exited the room.

Vulnerable. United. Determined. Drawing strength from each other.

He couldn't help but think of how the three of them must have been very much like this when their beloved aunt was murdered by the man who was supposed to love Vivian, to have loved all of them, but turned out to be a monster.

Bel made a faint sound low in his throat.

Landis turned toward him. Bel, not much more than a boy himself at the time, had seen the three cousins in that moment they'd discovered Vivian was dead. He clearly was thinking the same thing.

Then Bel shifted his gaze to him. And Landis saw those memories replaced by a new observation.

Without any difficulty at all, he read his partner's unspoken words.

That's as bad as it gets?

Hell, no.

It just got worse.

From the wife of a cop in a coma to the widow of a cop gunned down in his own driveway.

A lot worse.

CHAPTER SIX

THE TAN BRICK suburban house was compact. Along with a kitchen and combo living and dining areas, it had two bedrooms, bath and a half on the main floor, plus a partially finished basement downstairs.

Ally unlocked the unadorned front door.

Without discussion, Maggie took her arm, subtly holding her back while Landis and Bel went in first.

The miracle was Ally was standing at all.

First, she'd spoken with the doctors and nurses who had been on duty. Then a quiet conversation with Rachel about Chad's mother. She'd been given the mildest sedative—not much more than aspirin was all she'd accept. The plan was Rachel would take Iris to Rachel's father's place, but wanted to wait for the pill and time to have some effect.

Then Ally insisted on speaking to and shaking the hand of every single one of the people—uniformed or not, Piscattoway County or not—who had come to show their respects.

It took more than an hour.

Tanner spent the time looking at nametags for any of the people Bel gently extracted from Ally.

He spotted S. Wuertl on a nametag. A neat, self-contained woman who couldn't have been very experienced four to six years ago, which is about when she'd have been partnered with Chad. Her exchange with Ally wasn't any different from any of the others.

A tall, thin officer with the nametag F. Brentford was a possibility. He looked worried, but hard to read anything into that under the circumstances. Might be how he showed sorrow or sympathy. Or he might be worried about something else.

No sign of a Paulz or a Selton. Not even Mark Northcutt. Could be odd that none of them showed up or could be a quirk of scheduling. Departments would shuffle around to try to let relatives and close friends be on hand in these circumstances. But sometimes it couldn't be done.

And with the possibility that Chad could have died anytime these past four years and six months, it was a hell of a long vigil to schedule around.

Ally had a low-voiced exchange with the PCPD's chief and a guy in a suit with him. A few words escaped their circumspection. *Arrangements, tomorrow, decisions, as much off your shoulders as possible,* and—a second time—*tomorrow.*

The same nurse as before took Maggie aside and said something Maggie agreed with, judging by her expression. There'd been a phrase that sounded like *if not for her, the rest of your family...*

So Landis wasn't completely surprised when Maggie declared they were stopping for food and communicated that edict to the other vehicles. Their three-vehicle caravan—no longer lights and sirens now—quietly hit a drive-through of a relatively healthy fast-food place, then parked in a back corner. From Landis' observation, Schmidt wolfed down his food while everyone else picked at their orders.

Maybe they'd see if there was something that might be more appealing in the house after they finished clearing it.

He and Bel covered the main floor in short order. He jerked his head toward a back landing. One door led to the basement, another to the garage, and a third to outside. The outside door was locked and showed no sign of being messed with. While Bel watched the basement door, Landis cleared the garage. Not a hard job with no vehicle in it and no enclosed spaces for anything bigger than a mid-sized dog.

Bel started down the basement steps first.

Nothing there, either.

It was as neat as the main floor. With a finished area with a second TV—slightly smaller than the one upstairs—a sofa, two older chairs, a coffee table, and a corner that felt oddly empty. The unfinished side had the washer and dryer, plus one set of shelves with pantry supplies and two others with labeled storage bins.

With the house cleared, he saw Belichek shift from security to investigation. His gaze took in far more than the objects it rested on.

This house was a two-fer for Bel's observations, which often focused on the victim first.

The home of Chad Northcutt, victim of the shooting outside it four-plus years ago.

The home of Ally Lindell Northcutt, would-be victim of the shooting at the courthouse today.

When they returned to the main floor, the cousins, J.D., the Chancellors, and Schmidt were in a tight cluster inside with the front door closed.

"Clear," Bel said.

Ally stared straight ahead at a wall with a generic print of a forested landscape. "Thank you. I'm… I'm going to change. If you'd like anything—"

"We can find it ourselves," Jamie said. "But do you want me to come with you and—?"

"No, I'm fine. Thank you."

She paused another long moment, as if trying to recall how to start walking, then turned and went down the hall.

Jamie moved into the kitchen. "Does anyone else want water? Or something else to drink?"

Landis absently declined.

His attention slid from the forested landscape to a print of a man on horseback, leading a pack mule through rocky terrain under a stark blue sky. Another large print beside the fireplace showed a sunset reflected in water in what—incongruously—appeared to be the Arctic. He'd bet the print had been displaced from over the fireplace by a TV that took up every inch to the ceiling and extended wider than the mantel.

The furniture matched an unimaginative man-cave recliner in front of a TV that could have been a highway billboard. But the art on the walls surprised him. The prints could have been in any hunting cabin on the continent.

Nothing by Ally hung on the walls.

He thought of the painting by Ally he'd seen over the fireplace at Jamie's house. It was *art*. Why in hell did she have this generic crap on the walls of her home when she could have her own work?

He remembered Jamie saying months ago that Ally's husband didn't like her painting and that explained why her signature on her work wasn't Allison Northcutt. It was T-something Lindell.

Theodora. That was it. Her real first name. Allison was her middle name.

The mammoth overstuffed brown leather chair with a built-in table extending from one arm squarely faced the TV screen. He could see rings on it from beer cans. Two tweed chairs sat at right angles to the behemoth. Neither with a good angle on the TV. The leather chair's view would barely pick up the tweed chairs peripherally. No sofa offered a place where visitors or residents could look at each other while they chatted.

A closed laptop sat on the rectangular table in the dining area, with sliding glass doors to the outside beyond it. A neat stack of papers and a coaster awaiting a drink sat beside the laptop.

It was clean, neat, and lifeless.

Except for where the members of their party drifted toward the living room seating area.

Except Maggie. She stood directly in front of him. "You knew my cousin and never thought to tell me?"

"Long time ago. Didn't really know her." He regretted the second sentence immediately.

Maggie jumped on it. "What the hell does that mean, didn't really know her?"

"Because she married Chad," Jamie said.

Landis shifted his gaze to the younger woman. She looked sweet, but sometimes she was scary.

Fortunately, Maggie took it more generally. She snapped her mouth closed on whatever argument she'd meant to pursue. After a beat, she said in a different voice, "I never understood that, either."

"I did."

The rest of them looked at Jamie.

"She wanted family," she said. "She wanted *his* family."

"Good God," Maggie said.

"Not the way they turned out." A bit of impatience came through in Jamie's voice. "The way she wanted them to be."

Something alerted him and he turned to find Ally standing where the bedroom hallway opened to the living room, still wearing her court clothes, with the smear of grit on her left thigh from where he'd brought her down to the plaza surface.

She opened her mouth twice before words came out.

"I… I think… No. Not that I *think*. Someone *has* been in the house."

CHAPTER SEVEN

DANA CHANCELLOR CRUMPLED to the floor.

"*Mom.*"

Jamie was to her side instantly, but Wes already had her in his arms. "She's okay, Jamie. She's okay."

Bel looked up from the hold he'd taken on the woman's wrist. He nodded to Jamie.

Dana moaned slightly, then blinked. "Wh- what happened?"

"You fainted." Wes looked into her face a moment longer, then, apparently satisfied, addressed Jamie. "She hasn't been sleeping well. I don't think she slept at all last night, worrying about… And then with everything today… She should get some rest now."

"Of course. You two go with—"

"Nobody's going anywhere yet," Landis said.

"Surely Officer Schmidt can take Aunt Dana and Uncle Wes home now and let them—"

Landis had his phone out and cut off Ally. "Nobody. Anywhere. I'm contacting the Piscattoway Department. They'll need to work this scene."

He walked out the front door, not waiting for further discussion. There was no discussion on this.

He didn't call 911, figuring the call about a house with no evidence of forced entry wouldn't elicit the response he wanted without a lot more talk and time than they could spare. Faster to go to someone who knew the background. Palery's contact took over after Tanner's brief explanation.

By the time their conversation ended, Bel had everyone squared away and confined to the area they'd already disturbed.

They'd settled Dana into the oversized chair, wrapped in a thick knitted throw. Wes and Jamie sat on the floor at either side of her. Ally sat in one of the tweed chairs, Maggie in the other, her arm stretched across the small gap to touch her cousin. J.D. half perched on the arm of Maggie's chair. Schmidt had a position by the front door. Bel sat on one side of the hearth with a clear view to the sliders and, beyond the kitchen, to the back door.

Landis sat on the other end of the hearth.

"They'll be here shortly." Everyone looked at him. He looked back at Ally. "What makes you think someone was here?"

"I shouldn't have said *I think*. I'm sure." For all the confidence in those words, her voice remained unnaturally calm. "I have a jewelry box with a drawer in it. If I'm not careful, the chain of a necklace hangs out. Every time. But I am careful. Every time. Aunt Viv gave me that necklace."

Her hand went to her throat. Jamie echoed the gesture. Maggie started to, until she caught herself.

"Gave one to each of us," she continued. "The chain was not hanging out when I left this morning. It is now. When I saw that, I stopped just inside the doorway. One of Chad's drawers isn't fully closed. You have to lift it a bit to get it to fully close. Also, the bed skirt is different from how I left it. I changed the sheets this morning. When I do that, I adjust the bed skirt and make sure it's hanging down even and straight all around."

From the corner of his eye, he saw Jamie pull her bottom lip in between her teeth. Something about this recitation bothered her.

To Ally he said, "Okay." He looked around. "Has anyone besides Bel and me left this area?"

The unanimous answer was no.

One benefit, he thought dryly, of being emotionally exhausted from a draining court case, being shot at, racing across the metro area, then hearing a relation—whether close or not—had died. The witnesses sure didn't mill around a lot.

"Anything in here touched or different?" Bel asked her.

She looked so long and took so long to respond that Landis began to wonder if she'd forgotten the question.

But when she said, "No," she meant it.

THE RESPONSE TIME was decent.

The first Piscattoway Police Department vehicle was a lone patrol officer.

Landis met him outside, identified himself, sketched the background. After explaining the reason for the call briefly, he recommended the officer remain outside, where he could better spot any movement in the neighborhood.

A second patrol vehicle barely beat the shift supervisor and a property crimes detective who arrived separately. With the street covered, the patrol officers split, one going up either side of Ally's house toward the back.

Landis met the supervisor and detective on the front walk and gave them the complete rundown. The supervisor tuned in and out of his report as he deployed additional officers arriving on the scene.

Palery's contact must have told them the connection to Chad or the rest of the Northcutt law enforcement clan or there would not have been this kind of response.

"Say that last part again," the supervisor said to Landis.

"The only members of the party to leave the entry area and the living room area adjoining it were my partner, Detective Belichek of the Fairlington County Police Department, me, and the homeowner Allison Lindell Northcutt.

"Detective Belichek and I cleared the house when we arrived. Two bedrooms and a bath down the hallway to the right of the front door. Guest bedroom is at the front of the house, master bedroom to the back of the house. Living room is on the left, dining room behind it, with sliders to the outside. All undisturbed. Kitchen, garage, exterior door to the back, basement also showed no disturbance.

"Mrs. Northcutt walked down the hallway toward the master bedroom. By her account she immediately noticed things out of place from the doorway. She said she did not enter the room. She returned to the entry area and informed us of what she saw."

The property crimes detective, who'd identified himself as Edward Tancroft, had taken notes while Landis said this the first time. During the repeat, he'd stared at him as if he could find added meaning in Landis' face. He couldn't. There wasn't any added meaning and even if there had been, Landis didn't let it show.

"No visible signs of forced entry," the shift supervisor repeated.

"None."

"Tough day on the lady." That invited Landis to say it might all have been her imagination. Set this up as doing their duty and displaying appropriate sympathy, but treating the possibility of a real crime with a grain of salt.

Landis slammed that door. "Tough lady. Who was shot at today."

"Out of the house for, what? Twelve hours or more?" Tancroft asked. "Plenty of time for a careful job."

"Yeah, yeah," the shift supervisor said. Not happy—no doubt he was already mentally reassigning personnel—but compliant after his foray down the easier path was rebuffed.

The supervisor and detective shifted slightly, edging Landis out of what had been a circle. He got it. He'd given his report. They had no more use for him. He'd've done the same.

He stepped back to make it easier on them and show there were no hard feelings.

An awareness of new arrivals, which he'd filed away to be dealt with later while he talked to the two members of the Piscattoway Police Department, came to the forefront of his attention.

One of the additional patrol officers, stationed at the end of the driveway—just about exactly where Chad Northcutt was shot, judging by the crime scene photos Landis saw years ago—was waging a battle to keep out Iris Northcutt.

"I'm sorry, ma'am," he said over and over, shifting from side to side to block her as she tried to go around him. "No one's allowed—"

"I'm not nobody, you idiot. I demand to go inside and talk to the officer in charge. I'm *Iris Northcutt*."

That began a family history of the Northcutts in Piscattoway County Police Department history that might baffle the officer, but didn't stop him from inserting his bulk between Iris and the house. She didn't relent—verbally or physically, including drumming at his chest.

If this was her sedated, they definitely hadn't given her the good stuff.

A vehicle in the driveway of the house across the street sat slightly askew, with both front passenger doors open.

Rachel Northcutt, still in uniform, but not appearing quite as pulled together, had clearly lost the battle to take the older woman somewhere other than her home. She silently stared from behind Iris. Neighbors had come outside, but remained on their own front stoops.

Iris Northcutt's carrying voice expressed no concern about Ally, but plenty of possessiveness over *Chad's things*.

Landis closed the distance to the end of the driveway by half then drawled at her, "If that's really your worry and not just nosiness, you'll let the officers do their jobs."

She huffed and called him a few names.

Unmoved, he added, "Piscattoway County Police Department's acting professionally in dealing with this situation. With all your talk of the Northcutts, seems like you'd try to do the same."

Iris Northcutt turned crimson. Not only her face, but her scalp, her neck, and he'd swear her hands showing beneath the wide cuffs of her blouse. But she did make her exit, her outraged posture suitable to a melodrama.

As she turned to follow Iris, Rachel tossed him a quick grin.

The shift supervisor looked scandalized. The detective—Tancroft—looked interested. The patrol officer grateful.

Landis lingered outside, mostly to be on hand to turn back another charge from Iris Northcutt.

The crime scene van and techs arrived not long after and took possession of the house ... except for the occupied living area.

Then the questions began in earnest.

CHAPTER EIGHT

THE PISCATTOWAY DEPARTMENT did a thorough job, especially for a scene with no sign of a break-in, no property obviously taken, and—as they soon found out—no fingerprints in much of the master bedroom.

No fingerprints at all.

That pricked the hairs on the back of Landis' neck when Detective Tancroft eventually showed the two detectives from Fairlington the room.

No question—if he'd had any before—that Ally was right. Someone had been in there. Had to have been to wipe those surfaces clean. Deliberately, thoroughly clean.

"Unless she did it herself," murmured the shift supervisor who'd left earlier and only just returned, likely alerted by Tancroft that the scene was winding down.

"She didn't," Bel said before Landis could.

The four of them were standing on the front walk, watching the scientists wrap up.

The guy looked at each of them, then down, but his jaw set. "Gotta be a real upsetting day for her. Her family getting shot at that way, then her husband dying. Easy to forget what she did before leaving. A little dusting, absent-minded like."

"She's certain. She's credible. She's not absent-minded." Landis kept his words calm and even. He backed it off even more in the interests of cross-river cooperation by saying with something approaching humor, "And according to your people she would have had to do a job worthy of a tech clean room on those surfaces while skipping the ones in between them."

"And why the bed skirt?" Bel asked. "Anomaly."

His partner did love his anomalies. Said the pebbles of evidence built the mountain of truth and plenty of pebbles came from anomalies. Said it all the damned time.

Landis could only be thankful his partner didn't say it now.

"The evidence techs took the bed skirt already, so if there's anything there, the lab can find it," Detective Tancroft said. "Doesn't seem to be anything missing in the room—in the house—so that's good."

Landis didn't agree with him, but kept that to himself.

"We'll see what the scientists come up with in the lab. In the meantime, the techs got through the second bedroom a while ago at Mrs. Northcutt's insistence—Allison Northcutt—" He added the clarification presumably because they were all aware of Iris Northcutt's seething presence across the street. "—and the older lady and gentleman—her aunt and uncle?—have gone to bed. The techs will let you know when they release the rest of the house. We'll leave you now and be in touch when we hear anything."

After thanks and good-byes, he and Bel went inside.

Near the front door, Schmidt sat on one of the dining room chairs, which showed signs of being fingerprinted, as did other visible surfaces in the vicinity.

Dana and Wes Chancellor were gone, confirming Tancroft's statement.

Ally now occupied the big chair. Jamie was back in a tweed chair. J.D. sat on the floor beside Maggie's chair, leaning against its front corner.

Bel and he returned to their positions on the hearth.

"The big question is what were they after," Maggie was saying.

"I can't imagine." Each time Ally blinked, Landis thought her eyes might stay closed. Wished they would.

"There's a bigger question," he said, tagging onto Maggie's words.

"What?" she asked, alert, as always, to other angles.

"Did they get what they came for? If they didn't, we can expect them back.

"Whoever was in the house didn't go past those limited areas in the bedroom. The fingerprint techs will have to go through everything they gathered, but so far nothing unexpected elsewhere. But those areas Ally spotted showed no fingerprints. None."

"But mine should be…" Ally's protest gave way to recognition. "They aren't there because whoever was in the house wiped where they'd been."

"Right," Bel said. "The techs spot-checked elsewhere and there were fingerprints like you'd expect in those areas, which matched yours."

Maggie immediately asked, "How do they have your fingerprints?"

Ally's eyes closed, then opened in a slow, weary blink.

Jamie jumped in. "They took them when Chad was shot."

"As if they were looking at Ally for—"

"We would have, too, if it had been Fairlington, Mags," Bel said. "To eliminate if nothing else."

"Better have been for nothing else. Did they take Iris'?"

"She wasn't living in the same house where Chad lived," Ally said reasonably.

"Might as well have been for the amount of privacy you had—*have*."

With a faint smile showing in his eyes at Maggie's feistiness, J.D. said, "Go back to what you were saying about the question of whether the person who came in got what he wanted. You're thinking he stopped after those few spots because he *did* get what he came for—or she."

"That's one possibility. The other was the search was interrupted."

"Either way, they're not likely to come back tonight." Jamie looked toward Ally as she spoke, clearly thinking they should end this.

"There are things we should know tonight," Landis pursued. "Ally, was there anything in any of those spots missing or that you can think of as potentially something somebody would be after?"

"I told the officers. There's nothing missing. I'm sure of that. I went over it with that PCPD detective. Nothing's kept under the bed. Chad's drawer was where he kept his underwear. My jewelry box… I have a few eighteen-carat gold pieces—earrings, necklace, bracelet—but none of those were touched. And, again, nothing's missing."

"What could someone have been looking for in those three spots?" J.D. asked. "Under the bed sounds big, in the jewelry box sounds small, and the underwear drawer sounds in between."

"Goldilocks and the three bears," Jamie murmured.

"Except nothing was just right," Bel said.

She sighed. "So, what next?"

With his head down, Landis said, "Two directions."

"What two directions? Heading where?" Maggie's impatience nipped at the brim in those rapid-fire questions.

With his usual unhurried thoughtfulness, Bel said, "The shooting is one direction to pursue. The break-in's the other. For us, anyway. PCPD will follow other directions, including what forensics discovers."

"Shootings. Plural," Landis said.

Bel said, "Okay. Yeah. Starts with the shooting of Chad."

"No." Ally's sharp voice drew everyone's attention. "That was years ago. It has nothing to do with what's happening now."

"It has to be looked at. No question," Maggie said. "It's logical. The Piscattoway department's never found out who shot Chad or why. And with that open—especially the *why*—that has to be a line of inquiry now."

"More than four *years* ago. There can't be a connection."

"Ally—"

"No, Jamie. I won't be quiet. It's a waste of time to look back. I won't do it. I'm not spending my time and energy doing that. We could have been shot today. Chad died today. If that doesn't tell all of us there's no more time to waste, then we're not listening. I'm moving forward. Forward, not backward. Not looking back to what happened years ago or even before that."

They all looked at her. Aware it was the first crack in her calmness in this interminable day.

"We're all tired," Jamie said placatingly.

"Yes. Of course, you all are. You should all go now. Thank you—that's inadequate, but, *truly*, thank you all for what you've done today. Aunt Dana and Uncle Wes should stay and sleep through the night, but the rest of you, go home now and—"

"*Hah.*" Maggie's sound wasn't a laugh. "You think we're leaving you here on your own tonight or any time soon? No way. You're coming home with us."

"I can't. I have to be here in the morning. For the meeting with the department about the funeral arrangements. And for Iris."

This time Maggie gave a near growl, but didn't verbalize her feelings about Ally's mother-in-law. "Fine. Then we're staying here with you."

"You don't have to—"

"I am."

"With the patrol outside, there's no reason—"

Jamie looked around at the group, ignoring Ally's protest. "Maggie and I are staying. J.D.?"

"Staying."

"Bel and Tanner—?"

"Need to check in with the captain in Fairlington. Schmidt will stay here," Bel said. "We'll be back in the morning."

✧　✧　✧　✧

BUT THEY DIDN'T leave immediately. Not even in the next hour.

Landis supposed Bel was reluctant to leave Jamie.

As for him, he was just reluctant.

Jamie came into the living room. She waved J.D. not to get up from the tweed chair she'd previously occupied and flopped into the big chair, which almost swallowed her. "Both my parents are asleep. Ally's door is closed and there's no light on."

The other two cousins had a hard time persuading her not to give up her bed to them or to Maggie and J.D. or even to share it. Maggie bluntly said Ally was the one who needed the best shot at a good night's sleep because she was the one who had to keep functioning.

Ally had looked at Maggie Frye's expression and sighed deeply. But she did go to her bedroom.

"You two should get going," Jamie said, focusing on Bel. "You won't get much sleep tonight."

"We'll be fine."

"Jamie," Landis said abruptly, "you reacted to something Ally said."

In genuine surprise, she asked, "I did?"

He allowed for no doubt. "When she told us how she knew someone had been in the room. The chain of the necklace in the jewelry box, the drawer in the dresser, the—"

"Bed skirt," she confirmed. "Checking the bed skirt every time she changed the sheets. It surprised me. Ally never used to be as neat as she is now."

Landis felt a muscle that had been pulling from the side of his neck to his shoulder ease slightly. She didn't disbelieve Ally's account. She wondered at the change in her.

"Anal," Maggie muttered.

"She was never a slob," Jamie said. "But she had other things to do, you know? More important things to spend her time on. Painting and art and ... oh, all sorts of things."

"Not bed skirts," Maggie said.

Jamie turned a grateful expression to her cousin. "Exactly. Straightening a bed skirt every time she changed the sheets? That's not our Ally. That's..."

She glanced toward Maggie. This time the oldest cousin didn't supply more. Jamie lifted her chin. "That's Iris Northcutt. Or it's Iris Northcutt picking at everything Ally does."

"Since Chad was shot or before?" Bel asked.

"Worse since, but before, too. The woman was on her constantly. About the house. About how things had to be done the way Chad liked them—which was the way Iris likes them. About not having a baby. You heard her. Awful things. Just awful."

"When all the time, that woman was worse than a human chastity belt. If Chad wasn't a eunuch, it wasn't for Iris' lack of trying." Maggie's rat-a-tat-tat words came out in a delivery he'd heard her use effectively in court.

Jamie stared at her cousin an instant, then began to splutter with suppressed laughter.

"I mean it," Maggie said, terse.

"I… I know. And you're right. It's just—" Jamie put her hands over her mouth to tone down the volume.

J.D. chuckled and even Maggie's fierceness eased.

Landis caught a small movement in the shadow at the end of the hall.

Ally. Going back into the darkened bedroom, then silently closing the door.

Bel made a low sound in his throat no one else heard. He'd seen Ally, too.

CHAPTER NINE

LANDIS LOOKED OVER as Bel got into the passenger seat of his vehicle uninvited. This was getting to be a habit.

"You're giving me a ride," his partner announced. "Leaving mine here so Jamie and the others have transportation."

Because Ally's vehicle and everyone else's were in Fairlington. He should have thought of that.

"Right."

They started in silence.

This time he was the one who didn't let it extend.

There were things he wasn't telling. That was okay. They weren't joined at the hip. Each entitled to a private life.

But this part wasn't private life. This was the job. Letting this ride could endanger their partnership...

A small bubble of amusement so dry it burned his throat rose up.

...Not to mention it was pointless because Bel would find out sooner rather than later anyway.

"You know a task force was investigating Chad Northcutt for corruption when he was shot?"

"Heard." Bel kept looking out the window on his side.

"You heard at the time he was shot or later?"

"Not long before."

"Did Maggie know?"

"Not from me."

Didn't mean she didn't know, but it was far less likely she did know yet never mentioned it to Bel. Less likely. Not impossible.

If she did know, would she tell Ally?

Probably.

Maybe not right now, but eventually.

Shit.

He jerked his mind back to *now*. Could only clear one hurdle at a time.

"I was on that task force."

Bel slowly turned his head toward him. Driving kept Landis focused ahead.

"When?"

"Joined about five months before he was shot. Left about two months before."

"You went on a task force investigating someone you graduated from the academy with, hung out with—"

"Not a lot."

"—and was married to a woman you were interested in—" Bel's tone underlined that he thought he was vastly understating the case. "—before they got married. I'm presuming you didn't tell anybody about those connections or you wouldn't have been given the assignment."

"I was asked to be on the task force. I didn't seek it out. It was broader than just him. Though it did focus strongly on him." Because he was the tip of the iceberg that showed above the surface. Certainly by the time he'd joined the task force, Northcutt was top priority.

"But you knew from the start that Chad Northcutt was being looked at."

"Not immediately. He wasn't a best buddy or anything." He almost added that he could be objective about the guy, but Bel wasn't above taking that into dangerous territory.

"You had to know soon enough that he was a focus. Central to it."

"Yeah."

"And you stayed with it."

He didn't respond. He'd answered the other statements as if they'd been questions. Not this time.

"Until?" Bel pushed.

"Until I thought I wasn't the best fit for the job and went to my supervisor."

Bel studied him. Making no secret of it.

Landis kept driving. The roads weren't jammed at this hour, but it never paid to ignore what was ahead and behind you in D.C. metro traffic.

When Bel spoke again, he picked up as if the period of scrutiny had never intervened and formed his own answer to the question. "Until Ally came into the picture. They were looking at her."

"Never seriously."

"Was that your judgment or the judgment of the task force leadership?"

"It was a fact. As far as I was concerned, she was the wife of a subject."

"Not sure even that would stop you. Hope to God it would, but—"

"You think I'd jeopardize an investigation?" His grip on the wheel stiffened.

"You've been edging closer and closer to it and you know it. Sleeping with a judge for God's sake."

"Not one we appear before."

"Now. Who knows about the future? It could taint a whole investigation, stop a prosecution."

"And you falling in love with the intended victim-slash-primary suspect didn't have that potential on the Chancellor case? Get off your moral high horse, Belichek."

Bel stared down. Maybe at his hands on his knees or his feet or something in between. Landis didn't spare the attention to determine which.

"You're right about that. I risked it. I knew I was risking the investigation, my career, the prosecution. And you know how grateful I am that you—"

"Shut up about that crap."

"I am grateful. But I'll also say this, Landis, the volume of risk you've been swimming in these past years by following your dick where it wants to go makes my one venture into risk a drop in your ocean. But if you tell me…"

"I'll tell you. Not because you're asking, but so we're damned clear—in fact, I will go on record as swearing that this investigation is in no jeopardy from anything I did. Ever. Including with Ally Northcutt."

"Did you sleep with her after she married—?"

"Never. I never slept with that woman, before she was married or after and sure as hell not during the investigation into Chad."

Bel's eyes narrowed. "Are you turning Bill Clinton on me? Parsing phrases? Didn't sleep with her, but what about—"

Landis' jaw went rigid. "Never had sex with her. Never had anything close to or resembling sex with her by *anybody's* definition. Nothing. No contact with her from well before she married Northcutt until today."

Bel stared at him for two, three, five beats.

"Okay." His fingertips thumped his knees. "Okay. But you said you did know her."

"Yeah. Just like I said. Fiancée of a guy I'd gone to the academy with when I still hung out with some of that group. Before I drifted away from them."

This silence lasted a good couple miles.

Abruptly, he asked Bel, "What made you so sure I knew her?"

Bel slanted him a look he couldn't untangle—not good for partners. "That pen you mashed."

"What?" Landis' confusion was genuine.

"Remember when you broke that pen first time we talked to Hendrickson York at the Sunshine Foundation, early after the murder at Jamie's house."

"Yeah." Almost his usual tone. Maybe a trace of caution, but that was understandable.

"York started talking about Jamie's cousin not lending her name to help with the foundation and having antiquated ideas about justice and law enforcement and you started clicking your pen the way you do to remind me not to get fired up.

"I thought the guy meant Mags. I thought you were pissed at him for dissing her, the way I was, and you were reminding yourself to stay in control. Then you mashed it so hard you broke it. I looked forward to giving you shit for sticking up for Mags, if only by mashing a pen, but never got around to it."

Now Landis recognized the need for caution. He said nothing.

"Realized my error today when I saw you look at Jamie's *other* cousin. It was Ally Northcutt you were thinking of when York's criticism pissed you off."

Landis' chuckle sounded normal. As it should.

"You've gone soft in the head along with falling in love, Belichek. Never was anything between us worth mashing a pen over. I'd encountered her a few times. That's all. Then I was on the task force and she was the wife of a subject. Nothing to say she was involved and a lot to say she wasn't, but didn't matter to me except for how it affected the investigation. My job was to investigate Chad Northcutt."

Bel expelled a breath. But he didn't say any of what was in that exhalation, so Landis didn't argue with it.

His partner shifted away from Ally Northcutt. "What was the case?"

"As far as I know, it's still ongoing…"

"Department business. Your business." It was a pledge. He wouldn't speak of it beyond the two of them. Not even to Jamie. Or Maggie.

That bought Landis space, time. … Unless Maggie already knew. In which case, she was likely telling Ally right now.

"Corruption. Your standard variety pack. Bribes, aligned business interests, money that never made it to the official forfeiture program."

"Drugs?"

"Maybe the only thing that didn't seem to be suspected."

"Because he was smart? Careful?"

"Neither. That's why he was being looked at. He was the visible bit that kept bobbing up above the surface of the dirty water. They figured there was lots more beneath. Hoped to get him tied up enough that he either led them to the others or had to give them up to save his skin."

"The wife would be a natural lever to try to pry him loose. And who better than someone who knew her—?"

"She wasn't. Nothing like that said to me, never hinted."

Bel made a sound in his throat.

"Don't believe me? Don't trust my judgment?"

"Trust my life to you pretty much every damned day, Landis. Believing's not it, either. If you look at yourself as clearly as you look at other people, you'll see—and admit—dealing with women is the one area you let something other than your head lead you—and I'm not talking about your heart. Though this time—"

"Do you want to hear this or do you want to moralize over me?"

After a pause while he knew his partner was thinking through the path each choice might lead to, Bel chose. "Talk."

"As I said, Chad Northcutt wasn't alone in the corruption, but he was the only one who popped up now and then out of the holes in the ground where they lived. He was visible. That's why they focused on him. It was all connected to the job. That puts Ally out of it. He never—*never*—let her into the job. That I can attest to from knowing them early on." He kept any edge from his voice, even though it underlined that Bel was totally off the mark accusing him of being influenced by anything other than the facts. Then or now.

"Rumor was he kept records. Somewhere, somehow. Nothing firm. The thought was that if we kept a close enough watch on him, we could get hard evidence. Didn't succeed while I was on it. They couldn't have after I left or we'd have heard about it."

"Exactly how long before he was shot did you get off the task force?"

"Six weeks."

Bel grunted—a neutral acknowledgment of information. "That's why you were so interested in the answers to my questions to Ally about Chad's partners."

He had not betrayed his interest in any way. Only Bel would have picked up on that.

"Task force had anything about any of them? The first partner?"

"He got attention because he was Northcutt's longest-term partner. Smart, too. On the other hand, Shindell Ortiz left before the first known instance of Northcutt taking money from a citizen on a traffic stop. Nothing in Ortiz' record—previous or after joining the FBI—indicates any involvement. He stayed in touch, but hadn't seen the Northcutts except a couple times from when he left until I left the task force."

"What about the revolving door partners?"

"Nothing specific known about any of them. By the time I came onto the task force, Northcutt didn't have regular partners anymore because of the change in department policy. They probably checked out those revolving door partners, but I wasn't on that."

"No, you were on Northcutt." Bel didn't hide his disapproval.

Landis ignored that. "I'll circle back and talk to the people who organized the task force, see if there's been anything. I always thought the foursome—Chad, his cousin Mark, Dewey Selton, and Ethan Paulz—were worth digging into. They spent time together. A lot of time. Those trips to the Eastern Shore—perfect for divvying up takings, getting rid of anything they didn't want coming back to them, even planning, or otherwise problem solving."

"Anything on them?"

"No. I wasn't given my head to look into it. Ordered to stick with Northcutt."

Bel turned to him a moment, then went back to staring out the windshield.

"And then you quit the task force. Letting the bosses think you were being a diva because you didn't get to follow the lead you liked." No need to answer that statement, either. "Couldn't have done your career any good."

"I survived."

Bel scoffed with a sharp exhalation. "Not what you could have expected from being put on a task force so early in your career. Couldn't have had exactly a meteoric rise after that or you wouldn't have gotten teamed with me."

Tanner grinned briefly. "They thought we were going to fall on our asses. Damned satisfying to prove them wrong."

"Damned satisfying to solve murders."

"Yeah, yeah, Mr. Goody Two-shoes."

A snort from Bel was as good as a belly laugh from someone else.

"Hear any more about the task force after you left?"

"Nothing big broke—I'm sure of that. As far as I know, the operation went quiet. Then, with Chad out of the picture, there wasn't a thread I ever heard about to follow back to the rat's nest. Don't know officially, but I expect the task force closed up then. Doesn't mean the rats turned noble. Doesn't mean they stopped supplementing their salaries in all sorts of ways. Especially…"

"Right. This attempt on Ally. The break-in. Have to consider the possibility that Northcutt's former associates think she might know something."

"That's why you asked about his partners, thinking they were likelies for the shooting."

"Obvious possibility. When they say start with the nearest and dearest and the guy's a cop, you look at partners. But—?"

Landis finished the thought. "Why now? If they were worried about her knowing too much of the operation, they'd have acted at the same time they dealt with Northcutt. If they thought she had something of theirs—information or money, they'd have broken in back then and every day since until they found it."

"So, something's changed. And the most obvious thing is that Chad Northcutt was failing and is now dead."

"And Ally most likely inherits," Landis said.

Bel nodded slowly. "Maybe somebody doesn't want her to do that. We need to find out what she inherits. Something that could have been hidden in the house. Small, or the jewelry box doesn't make sense."

One of their familiar silences fell. It felt like gears smoothly meshing.

Bel broke it. "The timing."

They'd been following the same track.

"That job on the house required time to be that unobtrusive and leave no prints," Bel continued. "They had to jump on it fast and go faster if they didn't start until after the word came that he'd died. Or else they knew he was headed that way."

Tanner shook his head. "Had to be earlier. Had to know he was headed toward dying or why shoot at Ally at the courthouse?"

"Yeah. Good. So, we find out when word reached his department and who heard it."

"And who was free to come over to Fairlington and take those shots."

"Yep. Nothing official. Just conversation. Best opportunity is going to be overhearing the conversations around—but just out of the hearing of—the widow. We're going back tomorrow and we're sticking there."

Landis grunted acknowledgment.

The only person who would look forward to that prospect less than him was Ally, if she knew what was coming.

He was glad she didn't. She'd sleep better not knowing.

—DAY 2—

WEDNESDAY

CHAPTER TEN

LYING ON HER side, Ally stared at the sliver of earliest light between the frame and the lowered blind that outlined the window to the backyard.

Tanner Landis.

How was that even possible?

He had been the lead detective on Jamie's case? How could she not have known that? Heard his name? Made the connection? ... Been prepared for it.

Easy.

Because at the start, when the police thought Jamie was dead, and Ally ignored Iris' protests and drove to the Chancellors' house in Virginia with dawn barely prying the dark from the sky, they'd focused on any possibility that it was a mistake. She'd scoured her brain for every fragment of casual conversation with her cousin to produce a lead to a place she might have been.

But Jamie wasn't there.

As the hours unrolled, they incrementally squeezed the life out of their hopes. Heartbroken, they certainly didn't sit around chatting about the police—and specifically the lead detective.

And later, all her contacts had been with Detective Ford Belichek—the man who'd long been Maggie's friend, the man who became much more to Jamie.

Ally frowned.

All her contacts…

They *had* all been with Bel. Was that an accident? Or had Tanner…?

It didn't matter. It wasn't important. Not even a question to contemplate when there were far more important ones.

Like, *What happens now?*

For more than four years, she'd been in an unchanging bubble, where time passed, but never got anywhere. She couldn't believe it was over, couldn't imagine anything outside of it.

Death did not stand as the opposite of life in Ally's experience.

The opposite of life was waiting.

As Chad's body had these past years.

As she had.

Every day showering, dressing, going to the facility. Every day sitting beside Chad's bed, reading to him, listening to the doctors, winning over the nurses. Every day feeling his mother's silent condemnation that she hadn't managed to save Chad, not the day of the shooting or any day since.

Some days also hearing the not-silent criticism that she wasn't sorrowful enough, she wasn't determined enough, she wasn't loving enough to pull Chad through.

How would her mother-in-law be now?

Taking last night as an example, not easy.

Ally resisted the urge to get out of bed and prowl silently.

She didn't worry about waking anyone. She'd perfected the ability in the years living here with Chad.

Unless he woke and reached for her—something he'd rarely done after the first few months—he never knew.

But where she wanted to prowl to now was out of reach.

She couldn't look out any of the windows at the front of the house without intruding on Aunt Dana and Uncle Wes in the second bedroom—never called the guest room, because it was destined to be a nursery—or her cousins, J.D., and that poor officer in the living area, making do with pillows and blankets on chairs or the floor.

Looking out the front windows in a way that she couldn't be seen from across the street had become an ingrained habit. Almost a talisman of sorts. Proof that she existed separate from the image reflected back to her by the Northcutts. At least Iris and Chad.

Iris' house stood directly across the street.

It was the house where Chad and his older brother, David, had grown up. The house their father, David Senior, had occupied until his death.

Yet everyone referred to it as Iris' house.

The kitchen was at the front, with a good-sized window looking out toward the street—and across it to her son and daughter-in-law's house. The first time Ally saw Iris' house, she'd thought the floor plan was a bit odd, but hadn't recognized its ramifications.

Instead, she'd thought it was endearing that Chad lived across the street from his widowed mother and the house where he'd grown up.

Most of all, she'd been too smitten with the idea of geography reflecting the Northcutt family's closeness. Rachel lived within a mile, her father three blocks from Iris. More Northcutt in-laws were in the next neighborhood north. Chad's brother and family had lived four blocks away. Until his tragic death and his wife's subsequent move with their children back to her family in Illinois. Dotted in between were the homes of a number of Piscattoway County Police Department officers.

That's what she had first seen.

The coziness. The interconnectedness of one family and the broader law enforcement family—close enough to share the good and hard times.

Gradually, she'd come to see Iris' kitchen window as something very different.

A command post to observe and direct the battle. Because that was how the woman saw life. A constant battle to make sure the Northcutts received their due in every way possible.

In the first year or so of her marriage to Chad, the observing seemed the worst of it.

That's when she'd wanted privacy with Chad. Intimacy that had nothing to do with physicality. To build a true relationship.

At that point it had seemed Iris' presence was the impediment.

The way she knew exactly when Ally left the house, how long she was gone, and what she brought back. Ally could almost believe that kitchen window had X-ray capabilities. It would explain Iris seeming to know each item in the grocery bags or shopping bags brought in.

She commented on all of it. Much of it critically.

How much worse that all became since the day Chad was shot.

What happens now?

She'd wondered something slightly different that morning, four years and six months ago when she pretended to sleep until Chad left.

He hadn't touched her or spoken to her before he left. She'd been so relieved. Afraid what her face, even her skin might reveal to him.

She'd decided that to be safe, she'd stay in bed until she heard his vehicle starting. Then she would get busy.

Waiting, her heart took an extra beat, hard, and reverberating against her ribs like a bass drum resided there.

Any second now, she'd start on her journey. She'd take back her life, herself. It would be difficult and possibly dangerous. But she would do it.

The sound of his vehicle starting never came.

She'd been listening so intently that even when the sound of a different vehicle accelerating rose, she didn't doubt herself, didn't think maybe she'd missed Chad's truck starting somehow and that this acceleration was his vehicle pulling away.

She was sure it wasn't.

She held her breath, not letting even that automatic sound of air in and out to interfere with hearing what came next.

A sudden flurry from birds disturbed by something, a second acceleration—this one away from the house—a pause of utter stillness, and then the otherworldly keening shriek of her mother-in-law.

Ally had pulled on an oversized hoodie over the tee and sweatpants she'd slept in as she ran to the front door.

Her phone—her regular phone—was in the pocket of the hoodie, where she'd deliberately stashed it the night before. That wouldn't have stopped Chad if he'd really wanted to find it. That's why she'd put it there.

Out in the open wouldn't do. Too obvious. Had to be somewhere he'd have to search for it hard enough to be satisfied he'd found what was hidden.

The precaution hadn't been necessary. Like all precautions, though, its necessity or lack of necessity only became apparent in hindsight.

Last night, when he came in and she'd been pretending to sleep, she'd known he'd been drinking hard. From the smell and from the way he moved around the room. If her phone had been visible, he might well have grabbed it, but he wasn't in a searching mood.

So it stayed safely in that pocket until she pulled it out to call 911.

She'd had other plans for this phone—and the one truly hidden— that day. Not to tell a calm dispatcher that someone had shot her husband in the head in the driveway of their home and, yes, she was quite certain he was dead.

Except he wasn't.

Iris hated her for saying it. Starting in the waiting room that day even before they took him in for surgery. "You said he was dead. You told 911 he was *dead.*"

How many times had Iris tasked her with that? She'd never answered back.

Part of her wondered if Iris was right, if she *had* wanted Chad to be dead.

But it was a small part of what cut into her and kept under layers of numbness.

Neither of her cousins had approved of her numbing routine before Chad was shot. They hadn't known how necessary it was.

After the shooting, they accepted it for a while. But as the months passed to a year, each thought the self-protective mode had run its course and she needed to be aware, alert. To not be numb.

She'd expected that from Maggie. In fact, her formidable older cousin had lasted longer than Ally would have expected before speaking her mind that she could support Chad without sacrificing her entire life to his hopeless situation. Not to mention getting out from under Iris' thumb.

Jamie agreed with Maggie without saying a word. Her younger cousin remained supportive and entirely unconfrontational. Yet Ally knew Jamie chafed at Iris' strictures and Ally's confined schedule.

It was only one reason it became harder to be around them.

And another reason they couldn't understand but that made numb a necessity.

If she'd acted…

But she hadn't. Caught by her own hopes, her own weakness.

Standing in the driveway, telling the 911 dispatcher that her husband had been shot in the head. In that moment, she had known that she would not—could not—let anyone else pay the price for her hesitation. No matter what.

CHAPTER ELEVEN

CAPTAIN WILSON PALERY didn't do anything as overt as raise his eyebrows as he pulled up a chair to the end of the diner booth's table, where Landis occupied one side and Bel the other.

But his question about why this wasn't a one-on-one breakfast came through clearly.

"Events yesterday after we talked changed the play," Landis explained. "Bel needed to know the background."

The server brought his steak and eggs, Bel's oatmeal, and coffee all around.

"Sir?" she asked Palery.

"Just coffee," he said.

As soon as she was out of hearing of their isolated booth in the back, Landis said, "I knew Chad Northcutt in the academy."

"Friends?"

"No. Not the opposite, either. After the academy, we were both part of a loose social group. You know how it is. As time went on, our paths didn't cross as much."

"Okay. Did you interact with Ally Northcutt during the investigation around the attempts on Jamison Chancellor?"

"Not at all." Did the chief of detectives make his question specific on purpose? Or was Landis lucky. Either way, he moved on quickly. "There was a task force investigating Chad Northcutt. I was on it for a short time early in my career."

"The black hole mystery assignment in your work record."

"Yeah."

"Got off it because you knew him."

"Not right away. I thought I could do it. But it got complicated with surveillance. Wasn't right if I couldn't pull my share, but it was too big a risk I'd be recognized."

Palery narrowed his eyes at him. Letting him know he suspected there was more, not feeling the need—at the moment—to find out all the details, but reserving the right to insist on them later.

Bel said his first words. "Why didn't you mind not crossing paths with him as the social ties from the academy loosened?"

Chewing, Landis held the question for an extra two beats. He could sidestep it, evade it, smooth it over. Bel wouldn't let it go. Not when he used all those words and defined his question carefully.

Landis swallowed his food.

"Didn't like the way he smelled."

The other two men accepted that with a blink.

"Dirty from the start?" Palery asked.

"No evidence."

"You could see the potential," Bel said.

"Too strong."

His partner gave him a quick, searching look. But his words were slow and deliberate. "His family."

Palery said, "What about his family? The Northcutts are known for their law enforcement heritage."

"Yeah," he and Bel said together.

"You think that's fake? My father knew the grandfather. Respected him."

"Could've been a lot of pressure on Chad Northcutt. The weight of those generations before," Bel said.

"Chad and his brother," Landis added slowly.

"What about the brother?" Palery said.

"Might be worth looking into him, too. Might throw more light on Chad."

"Thought his brother died on the job. Hit by a careless driver during a traffic stop, wasn't it?"

"DUI stop. And hit by a DUI."

"That's tough. Anything in it?"

"We'll look," Landis said.

"Iris Northcutt is … interesting," Bel said.

Palery looked down to his coffee cup, as if surprised to find it empty.

The server immediately slid in and refilled it, then topped off the other two cups. Landis and Bel were better tippers, but Palery was the chief of detectives and this place served by rank.

To Landis' surprise, Bel continued when they were alone again. "Did her best to shove the widow into the background and take the spotlight herself."

"The woman did just lose her son." Palery's neutral tone soft-pedaled some.

Still, Landis felt words of protest pushing up his throat.

"Allison Northcutt just lost her husband. Though you could say both of them sustained the loss more than four years ago," Bel said.

Landis realized his partner had spoken to keep him from needing to. Probably did a better job of it, too.

"Well." Palery drank more coffee. "Put family dynamics aside for now. Facts would be nice. We've got to get formal statements from those people."

"Today?" Landis asked.

Palery drank more coffee.

He did that to give himself time. It meant the man drank a lot of coffee, but he also had a record for making sound decisions.

Bel dropped in. "Funeral arrangements."

That elicited another sip.

After he swallowed, Palery said, "Play it by ear today. We'll talk at the end of the day. In the meantime, we've got a lot of video from the scene to examine. Three good angles. If you want to come back to the bureau to view some."

Landis exchanged a glance with Bel, who said, "Some. Before we go back to Maryland."

"Good. There's also some progress from yesterday. No smoking gun. But there's an office suite that's between tenants, so unoccupied.

The window's open. There are marks on a windowsill overlooking the plaza that would fit.

"Its location matches what you two and the security detail said, as well as the first rough estimate of trajectory. Yeah. They found the bullet in the planter, a couple feet from where Mrs. Northcutt and her cousins were. Another impact point on the concrete edge of it. There's not much left of that bullet. They'll work both, the office suite, and keep checking for more. Also going through the video and security camera coverage. So far nothing, but there's a lot more to go."

"What about the chance this is tied to the court proceeding—the plea deal?" Landis asked.

"Nothing's turned up about someone being against the plea deal. No public or social media blow ups about the proceeding—we were watching before and none then, either. He hasn't had any visitors or correspondents except the lawyers and their people—all professionals. None seem likely to turn to zealotry."

"Seem likely." Bel's murmured repetition raised a doubt.

Palery's *huh* recognized it. "Not done looking into them. Not done looking into any of it. C'mon, let's go. Don't have all day to sit around drinking coffee."

Which was Palery's idea of a joke, because he usually did sit around all day drinking coffee … while also doing his job very well.

✧　✧　✧　✧

THAT WAS DEFINITELY the guy. Didn't take a fucking genius to figure that out.

This wasn't nearly as hard as they made it out to be. First try and he'd found the guy.

He'd been sure yesterday at the courthouse.

He snorted a laugh to himself. Could say he took a shot.

Hadn't turned out the way he'd hoped, but that was okay, too, because he slipped away with nobody paying him any attention at all. But he hadn't slipped all the way away. Just to outside where the police tape kept back the gawking idiots. And he'd stayed long enough to see the vehicles come out of the courthouse parking garage, one after the other, with Landis driving the third one.

He'd snapped a quick photo.

Gotcha, you bastard.

That had felt almost as good as the night he'd found the guy online.

That part hadn't been as easy as it sounded.

Sure, he had the name and the department, but these guys didn't go out in the open like ordinary people. They hid away. Plenty of images of badges, including way old ones. But not of the man behind the badge.

His thoughts gave that phrase the sneering twist it deserved.

But the Internet was forever, and he'd found raw video from some bystander at a murder investigation a while back. Unidentified voices said, "That's the officer in charge. Heard them call him Landis."

Those unidentified voices had sounded horrified, scared. He'd been thrilled.

Gotcha, you bastard.

That video also gave him clues about which case it was. He found it soon enough. The problem was there was so much coverage that it would've taken forever to slog through it. But he'd been smart about that, too. Instead of trying to go through it in order, he jumped to the past few months. That cut it way down. That's where he found out about the hearing at the courthouse yesterday.

He'd thought that would be the last piece he'd need. But yesterday hadn't turned out the way he'd hoped.

That was okay, he reminded himself. He'd keep at it until it did.

That's why he was back today. Watching from half a level up in the parking garage, able to look through gaps to see the elevator doors not far from the car he'd spotted as he'd slowly, carefully, checked all the vehicles when he'd arrived this morning.

He'd seen the car yesterday with the asshole driving. He'd also seen it before that.

Anybody asked, he'd already decided to say he was looking for his friend's car left here overnight because it wouldn't start. And then he would have discovered he had the wrong address, and slunk away like he was all embarrassed.

Needed to think these things through ahead of time so you didn't get nervous and blow it.

But nobody asked. Nobody paid him any attention at all. Like always.

And he'd waited. Patient. Quiet. In the shadows. Forgotten.

Until, here came Tanner Landis again. Getting into the slick car with that same guy he'd been with yesterday like he owned the world.

Landis got behind the wheel. The other guy got in the passenger seat.

That other guy… Fuck it. Collateral damage. Not his fault if the guy hung around with the asshole named Landis.

CHAPTER TWELVE

"**Ally, dear.**"

Dana Chancellor's tone from behind them made Ally, Maggie, and Jamie turn to look at her from where they were cleaning up the kitchen after breakfast.

For an instant her aunt looked at the three of them with an expression Ally would love to paint. Someday. If she could capture it. Because it was complex. There was love for the people Dana saw now, mixed with nostalgic love for the children they'd been, and a dose of sorrow that those earlier days were gone. With a hint of the horror that divided the two.

But when Ally blinked, she saw that Dana also wore a worried frown that matched her tone and neither had to do with the past.

"What is it, Aunt Dana?" she asked.

"Your mother." Dana reached for Ally's arm and added, "No, not here."

Maggie had spun around and looked toward the front door.

Belatedly, Ally realized she'd done the same thing.

"Your mother messaged me last night… She heard news of the shooting at the courthouse somehow. And then news people picked up on Chad's death, too, and with both events involving you… She said she's been getting a lot of calls. She tried to call you."

They'd been spared all such calls, as well as condolence calls and crackpots by putting their phones on Do Not Disturb. Such an action never occurred to Greta Frye Moban Lindell.

Ally couldn't regret that Do Not Disturb had also stopped her mother's calls. No doubt her father's, too.

Dana continued with ripping-off-the-bandage speed. "She's coming today."

"*Mo-om*," Jamie protested.

Maggie groaned.

Ally might feel like groaning, but what was the point? Her reactions never altered—or slowed—her parents' actions. Hadn't when they were together and certainly not since they'd divorced.

Dana defended herself. "She *is* Ally's mother. I couldn't very well tell her *not* to come."

"Yes, you could have, Mom. You could have told her we were all taking care of Ally and nobody has any time to pay attention to her."

"Jamison."

"Attagirl, Jamie," Maggie said.

"You, too, Margaret. I know she can be difficult, but..." Dana interrupted her scold. "You're right. I should have told her not to come. I let my thinking be clouded by how I felt yesterday with you girls in danger on top of all the horrible worry about Jamie."

Ally squeezed her hand. "It's all right, Aunt Dana. She would have come anyway."

Greta Frye Moban Lindell was nothing if not single-minded about certain things.

It was how she'd taken on and led the effort to build a garden on land reclaimed from the ravages of Pennsylvania coal mining ... well after such coal mining had made her first husband rich. That's how they'd met. As a college student, she'd gone to lobby him to rehabilitate the land, he'd married her, died two years later, and she'd had her gardening dream ever since.

Don't ever mention to her that Pittsburgh's botanical garden was the *first* built on reclaimed land. *Technically*, she might concede, but then you would hear for hours, perhaps days, how much better her garden was, both in its approach to reclamation and its result.

No, Dana telling her not to come wouldn't have stopped her. Nor would Dana ignoring her message.

Once Greta wanted something, nothing stopped her.

Though Ally couldn't imagine what her mother might want that would make her decide to come.

Among other factors, it was odd that she would leave her gardens now. Even in the dead of winter, much less May, she said there was something needing to be done in or for her gardens. Just as her father claimed work kept him in Pittsburgh.

Neither of her parents had ever been to this house in the years she'd lived here. They'd barely made it to the wedding. In fact, had left the reception, her mother immediately after her father, before the bride and groom did.

In fairness, they came immediately after Chad was shot. Almost simultaneously, but of course separately. She had barely registered their presences at the hospital. They'd stayed… She didn't know where they'd stayed. A hotel, presumably, because she remembered them at the hospital again. Though she couldn't have said if that was the next day.

Her cousins, as well as Aunt Dana and Uncle Wes, provided the practical and emotional support that got her from the first shock into the numbing routine. One good thing, her parents hadn't even been a distraction at the time. She was too focused on other things.

How long did they stay? Not long, she was sure. And once one left, the other would have gone, too.

That never changed.

Ally's theory was that neither was willing to leave Pittsburgh when the other was there because of the weird, enduring need to know what the other was doing at all times. Each couched it in terms of avoiding awkward encounters, but if that had been the motive, they should have been *glad* to get out of town.

Dana sighed. "Well, yes, dear, I'm afraid you're right that she would have come anyway. But I made it worse, because—"

"Uncle Kurt also messaged you and now he's coming, too," Jamie said.

Of course.

"Yes, I'm afraid so."

"*Mo-om.*"

Ally went to her aunt, miserable even before Jamie's remonstration, and put an arm around her shoulders. "You couldn't have stopped either one of them. Don't worry about it."

But Ally did worry.

Useless, she knew from a lifetime of experience.

She used to worry *for* them.

She'd gotten over that a long time ago. She'd recognized them for who they were and that they could not become different people. She'd gone in search of a real family.

And her worry became about minimizing the turmoil they wrought in her life.

✧　✧　✧　✧

PALERY MADE CALLS while the tech set up video for them to view at Bel's desk.

Landis saw his own face as he dove at Ally.

Not obvious to other people, he thought, except maybe Bel.

But seeing it now, what he'd felt in that instant—

He breathed. Slow. Precise.

"Let's see it again. Slow motion."

This time to see if he picked up anything new, anything useful. Like better information on if he'd been totally wrong about the shooter aiming at Ally.

"Might not have been aiming at Ally." Bel's mutter proved they'd followed the same mental track.

"Aiming at her makes him a lousy shot. Not aiming at her makes him a *really* lousy shot."

Bel grunted acknowledgment of the point. "Not aiming at a specific target?"

"Can't take the risk of acting on that supposition and being wrong."

"True. But don't want to get too tied into one way of thinking and miss other possibilities."

His turn to grunt acknowledgment of a point.

"Really got into that, didn't you, Landis?"

Terrington, from behind them. Leering, no doubt.

"Jumping in front of a bullet?" Eddy Knarr asked from his desk. "You should try it, Terrington."

Low chuckles scoffed at that likelihood.

With unerring timing, Palery emerged from his office.

"Queue them both back to the start," he ordered the tech. Then added, "Bel, Landis, you stay. The rest of you get back to work."

The phrasing spared a direct reprimand to Terrington, the only one not at his desk working. He moved away without comment.

"Run all three straight through, real time," Palery ordered.

When they finished, the silence lasted until Palery said, "Thanks" to the tech, then "My office," to the two detectives.

Landis and Bel sat in what might be the guest chairs in some offices. In the chief of detectives' office, they were more like the inquisition chairs.

Palery took another beat, looking out at the desks beyond the glass wall. "Don't start thinking I'm soft on Terrington."

That surprised Landis. If it surprised Bel, he didn't show it.

"The rest of you ride him hard enough, I don't need to. If I did, there'd be no hope of making some kind of detective out of him someday. No—Don't say it." Though neither of the partners came close to saying anything. "You might not think he has potential, but that's why I sit in the boss' chair and earn the big bucks. Don't mind you riding him—within reason—but don't start thinking I'm soft on him, because I'm not. Not on him. Not on any of you. Now, what about that video. Bel?"

Without hesitation, he ticked off the obvious points. A group walking in the center of the plaza at a sedate pace, with no obstructions from the presumed position of the shooters. Far from an impossible shot.

"Second one a little harder, because they were all reacting, especially with Landis and J.D. Carson bringing people to the ground. Then me. But also not impossible."

"Yet two misses. Bad shot? Or purposeful misses?" Palery's questions were meant to be answered, but not until they had facts lined up to answer them. Now it would be speculation. "Landis?"

"Agreed. Can't bank on either a bad shot or purposeful misses. Too risky. And something else."

"Yeah?"

He'd have his say anyway, but Palery's invitation eased the entry. "We're not working investigation first on this—Bel and me. The rest of you can. But we have to work security first. And I don't care that Piscattoway would say they're primary security. They're not. Maybe they can't be." He granted them that much leeway, but no more. "We are. Security first, investigation second."

Bel grunted emphatically.

Palery looked at the other detective, then back to Landis.

"You're not on the Fairlington County Police Department payroll to protect citizens of Piscattoway County, Maryland."

"Bullshit. Sir."

Palery wiped a hand over his mouth. It didn't completely mask the mouth twitch, though whether at the *Bullshit* or the *Sir*, no telling.

"If you want to go with straight self-interest, letting Allison Lindell Northcutt get killed ties investigating the shooting at the courthouse into knots on top of knots. Keeping her safe is the best thing for the investigation and therefore for Fairlington."

"But even if it weren't, you'd make security your top priority."

"Yes, sir."

"Yes, sir." Bel added to his echo, "Ally and all of the family members."

Palery would give them some room to maneuver. For now.

"Got background on that task force." He looked at Landis from under his brows. "They liked your work. The task force officially disbanded six months after Chad Northcutt was shot. Only extended that long in case he pulled off a miracle and came around. But with him out of the picture, they had nothing to go on, nothing to tug to try to get it to unravel."

"Does that release Landis from keeping it quiet?" Bel asked.

"Any revelations only for the good of this operation," Landis inserted.

Palery snorted. "For the good of the operation—security and investigation. Within reason. *My* idea of reason, not yours. Get out of here you two. Get back to Maryland. Where you will work *both* angles of this job."

CHAPTER THIRTEEN

THERE WERE OTHER memories. Ones he wasn't sharing with Palery, with anyone.

He'd been friendly with most of the people at the academy, including the instructors. No reason not to be.

He just wasn't part of a group from his class that hung together all the time.

That was fine with him. He preferred being solo. Independent.

A couple of the guys in the group invited him fairly regularly. He made a point of saying yes often enough to not be considered a complete outsider.

He said yes more often after meeting Chad Northcutt's fiancée at one of the regular gatherings at Mikey's, a semi-dive bar between the academy and headquarters.

She wasn't the most beautiful—there were a couple stunners in their class and among the girlfriends and wives. He never did know exactly what made his scan of the room stop abruptly the first time he saw her. Whatever it was, it didn't evaporate the first time he talked to her. She was smart with a quick intelligence that made links not obvious to most. She was nice to everyone. She was quietly but dryly funny.

It must have been the second time he'd seen her that he'd automatically recognized she was an attractive woman. Probably got a glimpse of her legs.

They were long, with a curve that promised an element of power. He liked that.

But no matter what collection of pleasant-to-look-at parts she possessed, she had one insurmountable thing going against her. She was engaged to Chad Northcutt. Being engaged to anyone was a major impediment back then. But he didn't particularly like Chad and he didn't respect him. That sure as hell called her judgment into question.

So he chatted with her, spent some pleasant time with her. But nothing special.

Until…

One night, arriving at Mikey's late to join the group from the academy, he'd come across her sitting at a picnic table in the shadows left by the overhead light. She had a pad in front her. About half again as big as a sheet of printer paper. She stroked across it with first one pencil from a small case sitting open beside her tote bag, then another pencil. Sometimes long strokes, sometimes short and feathery marks, sometimes circular motions.

"What are you doing out here alone?"

She'd been so absorbed in what she was doing she hadn't noticed his approach. She jumped and that gave him a brief view of the pad.

Dark and light radiated across the page. That was all he caught before she quickly adjusted it so he couldn't see.

"The smoke gets thick inside. I cough," she said with a shade of ruefulness, as if she bore responsibility for coughing in a smoky dive. She stopped moving her hand across the paper. "It's disruptive."

He'd bet Northcutt said that to her. He didn't put it past the guy to say it in front of all the rest of them, too.

"It's a pit in there. You're better off out here. We all would be."

She didn't return to her drawing, though he caught movement from the corner of his eye, as if her hand twitched with the desire to keep moving.

She smiled. "Not exactly an oasis out here, either."

"Better for sitting." He matched the words with action by swinging one leg over the attached bench, then pulled in the other to sit opposite her. "And talking."

She smiled.

And she resumed moving her hand.

She held the pencil toward the end of it, angled on its side, not using the point. Light strokes, then changed her hold and crossed the original marks with new ones.

He told her a couple amusing stories from his past two weeks of patrol.

The year before, when he'd been hired right out of the academy by the Monacan Police Department, his friends had been polite. Chad and his cronies had said, "Where?" Or the ones who thought they were clever, "Did you say Mayberry?"

Yeah, it was considerably smaller than a lot of the departments his classmates went for, especially then, but he figured it would give him a diversity of experiences faster than he'd get elsewhere.

He was right.

When he tried to get Ally to talk, she avoided herself as a topic. She'd respond, just not about herself.

To show her how it was done, he kept talking. A lot. Not the way he did now, but with his heart and hopes hanging out all sloppy, like a piñata waiting to be whacked until it spilled all over.

After a few minutes, she flipped to a fresh page. As she did, he saw more clearly what she'd drawn on the previous sheet.

A spiked starburst of light sprayed out from the intense light of a sun lodged on the right side of the page. The shadings between the spikes created movement, like the light of a solar system extending out and out and out. Yet it couldn't have been a solar system, because he'd spotted an evergreen branch in front of one part of the light sprays.

While he talked, he found an excuse to turn around, looking for the inspiration.

It was an ordinary light on a pole. Mist surrounded it, but even knowing what he was looking for, he didn't see what she had seen. What she had created.

Now she was on to something else. Working with the pad angled—on purpose or not—so he couldn't see it as he told her about how he planned to investigate corruption, to root it out, so people with the public trust deserved it. He'd talked about how he would follow the money. He'd talked about how he'd never take a promotion that would take him away from direct investigating.

Charcoal, he realized. She was sketching or drawing or whatever defined what she was doing with charcoal. It stained her hand, and added a smudge along the side of her nose.

"Special paper?"

"Vellum. It holds the charcoal best because of its texture."

He talked on.

He talked to Ally Northcutt for hours that night. Telling her things he'd told no one else. Including how he intended to rid the world of corrupt officials.

She talked a little, too. Mostly asking him questions.

They'd laughed some. Not loud, not raucous like what came from inside, reaching them here as echoes. Their amusement was quiet, easy, relaxed.

As they talked, she continued working.

After laying down the darker color that also marked her hand, she used a paintbrush in controlled, circular motions to soften the tones. Then she fit a piece of tissue over her index finger, circling the paper's surface with the tip, smoothing out the transitions from light to dark.

He had to look away from that motion—too easy to get caught up in what that finger might feel like circling his surfaces.

Chad Northcutt never came out, never checked on her.

At one point, apparently not thinking about it, she shifted the pad to get a new angle on the paper, and he caught sight of what was there.

"Hey. Is that me?" He interrupted telling her about a conversation with an FBI agent about a potential career track for fighting corruption.

It was. The features, the haircut. She'd portrayed him from the shoulders up, leaning forward slightly. Intent.

A tuck of concern instantly appeared between her brows and she pulled the pad to her protectively. "I hope you don't mind."

"Hell, no. You made me out better than I am." The interesting thing was she hadn't focused on individual features. They were more an impression behind the intensity.

"Too bad everybody doesn't see me that way," he said, inclined to be amused.

She declined to respond with similar flippancy. "They would if you didn't stay behind that armor." Her quick gesture indicated his attire. Nothing fancy, but several steps up from what his fellow off-duty officers inside would be wearing.

"But you didn't include any of my clothes."

"No, I didn't."

"Clothes or no clothes, I look smarter." He grinned, teasing a bit with the reference to no clothes.

The tuck of concern remained, but she smiled back. "I draw what I see. I paint what I see. What's there. I don't make it up."

That sounded like defense against a criticism. That idiot Chad Northcutt? Probably.

But she was right. She'd gotten the light on the pole and she'd made him recognizable.

But she was wrong, too. She'd seen more than was there. She'd added—herself?—to these two drawings.

"I saw a bit of that other one you were working on—the light from the pole. I didn't know you could do that with pencils."

"They're not regular lead pencils. They're charcoal pencils."

She gestured to the small open case, which held her tools.

"You could've put one of those sprays of light behind me, too. Or gone all the way and given me a halo thing like they used to paint on saints."

She grinned. At ease again. "A halo? That doesn't fit you at all."

She returned the pencil to the case and took out something new. A chunk of charcoal, he supposed. About as long as one of his fingers and wider. Her index finger extended down the charcoal, guiding it, angled across the paper.

"Not a halo like just a round circle, but those pointy ones."

"A starburst. I had a painting teacher who called them corona halos."

"Have you been painting long? Not that this is painting. I don't know much, but I know that."

"Painting, drawing, sketching … all my life. It—" She paused. Not hesitating over what she was about to say, but making sure she said it accurately. "—makes sense of what I see around me."

That neared his sense that she put herself into it.

Not something he'd say to her. It would make her uncomfortable.

After that, they talked every time they crossed paths. Sometimes in snatches. Never as long or as openly as that night. Often with other people around.

But he knew.

And he was sure she did, too.

That drawing of him… She had to know.

That's what he'd thought in the moments when he watched her use a paint brush, then her tissue-wrapped finger to go over the darkness she'd laid down on the paper, changing it to something lighter and deeper.

That's what he'd felt when she eventually closed the case and pad and slid them into her oversized bag and went in to find Chad.

As if that weren't hint enough.

What an idiot. He should have paid attention.

Soon enough, he'd had to realize what really happened that night.

He'd talked a lot of crap and she'd pretended to listen to him, humoring him while thick smoke billowed out from her husband-to-be and the others whenever anyone opened the door.

He'd taken what she drew for who she was.

Wasn't her fault he'd created something of her she wasn't. Nobody was.

He'd learned. Eventually. And he'd moved on.

***D*AMN. H*E'D LOST* fucking Landis.**

Did fine following the vehicle out of the parking garage and through the nearby streets, but Landis slithered away coming through that Interstate pretzel just this side of the Potomac.

Didn't help they weren't in a marked car. It blended into a torrent of traffic. No sign of it at all after he'd crossed the river. Crossing the river had seemed the most likely. That's what he'd figured after that news story that linked yesterday's shooting in Fairlington with a woman whose husband died in Maryland yesterday. Some former cop who'd been a vegetable since being shot in the head years ago.

He didn't get the whole connection, not even after watching the TV report several times. Though it seemed to be saying there was more than coincidence. It referred to an article in the *Washington Post* about something to do with the woman, but if it had been important, it would have been on TV.

No matter what, it had been a bad day for her, he thought with a lift of one corner of his mouth at his dour humor.

He looked for a place to turn around and get back to Virginia. Still seemed most likely Landis had crossed the river into Maryland for something to do with this woman or whatever, but too many potential options. Even if he'd had the woman's address.

Better to turn back and pin down where she was.

He had something to thank her for. She'd be how he tracked down Landis again.

✧ ✧ ✧ ✧

PISCATTOWAY COUNTY POLICE DEPARTMENT

ADDRESS: 1567 Gardington Rd.
REASON FOR CALL: Report of breaking and entering
RESPONDING OFFICER: Det. E. Tancroft

I responded to a report of a breaking and entering at the home of Allison Lindell Northcutt, 1567 Gardington Rd.

Det. Tanner Landis (Fairlington, Va., Police Department), who had reported the breaking and entering, told me a group had arrived at the house on Tuesday, Nov. 9th at approximately 21 hours 53 minutes. He

said homeowner Allison Lindell Northcutt went to the master
bedroom. The remaining members of the party remained in the living
room area. The individuals in the house in addition to Allison Lindell
Northcutt and Tanner Landis are:

> Det. Ford Belichek (Fairlington, Va., Police Department)
>
> Officer Rodney Schmidt (Fairlington, Va., Police Department)
>
> Margaret Frye, Assistant Commonwealth's Attorney, Fairlington
> County, Va.), cousin of Allison Lindell Northcutt
>
> Jamison Chancellor, Fairlington, Va., cousin of Allison Lindell
> Northcutt
>
> Dana Chancellor (mother of Jamison), Idlewild, Va.
>
> Wes Chancellor (stepfather of Jamison), Idlewild, Va.
>
> J.D. Carson, lawyer, Bedhurst, Va.

Landis said Allison Lindell Northcutt was absent from the others for
approximately three minutes. On her return to the living room area,
Allison Lindell Northcutt reported to the group that someone had
been in her bedroom. Landis called Piscattoway Police Department
Captain I. Malek, who contacted dispatch.

I arrived at 22 hours 47 minutes.

Forensics technicians L. Oswall and B. Fraine arrived at 23 hours
04 minutes to process the scene.

I questioned Allison Lindell Northcutt separately from the others.
She said she had left the house at 7 hours 30 minutes to attend a court
hearing in Fairlington, Va., connected with her cousin, Jamison
Chancellor. Allison Lindell Northcutt said she had changed the sheets
before leaving the house. A set of sheets was in the washing machine,
not yet washed.

At the conclusion of the court hearing in Fairlington, Va., at approximately 12 hours 38 minutes, Allison Lindell Northcutt and the
family members with the addition of J.D. Carson, were leaving the
courthouse when shots were fired in their vicinity, according to Det.
Tanner Landis.

At approximately 14 hours 55 minutes, the party transported from

Fairlington to the Chate Long-Term Care Facility in Rock Creek County. Allison Lindell Northcutt's husband, Piscattoway County Police Department Officer Chad Northcutt, had been cared for there since being shot four years ago. Allison Lindell Northcutt was informed his condition had worsened and he was not expected to survive.

He died at approximately 7 hours 45 minutes.

Allison Lindell Northcutt said the entire party listed above returned with her to her residence at approximately 9 hours 26 minutes. She said she went to the master bedroom with the intention of changing her clothes. She said she immediately noticed a chain from a necklace hanging outside of her jewelry box in a way she said she had not left it in the morning. Further, she said a drawer in a bureau she identified as belonging to her late husband was not closed as it had been when she left in the morning. She also said the bed skirt was pulled up in two places, which she would not have left when she changed the sheets in the morning.

Officer R. Honnie and I questioned the other witnesses. Each corroborated the accounts and times as reported by Det. Tanner Landis and Allison Lindell Northcutt. Individual witness reports attached.

Evidence collection finished at 0 hours 16 minutes.

There was no sign of forced entry at the house.

Allison Lindell Northcutt said she is certain she locked the house. She said no spare key is left on the premises. She said Jamie Chancellor is the only person with a spare key.

Senior evidence collection technician L. Oswall called me to the bedroom to inform me that there were no clear fingerprints in the areas Allison Lindell Northcutt indicated.

PISCATTOWAY COUNTY POLICE DEPARTMENT
FINGERPRINT REPORT

ADDRESS: 1567 Gardington Rd.
REASON FOR CALL: Report of breaking and entering

RESPONDING OFFICER: Det. E. Tancroft
FORENSIC TECHNICIAN: Lucy Oswall

Latent fingerprints were absent from the areas the homeowner, Mrs. Northcutt, indicated had been found disturbed.

Specifics of those areas:

A wooden jewelry box, 38 cm wide, 32 cm deep, 22.3 cm high. Interior and exterior examined.

The top, sides, and front of the bureau the jewelry box sat upon.

A second bureau, between the closet door and the bathroom door, which the homeowner said held belongings of her husband, the late Chad Northcutt. Top, sides, and front. The top two drawers.

Bed skirt on king size bed. Focus on the side of the bed closer to the hallway door and the half closer to the foot of the bed.

The surfaces were consistent with having been wiped with a cloth and mild cleanser. Remaining latent prints were severely blurred, including those that would be expected on the jewelry box and bureau identified as belonging to the homeowner.

Other areas of the bedroom and bathroom did not show evidence of being wiped. We lifted multiple prints in other areas of the bedroom, bathroom, and potential points of entry. All were consistent with those of the homeowner.

We collected the bed skirt in place on the bed. We did not process the bed skirt based on the lack of latent fingerprints on the other surfaces. By collecting it, we do preserve it for potential further processing.

CHAPTER FOURTEEN

"**You ever read** the report on Northcutt being shot, Tanner?"

Bel's question as Landis drove them back to Maryland, reprieved him from memories.

"At the time. Not since."

"Schmidt sent us copies about four-thirty this morning."

"Proving to us he hadn't fallen asleep?"

"Nothing else to keep him awake. Judging from his hourly reports, backed up by what we've gotten from Piscattoway, all was quiet overnight."

Landis snorted his opinion of what they had gotten and would get from PCPD.

"So, he used his down time to dig up the report on Northcutt being shot. That's enterprising. We could ask him to look for other reports. Thought the one on Northcutt's shooting sure wouldn't keep him awake, from what I remember."

"Already asked him for what else he could scare up. But maybe they added to the shooting report since you read it. Interesting reading in some ways."

He cut Belichek a look. A quick one considering traffic on this bridge over the Potomac. They were fortunate they weren't among the streams trying to get into downtown D.C., except they had to cross those streams to skirt the southern edge of the District then go east to reach Ally's home. And, despite the traffic engineers' best efforts, that required fortitude.

"What's interesting?"

"It's a little thin. Except the list of officers on the scene."

"Half the department. And if it hasn't been fleshed out since I saw it, it was a *lot* thin for the shooting of a cop." Though that was interesting in its way. Attacks on law enforcement usually garnered maximum attention and investigative power.

"Guy who wrote it is gone."

"Retired?"

"Retired a year after the shooting, then died of a heart attack eight months later."

Not an uncommon story among law enforcement. Often didn't retire until a major health scare, waiting too late to improve their health enough for a lengthier retirement.

"What else interested you?" Because he knew Bel wasn't done.

"Suburban street. Weekday morning—when people getting ready to leave for work were likely to be around, yet only one person saw anything."

"The neighbor woman."

He'd found an opportunity to talk to the woman himself. She might have thought he was local, though he didn't say so. She didn't make any secret of it that she liked Ally, steered clear of Chad, and didn't like Iris.

"And she didn't see much."

Enough to immediately clear Ally of direct involvement. Piscatto-way also investigated the possibility of murder for hire, no doubt with one eye on the wife, but that never turned up a hint of anything.

"She got a partial plate," he said.

"Yeah. Which led to a car burned practically to ash. All silence beyond that. Fortunate for the shooter."

"You're thinking someone else *did* see something? Chose to keep it to him- or herself?"

"Possibility."

"Another is the shooter knew the neighborhood and knew that particular time was safe because of the vagaries of the schedule there. Although…"

"Yeah. Even someone who knew the neighborhood well, why risk it?"

"Right. Because there were almost sure to be safer opportunities for the ambusher during most of Northcutt's patrol shifts. Parked somewhere, writing a report. Or going up to a vehicle he's pulled over, drive alongside and…" He raised one finger. "So, yeah, safer opportunities, but maybe not more *certain* opportunities. Wouldn't know where he'd be at any given time on patrol shifts. Shit happens. Can't be sure where and when. Which might tell something about the shooter."

"Yup. Chose a time and place because of the certainty of getting a shot at Northcutt, because the shooter didn't have the free time to stalk Northcutt, waiting for a good opportunity."

"So that makes it more likely the shooter was gainfully employed at the time. Another explanation could be time pressure. The shooter had to get him dead right then. Couldn't afford to wait around for the right opportunity, had to make it."

"Yeah. Court cases?"

"Northcutt wasn't appearing in any when he was shot. Wasn't scheduled for any until the next month and none of those were major. Piscattoway PD covered that angle eventually. No parole hearings coming up, either. But there was something… Wasn't he in on a bust of a high up drug seller? Not right before he was shot."

"I read that… Hold on." Belichek scrolled through screens on his device, apparently looking at the report Schmidt had sent. "Got it. Four months before the shooting. Routine traffic stop, backed up by Dewey Selton."

"One of his cronies. Northcutt made the stop with the guy coming off the Interstate. Speeding."

"As people do, coming off the Interstate," Belichek said mildly.

Landis eased his foot off the accelerator. "But not much of a haul. Would have expected a lot more from that guy."

"Maybe he was too smart to carry more than a few hundred dollars and enough crank for a small party."

"Look at his sheet. He doesn't go for small parties. And I don't recall any signs of major intelligence."

Belichek was silent, reading. "Agreed. On the other hand, no violence on his sheet."

"Street smart enough to have someone else do his dirty work. Could be what happened here, too. The shooting wasn't right after the stop, like you'd think would happen if he lost it and went after Northcutt. Also wasn't close enough to a court date that disposing of the arresting officer might occur to him as a way to solve his problem. Not to mention that bust wasn't that big a deal in his career *and* he still had a chance to beat it by working through the court system, letting his lawyer try to make it go away."

"Can't tell if you're saying he's worth a look or not," Bel complained.

"He is. Eventually." He cleared his throat. "First question."

It was their routine, even if this was nothing like routine. For starters, it was a very delayed start to their routine, which usually followed the first glut of information on a case.

But they'd been rather busy yesterday. Hard to tell when one intake of info stopped and the next one started.

He hadn't realized he'd paused until Bel nudged, "First question is?"

"Not original. But the big one's got to be are they related— yesterday's shots and Northcutt dying."

"Chad's shooting, too. Even separated by four-plus years."

"Yeah. Possible. Good. And the break-in. As you said, we've asked those already. Still, good questions. You said the big one. What's your first small question?"

"Smaller, not small. Who was the target at the courthouse?"

"Ally." Landis drew in oxygen. Exactly as if his own answer knocked the breath out of him.

Bel gave him a look he didn't like. But his partner didn't say anything, so pushing him would make it a big deal.

He stayed with the case. "Trouble is, does answering the connection question give us other answers or do we need to first get the answer to yesterday's shooting to answer the connection question? Or..."

Another time he'd paused that didn't become apparent to him until

Bel nudged. "Or what?"

"Or do we need to get the answers surrounding Chad Northcutt being shot in the head in his driveway to unravel any of the rest?"

"Chicken or egg," Bel summarized. "Can't know yet. Just started collecting pebbles. Keep on going and eventually we'll see the mountain. You don't start with a vision of the mountain and fit the pebbles in."

"I know, I know."

"The pebbles tell you what the mountain's going to look like as you add them one by one."

Belichek had pebbles and mountains, he had his own way of thinking of investigations.

Started at the core—the victim—and worked out in circles or layers around them. Though he'd never encountered an investigation where any one layer remained consistent around the core, like rings on a tree. Instead, the layers bulged and flattened, bubbled and went sideways, depending on what there was to find out about their contents and when it was discovered.

"God, you and your damned mountain and double-damned pebbles," he grumbled.

"Yeah," Bel said placidly. "But having both the chicken and egg—even not knowing which came first—is better than just having one. Besides, insurance."

"Right." If Palery closed them out of the courthouse plaza shooting, they'd keep investigating, approaching it from the other angle.

Neither approach was what you'd call easy, but at least they had two.

"Second question," Bel said thoughtfully. "Why shoot at Ally Northcutt?"

"Connection to Chad. Whatever he was up to."

"Not proven he was up to anything. Suspected. Not proven."

"He was. Besides—"

Even as he wondered if there was a chance Bel would not follow up on that bitten-off word, he knew it was a futile hope.

"Besides," Bel started, leaving no doubt, "you think there couldn't be any other reason for somebody to go after Ally. No reason someone could want to shoot her in her own right."

"It's logical. She hasn't been making enemies of criminals like Mags has by prosecuting them. She hasn't been dealing with the public, asking for money, supporting people who might—or might not—be worthy of support like Jamie. She's kept to herself. Even when all the media was clamoring for the tragic wife story right after Northcutt was shot, she didn't do stories, didn't appear in the media. And you can bet there've been requests for anniversary stories."

"She does keep to herself. When she and Mags and I were checking for things in Jamie's house, she could pinpoint when she'd last been out with Jamie. Five or six months earlier. Jamie said before that, it was when that aunt of Chad's came to visit—one of the few people Iris Northcutt considered acceptable to sit beside Chad's bedside all day—and Ally attended a Sunshine Foundation event."

Jamie started the Sunshine Foundation to honor their Aunt Vivian Frye.

"Long time between outings," was all he said.

Bel turned his head and studied him anyway.

He ignored his partner's attention. That wouldn't make the attention go away, but it didn't encourage it, either.

He turned into Ally's street.

CHAPTER FIFTEEN

LANDIS AND BEL arrived at Ally's house just behind two official cars from the Piscattoway County Police Department.

"Sloppy," Bel grumbled when the uniformed officer waved Landis into the cordoned off space in front of the two Northcutt houses, not appearing to notice they weren't part of that official motorcade.

As they exited, they recognized the police chief and a deputy chief they'd seen last night getting out of the lead car, which also boasted a driver. Two more men and a woman got out of the second car.

"Division commander, chaplain, and somebody who specializes in liaising with bereaved family," Tanner speculated.

The group met in the street and looked toward Ally's house.

Before they could move in that direction, however, Iris Northcutt opened her front door.

She wore unrelieved black, including a skirt to her ankles.

In contrast, her voice was loud and commanding. "This way, Chief."

The man paused, turning his head toward her.

She stepped back, still holding the door open.

He glanced over his shoulder toward Ally's door, which remained closed. Then he turned and headed toward Iris, with the others falling in line behind him.

Without discussion, Landis and Bel wasted no time going up the walk and knocking on Ally's door. Schmidt let them in.

"Ally needs to get across the street," Bel said to Jamie, who'd come around the corner from the kitchen.

"Iris shanghaied the brass when they were on the way here," Landis added.

Maggie came out of the kitchen, one hand clasped around Ally's wrist, drawing her along. "Of course, she did. C'mon, Ally."

"It doesn't matter. Really." She resisted enough to stop Maggie's progress.

Dana put an arm around Ally's shoulders. "You have been so strong for so long, Ally. You need to be stronger a little longer. To do what's expected of you a little longer. This will be over eventually. Truly. Just keep moving ahead."

The look between the two women held.

Air streamed out between Ally's barely parted lips. "You're right." She used her other hand to remove Maggie's unresisting hold on her.

Maggie fell in line behind her, then Jamie, though Jamie turned back and asked "Mom?"

"I'll stay here. Those cleanup people Maggie called should be here soon." Maggie must have called one of the firms that specialized in crime scene cleanup. Ally's house might be a mess from the investigation by civilian standards, but it would be a walk in the park by crime scene standards. "I'll get them started. You girls are who she needs."

Bel went out right behind Jamie, one hand lightly touching her back.

Before Landis could follow, Dana Chancellor said, "Detective Landis—Tanner."

He turned, surprised at her using his first name.

"Ma'am?"

"This young man, Officer Schmidt, needs to get some rest. We've told him to sleep now that we're all awake and there's little cause to think there will be any danger, but he's refused. Will you please order him to at least take a nap?"

Schmidt flushed.

Landis sucked in his teeth to keep from laughing at the guy's reaction to Dana Chancellor treating him like a kindergartner at Rest Time.

The guy did look tired. But they'd all worked longer stretches than this. A lot. Still, the trick was to rest when you could and they didn't need Schmidt on guard right this second.

"Anything to report? Beyond what you already sent."

"No, sir. Just… the absence of something, I guess. The Piscattoway crime scene techs reported no sign of disturbance in the yard. Before Mr. Carson retired last night, he and I raked the lawn for a width of three feet from the back of the house, starting at the southwestern corner and ended with the gate in the fence at the northwestern corner of the drive." His gaze shifted fractionally toward Dana. "There was no sign of disturbance in the dew this morning."

"Your idea or his?"

"His." No hesitation. Score one for honesty.

"Good job. Go take a nap, Schmidt. But—"

"There's a sofa in the basement," Dana inserted.

"—on the sofa in the basement," Landis dutifully added. "But before you do, lock up the house. And nobody leaves or comes in until we come back. Understood?"

"Yes, sir."

Dana nodded, but it had less the feeling of acquiescing to his order than benign approval that he'd followed hers.

Landis left and heard the front door lock after him.

Across the street, he caught up before Rachel closed that door behind the newly arrived contingent.

From the doorway, the kitchen opened to the right. A short hallway straight ahead led to the living room.

"Please, please, come sit here, Mrs. Northcutt," the chief said from where he occupied the edge of a sofa upholstered in fabric with improbably large and black flowers of some kind interspersed with deepest green stems and leaves. All the other Piscattoway department representatives stood, crowding the room. "Er, uh, Mrs. Chad Northcutt."

"Please, call me, Ally." She offered her hand and he took it.

But when he started to draw her down to sit beside him, she stepped back closer to Jamie and Maggie, who'd accompanied her in her advance into the living room, and lightly clasped her hands in front of her. "Thank you, I'll stand."

Iris sat in a chair in the same deepest green, which resembled the big chair in her son's living room. Her position put her against the backdrop of a wall covered from floor to ceiling and side to side in photos, plaques, and mementoes of the Northcutt family's police service.

"I was just telling Chad's mother, that the department will do everything it can to make this period less difficult for all of you. Though we can't take away the pain and the loss, we can share in it with you at a fine young man and excellent police officer being taken from us so senselessly."

Landis could swear the man had said the same words in a news clip after Chad was shot. Might as well recycle them.

Ally lowered her head in dignified thanks.

"And these officers—" He indicated the others. "—will all help in any way they can to lighten the burden of planning the funeral, as well as other practical matters. Of course, under your guidance."

"The funeral is what matters now," Iris said. "A proper farewell for a Northcutt."

Landis looked at her positioning against that remarkable wall more closely. One area was not covered as thickly. It was the area directly behind her chair. It had the effect of making her, sitting in her chair, appear to be the largest piece—perhaps the most important?—in the collage.

The chief heaved himself to his feet and gestured to one of the other men. "Certainly, certainly. And our experienced officers will help you with that every step of the way."

He edged between the sofa and coffee table, then gestured to the gray-haired officer who'd come forward that he should replace the chief on the sofa.

"This is the man who will discover your wishes—" He looked directly at Ally. "—and make sure they are met. I know he will help you through each step of this. It was my honor to come to pay my respects today to you—both of you—and to get this process started," the chief continued smoothly as he subtly moved toward the front door.

On his way, he gave an eye signal to the assistant chief and division head, who immediately split up, one going to Iris, the other to Ally. They murmured condolences then, as if choreographed, swapped spots.

The assistant chief put his hands over Ally's.

She didn't withdraw from the touch, yet Landis sensed an instinct to jerk away.

Honesty compelled him to admit that the trouble was, he didn't know if that was her reaction or what he wanted her to do.

He shifted around to make room for the two officers—their condolences finished—to get past him.

From behind him, he heard Rachel Northcutt, just inside the entryway to the kitchen.

"Thank you so much for coming, Chief. Before you go, you must try these pastries Officer Cartoukis brought this morning."

With that offer, Chad's cousin successfully detoured the chief into the kitchen. That backed up the division commander and assistant chief in the entry from the living room to the hallway because they didn't want to walk out ahead of him.

Landis moved out of the hallway and into the living room to give them room, a move acknowledged by the assistant chief with a nod.

The move brought him next to the remaining officer. A chaplain. She listened to the officer sitting on the sofa.

"…for Piscattoway County Police Department. And as an active-duty death, Chad's funeral—"

"Line of duty," his mother said.

"—can include… Ma'am, Chad's death was active duty."

"Line of duty."

Red showed around the top of the man's collar. "Ma'am, there's a firm definition of what constitutes a line of duty death to determine the benefits for the widow and—"

"I don't give a damn for your firm definitions. Care even less about the money his widow will snatch up. My boy will have a funeral as befits an officer killed in the line of duty. Get Archie over here."

The man hesitated, sending a look toward Ally.

"Now," Iris cracked out.

He went.

"Ally." Maggie cupped one hand around her cousin's clasped hands.

"No."

"The choices should be yours—"

"No." She brought her unfocused gaze to Maggie's face. She spoke so low he doubted anyone else could hear her, possibly not even Jamie on her other side. "Let her. She wants to. Maybe she needs to. I don't. Let her."

CHAPTER SIXTEEN

IRIS STEAMROLLED THE Chief of the Piscattoway County Police Department—a k a Archie.

He told the gray-haired officer that they wouldn't bother with the technicalities at this point and the services would include whatever the Northcutt family wanted. Then he got the heck out of there, not tempted to delay a second time by anything in the kitchen. The assistant chief and district commander went with him.

Under Iris' dictatorship, it soon became apparent the funeral would include all the main points of a line of duty funeral. The flag-draped casket, an honor guard, badge shrouds, bagpipers, a bugler to play *Taps,* a formal procession to the cemetery, flag-folding ceremony, and a reception afterward.

"That's a lot," the chaplain said softly. "It will make for a very long day—two long days, with the visitation the evening before. That can—"

"Doesn't matter how long a day or days. It's no less than Chad deserves. Should have the twenty-four-hour casket watch and have his badge retired, too," Iris said.

Two of the few elements she'd previously agreed to forego.

"I was going to say it can be a drain for the mourners. I was thinking of Chad's widow, who—"

"Won't be a drain on *me.* All that matters is giving the Northcutt family the honors it deserves."

The chaplain faced Ally. "Mrs. Northcutt?"

"We've settled." Without unclasping her hands, she pointed with one finger to the written list that had been put together.

"Very well," said the gray-haired officer. Not approving, but moving on. "We also need to talk to you, Mrs. Northcutt—Ally—about Chad's life insurance and pension."

Iris cut in. "For God's sake, she can at least wait to start benefiting from his death until after he's buried."

The harshness startled everyone in the room into silence.

"That's a conversation that can wait a few days and doesn't need to involve Chad's mother," Jamie said smoothly.

"Unless I'm the beneficiary." She added, "Not that *I* care about the money."

With more than a little relief, the beleaguered gray-haired officer said to Jamie, "You're right, it can wait until after the funeral. Then we'll set up a time with Mrs.—with Ally Northcutt that's mutually agreeable to go over the details."

That announced to all that Ally was, indeed, the beneficiary. A fact that caused Iris' face to darken toward magenta, whether at being proven wrong or the loss of the cash was unclear.

✧   ✧   ✧   ✧

THE REMAINING POLICE department representatives stood, and Ally used that shift to prepare for departure, too.

She said a few words to Iris, then started for the door.

The chaplain stopped her before she was all the way out. The woman must have mastered the ability to murmur for one set of ears only, because Landis didn't pick up anything she said.

Jamie, followed by a reluctant Maggie, stepped up to speak to Iris after the gray-haired man finished what sounded like a canned speech.

But even after the chaplain released her arm, Ally didn't make a clean escape.

Chad's cousin Rachel stood in the kitchen doorway as she had with the chief, like some funereal banquet siren.

"Ally, if you would please take some of this food—"

"No, thank you, Rachel."

"You know we can't possibly eat it all, even when the rest of the family arrives. And by rights, it should go to—"

"Really, no. Though I appreciate your thought."

"At least some of the flowers…"

Ally's mouth lifted into a smile that had no life behind it. "No, thank you. We're fine. Honestly."

"I hope you'll come back when the rest of the family comes. I know they'll want to see you."

Neither her expression nor her voice betrayed her, but Landis knew that Ally Northcutt doubted the Northcutts' eagerness to see her. "I'm not sure I'll be able to. More of my family will also be arriving today."

"All the more reason to take some food."

Ally produced a smile. "Thank you, no."

When she left, the rest of them spurted out through the bottleneck created by the short hallway. Jamie and Maggie hurried to catch up with her.

On the way back across the street, Bel detoured for a quick word with the officer who'd earlier waved them in without checking their IDs.

Landis slowed his gait so they met where the walk started toward Ally's front door, which Wes Chancellor held open for the cousins. "Ream him a new one?"

"No. Asked how all the offerings got to Iris' house. She came out early this morning and told him that's how it would be and to tell anyone who relieved him. Then I suggested more care in checking vehicles."

Landis snorted. "Reamed him a new one, Belichek style."

In the house, Maggie had her hands on her hips, addressing Ally. "…not going to ascend to sainthood for letting that woman steamroll you. Sit down for heaven's sake before you fall down."

Ally sat in one of the two chairs facing the front window. "Happy?"

Maggie's grim satisfaction likely came from recognizing the tang of smart ass in that reply, even as she said, "No. Far from it. But it's a start." She waved at the rest of them. "All of you sit down."

Landis kept his observations to himself that she was in full court mode, with her standing and everyone else sitting. Wes directed Dana to the big chair, then accepted with thanks a dining room chair that J.D. put next to it. Jamie sat on the floor near her mother. J.D. brought up another dining chair and took it, leaving the second upholstered chair beside Ally for Maggie if she ever landed. Bel took his same spot on the hearth and Landis followed suit.

During this, Ally said, "I'm not going for sainthood, Maggie. It's easier for me this way. I don't have any interest in making the decisions about the funeral or any of the … ritual."

"Letting Iris make the decisions might be easier for you in the moment, dear, yet make the funeral and the events around it more difficult. I don't know the details but I can only imagine a police funeral with full honors requires a great deal of the widow." Dana glanced at Bel and him. They confirmed with nods. "To perform those duties when you gain no solace from the ceremony…"

"I'll be fine, Aunt Dana."

"At least you could accept some of the food," Jamie said. "You'll need it if people come by here."

"They won't." She said it with matter-of-fact confidence. "You mentioned solace, Dana. Well, that food is solace to Iris. Not to eat herself or even to serve to others, but to have it arrive at the house. To know with each delivery of a dish that another officer, another family has acknowledged the Northcutts in a tangible way. Can you understand that?"

Maggie was the one who said, "Yes." Then she added. "That's interesting, though, isn't it? The gifts of food acknowledge the Northcutts. Not necessarily mourning Chad."

"Oh, Maggie, that's too strong," Dana started.

Jamie interrupted her. "No, it's not, Mom. Not if you'd seen Iris in action about the funeral arrangements. She was so fierce about what was owed the Northcutt name, her attention all focused on getting the pomp and circumstance honors while she hardly seemed to remember that it should be about Chad. So Maggie's right. But Ally's right, too, and she's very generous to recognize that it does help Iris and accept it."

"Of course she is," Dana said immediately. "She's always been generous."

Ally smiled slightly. "Thank you, Aunt Dana."

Surprisingly, Maggie was the one who turned the conversation. Not surprising was the direction she turned it in.

She pivoted and with a single glance put the two of them sitting on the hearth into an imaginary witness box.

"What have you got on the shooting?"

Dana squeezed her eyes shut for a moment. Everyone else, though, gave them their full attention.

"More important than what we've got is what we need." Landis deliberately looked at Ally. "We need to ask you questions, Ally. Is there somewhere we can go and—?"

"You can ask in front of my cousins."

"No." His bald negative triggered something deep in her eyes that wasn't quite strong enough to reach the surface. "Better to talk to each of you separately."

"C'mon, Landis, be realistic," Maggie said. "As if we haven't already talked amongst ourselves about this. Besides, we outnumber you. If the two of you each talk to one of us at a time, this will go on forever."

Apparently sensing his concession, Jamie asked, "Questions about what?"

"Chad, for starters."

Maggie expected that. Ally remained stoic. Jamie's eyes widened slightly. "You think what happened yesterday has something to do with Chad? With his dying? Or with his being shot?"

This time he left it to Bel to respond.

"We have to consider any possibility."

"But it's not just any possibility, is it? You must be sure the shooter was aiming at Ally. Otherwise, Chad wouldn't be the first thing you focused on."

She had logic on her side. But Bel didn't fold. For the good of the investigation or an effort to protect her from what they already knew?

"We're small cogs in this investigation, Jamie. We have a narrow focus. There are a lot of people looking at other aspects, all feeding into Captain Palery, who's got a lot of people looking over his shoulder. The powers that be don't take kindly to anyone shooting at people on our courthouse grounds."

"And you two got stuck with us?" Her mouth quirked.

Bel's mouth didn't, but the way the two of them looked at each other, it might as well have.

"Do you really need to talk to Ally alone?" Jamie asked.

Before Maggie could express the protest Landis saw welling in her, Bel said, "Not yet. Let's get an overview first. Let Ally respond, but if either of you has insight or a different take, we'll get to that after."

"Are you *sure* Ally was the target?" Maggie asked, despite being experienced enough to know that *sure* was a rarity in investigations.

"No. Can't be sure. Certainly not yet. But considering the trajectory and where the bullets hit, it's not only a hypothesis we have to consider, it's the most likely place to start. And in case it's the right hypothesis, we don't want to take any chances with safety measures or—"

"You better not," Maggie said.

"In addition," Landis smoothly continued for Bel, "the timing of the shots at the courthouse, Chad's death, and the break-in sure catches our attention."

"In other words, you might not know why this is happening, especially why now, until you catch the person."

He turned to Ally's calm voice. "That's right."

"*If* you catch the person."

"We will."

She didn't buy that, but she didn't express her disbelief.

Bel looked at him, inviting him to start the questions.

Fine. This wasn't different from any other investigation.

"Let's go back to before Chad was shot. Think about the month before. Day-to-day life. Was—?"

"The shooting wiped out all the day-to-day."

His gut hardened. She was too quick, too defensive. There was something and she intended to hide it.

He didn't come close to looking at Bel, but felt his recognition of the same conclusion. From the corner of his eye, he caught Maggie's frown at her cousin.

But his peripheral vision also caught Jamie looking from Ally to him and frowning. What was that about?

"—there anything out of the ordinary?" he concluded.

"If there was, the shooting wiped that out, too."

"Let's take it a piece at a time. Did Chad introduce you to anybody new? Bring anybody new home?"

"He never brought people home. He wanted to keep home and work separate. As a result, there weren't opportunities to introduce me to people."

He shut down memories of when he'd first known Ally and saw Chad separating her from his work life.

"Still, it must have happened sometimes. Did it happen in the month or two before he was shot?"

"No."

"Did he talk about anybody new?"

"He didn't talk about work."

The rhythm of her answer was off, with a gap between *talk* and *about*. As if she'd meant *He didn't talk* as a complete statement, then tacked on *about work* to soften it.

"Even if you only overheard, say, him talking on the phone or to his cousin—"

"No."

He leaned back, aiming at casual, but watching her closely.

"Did his behavior change in any way in the weeks before the shooting?"

As her eyes went unfocused, her lips parted, and he anticipated another negative. Then she pulled in a breath before pressing her lips together.

Another beat passed before she spoke. "He... he might have been more on edge than usual."

"How?"

"Nothing specific."

She had the brakes on hard. Would pushing her gain any ground? Or was the best hope letting it go for now, coming back later.

The decision was made for him when there was knock on the door.

He went to it, saw three men and a woman on the front step whom he recognized as being at the long-term care facility yesterday.

He opened the door and they came in carrying covered plates.

Rachel's doing?

With the option of pushing Ally for more information closed, he'd have to hope time might help.

CHAPTER SEVENTEEN

AFTER PUTTING MORE chairs around, he and Bel retreated to out of sight in the kitchen.

Before they could say anything, though, Maggie came around the corner from the living area with a social smile still on her face that might otherwise have made him laugh. J.D. was with her.

Her smile evaporated in the heat of her intensity.

"What the hell is going on?" she demanded in a voice that wouldn't carry more than a couple feet but still intended to dominate.

Bel started to say something, but Landis talked over him. "Are you asking as Assistant Commonwealth's Attorney Margaret Frye or as Ally's cousin Maggie?"

She gritted her teeth. "The former."

"Then, sorry, J.D., but…"

He raised both hands with laconic ease. "I feel a sudden need to scope out the trash can situation, since I predict we'll need those services soon."

As he passed Maggie on the way to the garage door, she stroked his arm.

"Oh, here you are," Dana said absently, entering the kitchen with her gaze bouncing from cabinet to cabinet. "Ally says she's sure she has paper plates, but she's occupied. Do you know where they are, Maggie?"

"No idea, Aunt Dana."

"I suppose I'll just hunt."

"Outside," Bel said under his breath. "Out back."

They exited the back door, staying out of view of the sliders, the window over the kitchen sink, or anyone looking from across the street. Which left them in a tight bunch not quite to the back corner of the house.

Succinctly, Landis told her about the suspicions of Chad, his joining the task force then leaving it, and his own conclusion that Chad was dirty. He should be getting succinct with this now, the number of times he'd told it lately.

"…logical working hypothesis is that his actions led to his being shot."

"We'll talk about your never telling me this when we have the time that subject requires, but now—"

"Bull, Mags. You know I couldn't tell you. Or anyone."

"—what matters is whether this endangers Ally."

"Agreed. What argues against it being connected is nothing happening for the years since Northcutt was shot. What argues for it is stuff happening now, with his abrupt decline and death."

"Abrupt decline. Do you think…?"

"No reason to think anything was involved beyond nature. But it's worth some questions to be sure and—"

"Not you guys. Too good a chance it'll get back to Piscattoway or—worse—Iris. I'll do it. Don't look at me like that. I'm not always a bulldozer. Have to be with you two because you don't understand anything else, but I can be subtle when it's called for. Let me do some on-behalf-of-my-cousin's-peace-of-mind poking around and see if there's any *there* there."

Not waiting for their agreement, Maggie said abruptly, "When Chad was shot, I looked into it. As much as I could with his department resenting the hell out of anyone from across the river."

"Especially anyone in a prosecutor's office."

"Fine. I get your not-so-subtle point. I should have asked you and Bel to look into it. Except you were almost brand new and I was leery, since Bel's previous partner was a prick. *More* of a prick." She tried to mask she'd almost paid him a compliment.

"Aw, Maggie. You touch me deeply."

"I'll touch you all right and deeply, if you do anything to hurt my cousin. And I don't care what that does to our working relationship."

"I can always console myself that it could have been worse. You could have been a defense lawyer."

She glared at him before spreading her more neutral focus to include Belichek. "The bigger question is what are you two going to be doing?"

"We have to get answers from Ally," Bel said.

"Now? Can't it—? No, never mind. I know it can't wait. It's just… The poor kid. Dammit. It wasn't enough Chad made a lousy husband in addition to dumping her into the clutches of his mother's Northcutt obsession? And then, after he's shot, Ally's sense of duty and what's right held her captive. No matter what the rest of us said… Fine, fine, I'm done… Now we have to wade through the tide of condolers."

BEL REMAINED OUTSIDE after the other two went inside.

He didn't admit to himself he hoped Jamie would come out until she did.

She walked right into his arms and they kissed.

But only once, because more and he'd be hauled up on indecency charges.

"Don't worry so much, Ford." She stroked his forehead and smooth furrows there he hadn't been aware of. "You'll figure it out, you always do. You and Tanner, together."

"It's Landis I'm worried about."

"Ah."

"Do you know the history between them?"

"No. I know there's a strong connection. I also know Ally never would have cheated on Chad, so if that's what you're worried about…?"

Was it? "I don't think so. Landis has been… Not falling. That's not right. But sort of skidding sideways for a while. If he falls…"

Then Jamie—his miraculous Jamie—touched his cheek.

"You would pick him up, Rutherford Belichek. But I don't think you'll need to. He'd already fallen. What you see as skidding sideways is more like reaching for footholds as he climbs back up. He has a way to go, but he's not alone anymore."

She pulled in a slow breath, tears sparkling her lower lashes. "Neither of them is."

✦ ✦ ✦ ✦

THE TIDE HAD ebbed when Maggie returned from escorting stragglers out and warned, "Greta is here."

She added, apparently to J.D., but probably for the sake of the Fairlington detectives, "Ally's mother."

Jamie looked out the front window toward the end of the house's driveway.

"Not there. Look beyond the members of the media."

Parking in the driveway would have eliminated her mother's exposure to the cameras.

She had parked on the street, two houses down, beyond where the patrol officer had contained three media stringers with video cameras.

"Oh, dear."

Ally's reaction echoed Jamie's, though she might have expressed it differently.

She emerged from her car with a swirl of fabric layers and scarves.

The three bored guys brightened and met her on the sidewalk with their cameras.

The officer looked uncertain for a moment, which was plenty for Greta Lindell to clasp a dramatic hand to the V of her blouse and take control.

Only phrases and words reached them. That was enough.

"Tragic … immediately, even though… vital time for the season… Gardens reclaiming ravaged land … But a mother's horror… Rushed to her side… and important fund-raising…"

"Taking the time to give an interview," Maggie muttered.

Ally sighed.

Jamie put an arm around her shoulders and Maggie said a curse word, each empathizing with her in her own way. At the moment, Ally trended toward Maggie's reaction.

One of the guys lowered his camera.

Greta's voice rose, her hand again clasped to her bosom.

"Please. Please, all of you. No more questions. The website I gave you provides more background on my garden reclamation."

Her dramatic pause allowed time for the wandering camera to return to her.

"Please. I need to see my daughter now. To offer her what only a mother can."

Ally didn't doubt for a second that there were tears in her eyes as she moved past them and headed toward the door.

At least Greta provided the perfect excuse for not going back across the street for the awkwardness of accepting condolences from other Northcutts, who were aware of how Iris had faulted and derided her.

✧ ✧ ✧ ✧

GRETA FRYE MOBAN Lindell hugged Ally.

As Jamie and Maggie said hello to her, her gaze shifted past them to the sliders. She walked to them, looking outside. "This is deplorable. No effort at all, Ally?"

"She's been at her husband's bedside every day for more than four years," Maggie said sharply.

"A few moments, plants make such a difference in this world. She could have taken the time to make that difference. He would not have noticed that she wasn't there—that was the issue, was it not?—and the world would have been better for it."

He would not have noticed that she wasn't there—that was the issue, was it not?

Before anyone summoned a response to that—and Landis' money would have been on Maggie being the responder—another knock came at the door.

Maggie strode to it, as if needing something to expel her pent-up energy. She opened it fast enough to catch the people outside not totally prepared.

From Landis' spot on the hearth, he saw their unguarded emotions. Rachel Northcutt led the group. Her expression reflected determination. To do the right thing? Or something else?

The man beyond her right shoulder—not giving anything away—had enough resemblance to Chad and to Rachel to say he was a Northcutt for sure.

The man on her other side, being shorter and heftier, did not. But Landis was prepared to guess he was Chad's uncle. Mostly because the third male in the group was a clear blend of this second man and the woman with him from the same vintage—father, mother, and son. And the most likely grouping matching that description would be Chad's cousin Mark, along with his parents, Chad's uncle and aunt.

In that case, Mark Northcutt Junior would have preferred to be almost anywhere else at the moment. His presumed father came in a close second on that scale, while his mother's dominant reaction being curiosity.

He sent a look at Bel and saw they were on the same page.

"Oh, hello, Maggie," Rachel said. "We wanted to come pay our respects to Ally. This is my father, Preston, my uncle, Mark Senior, and aunt, Susan, and their son, Mark Junior."

Maggie nodded to each. "We met at the wedding."

They muttered acknowledgments that left it unclear whether or not they remembered the meeting.

The aunt zeroed in on Ally. She crossed the threshold first, followed by her son, helped along by a firm hand to the back from his father. Rachel's father came last. Interesting, considering he had the most presence among the group.

Ally stood to receive them. Their greetings were awkward, but not unkind.

Rachel remained where she was.

In order to follow the path her relatives had taken, Rachel would have needed to sidestep, because Maggie blocked her straight-ahead path, looking at her.

Rachel did not sidestep, but returned Maggie's gaze, neither woman precisely unfriendly. Not overtly friendly, either.

"Ally said you helped her, especially after Chad was shot," Maggie said.

"I tried."

"But Iris blocked your efforts."

She exhaled. "Thought it would be good for Ally. Maybe help her move on. Iris put a stop to that."

"How could she? It's Ally's house."

"Not exactly. The way it works is a family trust owns half of each member's house. And Iris controls the trust."

"All the Northcutts—?"

"No, no, not all. This branch of the family. It's the descendants of one Northcutt, who was the grandfather of my dad, Mark Senior, and David Senior—that was Iris' husband. But even without the trust, Ally wouldn't go against what Iris wanted. Soft-hearted, as you must know."

Maggie didn't follow up on the soft-hearted comment. "This trust includes your house?"

"Including mine," she said evenly.

"This is brave of you, then, coming over here," Maggie said.

Rachel half-grinned, half-grimaced. "Aunt Iris—she's not really my aunt, but that's what I've always called her—is taking advantage of a gap in the stream of visitors to take a rest right now. And a neighbor is manning the front door in case someone comes by while we're here."

Possibly reminded by that reference of the expectations of hospitality, Maggie swung the door wider, clearing a path inside for Rachel.

Rachel Northcutt hugged Ally then said hellos all around.

Belatedly, the other Northcutts also hugged Ally, the embraces made more awkward by the delay.

At the end, Ally said, "Let me introduce you all to my mother, Greta."

"Greta Frye Moban Lindell," her mother expanded, stepping in front of her daughter, "of the Moban Gardens of Pennsylvania."

Uncertainty ruffled the surface of Rachel's poise for an instant, then she rallied. "Of course." She gave it enough emphasis to make it plausible that she knew what the woman was talking about. "It's a pleasure to meet you."

She then took over the introductions, while Jamie offered refreshments.

Landis tipped his head toward the front door and Bel agreed.

CHAPTER EIGHTEEN

THE MURMUR OF voices came from inside, the sounds of the weary and bored low-level journalists drifted to them from past the Piscattoway patrol vehicle, and a car started down the block.

A quiet, tranquil neighborhood, where someone had driven across this lawn, shot Chad Northcutt in the head, then driven away.

"We need to talk to that witness again."

"Again?"

"The neighbor who saw the car and the muffled figure that was its driver." He jerked his head in the opposite direction from the patrol vehicle. "Used to live down there. Don't know if she's still there."

"Get Schmidt to check. We need to talk to other people first."

He didn't respond. He knew who Bel meant.

"Yeah." He turned and looked from the patrol vehicle to the front of Iris Northcutt's house, to the neighbors on either side of it, then pivoted and did the same survey on this side of the street.

"How desperate would somebody have to be to come here and break in with a marked vehicle out front?"

"So, they didn't. They broke in before the vehicle got here. Ally left at seven. That left a lot of time to break in."

"Neighbors have a view, too. Next door, across the street, and behind could all see someone going in or out the back door."

"During a work day, kids in school. Biggest danger was probably Iris, but, even if she'd been home, she doesn't have a view of the back door. But, yeah, some measure of desperation."

"Versus the shooting."

Slowly, Bel said, "Yeah. Desperate enough to come here, but cool enough to minimize risks with the timing. By contrast, the shooting from a distance. Lowered probability. Shooter was willing to accept lower probability to minimize his risk of getting caught."

"That…"

Landis' thought died as the Northcutt group emerged from the front door.

He prepared to exchange nods as they walked past. Instead, the cousin, Mark, stopped in front of them and the others followed suit.

"I remember you." He directed that at Landis.

"I remember you, too."

"You and Ally were always talking. I know all about that."

Landis didn't make much effort to stop one corner of his mouth lifting. He didn't keep his reaction out of his voice either.

"Yeah. Talking. That's real bad."

"Well, Chad didn't like it. The two of you—" He searched for something and fell back on what he'd already used. "—talking. At Mikey's. Outside," he added, as if that were significant.

"Then he should have made her comfortable inside. Instead of letting her—and everybody else—know he preferred spending his time with the guys. Never mind there were other wives, fiancées, and girlfriends there."

Mark Junior appeared struck by that, but stubbornly repeated, "I just know he didn't like it."

"He could've come out and joined us any time. How's that for a concept—he could have talked with her himself."

"But what are you doing here *now?*" Mark's question tinged toward triumph.

His uncle answered, addressing Landis and Bel. "Understand you two kept Ally and her family safe yesterday during that shooting in Fairlington. I'm—we're all—grateful for that."

"Very grateful," Rachel echoed, while the others murmured agreement.

Landis' cynicism wondered if including the location of the shooting was a dig—somebody shot at Ally in Fairlington, here in

Piscattoway County all she had to deal with was an unobtrusive break in.

But he knew his role with Bel was to be the social partner, so he quieted his cynicism and said, "We're all grateful it wasn't a whole lot worse. Though there's no way to miss it was a real hard day on a lot of people. Our condolences to your family on the death of Officer Northcutt."

"Thank you" murmurs came from them all except Mark Junior.

After a pause, he caught up. "Yeah, thank you. It… It doesn't seem real." He rubbed a hand over the short hair on the top of his head and that seemed to shift his attitude. "Hasn't seemed real since he was shot four years ago. Kept feeling it had to be some big mistake and I'd wake up and everything would be straight, you know? And after a while I started thinking *he'd* wake up. I mean, it was real that some asshole shot him, but still, I thought he'd wake up and he'd be himself and it would be okay.

"But yesterday… Well, took me back to that day. Same sense of… like I said, *unreal*. I was on duty when I got the call. Took a while to arrange coverage for me, but as soon as I could, I got over there. I was glad you were already there, Uncle Preston. To represent the family."

"Heard from a friend when the department got a call from Fairlington PD." The slightest pause before *Fairlington* indicated a measure of distaste that the notice came through an outside agency.

Rachel patted Mark Junior's shoulder. "I was at the dentist and had my phone off, so I didn't get there as fast as I wanted, either. But when I heard, I went right over to the Chate."

"Didn't come here to pick up Iris?" Bel asked.

"No." The Northcutts shifted and obscured quick, furtive smiles. Rachel added, "Iris does not like to be driven. She insists on being the driver. I arrived at Chate Center right behind her and caught up with her at the door. Not that she'd thank me for staying by her side. As I heard when I tried to persuade her to stay at my dad's place last night. In the end, all I could do was trail her back here."

"You did the right thing, Rachel," Mark Senior said. "No matter what she says."

Rachel grimaced, likely at the reminder of what Iris had said and would say, rather than at her uncle's support.

Mark Senior continued, "I didn't get the word until your aunt came to find me. And then I saw all the messages and calls on my phone, but I'd been occupied in the garage with a woodworking project and didn't hear most of them. Ignored the rest. I've been enjoying that perk of retirement, but this time… By the time your aunt and I got there, he was gone."

His eyes went shiny, but his voice remained steady when he added. "Well, we'd better get back…"

He tipped his head toward his sister-in-law's front door.

They all shook hands and wished each other a good day, then the members of this branch of the legendary Northcutt law enforcement tribe started with apparent reluctance across the street to the other house.

J.D. Carson came out the front door, with the air of a man confined too long.

Possibly also the air of a man who had listened and waited for the conversation to end before emerging. He left the door open behind him, and they could see the living room had emptied.

"Where is everybody?" Bel asked.

"Maggie and Jamie are loading the dishwasher in anticipation of the next wave. Dana distracted Greta by suggesting they go out back to look at plants. Wes went downstairs to see if Schmidt's hungry. And Ally said she was going to the restroom," J.D. reported. "Suspect it was the one place she thought she could get time to herself. Making any progress?"

"Too early."

"Looks like pea soup to you, too, huh?" he drawled.

Bel grunted agreement.

"I've been sent on a mission of mercy—the coffee supply's running low." He seemed cheerful about it.

Landis couldn't blame him, since it got him away for a while.

Although a smart man would probably keep driving. The guy was nuts for Maggie, to go through this voluntarily.

"Anything I can pick up for you?"

"A clue would be nice," Landis said.

"I'll keep my eyes open."

He walked away, not quite pulling off an air of unconcern. Landis had seen his military record. If J.D. Carson wasn't aware of everything around him at that second and all the others, Landis would be shocked.

"He's good for Mags," Bel said.

"Seems mutual."

"Yeah." For his partner, that was practically gushing. Bel switched topics without a pause. "Cousin's not a fan of yours."

"Mark? Still trying to curry favor with his older cousin. Used to tag along behind Chad."

"Interesting then that he was so eager."

"To tell us he was on duty when word came about Chad dying, the break-in here, and—coincidentally—was just after someone shot at Ally in Fairlington. Yeah, sure was."

"Are you so certain Ally was the target because of logic or because of your fear that she might have been and you don't want to take any chances?"

"What makes you think I'm so certain?"

"Your face. I watched that video of yesterday, too."

He scoffed with a snort.

Bel didn't buy it.

Landis chose to move past that, as if it didn't warrant discussion. "Still, it's true it's a hell of a lot harder for anybody on-duty like Mark Junior or Rachel to get away, though not entirely impossible. Uncle Mark Senior doesn't have an alibi at all."

Bel grunted—acknowledging without trying to fit those facts in anywhere, never forcing pieces into an image he'd formed of the case. Ford Belichek had taught him more about keeping an open mind, while letting the evidence lead to the rightful conclusion, than all the training he'd ever had.

Which reminded him of his role in this partnership.

"This is an opportunity to get more from Ally." It wouldn't have been natural for him not to point it out.

"You." So simply, Bel handed off the assignment.

He could argue. He could ask why. Either response opened too many doors.

He went inside, and turned to the right toward the bedrooms.

✧　✧　✧　✧

ALLY NORTHCUTT SAT on the edge of the bed, on the far side, facing the closet. She had one knee pulled up on the surface, angling her body in such a way that she had to be aware of someone at the door.

She didn't acknowledge him.

He walked into the room, completely into her field of vision. Except her unfocused gaze spoke of a field of vision a thousand miles away.

He leaned against the dresser with the jewelry box on it, eyeing the wooden box without touching. It was about fifteen inches wide and ten deep. A drawer with two pulls extended across the bottom half. A lid gave access to the top.

No sign of the chain that had spilled out of it yesterday or of anything else awry. The cleaners had done a good job.

When he turned from the jewelry box to her, he found her returned to the here and now, watching him.

He returned the look.

It wasn't like their time at Mikey's.

They weren't strangers, which would be neutral. More like acquaintances with distrust.

"I want some time alone," she said.

"That's an indulgence we can't afford."

"*We?*"

"We're not going away, Ally. Not Bel, not me, and not the rest."

"You think because you saved my life that you can—"

"I didn't. That bullet had already missed you when I tackled you."

"Oh." She blinked, clearly not sure if that was better or worse. Neither was he. "*Tried* to save my life. Or, anyway, risked your own.

Putting me under an obligation."

"No obligation. Doing my job."

"Of course." She looked away, then back to him. "No—Wait. That was the first shot. The one into the planter. What about the one that hit the plaza? That would have…?"

He felt her pulling the truth out of him. "Yeah. Maybe."

She stood abruptly and he thought she would leave the room. Instead, she moved to sit on the bench at the foot of the bed.

It put more distance between them, but was that the only reason?

He didn't let his thoughts go down that path. Not down any path except what he needed to get straight between them now.

"We have to talk, but you can relax, Ally. At least about one thing," he added dryly. "I won't bother you. You can—you have to—focus on what's important. On what's going on."

CHAPTER NINETEEN

SHE'D HAD DREAMS when her motions and mental processes were slow-motion while the rest of the world operated double-time. She felt like she was in one now.

"Bother me?"

"With unwanted attentions. I got it when you first made it clear. Got it again last night. Believe me, if I could, I'd give you what you want and get out of your hair. I can't. I'm going to do my job, which is what you need." With a lazy grin, he added, "And get another gold star on my career report card."

"Why did you make sure our paths didn't cross during the investigation into who wanted to kill Jamie?"

Maybe her mental processes weren't as slow as she feared. Not judging from his fleeting expression of not being prepared for that question.

He recovered fast.

"Make it easier on you. Didn't want anything awkward, especially not if it directed any attention away from the investigation."

"Or resulted in you being taken off the case?" Her question had an edge. She didn't regret it.

Not until he took hold of it and sharpened it.

"Or that. Being lead on that looks real good on my record." He grinned. The grin that said he knew exactly how attractive he was and how to get what he wanted.

She realized she didn't believe what his words implied. But maybe her mental processes weren't that hot after all.

"Just wanted to let you know I'm here to do my job. Won't bother you," he repeated.

She wasn't sure she believed that, either.

"Okay."

She had to remember it was oddly easy to talk to Tanner Landis. It always had been.

Probably because he knew the people, the history, the law enforcement life. All things her cousins couldn't totally understand, all things her parents didn't try to understand.

But she needed to be careful of how easy it was to talk to him. For her own sake and his.

✧ ✧ ✧ ✧

"WE'LL GO OVER every step." He leaned back, looking at her from half-lowered eyelids. "This might stir memories, thoughts. Don't dismiss them. Hold onto them. Tell me. Or Bel. Even if it doesn't make sense to you and you don't see the significance."

"Okay." She would tell him or anyone everything she knew about yesterday's shooting.

"You got up. Regular time? Anything unusual?"

"About half an hour earlier than usual. I wanted to be sure to be at the courthouse on time. Other than that, nothing unusual."

"Changed your sheets."

Her mouth shifted, not quite lifting. "That's not unusual. This is the day I do sheets. Strip the bed, put clean sheets on in the morning. Wash, dry, fold, and put away the other set when I get home from the Chate Center."

"Any phone calls? Someone hanging around?"

She thought a moment, then shook her head. Strong enough to swing her hair slightly. "No."

He took her through the drive to Fairlington—boring despite the vagaries of traffic. She met the rest of her family at Jamie's townhouse in historic Old Town Fairlington. They condensed to two vehicles and drove to the courthouse.

One of Maggie's junior colleagues in the Commonwealth's Attorney's office escorted them to a meeting room, where CA Vic Upton explained the procedure, which Maggie had already explained "and she did a better job of it," Ally said.

"It sounds routine for a plea deal. But anything strike you?"

"No, though I have nothing to compare it to."

"Notice anyone you didn't recognize in the courtroom?"

"Yes. But they seemed to be media, defense lawyers, law enforcement, people associated with the CA's office. One I now know was Captain Palery. Maggie definitely knew most of them. No one who seemed out of place to me or who drew a reaction from Maggie. She'd have told you if there was."

"She would. If she remembered. That's why we go over and over and over the details. Something you saw might trigger more for you or Maggie or somebody else. Every detail counts."

He took her through leaving the courtroom. The brief news conference, with the media satisfied when Vic came out of the courtroom and went into giving-a-statement mode.

She was aware of the security detail escorting them out the main doors, then angling wider, officers at each side of them, but giving them space.

"Nothing outside until the moment—"

"Wait. Slow down. Close your eyes. Remember coming out the doors. Smelling the fresh air. Feeling the plaza surface under your shoes. Hearing the traffic on the street in front—"

"And birds. I heard birds."

"Good. You looked to see where they were?"

"I did." She was bemused that he guessed that. "They were in those parallel lines of trees on either side of the main area of the plaza."

"You had to look up to see them."

"Yes."

"What else did you see when you looked up? No, keep your eyes closed."

"The sky." She humored him. "The rounded tree tops up against the sky, with the courthouse building behind them. That was looking directly to the side. Then as we started forward, I looked that way. Down the length of the plaza, then the buildings across the street."

"Notice anything about the buildings? Anything unusual or—"

Her eyes popped open. "You think that if I'd been noticing, I would have seen a sign of the shooter. Be able to tell you where he shot from, maybe who it was—"

"Don't worry about what you think I think. Just remember. Best you can. Everything you can."

"We'd linked arms, the three of us, with Jamie between me and Maggie. J.D. past Maggie, Jamie's folks behind us. We'd reached the second set of steps—you know how they had three steps then a flat section, then three more steps. We got a little out of sync and with our arms linked… We paused a moment at the top of that set of steps, getting back into rhythm. Then—Well, you know what happened."

Did he interpret her reluctance to describe how he'd tackled her as having more to do with the bullets than his presence? She wasn't even sure herself.

He went another direction.

"What were you thinking about?"

"When the shots were fired? I thought… I remember seeing that J.D. had Maggie and Jamie. And he put his body between them and the direction of the shots—what seemed like the direction of the shots to me."

"Where?"

"Across the street." After a beat, she added with less certainty, "And above us."

"Go ahead. What else did you think?"

"I remember thinking he'd make sure they would be okay. I released Jamie's arm, so she could get lower. Behind us, her folks started huddling down, though reaching toward us. I remember thinking they'd be okay, too. And the lawyer. And then I was going down. You… You knocked me to the ground."

"Were you aware of anything else? Anything out of place? Something that caught your attention?"

I remembered your scent.

She gave him a side-eye, then looked down at her hands. "I couldn't hear well. Everything seemed to come from a long distance. Was the shot that close that it deafened me?"

"Both were close and one hit the concrete just outside the nearest planter area holding the trees, but that shouldn't have affected your hearing. More likely the adrenaline."

"Two shots? There were two shots? I only heard one."

"They were close together. The first hit the dirt in that planter. The second one hit the concrete."

She'd been close to the side of that planter. Her next step… Would the second shot have hit her if he hadn't tackled her?

She licked her lips. "Boy, I really failed as the heroic shot spotter. Looking at birds instead of—what?—a figure in a window, a glint off a scope?"

"Most scopes don't glint these days."

"See? Failed again."

"Relax, Ally. We know where the shots came from. We don't need you being the heroic shot spotter."

Her shoulders eased. She even edged toward a smile as she said, "Why? Because you or Bel already was—in addition to those flying tackles and putting yourselves at risk."

"I wish. Might've been worth one of those nice shiny stars on my record. Instead, it was grunt police work. Guys going office to office, floor to floor, and finding one with marks on a windowsill. Then the lab folks burning the midnight, noon, sunrise, and sunset oil to confirm that was the spot. What we need from you is to keep going with this step-by-step account."

She tilted her head. "Inside. Checking each other to be sure everyone was okay. Then into that courtroom. My hearing still seemed odd, but there was little talking. Almost none other than when you and Bel were in the room. Jamie started to say something once and Maggie glared at her, then looked at that detective—his name starts with T— and I had the feeling Maggie was specifically saying not to talk in front of him."

"Terrington. And that's a good rule to follow."

She did smile this time. "On the other hand, what was there to say? None of us knew anything. We were all in shock."

"And then came another shock."

"The phone call," she agreed. "And you know what happened at the Chate—"

"Wait. Go back to the call. Who called?"

"Dr. Sala."

"What did he say, exactly."

"He said Chad was dying. That wasn't how he worded it. He used technical language, but that's what he meant. He said it was hard to predict, but that sometimes things accelerated at that stage. He thought it wouldn't be long.

"I asked about the family—Chad's family—I needed to know who to call. He said a nurse was calling Mark Senior and Junior. Then he said Dawn was there."

"You asked about Chad's mother."

"Oh, yes. I was surprised he hadn't mentioned her. Then he said she wasn't there. He said he'd tried to call her. Dawn asked him to call when things started … declining. I mean, she asked him to call Iris."

Calling her had been the doctor's choice, not the family's request.

"What about that surprised you?"

She felt a frown form.

"What about it surprised me? I guess… I guess that after all the days and months and years of being there, Iris wasn't there when he… When it was near the end. Which wasn't reasonable of me. Not even Iris could be there at every possible minute. Usually, if she wasn't going to be in the next day, she'd tell somebody. She hadn't said anything to me, but she must have told the staff. She *had* arranged for Dawn to be there. Chad's aunt," she filled in.

"I know. Also Mark Senior's sister and Mark Junior's aunt."

"Uh-huh. She's a nice person. Not at all…" Her words stalled.

Not at all … like Iris.

She might as well have said it. He clearly interpreted her silence as being filled with those words.

"Not at all hyped on the Northcutt mystique, huh? That makes Aunt Dawn an outlier."

A quick smile surprised her. It was gone as she said, "She's—she was—good with Chad. Kind. Talked to him like he could understand. Chatting away."

"How was Iris with him?"

"Fierce. She told him she wasn't giving up and he better not, either. She'd talk about seeing people he knew and who had asked about him. She'd talk about some new treatment she had high hopes for." A short sigh. "She told him any time I ever tried to make changes at the house and how she stopped me, so when he went home everything would be as he left it."

"And you?"

"I mostly read to him. Especially about sports, because he loved them. Anything positive about the Piscattoway PD. Never anything critical because…" She hitched one shoulder. "Some general interest articles I thought might interest him."

"There's a corner in the basement that's empty. Off to the side from the sofa and TV. What usually goes there?"

It surprised her. It shouldn't have. It wouldn't have if she hadn't let her guard down.

But why not tell him? Or anyone? It wasn't something that mattered now. "That was my area. For painting."

"In a basement? What kind of light would you get in the basement?"

"The smells gave Chad headaches. Solvents, paints, even…" She paused, then rushed it. "Charcoal."

He kept any reaction to himself.

"With that and concern about my not getting pregnant… I packed up my things and put them in a storage locker. Chad didn't know that. He thought I got rid of everything. I… I discovered I couldn't."

Jamie appeared in the doorway. "Ally? A couple officers are here who say they knew Chad."

She immediately stood and left the room without hesitation.

She was aware of him following slowly.

CHAPTER TWENTY

SHE'D SPENT MOST of the time he'd questioned her with a little tuck between her brows.

He remembered that tuck from when she drew that night outside of Mikey's. He'd seen it, too, when he spotted her in an art class.

That was after he'd left the task force.

He'd been to the little gallery where she'd told him she sold some of her work. He'd had no idea she took classes there. He'd spotted the open door into a studio down a hallway, but it wasn't until he moved to the other side of the gallery that he'd spotted her.

She easily could have seen him before he'd realized she was there. Except she was lost in concentration, that tuck between her brows as she worked on a canvas he couldn't see.

He'd left immediately.

That had been a close call.

He hadn't been ready to see her, to talk to her. He sure as hell hadn't been ready to have to report a contact with her to the head of the task force, who already wasn't happy with him for leaving.

What was he doing? These memories weren't going to get them anywhere on this investigation.

Assess what she said. How she said it.

Like pulling up short of what she really thought of Iris Northcutt.

Ally had been fully prepared to stonewall. She was a champion stonewaller. That's why he'd redirected. Doing an end run.

Which brought up a more important question than all the ones she'd answered.

She was a champion stonewaller, but was she a champion dissembler, too?

He had a flash of her in the courtroom in Fairlington, the phone still in her hand. She'd first said Chad had taken a turn for the worse. Then the jerk of her head and the plain words *He's dying.*

She'd immediately rejected her own soft-pedaling.

Ally didn't turn away from harsh facts. She didn't try to pretty up the truth.

So what the hell was she working so hard to keep to herself?

Because there was something.

He was going to find out.

✧　✧　✧　✧

"ALLY, HOW HAS Chad left his things?" Bel asked.

She looked at him quizzically. "They're all still here."

"His will," Tanner said. "Who inherits what?"

"I… I don't know for sure. We made simple wills when we got married, with everything going to the other one. If we died at the same time, or within a week of each other, my share went to the Sunshine Foundation—"

Jamie made a sound.

But that didn't derail Tanner. "Not your parents?"

"No." She didn't waste any time on that word. "Chad's share went to his mother, along with a bequest to his niece and nephew—David's children."

"No later will?"

"No." This negative had doubt strung out behind it. "Not that I know of. I mean, I know the medical authority was still the way we'd agreed at the time we did that will, but I suppose he could have left that and changed the will."

"You were his medical power of attorney?"

"Yes."

"Then why on earth did you let Iris push you around?" Maggie asked.

"Because she needed that. I didn't."

The simplicity of it quieted even Maggie.

Tanner came back to the point. "Didn't you look at the will after Chad was shot?"

"No. My focus was on the medical status, not … beyond that."

"But it's happened now, Ally," Jamie said. "You need to know what the will says, especially if there's been another one."

"I suppose it's in the safe deposit box, along with the deed, our passports, things like that. I'm sure it isn't in the house. I've been through all his papers here. And that's where the medical power of attorney was—the safe deposit box. I never thought to look for the will then."

"You haven't looked at the safe deposit box since?" Tanner asked.

"Nothing in there applied to my life since Chad was shot."

"It does now. Where's the bank?"

"Can't that wait until—?"

He cut off Ally. "No. There could be something of investigative value in there. Or not. We need to know either way, not have it dangling. If we go now, we can get there before the bank closes."

✧ ✧ ✧ ✧

MAGGIE WENT WITH in case they hit any legal snags. They didn't.

Ally opened the safe deposit box and held out two wills. Tanner took them and started reading, while Bel asked her, "Mind if I…?"

She nudged the box toward him in answer.

They finished about the same time.

"Same, original wills. Ally inherits."

"Nothing else of interest in the box," Bel said.

Back in the vehicle, Ally said, "Nothing there, so, we could have waited."

"Knowing which pebbles don't belong to the mountain is vital," Bel said.

Maggie's groan saved Tanner the effort.

"Pebbles? Mountain?" Ally asked.

"Now you've done it," Maggie said. "Bel's going to explain his approach to investigating."

And he did.

✧ ✧ ✧ ✧

JAMIE GREETED THEM at the front door with a grin.

"My amazing mother took advantage of Greta complaining about people coming and going so much here to convince Greta that she needed her rest and wouldn't get any here. She and Dad are settling Greta in the closest hotel that met her standards."

"Bless Aunt Dana," Maggie said.

Jamie's grin drooped. "And in the nick of time."

Tanner turned to follow her gaze over their shoulders.

A man in a quality suit made for him and with distinguishing gray at his well-barbered temples walked up the walk toward them.

Tanner shifted his weight to block off Ally, but she circled him and met the man.

"Dad."

"Allison."

For a moment he expected the man to shake her hand like a business associate. Instead, he took her by the shoulders and kissed her on each cheek. Like some dictators or mafia bosses.

"I told you he'd be along anytime," Maggie said under her breath to J.D., but audible to Landis, too. "For two people divorced for twice as long as they'd been married, they have some odd ESP going that informs one when the other's had contact with their daughter, making Ally their never-ending scorecard."

Jamie leaned toward Bel as she spoke in an undertone, but her gaze was on Landis. "Only break she ever got was at Aunt Viv's, until she went out on her own."

Ally and her father came toward the door.

Jamie stepped forward to greet them, tugging Maggie by the sleeve. "Uncle Kurt, hello."

Inside, with the introductions made, Kurt Lindell's gaze scanned the room, probing down the hall to the bedrooms, then toward the kitchen.

"Mother's at a hotel." Ally's voice held no intonation.

"Which one?"

Jamie told him, chatting on about how her parents were helping her settle in because there wasn't enough room or peace at the house. She interrupted herself to say, with a hint of relief, "Oh, look, more visitors are coming."

WHAT ALLY THOUGHT of as her earliest memory was being scooped up by her father from a stiff chair where she'd been looking at a doll the tall, thin woman called Aunt Moban had given her.

It was a porcelain doll. An antique. Accompanied by instructions to not hold it that way, to be careful, and to note details about the dress that made no sense to Ally.

The woman said other things, too. Things that made her father angry.

"…got her pregnant so she'd marry you and you'd get your hands on the Moban money…"

He'd wrapped her coat around her, not bothering to button it. She left the doll on the chair.

"C'mon, Allison. We're going."

He'd crammed her red knit hat and matching mittens in his pocket and grasped his wife's arm, hurrying her to the door, too, though Greta resisted.

"We're not staying here to be talked to that way."

She remembered her father's words. She remembered the anger vibrating through his body as he held her against his shoulder. She remembered a different anger in her mother's eyes.

Over the years, as memories of milder variations of that scene filled in the gaps of her understanding, she recognized that the sister of her mother's first husband heaped verbal abuse on all around her.

It flowed past her mother, who had no attention to spare beyond her gardens.

But not her father.

Because he resented the denigrating invective directed at Greta as a gold-digger or to get away from the woman's accusations that he had married Greta for the Moban money?

Other early memories centered around her dad coming home being the best time of the day.

He was handsome and intelligent and he asked her serious questions. Not fluff about "how was your day, dear?" or "did that nice Peterson boy notice your new haircut?" But probing questions about what they'd studied in school—as probing as you could get at that age—or what she'd drawn that day. Questions that made it seem like he was really interested.

That eroded over the years, though she'd treasured the times it still happened. It ended when she was eight.

That day she kept checking out the window, looking at the time. But he didn't come home.

Her mother called her for dinner. There were only two places set at the table.

Even her mother's vague explanations eventually arrived at the word *divorce*.

"Why? Why are you divorcing Daddy?"

"I had a feeling…"

A *feeling*? She sent him away over a *feeling*? Ally couldn't believe it, and for once Greta appeared to read her daughter's reaction.

"When one lives with a man for fifteen years, one gains a sense of these things."

"What things?"

Her mother turned a vague look to her. "There's another woman."

Ally stared at her. Unable to process the words at first. Not their meaning—she understood that. But what did it have to do with *her*? Why would it mean she had to lose him?

"Your father was unfaithful," her mother said.

Not to me, he wasn't, she wanted to scream.

Then her mother's earlier words echoed in her head. *I had a feeling.*

"How do you *know* he was unfaithful?"

"I just knew. I had this feeling—"

"Feeling? You've ruined my life for a feeling?"

It was the only time in her life Ally screamed at her mother.

It made no difference.

Neither did saying she wanted to live with Dad. That was never considered as far as she could tell. Not by her mother, not by the courts. Not by her father. Especially since her mother's first marriage was to a Moban.

As a teenager, she'd tried logic.

"But if he married you for money, Mother, why would he risk that by fooling around with someone else?"

"Because the Moban money had done its work by then. It had given him the entrée to the circles and the professional connections that built his career. Without that it would have taken him decades longer to have achieved what he had to that point."

"But if professional ambition was his only motivation for marrying you, staying married would have put him farther ahead."

"You know what they say about animals chewing off their own legs to get free of a trap." Her mother never looked up from a plant catalog. "He was willing to give up the top level of success to achieve his freedom."

In college, she had called Kurt Lindell and asked flat-out if he'd cheated on Greta.

"I am not going to discuss my marital fidelity with my daughter."

"It's not like I don't know about such things, Dad. And it's been years. What difference can it make to you now?"

"I am not going to discuss my marital fidelity with my daughter."

"Did you ever love her, Dad?"

That brought only the sound of breathing for so long she began to hope. "I'm not going to discuss this with you."

"Do you still love her?"

"Good-bye, Ally."

Had Kurt Lindell married Greta Frye Moban for her money and connections as a widow? Or had Greta's insecurities driven Kurt away?

Insecurities pounded into her word by relentless word by her domineering sister-in-law?

Their daughter didn't know.

She doubted they did.

CHAPTER TWENTY-ONE

THE FLOW OF visitors picked up as neighbors came home from work—with their credentials checked by Schmidt.

Landis spotted the woman he'd talked to at the time of the shooting, avoided her to preserve any confusion that he'd been local and official when he'd talked to her then. But he pointed her out to Bel, who walked out with her.

He noted a lack of enthusiasm as neighbors left Ally's house and headed across the street to call on Iris.

Shortly after Bel and the neighbor woman left, there was a break in the flow.

Ally said she wanted to return a few personal phone calls.

After fifteen minutes, he went down the hallway to tell her a clot of headquarters types from PCPD were headed this way, having visited Iris first.

She was smiling and talking warmly on the phone. She looked and sounded more like the Ally he remembered. He heard the name Shindell and recognized it as Chad's longest-term partner, who'd left for the FBI.

"…of course I understand. I'm so grateful you're coming later on, Shindell. I hope we have a chance to really talk…. Yes, me, too… Oh." She'd spotted Landis. "Just a moment."

She held the phone to her breastbone.

He explained his purpose for being there, then left, not waiting for her to end the call.

She returned to the living room as the headquarters types came inside. She did not look at him.

The public information officer asked Ally about making a statement to the media for the evening news.

Ally barely started to refuse when Maggie said, "I'll make a statement on behalf of the family, if you'd like, Ally."

Ally liked. So did the PIO—an Assistant Commonwealth's Attorney making the statement wasn't merely family. He escorted her out to make the brief statement like he'd won a prize at the county fair.

"PIO should be a tap dancer," a PCPD officer muttered to another.

"Wouldn't have his job for anything."

Unfortunately, that startling insight was about the only thing Landis picked up from threading through the groups, listening while he pretended not to.

Bel returned with a one-shoulder shrug that said he didn't think he'd gotten anything additional from the original witness.

The latter influx coincided with the end of the Piscattoway County Police Department's shift change.

This is what they'd been waiting for.

✧   ✧   ✧   ✧

"I HEAR FROM Mark Northcutt Junior that you two like fishing," J.D. Carson said to the two PCPD officers Landis and Bel had briefed him on.

Landis and Maggie stood on one side of the group, involved in a desultory conversation that allowed both to hear most of what the fishing pals said. Bel was on the other side of them, adding items to the buffet table.

Dewey Selton had a wiry, thin frame. He couldn't have met the height requirement for the Piscattoway County Police Department. His regulation cut for his black hair emphasized an unusually narrow forehead.

Ethan Paulz, half a foot taller and edging toward chunky, had the voice that would have matched Selton's body type—fast-paced, emphatic, repeating key phrases.

In contrast, Selton's speech came slowly, with thoughtful gaps.

Paulz said, "Yeah, like fishing a lot. A lot. You're…"

"J.D. Carson. I'm here with Allison Northcutt's cousin." Good move not mentioning which one, in case either officer knew of Maggie's position. They exchanged handshakes all around. "Sure would rather be fishing. You ever fished up in the mountains?"

That started a run of fishing talk that Landis hoped to hell Bel understood, because he didn't and he could tell Maggie didn't either.

J.D. dropped Mark's name in again. That led to memories of their fishing with him and Chad. Paulz' Eastern Shore cabin featured largely in that, as did Selton's boat.

"Nice to have a boat like that," J.D. said with believable longing.

"It's amazing," Paulz said. "He found a great one."

"Sounds like you didn't do so bad with the cabin, either."

"Can't take the credit for that. It fell in my lap. I inherited it from a distant relative. Could have knocked me over with a feather when I got the letter. Seems like he remembered me as a cute baby." He grinned. "Didn't even know the guy's name and he left me a cabin like that."

His explanation highlighted that Selton had said nothing about his prized possession, yet didn't sell Paulz' story, either.

"Amazing. Shame it had to end," J.D. said.

For once, Selton jumped in. "Shame what happened to Chad Northcutt."

J.D. grimaced sympathetically. "That must stick in your craw. Years pass, no answers."

"You could say that. You could also say it's fucked up," Paulz said.

"Had any ideas of your own?"

"Somebody wouldn't be walking around if we did." Paulz said it. Selton grunted agreement.

"Hard to lose a buddy like Chad. Good thing you have each other and Mark Junior, huh."

Their gazes slid past each other.

"Yeah."

EXCERPT from TASK FORCE ARIES FINAL REPORT

Final report from Interagency Task Force Aries, upon termination of its investigation into possible police corruption and/or other malfeasance, as well as conspiracy to commit such crimes in the Piscattoway County Police Department.

… In conclusion, this task force was officially terminated five months after the shooting of Piscattoway County Police Department Officer Chad Northcutt.

After the observation of Northcutt's meeting with fellow officers Dewey Selton, Mark Northcutt Junior, and Ethan Paulz at the latter's cabin on May 24-27, as described above, there had been no further off-duty meetings among them and no contact identifiable as furthering a conspiracy.

None of the remaining targets of investigation demonstrated any monetary transactions not explained by their ordinary income. Nor did the three gather at the Paulz cabin or elsewhere when not in the company of multiple others, such as at the hospital.

The shooting of Northcutt appeared to end their enterprise, if it had not, in fact, ended previous to that, since no activity was noted after the May 24-27 gathering.

At the time Northcutt was shot, we had correlated financial activities by him that could not be explained by his ordinary income with traffic stops made by him. (Chart 2) The outgoing financial activities consisted primarily of gifts, including of cash, to Iris Northcutt (mother) and Willow (girlfriend). (Chart 1)

The task force documented his meetings with fellow officers. (Chart 3) Based on frequency of contact both on-duty and off-duty, we focused on Dewey Selton, Ethan Paulz, Mark Northcutt Jr. (Chad Northcutt's cousin.) Those contacts are in Chart 4.

There was evidence of expenditures above their means by Selton (boat) and Paulz (cabin), but a further pattern had not yet been discerned for either subject. The investigation had not yet determined a correlation of timing or otherwise between the expenditures by Selton or Paulz and their on-duty activities.

However, none of the lines of inquiry involving those three subjects or any others had been exhausted when this investigation was halted.

An additional area of investigation would be the shooting of Chad Northcutt. If he was shot to prevent his giving away the enterprise, whether by carelessness or potentially agreeing to become a witness, finding who shot him would offer another door into the investigation. I have volunteered to lead such an investigation, to run parallel to that of the Piscattoway County Police Department's ongoing investigation into the shooting.

In the event that avenue is not pursued, it is advised, at the least, to continue periodic checks of the finances of the above-named potential conspirators.

✧ ✧ ✧ ✧

THROUGH ALL OF the visitors, Kurt Lindell stood apart. Not demanding attention as Greta had tried to do, but not helping as did Ally's cousins, J.D., and Dana and Wes when they returned.

Kurt approached Ally and said, "I better go now. I made a reservation at the hotel, but I don't want to lose my upgrade by getting there late."

"I'll walk you out."

Landis reached the door first, stepping out ahead of them to scan the area.

He gave them space for private conversation, but he didn't leave.

As far as he could tell, there wasn't much conversation—private or otherwise.

Ally stopped and her father went on.

Landis moved up next to her. For security.

Then he asked, "Why did he want to know which hotel?" without considering how that fell under security.

"Because if they stay at the same hotel, there's no risk of the other trying to score points on being closer or cheaper or more luxurious or … whatever. And they can keep an eye on each other. It all makes sense if you view it as competition."

"And you're both the judge and the prize?"

"I'm judge, jury, and bailiff, but never the prize. Never mind, it's nothing to do with—"

"I'm not a bad listener."

She knew that. It made him dangerous.

"What would you know about family? You stay as far away from the concept as possible. You wouldn't even talk about—" Almost immediately, she said, "I'm sorry, Tanner. I didn't mean—"

"Yes, you did. You wanted me to back off and it was an effective weapon. Don't apologize for being a crack shot with your weapon of choice."

She turned and went inside.

—DAY 3—

THURSDAY

CHAPTER TWENTY-TWO

THE THREE FAIRLINGTON officers took turns on the sofa in the basement. The two left awake split duty on the front door and back door.

As he and Bel traded off early on, his partner asked, "Is she telling us everything?" No need to specify who he meant by *she*.

"No. She's hiding something."

Protecting the Northcutt name? Why when Iris Northcutt treated her so badly?

Chad's memory? Maybe.

"Takes one to know one." Bel remained unfazed by the glare Landis sent him. "Seems like Chad might have been hiding something, too. Something people were willing to break in here to try to find. They'd have found it by now if regular looking would have found it."

"And, considering they had years and we've been on the hunt a few hours, means we aren't likely to find whatever the hell it might be."

"Where we might be able to beat them is by trying the inside route. Someone who knew him well."

Bel not saying her name, leaving it dangling out there for him to avoid was a challenge.

He met it. "Ally."

"Ally," Bel confirmed. "You should tell her what's going on. Ask her what she knows, what she might suspect about Chad, and see if she has ideas."

"If I go through channels for permission to reveal the task force, it could take—"

"Longer than the patience of whoever's targeting Ally. Besides, when have you gone through channels?"

"Yeah." Landis felt more like himself than he had since the moment of hearing that shot aimed at Ally.

Then his partner said, "So you and Ally have a lot more talking to do tomorrow."

Nothing happened the rest of the night.

Which meant Landis had far too much time to think. And remember.

✦ ✦ ✦ ✦

That last night at Mikey's...

HE'D HAD A lot to drink, celebrating without telling anyone else why.

Barely a year out of the academy and he'd been chosen to assist the Monacan department's senior detective, because they had two investigations going at the same time. No one else considered working with the guy a positive.

He was blunt, chewed and spat tobacco, and didn't like answering questions. Tanner figured all that was worth it because the guy closed cases. He didn't need a mentor explaining what he was seeing, he just wanted an opportunity to see it.

The case looked like it was a simple break-in at the office of the part-time mayor of the major town in their jurisdiction. A window pried open and the petty cash taken from the mayor's desk drawer.

The old detective moved through the logical and necessary investigative steps with speed and thoroughness.

The mayor didn't have any ideas, but his assistant mentioned a kid who a month earlier had pushed over planters making a mess at the small building's entry and knocking off some geraniums. That seemed the logical lead to follow.

But the old detective barked at him, "What're you staring at?"

And Tanner realized it was the computer keyboard.

"It's been wiped. Not like someone trying to clean it, but just the keys and where hands would rest. Also, there's a key drive missing." He pulled out the already fingerprinted drawer and four key drives lined up there with a gap in the middle. "First two were wiped, too. Fourth and fifth weren't. Someone could have found what they wanted on the third one."

The old detective grunted.

Then he got a warrant.

Then all hell broke loose.

The mayor had child porn on his computer. Local kids. Selling and trading it. Including the kid who'd trashed the geraniums.

The kid stole the key drive, after finding the one with his photos on it.

The mayor had also been stealing from the town. That seemed minor, considering, and that's probably why it got dumped on Tanner. But it helped.

Now, the mayor was in jail.

There was a lot more work to do, but after a solid week on it, the old detective told him at seven o'clock to cut loose for a night and get back to it in the morning. He also said Landis would be assigned to him from now on whenever there was an active case going.

He went to Mikey's.

To celebrate, he told himself.

As soon as he walked in, he looked for Ally.

It took more than two hours and the drinks to occupy them before he got her alone and told her his news—the only person he'd told.

She smiled at him. That smile that started in her eyes.

"Tanner, that's fantastic. What a great opportunity for you, and completely deserved."

She put her hands on his upper arms and leaned into him for a short hug.

He wanted more.

He wanted everything.

Too little sleep, too much celebrating, and with a sense of time and opportunity possibly never coming again, he stepped into her and tried to kiss her.

They were alone, of course—he wasn't that drunk.

He didn't reach her mouth.

She backed up, one splayed hand to his chest, the other fleetingly brushed his cheek.

"Tanner. Don't."

Not moving apart, not moving closer, they looked at each other, suspended.

"Ally—"

"I can't, Tanner. I'm going to marry Chad."

"You don't have to."

"I can't."

He could have overcome the resistance of her arm. He didn't. "That's not the same as you don't want to."

"Please, Tanner."

That's all. *Please, Tanner.*

He walked away. He didn't look back.

He went to his tiny, bland apartment, slept it off, and got back to work in the morning.

I can't. He'd thought of that a lot in the weeks after that night. It was an odd response. Wasn't it? Wouldn't a woman looking forward to marrying Chad Northcutt, a woman not interested in Tanner Landis have said, *I'm going to* or *I want to* or *I love him, not you.*

In the end it hadn't made any difference, because she married Chad Northcutt.

He didn't do anything stupid like going to the wedding or hanging around the church that day. Or going back to Mikey's.

He had seen her—now Mrs. Chad Northcutt—several months later at the wedding of a mutual friend, but he'd had no trouble steering clear of her. Or of reminding himself, when he saw Northcutt holding onto her arm more like a prison guard than a man guiding his wife, that it was none of his business.

Afterward, he advanced just the way he'd described to her, getting ever more difficult cases, working with other jurisdictions, attending additional training.

He always suspected the old detective recommended him for the corruption task force. Didn't have a chance to confirm that before the man died of a massive heart attack, sitting at his desk, reviewing case notes on a cold case.

However it happened, Tanner Landis got on a task force at a younger age than anyone else in the metro area. Reveled in the work, the mission. Even the target.

A fellow cop? Get him—or her—caught and out of the force as fast as possible. That's how he'd viewed that.

Chad Northcutt specifically? No problem. Never cared for his blowhard ways anyhow.

Until he'd realized the full implication of that particular mission.

Ally.

He'd been fully aware of the hit he'd take to his career by quitting the task force. Knocked clear off the fast-track.

Had he considered going to her, telling her what was happening? He didn't know.

In the end he hadn't.

Maybe it had been a half-assed non-decision, not investigating her himself, but not warning her, either. On the other hand, she'd chosen Chad.

He took the career hit, sliding back to patrol for a few months until the old detective kicked him in the butt.

He'd pulled it together then. Crossed the river—he'd always assumed that move happened with some combination of the old detective and the head of the task force providing the impetus.

The quick jump to the murder squad, partnering with Belichek, came as a surprise.

He quickly realized the partnership was expected to fail. It was unclear, though, if he or Belichek was supposed to be the one who tanked it. He'd decided not to. Bel hadn't needed to make a decision. He never tanked anything. They meshed.

These past years he'd been enjoying the job and himself. With women, with food, with a lifestyle. Not being so damned earnest.

Doing good work, experiencing good life.

He liked his life. Loved it. He wasn't going to screw with it. Never again.

LANDIS WALKED INTO the kitchen, crowded with everyone except the Chancellors, who sat at the nearby dining room table, and Schmidt, by the front door.

"I have more questions, Ally."

He sounded grimmer than he intended. Every pair of eyes except hers came to him. Hers and probably Bel's, but since those eyes were behind him, he didn't know for sure.

As if synchronized, the pairs of eyes shifted to Ally.

She kept her gaze on the towel she was using to dry a cutting board.

As long as he had their attention, "You're all coming to Fairlington later today. You need to give your statements first thing in the morning."

There were murmurs, but Maggie stopped them by saying, "I'm surprised Captain Palery has waited this long. It's more than reasonable."

"We can all stay at my place tonight and go to the police station in the morning," Jamie said.

"Your mother and I will go on home for tonight, then drive back," Wes Chancellor said.

Ally surprised Landis by not saying anything. She didn't even look like she wanted to argue.

"Good. In the meantime, Ally…?" He took half a step back, indicating she should precede him toward the bedroom hallway.

She paused.

"This has to be cleared up, Al." Maggie's tone, softer than usual, left no doubt. "They need to know everything you know, even what you don't know that you know. Until they do and figure this thing out, you're in danger."

"The representative from the police department is coming at one to go over the initial schedule for the visitation and funeral," Ally said.

"That leaves enough time to get started."

She cut him a less-than-friendly look at his cheerful words. But she put down the towel and cutting board, and preceded him out of the area.

He was aware of scrutiny from all directions as he turned to follow, but the only one he made eye contact with was Bel.

"Do what you're good at," Bel said quietly.

CHAPTER TWENTY-THREE

SHE CHOSE TO sit on the bed again.

He took the same position he'd held yesterday by the chest with the jewelry box on it.

There'd been a few moments yesterday it seemed they might be able to reach through the wall between them.

Not for anything like a relationship, but for him to do his job.

As Bel had reminded him.

As he had promised her that he was here to do, if he was any good.

As he needed to do.

"You quit art." His accusation didn't catch her as off-guard as he'd hoped, though her brows rose. "When you're damned good at it. That's wrong."

"How would you know? You couldn't have seen—Oh, of course. The painting at Jamie's. I forget you've known Jamie these past months. And I tend to think of all my work locked up in my storage area. Even when I'm at Jamie's and I look at it—really look at it—not just like part of the décor, it doesn't seem like I painted it. That's all so long ago… Before—"

"You quit art."

"I didn't. Completely." The tuck between her brows mirrored the irritation in her quick words.

"Did you keep working with charcoal?"

"No."

"Because it gave you away? He'd know from the marks on your hand? Harder to clean than paints? Harder to leave no trace he'd see?"

"What does this have to do with the shooting at the courthouse?"

"You're going to have to get over this, Ally. Stop thinking questions are personal. The answers might be personal to you, but the questions are my job. All part of victimology."

"Victimo—But… You mean you're investigating *me*? You *can't* be investigating Chad's shooting."

"Can't ignore the possibility of a connection."

"But…"

He caught a flash of something strong in her eyes—deeper than surprise. Was that fear? Then she dropped her head.

He looked at her for a long moment while she looked at her left knee.

"Did he—? Was he physical with you?"

She didn't look up from her examination of that knee. "Not the way you mean. He never hit me or really hurt me. Not even where the bruises wouldn't show."

He should have been relieved. He wasn't. There were a lot of ways of hurting someone without hitting them, including physical ways.

"*Not the way I mean?* What way, then?"

"He shoved me a few times. But he never hurt me."

He didn't like her insistence on that. "Did anyone else ever see him do it?"

Her mouth twisted, dismissing what she was about to say. "His mother. Possibly his cousin. I'm not sure."

"Mark or Rachel?"

"Rachel."

So, if Rachel saw it, she never talked about it to Ally. And that meant if Ally was surer that Rachel had seen the incident than she let on now, she'd have felt Rachel's silence cut off an avenue of potential support.

"Ally—"

"Really, Landis. This is unnecessary. Not only is my husband dead, but I assure you, he never physically injured me."

Carefully, he shifted the focus. "He seemed fine with you painting before you got married."

"Yes." She looked straight ahead.

"Even seemed proud of it."

"Perhaps."

"It changed after?"

She started to turn her head toward him, but must have thought better of it, because she returned her stare to straight ahead. "Yes."

"Other things changed?"

"Yes."

"Like?"

Her gaze flickered, her voice stayed steady. "Didn't want me coming out with the group from the department. Didn't want me to spend so much time with my cousins, the rest of the family." Her tone remained even, emotionless. The voice of law enforcement giving an unembellished report. "Said it was an insult to him and his family, saying they weren't enough for me."

He shoved aside anger—it wasn't what was needed now and even if it were what he was angry about and at whom was too tangled. He summoned professionalism.

"It's what controllers do." He didn't use the word abuser. Not after she'd rejected the idea so thoroughly. No need to add another wall. "They're experts at it. They cut off avenues of support, of pleasure, of sociability, of expression, and focus it all on them. It's hard for people on the other end to spot it. It's gradual. It's laid out as a matter of love and trust and loyalty. Doesn't have anything to do with any of those, but those are the buttons the controller pushes. At the start. When they need the other person's cooperation to make it happen the way the controller wants."

She seemed to look toward the jewelry box as she spoke. Thinking of that necklace from her aunt? "I know."

"So, you gave up painting." He said it mostly to give her a place to restart. It wasn't far from the topic of Chad's efforts to control her, but even some distance might help.

When he'd first seen the house's décor, he'd thought Chad Northcutt had crap taste to prefer schlock to Ally's work. Now he understood that Northcutt not liking her painting had less to do with aesthetics and more to do with her daring to pay attention to anything other than him.

"I didn't do any art in the house anymore. At first, he said the mess bothered him. Then the smells. Then he and his mother started saying the chemicals must be why I didn't get pregnant. Iris had a lot of theories about all that... Well, you heard her. I was barren."

"Bitch," he muttered.

She didn't voice agreement, but she didn't object, either. "So first I moved from the guest room to the basement. Then I moved everything out of the house. I had my things at a studio for a while. I was taking courses there. Then Chad found out I was leaving the house on a regular schedule—"

"His mother."

"Yes. And he objected, especially when he found out it was for an art class. Saying I must not really want a baby when I kept exposing myself to poisons. I kept telling him I was working in water colors, not oils, much less the lead-based wall paints that are bad for pregnant women. I'd given up oils, even though it's mostly the solvents that are a problem. Though some of the cadmium- or cobalt- or nickel- or chromium-based colors might be harmful. But I wasn't using those ever. And when he and Iris brought up the possibility, I researched it all carefully, even had the doctor write out an opinion. And after that, I gave up oils completely to satisfy them. But it didn't make any difference. Chad kept saying over and over that I was making it impossible for him to have a baby."

Big surprise. Chad Northcutt saw it as all about him.

"You quit the class."

The tiniest start of a smile crossed her lips. "It had ended, actually, about six weeks earlier. But the instructor let me keep working there. The problem was, he was moving to New Mexico, so my space where I could paint was gone."

He waited. He wasn't sure for what. An expression of grief at losing her art? Of frustration, anger, hatred toward Chad? He knew which he voted for.

"So, I took workshops," she said. "One-day or half-day sessions.

Different times, different places. No regular schedule. Mixed up who was offering them. Nothing he or Iris could track or pin down. I had a sketch pad I kept tucked up under a strap on the bottom of the bed. He couldn't smell sketching."

He sat back.

He didn't realize he was grinning at her until she blinked and gave him a small smile.

"You never gave up your art?"

She didn't answer directly.

"It became harder. There was a time I thought for sure he'd found my sketch pad. I put it in the storage locker, too. Then, after Chad was shot, I couldn't do the workshops, much less a class, because I'm at the facility every day. Was. *Was* at the facility most days. But I've started sketching. Sometimes even at the Chate if Iris isn't around. A few of the nurses … well, they let me know if she's coming and they've stored things for me so she wouldn't know. They've been wonderful to me. As well as Chad, of course. I wouldn't have survived even a few months without their amazing care."

She'd held onto her art.

In his head, he heard her words again after the call came from the long-term care facility. Facing the facts, not sugar-coating them.

He made a decision in that instant, but didn't act on it immediately because she spoke first.

"Do you know what Chad was doing?"

He slowly repeated, "*What Chad was doing.* What *was* he doing?"

"I don't know."

He saw her brace for him to push back at that, to declare she had known.

So he didn't.

"Then how do you know he was *doing* something?"

"He wasn't very good at deception. Even though he thought he was."

Now he did act on his decision.

"He was dirty, Ally."

CHAPTER TWENTY-FOUR

HE DIDN'T COUCH it in the softer guise of *we have reason to believe* or *we suspect*. He stated it as a fact.

Though he couldn't say *we have the hard evidence*. They didn't.

Her head snapped up. "*No.*"

For a moment that's all she said.

He left her to grapple with it, letting her see his certainty while he watched her.

"His family. His father. The tradition of Northcutt cops. The generations. It's not possible."

Did she realize her immediate, certain denial didn't include anything about Chad himself? Certainly not raising his character or ethics as refuting the charge.

"I was on a task force investigating suspected corruption."

"Investigating." Her voice was odd, like she'd repeated the word after being turned upside down. Maybe she had been.

"Cops stealing money, sometimes drugs from people they pulled over. Sometimes people passing through, sometimes locals, but not people they thought could bring it back to them. But there were rumbles. And Chad made mistakes that drew attention to him."

"You were in charge?"

"Not hardly. Strictly peon."

She shook her head. "You couldn't have been. You became a Fairlington homicide detective."

"You're missing a chunk of scut work in between."

"Being in on that kind of investigation early must have helped your career."

He said nothing.

She frowned. "It didn't," she concluded. "Why not? That should have advanced you to what you wanted to do—rooting out corruption."

"Didn't turn out that way."

"Were you pulled off?"

"No."

"You requested to get off."

"Connections could have compromised the investigation." He should have grinned at the irony of his using Bel's complaint against him now. He didn't.

"You knew you were connected to Chad before you joined the investigation. Unless… They didn't tell you?"

Was that what she wanted? To exonerate him of investigating her dirty cop husband? Not happening.

"They told me. I told them we'd been at the academy together, even though they knew. Also knew we weren't buddies."

She said nothing.

"He wasn't the connection that could have compromised the investigation. You were."

He didn't need to say that. She knew the implication. Why drive it home? As if punishing her for it being the truth.

He said again, "He was dirty, Ally." Not letting her knowledge of that truth retreat into wishful thinking.

He saw something happen in her eyes that he'd seen before when a spouse, a lifelong friend, a child, a parent recognized a truth they'd known for some time at the level of muscle and sinew, but never allowed into consciousness. Until this instant.

An overlay of haze edging across the iris, a change in focus as reality tilted the axis of their lives, of their familiarity with themselves.

"This will kill his mother," she murmured.

The way that harridan treated her and she wasted any concern over her?

"My job is to make sure it doesn't kill you."

For an instant that felt like centuries, her eyes met his.

He pulled in a breath. Her gaze dropped. To his mouth.

He fought the sudden need of his lungs to breathe faster.

He concentrated on speaking dryly. "Make sure it doesn't kill me, either. Because if I fail, Maggie *will* kill me." He cocked his head slightly. "With help from Jamie."

Her unexpected smile tripled the strain on his lungs. "They would, wouldn't they?"

"No need to sound so cheerful about it."

Her smile turned to a grin and, for half a beat, they grinned at each other.

As far as he could tell, they looked away at the same instant.

"I'm not cheerful," she said slowly. Then she asked, "Could this be why he was shot?"

"Possible. We didn't have enough to know who was involved with him, or who was in charge."

"Chad wasn't." She said it as a statement.

"No. There were rumbles he might have been in trouble with somebody, maybe lost something. Presumably something that could point back to the person in charge. Money, something else? We couldn't get a grip to find out. Rumbles weren't enough. And the operation went quiet after he was shot."

"But... How can you be so sure about this?"

When it took him too long to connect the question to what they'd been talking about instead of what he felt, she glanced toward him— not making contact.

He cleared his throat, hating the sound.

"That he was involved? Money. It drew attention to him."

She frowned, then proved she'd listened those nights in Mikey's. "Money without identifiable legitimate sources. But Chad didn't—*we* didn't—have money beyond his salary and my small inheritance from Aunt Vivian. Certainly not conspicuous consumption."

"Not spent at home, not on you."

This time she did not look away from his eyes.

"Another woman?"

"Yes. And his mother."

She didn't flinch at his confirmation, but did at the second part. "Iris? But she has her husband's pension, the benefits."

"Apparently she needed or wanted more. Either way, he was supplementing her income monthly."

"Or Chad *wanted* to give her more."

God, she was still trying to turn the guy into a saint.

He drove the point home. "By stealing it."

"By stealing it," she repeated. After a pause, she shook her head. "It goes against everything the Northcutts have stood for. You know about his brother? About David?"

"Died on the job."

"Yes. Not too long after their father died. That was before I knew Chad, but I could see... He tried so hard to take his older brother's place. He never did. His place in the family was always in his brother's shadow. When David died, the shadow covered everything else."

Maybe not such a saint in her eyes if she could describe his family dynamics so dispassionately.

"Did you have any sense of something going on with Chad on the job. Anything he talked about or..."

She was shaking her head. "He never talked to me about the job. Not even at the academy. I learned more from—" She stopped short. Too late to stop recollection of their long-ago conversations. "—the talk around the table at Mikey's. He didn't like that, but I didn't realize it until later. He said he wanted to protect me from the sordidness."

She didn't believe that.

He agreed.

Had Chad wanted to keep her separated from his work life to isolate her as much as possible? Not let her have connections with his work friends to exert more power. To keep her from finding out about his affairs?

Or to keep her at a distance from the activities that put the task force on his trail? Chad wasn't the sharpest, but he had to know Ally would figure it out if she possessed pieces of the puzzle.

Possibly all of the above.

"Did you notice conspicuous consumption by Iris?"

She considered it, then slowly shook her head. "Not that stood out to me."

"What about the other woman?"

"How would I know what he spent on her? I didn't know she existed. Besides, wouldn't I be the last person to know?" she asked dryly.

"Ever suspect he was cheating on you?"

"Yes." A bald statement of fact. She broke their look. Then a breath. "But I thought it was serial one-night stands. What you said… The *other woman* sounds like something regular, settled."

"It was."

"Do you know her? Have you talked to her?"

"No."

"But you know about her? Who she is? Who…?" That question ran out of steam. She tried to mask it. "I suppose it's the cliché of a hooker with a heart of gold?"

"Neither, as far as I know. She's a dental hygienist. She lives well above her salary. She appears to have help from men along the way doing that."

"Dental hygienist—Then it's not Natalie?"

"Natalie?"

"David's widow. I thought, maybe…"

"It's not Natalie Northcutt. Did Chad have a lot to do with her?"

"No. In fact… I don't know why I thought—"

"In fact, what?"

"Nothing, really. It's family—"

"In fact, what?"

She compressed her lips. "He was angry at Natalie for leaving after David's death, moving her and the kids to Illinois. A little town called Drago."

Weighing the family dynamic, he probed. "Don't imagine Iris Northcutt liked it either."

"No."

"This isn't the time to protect the Northcutts, Ally."

"She's lost her son," she said quietly.

I'm not losing you.

Not that way, he told himself. That was over and done with long ago.

And even then, he hadn't lost her—because he'd never had her.

But he was not about to see something happen to her now. Call it professional pride. Or what was due his friendship with Maggie and now Jamie.

"We'll send flowers to the funeral. But in the meantime, somebody shot at you and came into your home going after *something*."

"But if Chad took money or lost something of this person in charge and they had any thought that I might know about it, why wait until now to come after me?"

"You put your finger on what we're trying to figure out. What you're going to do is answer every question we think might help. Whether that is Chad or Iris or Natalie Northcutt's innermost thoughts or deepest, darkest secrets, you're answering." He pulled in a breath through his teeth and eased back deliberately. "And if you don't do it fast, I'll get Maggie on you."

Her eyes widened, then narrowed sharply. Not anger. A kind of amusement she wasn't yet ready to recognize as amusement.

"You consider my cousin a greater threat than your law enforcement powers?"

"Hell, yes."

She smiled. A flash, then gone. But in its absence, less shock, more alertness.

"So, what happened with Natalie leaving?"

"Iris didn't want Natalie to take the kids—David's son and daughter—to Illinois. That's natural."

"Why did she go, then?"

She started to say something, then stopped herself. "I need to call Natalie to tell her."

She looked around. For a phone, maybe a clock.

"You don't need to call anybody now. Let Iris do it."

"She won't," she said simply.

"I'll check that the Piscattoway department takes care of it if they haven't already. But go back to Natalie. Why did you think she might be the woman Chad was seeing?"

"I'm not sure I seriously thought that. It popped into my head. Because Chad so wanted to emulate David in every way possible. Right down to... Anyway—"

"Right down to what?"

"Right down to wanting children. A boy first, then a girl. It was part of the strain. We'd been married eighteen months and I wasn't pregnant yet. We weren't keeping to David's schedule. Then it was twenty-four months, then thirty, then..." The spurt of words ceased. "Then it didn't matter." Full stop.

But that wasn't something he could allow her.

"Why didn't it matter?"

"I had a miscarriage."

Trying to absorb her emotions, he heard Iris hurling words at her in the waiting room of the Chate ...*And barren on top of it.*

So they hadn't told Chad's mother that Ally was pregnant or when she miscarried. At least Chad had protected her to that extent from his mother.

Not that it was any of his concern what went on between them. Except as it applied to this investigation.

And it did.

"I'm sorry." How many times had he said words like these to interview subjects? With the right amount of compassion, while keeping his feelings under professional lock and key? Enough to be really, really good at it. "Grief like that can be hard on a marriage. Taking the loss different ways."

She looked straight ahead to the closet doors. "Yes. That's when I decided to leave him."

"*Decided to leave?* You'd decided to leave Chad. When?"

"It doesn't matter. I never left."

"You were going to leave, but he got shot before you could?"

"It doesn't matter."

"How long before he was shot?"

"Tanner—"

"How long?"

Her shoulders rose and fell with a deep breath that she did not allow to have any sound.

"That day?" he demanded. "That damned day? But he was shot and you never left."

CHAPTER TWENTY-FIVE

AS IF SHE'D said nothing remarkable in the past few moments, she said, "If anyone knows what was going on with him at work in that period before the shooting, I would have said it would be Iris. Chad talked to her about the job. About everything. But not this. If it exposed that he'd been dirty…"

At some level he thought she was trying to give him a chance to regain his equilibrium, as weird as that seemed. "He didn't tell her when you were pregnant."

"He didn't tell her because he didn't know."

He forced his mind to focus. He was asking these questions for a reason. To know what was going on with Chad Northcutt around the time he was shot, to paint in the background to that event, to help understand it, and find who was behind it.

To know if it connected to the shots fired at Ally.

To keep her alive.

"The miscarriage didn't drive us farther apart because I never told Chad that I was pregnant. Or that I lost the baby."

"Why?" How bad had it *really* been?

"Afterward, I thought realizing I was pregnant was what made me decide to leave. I didn't want him to know I was carrying his baby. I didn't—I realized I *couldn't* have him raise the child. His own baby. That sounds awful, but I know what it's like to… I couldn't.

"After, I didn't trust him with the pain of losing the baby. That marriage was dead before the pregnancy, it was buried before the miscarriage. That's when I started to plan.

"I'd read up at the library about leaving someone in law enforcement. About being very careful. I'd set up another identity. Two, actually. One for the first step away, then shed that and travel to a new city and state, then pick up the second one, so the two were never in the same place at the same time. I'd been saving up cash for quite a while. I had that and papers and clothes and things stashed in four places. If I could get them all, great, but if anything caused a problem—an accident that pulled in a police presence or *anything*—I'd let that one go and be fine with the others.

"I told no one. And I had backup phones and travel reservations and…"

"You planned all this to get away from him."

"I see what you're thinking and you're wrong. I swear, he never hit me." She pulled in a sharp breath, then released it. Her voice came calm. "But he wouldn't have let me go."

"Maggie and Jamie—?"

"Never knew. And I hope they won't have to now. It would hurt them to know I didn't ask for their help, but I couldn't pull them into the middle. They needed to be able to tell Chad they honestly had no idea where I was."

He didn't give her the pledge her words implicitly requested.

He'd do what was best for the investigation. And he didn't know what that was yet.

He moved from in front of the chest to sit on the bench at the foot of the bed. It sat slightly lower than the top of the mattress, so they were closer to eye level.

"You said he was on edge before he was shot. Could he have known or sensed—?"

"No. I'm sure he didn't. But it's why I hesitated about describing his behavior. Was he more on edge? I think so. Or did I project my nerves about leaving?"

"Makes sense. You were on edge yourself?"

"Yes. I was conscious of not letting what I was doing to prepare to leave distract me from what I ordinarily did. I was also conscious of not pulling away from Chad, from his mother, from … all of it."

"Okay. What did Chad do that made you think he was more on edge?"

She paused again.

She didn't pull in her bottom lip or clamp her teeth on it. She seemed to draw in and go blank.

"He couldn't ... settle. Usually, if he was home, he'd sit in his chair and he wouldn't get up until he went to bed. But that week, he'd jump up and go to the basement or even out to the garage. He left for work, then came back in because he'd forgotten something. Twice. At least twice. It's the only time I ever remember him doing that."

"What did he forget?"

She shook her head, but stopped abruptly. "His jacket, I think, the first time. The second time was his wallet."

"When he went to the basement or garage, what did he do?"

"He pulled storage bins out in the basement. Christmas decorations, which made no sense. He didn't bother with those even at Christmastime. I don't know what he did in the garage."

"I don't think you're projecting your feelings onto him."

"You mean because my being on edge didn't involve any action, while his did?"

"You're sharp."

She met his gaze for a beat. "He *was* on edge. But, before you ask, I couldn't say why he was on edge."

"Okay. Let's narrow the timeframe. The week before the shooting. What day of the week was it he was shot?"

"Wednesday."

"Tell me about Tuesday."

A sharp opening of her hands indicated impatience, but she said, "Totally ordinary. I was conscious of keeping it as ordinary as possible. Not to draw attention from Chad or ... or anyone."

His mother.

"Was he unsettled that night?"

"No. Or, I should say, I don't know. He didn't come home until after I was in bed. He'd been drinking. He went right to sleep."

"When was he off-duty?"

"Seven p.m."

"When did he get home?"

"After one."

Plenty of time to drink heavily. Or something else?

"Monday," he said. "What did you do that day?"

"Final check that I had all the important documents to take with me. Not kept all in one place, just in case, but knowing exactly what order I'd pick them up. Going over and over and over it. So I wouldn't have to think about it."

"You acted out how you'd leave Wednesday morning?"

"Not completely. In case… Not with Iris living across the street. I went through it mentally. Also, I dusted, then vacuumed, moving around in the order I'd get the documents. And checked on my stashed cell phone when Iris went out to lunch."

"When did Chad come home?"

"As the news was ending. He'd been at his mother's for a while then. He'd spend an evening with her every month or so, just the two of them."

"His idea?"

"No."

He nodded. "Sunday?"

"We had brunch at Iris' along with other family members. We always did unless Chad was on duty, but he was off that day. He'd been off three days—the whole weekend."

"He was around all weekend?"

"No. He was gone most of it. He slept in Friday morning, then left. He didn't come back until late. The next day, he stayed around until mid-afternoon, spent time out in the garage. He has a workbench out there."

"He was working on a project?"

"Not that I was aware of. He didn't do projects."

"You said he was in the garage until mid-afternoon Saturday."

"Yes, then he left."

He kept his tone easy. "Was that usual?"

"Yes." She said it quick, taut. "When he was off-duty on weekends, he didn't spend much time here. Except Sunday brunch. What was unusual that day was after I came home from brunch, Mark came over."

"Wait. I have to back up. Chad was upset. He and Rachel had words at the brunch."

"About?"

"I didn't hear. Nobody did. They went outside and they kept their voices down."

"Any guesses?"

"Chad was jealous of her promotion. He'd nipped at her the whole week before and she put up with it. Maybe she decided she'd had enough. Anyway, Chad left. Rachel came back in, pretended nothing happened, except Mark tried to sympathize with her while really trying to find out what happened and she snapped at him."

"I went home after we cleaned up for Iris, and Chad was there, in the garage. Startled me, because he usually left right after Sunday brunches. He was still there when Mark came about an hour later. That was even more unusual."

"What were they doing?"

"Talking. I thought it must be about the fight with Rachel. Chad must have gone in the storage bins in the basement because when I went downstairs the next day, they were open and there was stuff on the floor. I picked it up and put the bins back where they belonged."

"What was in the bins?"

She raised her hands slightly. "Christmas decorations. As I said, it made no sense at all. Unless—He was looking for something? The same thing the person who broke in wanted? But why wait more than four years and—?"

He went past it. "Go back another day. Thursday."

For an instant her face shifted. It was like suddenly seeing Ally sitting across from him outside Mikey's. The Ally who was about to argue with him.

Then that Ally was gone again, behind the protective ice.

"He left at his regular time," she said evenly. "But that was the day he forgot his wallet. He came back and was in a foul mood. Which was a blessing because his coming back like that... I was getting ready to go out, but he didn't even notice. With him off over the weekend, I'd decided to make it my last day to make final preparations away from the house and I wanted to get started to make sure everything was done. ... I felt like it stood out all over me. Exactly what I was planning. But he came in, cursing about his wallet and left right away."

"And when he got home that night?"

"It was late. I was in bed."

"Did he call when he was going to be late?"

"No. He said I'd see him when I saw him. I tried to have something he could heat up and eat for dinner if he wanted, but it was long past trying to plan meals."

"Wednesday, a week before he was shot."

A tiny tuck showed between her brows. She guarded her expressions so carefully that it felt like a victory to see that small reaction through the ice.

"More of the same. Nothing out of the ordinary."

Which meant Chad staying away, Iris watching her, and Ally working to escape.

"Why didn't you leave the day before he was shot—the Tuesday? You said you had everything ready."

"When he worked four on, the way he was scheduled starting that Monday, his mother used to insist on taking me out to lunch on Day Two—that was Tuesday. She said it was a ritual she had with Natalie—David's wife—and she started it with me after we were married. She'd done it less and less in the two years before he was shot, but once in a while... And when she did, she always sprang it on me."

"Like a pop quiz?"

She didn't smile, but her face eased.

"Probably. I couldn't take the risk that she'd choose that Tuesday. If I'd already left, she might sound the alarm right away. If I hadn't, it would still cut my lead time way down."

Another smart move on her part.

Not all women made it out when they planned to leave. But she'd thought it through, considered angles and contingencies. He bet she would have made it ... if Chad hadn't been shot in the head before she could.

She'd also have left everything she knew behind. From his point of view her parents weren't much of a loss, but for her to never see Jamie or Maggie again, that was a hell of a price to pay to escape her marriage.

"Why didn't you go anyway?"

She sucked in a small breath, like a desperate sip of oxygen.

He'd hit a nerve. But the hell if he knew what nerve.

"I'm not criticizing you, Ally. Or second-guessing. But you had everything set. He didn't deserve your loyalty."

This time her eyebrows popped up and she spoke with a tinge of dry amusement. "Maybe not. Though there was that in sickness and in health issue. Besides… Think about if I did stick with my schedule. Disappeared right after my husband was shot. You don't think the department might have found that suspicious?"

"Fair point. Doesn't mean you had to stay for years. At his side the whole time. Nobody who knew the truth would have judged you."

"But nobody knew the truth." She expelled a breath. "I wouldn't care if they did judge me, but how could I explain leaving? A lie? The truth? What would the point of that have been? Ruining the family name when Chad couldn't respond, couldn't take responsibility, couldn't…change."

"Was it really for his sake? Or Iris'?"

Another lightning glance toward him. He'd definitely missed something in this, but the hell if he knew what it was. Would Bel have caught it? Was his involvement—*previous* involvement with Ally clouding his perceptions?

And how the hell had he let this get so off track?

"Okay. This has been a long session. There will be more. Maybe a lot more. Until we figure this out. But you've got that meeting at one. You should have some lunch first. But is there anything else you can think of?"

With more wryness, she said, "I've thought of more than I ever expected to. You're good at this."

He rested his hands on his thighs. "A lot of practice." In his good cop voice—friendly, unthreatening, but still a cop—he added, "Going back over that time like this might stir loose some other thoughts. Grab onto them. Doesn't matter how small. Anything that surfaces in your memory, tell me or Bel. Got it?"

"Got it."

He stood and turned toward the door, then paused.

Surprising him—maybe herself, too—she asked, "Something more, Detective Landis? A question you forgot to ask?"

"One. Why?"

She twisted around to face him. "Why what?"

"Why did you marry him?"

Her expression gave nothing away. But he didn't have the sense of her face being unreal anymore. It was hers, Ally Lindell's, but closed up tight.

"Did you think I wouldn't?"

He felt like he'd been pulled up by a short rein. "I suppose I did."

"He treated me well—"

"You're going to tell me he treated you well *then*, at the start? More like he didn't treat you as badly. He dismissed your abilities, your brain. He blocked you off from his colleagues, your family." He held her gaze. "Your art."

"He couldn't have if I hadn't let him."

"Why did you let him, Ally?"

Her gaze slipped away from him, perhaps looking inside herself.

"I thought he had what I wanted. Family. I was wrong." She made a sound. Not much of a chuckle, but that's what he thought it was supposed to be. "How stupid is that? From my parents to Chad, I went from the frying pan to the fire."

"More like you were the frog in the water with it already partway to boiling, so when you got in with Chad you didn't notice the heat at first."

She blinked at him, but said nothing else, so he left.

CHAPTER TWENTY-SIX

"SHE'S STILL HIDING something," Landis said after filling in Belichek on the part of what Ally said that was his business.

They were out back, in that one spot not visible from inside the house or across the street.

Instead of responding to his statement, Bel said, "Feel vindicated that her marriage was shitty?"

"Go to hell, Belichek."

"You should, you know. The woman dared to pass you up for some other guy, it was justice he turned out to be an asshole. That's what the kind of guy you pretend to be would feel."

"Just because I don't go in for total assholeness myself doesn't mean—"

"Yes, it does. But I won't torture you by making you admit it. So, one interesting thing at least."

"Yeah. Chad Northcutt was searching for something—basement, garage."

"Could have been searching elsewhere, too. All those late nights."

"Or drowning his sorrows. Also could have been routine to stay out like that. Got the feeling it was."

"You could've asked."

Tanner didn't react to that. "Second thing. The fact that he couldn't find it had him on edge. Third thing. Northcutt was searching for something. Whoever came in here was looking for something.

"You're thinking what I'm thinking, Belichek. Why don't we say it? What he's looking for has something to do with the corruption.

Money, records, something. Having it gives him power. Losing it—and he had to lose it or he wouldn't have been looking for it—could be what got him killed."

"Logical. Still speculative."

"What isn't about this case?"

"No call for bitterness," Bel said.

"Like hell there isn't." But he did chuckle.

"Problem is, agreeing he was looking for something to do with the corruption scheme, which makes it the prime motive for why he got killed doesn't get us very far."

"Yeah. All we don't know is what it was, what it means, and where it is. Other than that, this makes everything clear."

"What could someone be looking for that could be in a jewelry box, a drawer, under a bed, on a workbench, or in a crate of Christmas decorations?"

"Can't be any larger than what would fit in the smallest, which makes it the jewelry box. That limits the size. So possibly a wad of cash, but not a big wad. Though why he'd put it in her jewelry box…"

"All sorts of reasons. What matters is what we're going to do next."

"Even though we don't know what we're looking for," Landis grumbled.

"Basement or garage first?"

"Before we start pawing through shit that's been sitting here five years—"

"Four years and six months."

"—something else Ally said. Asked. If we'd talked to the girlfriend. What was her name from that report?"

"Willow Spencer."

"Right. Might be worth a chat."

"Agreed. The Piscattoway record was thin there, too. We should try to track her down and talk to her. Between security duty and pawing through stuff."

✧ ✧ ✧ ✧

TANNER LANDIS COULDN'T have been any clearer. He was here to do his job. His questions weren't personal. And even if the answers were personal to her, they still weren't to him.

He couldn't possibly be that cool if…

A shudder caught her by surprise.

It shouldn't have. She had experience with this. A lot of experience.

More like you were the frog in the water with it already partway to boiling, so when you got in with Chad you didn't notice the heat at first.

Of all the things that had happened today, the past two days, this was what kept whirling through her brain.

More like you were the frog in the water with it already partway to boiling, so when you got in with Chad you didn't notice the heat at first.

Had she been conditioned?

Her parents. Chad. Iris.

Why should Tanner Landis be any different?

He had more cause. She had hurt him—at least she'd thought she had.

She was *glad* he was distant.

Glad and relieved and grateful he'd been clear that he was here for the job and nothing else. And had lived up to it.

Her words about deciding to leave slid out of her so easily after holding them so tight, so silent, so deep for years.

Only after she spoke them did she brace herself against his saying she could have—*should* have—left anyway, left earlier, never been with Chad.

Was that part of why she'd never told her cousins? Not all to protect them, but some to protect herself, too? Because she didn't want to hear that. Maybe couldn't hear it.

Enough.

She needed to think this through.

He was dirty, Ally.

At one point, Tanner's eyes flickered, almost like it was a trick of the light, except it wasn't. He'd been doubting that she'd fully accepted that Chad had been involved in corruption.

But she did believe it and accept it.

At some level she must have known all along or wouldn't she have been more shocked? More resistant to what he said?

Yes.

But the knowledge had been stored at a level she hadn't accessed for a long, long time.

The only way to get through the days and months and years of her marriage, before and after Chad was shot, had been to live on the surface, leaving the real her—the core of her—out of reach.

More like you were the frog in the water with it already partway to boiling, so when you got in with Chad you didn't notice the heat at first.

Would that mean she hadn't been utterly stupid to fall for Chad? Was it as reasonable as Tanner made it sound?

Or was he letting her too easily off the hook?

…you didn't notice the heat at first.

At first, but not forever.

✧　✧　✧　✧

THE SINGLE CAR garage had yard tools hooked on one side wall. The workbench was in an alcove at the back.

Tanner looked from the well-used ones on the wall to the new but dusty tools on the workbench.

"Complete set," he muttered.

Bel drew the inference. "Bought to have a set of tools. Not to do specific jobs."

Jamie appeared at the door from the house into the garage.

"Is this secret police business?"

"Yes," Bel said. "Any idea if Ally's moved things out here?"

"I doubt it. Maybe used the hammer and screwdrivers, putting them back where she found them. Other than that and using the handheld vacuum on the dust, no."

"Thanks, Jamie." Bel softened the dismissal with a smile. She leaned forward and kissed his cheek before closing the door behind her.

"Might get something. Worth a try," Landis said to Bel.

"Who?" It was less of a question than his statement about who would do the trying.

Call the Piscattoway contact and ask for evidence techs? And tell him what? They were looking for a long-shot thread from more than four years ago on the wild hare that it might connect to now and the very careful intruder. Even if they got the techs—no sure bet, especially since there'd be no prints from the break-in to try to match them to—would the results be shared with them in a timely fashion?

Fairlington techs? Not likely Palery would approve that nor the Piscattoway department like it.

"You had training in evidence gathering," he said to Bel.

"You, too. Neither of us recently."

"Schmidt would've had the training more recently."

Bel considered. "Might work."

CHAPTER TWENTY-SEVEN

WHEN ALLY DIDN'T appear, Maggie went to her, insisting she eat some lunch.

Even as Landis followed the discussion in the kitchen and dining area about the investigation into the shooting at the courthouse, he picked up Maggie's clear voice approaching. "And don't worry, Aunt Dana took your mother and Uncle Wes took your father out for lunch, which we all greatly appreciate."

He had his focus on his sandwich when Maggie and Ally appeared.

"…with your department running the official inquiry, how much leeway do you have on this end?" J.D. asked him.

"Don't know how long and how far Palery will let us run with investigating, especially if Piscattoway County PD raises a stink about us encroaching. We can argue the shooting at the courthouse gives us standing, but if we link it to Chad—or they link it to Chad beyond the obvious fact that his wife was a target—they'll have a point. It's likely they will make the link at some point and that means they'll make a stink at some point. First, as a result of knee-jerk territorialism and then a lot stronger if they get even a whiff that we're looking at a corruption angle."

"Let me see what I can find out," J.D. said. "I have connections from my Army days. Both Maryland state police and some federal. I can ask without rippling the pond."

Landis nodded once. "Good."

"Bel? You've been quiet," Jamie said. "What are you thinking?"

He looked at her for a long moment. Not irked with her for bringing it up—as far as Landis could tell, his partner rarely got irked at the woman for any reason at all—but, still, considering whether to deflect the question or answer it.

"There's one area of potential shooters we haven't hit yet," Bel said.

They all looked at him.

"What area?" Maggie asked. The answer didn't come fast enough for her. "Who?"

"Tanner's women."

He knew he didn't change color—he never did—but he couldn't do anything about the muscles of his face going rigid.

"There's no—" The muscles of his throat had tightened, too. "—possible connection between—"

"Let Bel talk," Jamie said.

"There've been women who wanted more from him. Who haven't let go. Who wouldn't appreciate seeing another woman who held his interest—"

Ally went blank again.

He cut across. "No way in hell."

"How would they know?" Jamie asked, alert, interested, impressed by Bel's whacko theory.

"The judge…"

At Maggie's almost dreamy words, he jerked his head around to her, then his partner.

"Belichek," he started in accusation.

Maggie's next words came with her usual briskness. "He never said a word. I have eyes, don't I? Thought the two of you were going to do it right there in the back stairway when I saw you a few months ago. Besides, Nancy said something."

God, if Nancy Quinn knew…

Maggie's assistant wouldn't blab, despite having an unrivaled regional network. But she also wouldn't cut him a centimeter of slack.

Talking over Jamie's small chuckle, Maggie continued, "But I also saw Angela DaSilva watching you when we arrived at the courthouse for the hearing. You were intent on putting people between you and our party coming off the elevator—didn't want to be spotted by Ally, presumably—"

"That's—"

"—so intent you might not have been as guarded as usual. Didn't click with me at the moment, but the judge's expression did."

"What was her expression?" Jamie asked.

"You know the saying about more in sorrow than in anger? But that could be a professional mask, hiding yet another woman ticked at Landis for throwing her over, and transferring that to Ally. If she had found out about your history—"

"That's bullsh—"

"Shut up," J.D. ordered. "We're considering this like everything else. For Ally's safety."

Tanner shut his mouth.

"But a *judge?*"

He didn't know if Jamie's disbelief was at him for being involved with one or that they were considering her as a potential suspect.

"Not the first woman to go off the deep end after the Landis treatment," Maggie said. "What about that one while we were digging into who tried to kill Jamie, Bel?"

"Uh-huh. She thought she had a future with Landis. Separated from her husband. Was not happy when Landis said there wasn't a future. And didn't give up."

"Haven't heard a word from her in months," he got out around his stiff jaw.

"After months of hearing far more than a word from her."

Jamie posed another question. "But how would that woman know his connection with Ally, much less that she's a rival—?"

"That's bullsh—"

Maggie interrupted. He was never going to get that complete phrase out.

"Same way as Judge DaSilva, only none of us happened to see her watching him lurking around watching Ally."

Lurking? "On the job and—"

"It fits with the personal nature of the search here at the house,"

J.D. said. "We've known from the start it wasn't people looking for quick money. They're digging deep and personal."

For the first time, a fizzle of unease at his nerve-endings passed through Tanner.

For a slice of a second his gaze met Ally's.

If he'd been the cause behind this—

"Bel, you're being quiet," Maggie noted.

"Already knew what I thought. Wanted to hear where you all took the idea."

"And?"

"Good amount of overlap, you all and me. As J.D. said, we need to look into them like anybody else. So, next step is looking into them."

"I can talk to the judge," Maggie said. "Discreetly, which means in person. Bel, you want to take the other woman? What's her name?"

"Rhonda Quesey. Yeah, I'll talk to her."

"What about Tanner?" Jamie asked.

Maggie said grimly, "We're keeping him as far away from those women as possible. But he is useful for security watch on Ally—our security watch, inside the local's."

He should have said *gee, thanks.* It's what his normal response would be. But he was occupied in not outwardly reacting to the prospect of running close security on Ally.

"I'll help," Jamie said. "I can't investigate those women or stuff dealing with Chad, but I can stick with Ally all the time. She'll come stay at my place."

Ally stood abruptly. "It's time for me to go to Iris'. I won't be long." Because she intended to let Iris do whatever she wanted. "No. None of you are coming. I know what I want and it's not any of you bristling about my position or—" Her eyes shifted toward her parents as they entered, Greta right behind Kurt, neither acknowledging the other. "—otherwise getting involved."

J.D. slowly rose from his chair. "Schmidt and I will walk her over and stick around until she's ready to come back." He addressed Ally. "Figure you'll trust the two of us to stay out of it?"

She smiled slightly at him. "Yes. Thank you, J.D. Although there's no need for you or Officer Schmidt to—"

"There is need. It'll set everybody else's minds at ease and that'll let Tanner and Bel get on with their investigatin'."

His deliberate strengthening of his drawl deepened her smile.

❖ ❖ ❖ ❖

THEY DID GET on with their *investigatin'*, but Landis' mind didn't feel particularly at ease.

After consulting Schmidt's notes about what he'd processed in the garage, they finished the one corner they hadn't previously gotten to. Then they'd split up—Bel to the basement, him to the attic.

Now, he backed down the pull-down steps to the attic to find Jamie at the bottom, frowning slightly.

"I don't think Ally stores anything in the attic. She never liked attics, even at Aunt Vivian's, where she had all sorts of dress-up clothes and things there. Ally would get us to take the clothes down to the second floor to try them on."

"Now you tell me."

Her frown disappeared at his fake grumble. He wasn't after Ally's storage spots. And her aversion to attics would have made it the perfect spot for Chad to hide something from her. Except there wasn't anything there.

It was the sparsest attic he'd ever seen. Rafters, joists, insulation. Not a single box in sight. He'd even gone from cavity to cavity, lifting up the sheets of insulation and poking them to see if anything was under or inside them.

Nothing.

"You're not really upset I didn't tell you because you would have searched anyhow." She tipped her head. "Are you not happy about Ally planning to let Iris have her way with the funeral and everything?"

"Police funerals are run a certain way. The widow takes precedence."

"This is the way Ally wants it." She studied him a moment longer. "No, I'm wrong. It *doesn't* bother you, not really."

"None of my business. Though I wouldn't mind seeing Iris' nose out of joint."

"So you say, but you don't mean that, either, because it would make things harder on Ally."

No reason to respond to that.

Her head tilt deepened. "And something else… Oh… *Yes*…"

He had no idea what she was getting at, but didn't like her expression. Like he was so transparent she had a closeup view of his backbone.

He pushed the steps up. When he turned back around, she still blocked the hallway.

"Of course. Ally not being treated as a *widow* makes it easier to ignore that she'd been Chad's *wife*."

"Bullshit."

He should have thought before that retort, because her face lit up.

Then it fell.

"What's wrong with you, Jamie?" Maggie asked approaching from behind him.

"Tanner's reputation for womanizing."

"How's that a problem for you? Do *not* tell me you're switching partners—in both senses of the phrase. I would have you committed and—"

"Thanks a lot, Mags."

Jamie ignored that and stuck with her topic. "Of course not. But if he really earned that reputation, it—"

"He did."

"—could be hard for Ally."

"Ally? *Ally?*" Before Maggie's voice finished skidding up, she jerked around to stare at him.

He raised his hands, sidestepping to gain enough space to ease past Jamie. "She's imagining things. I'm just doing my job."

Maggie scoffed with a short sound. "She better be imagining things. And you better do your job."

"I'm not imagining things," Jamie said calmly from behind him. "What I don't understand yet is how Ally's acting."

CHAPTER TWENTY-EIGHT

"Mom, Dad," Ally said to them when she returned from Iris', "we have to go to Fairlington tonight to appear at the police department first thing in the morning. You're welcome to stay here or find a hotel—"

"I'll come with you."

"I'll—"

"It's official police meetings, Mom. You can't. Either of you."

She'd recognized the benefits of going to Fairlington first while Iris went on about the funeral events. Then she'd thought of being away from her parents. And out of this house.

"I'm afraid there's not room, Aunt Greta," Jamie contributed. "My house is quite small."

She didn't mention that Maggie also had a townhouse or that Wes and Dana planned to spend the night at their home an hour or so south. On the other hand, she doubted anybody could imagine a scenario where either or both of Ally's parents stayed with Maggie.

✧ ✧ ✧ ✧

"Darn." Jamie tugged at the curtains at the front window of her living room in the narrow historic house she'd inherited from a maternal relative in Old Town Fairlington, Virginia.

They'd entered Jamie's from the back. As they started to file into the living room at the front of the house, J.D. said, "Curtains," and subtly blocked Ally, keeping her in the hallway.

Jamie had hurried forward to close them and block the view inside for anyone on the street outside.

The bottom of the curtain moved, but not the rings across the rod. "The rings are stuck where the rod fits into another piece. Bel, can you…?"

"Landis will. He's taller. Claims all sorts of perks because of that, about time we get something useful from it."

Landis grimaced at his partner, but immediately went to Jamie.

"I think it's caught on both sides, Tanner."

"I'll get it. Leave the genius to think deep thoughts."

From the hallway, Ally saw that Belichek had not moved from where he'd stopped in front of the fireplace, seeming to examine the painting she'd done of Aunt Vivian's park.

"What are you doing?" Jamie asked him.

"Looking."

"You've seen that painting a thousand times."

"See more every time."

Jamie turned her beaming smile toward Ally. "That's quite a compliment to the artist."

"It is," she agreed to placate her cousin.

Because he wasn't just looking. He was questioning the painting—interrogating it.

It unsettled her.

Nothing like the butterflies in the stomach edginess of awaiting a teacher's comments or a judge's verdict. Instead, a visceral urge to get between the detective and the painting.

Because, as much as she had no idea what his questions were, she also didn't know what answers it would give.

"Though I'm worried about the verdict."

She immediately wished she'd said something else—anything else—to break the silence, because Ford Belichek looked over his shoulder at her with a look that switched the interrogation from the painting to her.

"No need to worry about me. Landis is the aesthetic police," Bel said.

Ally's gaze, a little surprised, a little thoughtful, went to Landis' back, where he'd freed the rings on one side, and was pulling those curtains closed.

"That's only from the point of view of a heathen." His tone made her think they'd had this conversation before.

Belichek continued as if he hadn't spoken "He's taken a bunch of courses in art and historic architecture and such."

Landis, moving to the other side of the curtains, cut him off with a short chuckle. "First time you haven't griped about those classes. Usually telling me to shut up about what I've learned. Even though it's helped with cases, including the architectural history of our jurisdiction."

"True. I just don't want to hear all about them." Bel turned his head and met Ally's gaze. "They're not for me."

"Because you've got me carrying your ignorant carcass." Landis reached up to free the other set of jammed-together rings.

"Tanner are you—?" Jamie started.

But Belichek turned quickly to her, appearing to recognize in that moment that she'd been tracking the interplay all along.

"No need to defend me, Jamie," he said to her.

Ally watched them communicating with locked eyes broken only when Jamie's gaze shifted to Tanner's back then toward her.

Ally looked down before her cousin's gaze reached her.

"No *use* defending him, either, Jamie." Tanner lifted the rings over the lip of the curtain rod joint. "It's the truth. At least he knows he's an ignorant heathen."

"I love him the way he is."

Belichek reached out an arm. Jamie went to him and snugged up to his side. He put the arm around her shoulders and squeezed. "Atta girl."

"All set," Tanner pulled closed the other side of the curtains and turned back to them.

✧ ✧ ✧ ✧

"I GOT THE reports on David Northcutt's death," Schmidt said.

They were outside, waiting for the others.

Landis turned around. "David's?"

Schmidt looked a little uncertain. "I thought to be thorough, I should…"

"Good thinking," Bel said. "Have you read it?"

"Yeah. I can send you copies."

"Do that. But first tell us."

Schmidt visibly swallowed. "It was February eleventh. At 9:53 p.m. Officer Northcutt—David—had pulled over a suspected DWI in the northbound lanes of Piscattoway Parkway, where it's two lanes each way. He approached the vehicle, a dark blue BMW 4 series with Maryland plates. Do you want the registration plate number?"

"Not unless that's pertinent."

"No, sir. Officer Northcutt was at the window and asked the driver for his license and registration. A vehicle—a silver Subaru WRX—was in the left lane behind another vehicle, according to witnesses who'd been behind them and stopped after Officer Northcutt was struck. The Subaru started to change to the right lane in an apparent attempt to pass on the right. The lane change happened just short of where David Northcutt's patrol vehicle and the BMW were pulled off.

"The closest point of the patrol vehicle to the outside of the right lane was three feet and ten inches, well off the driving surface. The BMW was farther off.

"The Subaru crossed the outside line of the right lane, onto the shoulder, striking Officer Northcutt. The impact threw him twenty-eight feet ahead on the shoulder.

"The driver of the BMW said he had started to get out of the vehicle. Northcutt turned his head in the direction of the oncoming Subaru and shoved the BMW driver back inside. It saved the guy's life. But Northcutt couldn't get out of the way.

"The driver of the BMW, who was a doctor, tried to render aid until emergency services arrived. Officer Northcutt was declared dead on arrival at the hospital."

He cleared his throat, but didn't look up.

"The silver Subaru was rendered inoperable by the crash. Citizens stopped and found the driver passed out. He had regained consciousness by the time Emergency Services were on scene. He had no serious injuries."

He stopped and looked up.

"Who made notification?"

"Preston Northcutt."

"To Natalie Northcutt?"

"To Iris Northcutt."

He saw that Bel shared his reaction—Preston's response revealed him as firmly in the Northcutt pack.

CHAPTER TWENTY-NINE

Jamie flapped the fitted sheet to spread it over the pullout in her office, where Ally would sleep tonight. "In some ways, Ally, you're as bad as Maggie."

"Thanks a lot." Maggie snagged an opposite corner and tugged it into place.

"Shouldn't I be saying that?" Ally deadpanned.

Ignoring her cousins grinning at each other, Jamie said, "I mean it. Nobody could miss it that Maggie withdrew from the family, more and more as time went on. She stopped answering the phone, didn't return calls, had a hundred excuses for not seeing any of us. You were slipperier. You were there physically—at least sometimes, sure more than Maggie—but—"

"Hey."

"It's true. All the foundation events you missed, Maggie, and—"

"The foundation's your baby. I never wanted to be involved or—"

"Neither did Ally," Jamie said.

They both turned to Ally, waiting for her response. "Not particularly, but I wanted to support Jamie."

Her younger cousin repeated her flapping motion with the top sheet. "So, she came to Foundation events, but was like a wraith. Drifting through an evening, listening and nodding, but impossible to pin down or get your arms around or … or *read*. Closed off from all of us—from me."

At the sight of tears standing in Jamie's eyes, Ally felt an unfamiliar tightness in her chest. "I'm sorry, Jamie. I thought that even with not having much energy to be social, it was better to come than—"

"I know you've been tired—exhausted—but it's more than that. You shut us out because you didn't want us to know you were miserable." Jamie turned her head to Maggie, adding, "With Chad, but also with the rest of the Northcutts."

Maggie stiffened. "Did he abuse you? Get physical? A lot of law enforcement—"

"Nothing like that. No." To tell them everything now. To say all the things Tanner had drawn out of her… But what good would it do? They'd only feel bad that she'd intended to leave on her own, without their help and without a future that would include them. "It was my own expectations. I wanted what I hadn't had from my parents. A family. A close family." Her mouth twisted. "A sitcom family—not like the modern ones where everyone tries to out-dysfunction the other—"

"Yeah, you've had more than your share of that," Jamie murmured.

"—but an old-fashioned sitcom family where the lawn not being mowed on time is the big crisis. It was my fault for expecting—"

"Bullshit," Maggie inserted.

"Now you sound like—" She should have gone ahead and said she sounded like Tanner Landis. From their expressions, both cousins not only supplied the unspoken name, but read a whole lot more into the fact that she hadn't said it than warranted. Still, she went back to completing her thought, leaving the name unspoken as she smoothed a blanket over the narrow bed. "It was my unreasonable expectations."

"Those expectations are *not* unreasonable," Jamie said fiercely. "Having a family—a loving family—is the least you deserve, anybody deserves, but especially you. The problem was, you weren't ever going to fix your parents or their divorce by fixing your marriage to Chad, Ally."

"Like I could." She folded back the comforter Jamie supplied so she could pull it up if she wanted more warmth during the night.

"But you wanted to."

"Yeah, great. I tried to overcome my dysfunctional parents by letting myself be overrun by the Northcutts, who can make dysfunction look like a giant step up. No, no I didn't let myself be overrun, I ran into their arms. So desperately wanting to see what I hoped for that I refused to look at the truth. And then to keep the delusion going, I *willingly* gave up painting and independence and my brain and pretty much everything else that made me me. And giving up—"

She had to suck in air, because a memory of looking back at Tanner, sitting at that picnic table at Mikey's slammed into her diaphragm, knocking the wind out of her.

And giving up Tanner Landis.

Who had talked with her and seen her in a way not even her cousins had. Because they were busy with their own thoughts, feelings, and pursuits.

"Geez, Ally," Maggie said, "I'm usually the critical one, but you're tough enough on yourself that even I'm saying cut yourself some slack."

"Absolutely." After her emphatic agreement, Jamie added, "Besides, that was the past. Do you realize what you said the night Chad died?"

Ally looked at her in confusion, Maggie with expectation.

"You said, *I didn't want to lose that family. Didn't*, not *don't*. You had already shaken loose of their hold on you."

Her gaze flicked toward the stairwell, which strengthened an echo of Tanner's voice, carrying it up toward them.

She instantly regretted the glance. Too late. They'd seen it.

"Ally—"

"Don't, Maggie." She held her hand out as a stop sign. "Please. Don't. At least for now."

LIKE CLOSING CURTAINS made any difference.

Especially not when those women went up to the third floor and cast their shadows all over. He tracked them by backing up to a spot down the alley for the right angle.

Triumph welled in him. They thought they'd shaken him off. But they hadn't.

They were here. *He* was here.

Hell, this was a lot better. He knew this area, unlike being stuck over in Maryland. Not that he'd let that stop him. He wouldn't let anything stop him.

Because he wasn't pathetic and weak.

He knew what he had to do. He'd created a plan. And now he was following it.

Best of all, that asshole Landis would pay for what he'd done.

But he'd be patient. He'd keep following them. For days if necessary.

Until the time was right.

❖ ❖ ❖ ❖

ALLY HAD SENT them downstairs with the excuse that she wanted to settle in a bit.

She'd lingered too long.

She heard footsteps, knew whose they were.

She stood from the edge of the bed before Tanner Landis' head and shoulders appeared in the stairwell. "I've been sent to deliver a pillow. Got one too many downstairs and Jamie said you'd be without."

Which meant they'd been setting up for him to sleep on the first floor, on guard duty again.

"Meant to tell you earlier, PCPD confirmed they've notified Natalie Northcutt about Chad's death."

"Thank you."

"No problem."

He flipped the pillow toward the bed at the same time she reached to take it. Her hand deflected his aim, sending the pillow to the far side of the bed, then tipping over onto the floor.

"Sorry." He was up the stairs and edging around the foot of the bed before she reacted.

"There's no need. I can—"

"All set." He placed the pillow at the top of the bed, remaining on the far side.

He cleared his throat. His voice came out perfectly normal, with much of his old, dry humor.

"If Belichek had known this thing pulled out to a bed when we first started working Jamie's case, I never would have gotten him out of here. He practically lived here as it was."

She smiled, but her words were too formal, too wooden. "We all appreciated his dedication—and yours—so much."

"Doubt Dana Chancellor would agree. She was ready to tear me limb from limb for looking at Jamie as a suspect."

He was trying to put them back on a more casual footing, like they used to—

"She knew you weren't stupid enough to really believe that."

"Ouch."

From a wince, he smiled at her.

An abrupt intake of air made her realize she'd been holding her breath. She needed to get him out of here. But to have him edge past her again...

"Downstairs," she said. "We—I'm going to join the others downstairs."

She grabbed her phone and slid it in her pocket, then took two of the three steps that would bring her to the stairwell.

"Oh. The light—"

She stepped backward, intending to turn off the bedside lamp ... right into Tanner.

He'd come around the end of the bed and was immediately behind her.

She knew him. That individual scent she'd recognized the instant he tackled her outside the courthouse. No artificial aromas of products, but specific to him.

His body absorbed the impact, but not the repercussions. Those she felt echoing through her in pulses of heat.

His arm clamped around her above her waist, steadying her—did she need steadying from the physics of her motion being stopped so abruptly, or from those echoing repercussions?

His breath stirred her hair, brushed her cheek. And without seeing him she knew he was surveying for danger as the cause of her action. Finding none, his muscles' heightened alert eased.

No, that wasn't true. They didn't ease. They shifted, the tension and preparation for action moving from one set of muscles to another.

She felt the expansion and contraction of his chest against her back, the rhythmic expulsion still across her temple and cheek.

Under his arm, her ribs surged with her lungs' quick, sharp efforts to drag in air.

Other than breathing neither of them moved.

With the exception of the band across her ribs, he touched only her back from shoulder to hips. More of her was untouched by him than was touched. Yet he surrounded her, enveloped her. With his strength and heat and physicality.

And then she distinguished amid all the heat a more intense and specific heat pressing against her.

"Ally." A sound so soft, it seemed to be part of his breathing.

But if she doubted she heard it, she couldn't doubt the hardening evidence of his erection against her.

She didn't move, but her single word came strong and sure.

"No."

Before that brief syllable ended, he dropped his arm and stepped back. Her muscles clenched and strained to prevent a sway at the abrupt loss of support. Or a move to regain the contact.

She didn't look back as she went down the stairs.

—DAY 4—

FRIDAY

CHAPTER THIRTY

LANDIS HAD GIVEN up pretending to sleep a while ago, though the sky had only reached the point of thinking about showing off some sunrise colors.

He wasn't officially keeping watch. They had unmarked cars in front and behind the house, increased patrol in the area.

He probably could use the sleep, but it didn't come.

He sat at the desk in the small library between the living room and a glassed-in patio room with a pad of paper and a pen.

He hadn't written a thing on the pad when he heard Belichek on the bottom third of the stairs.

"We're getting carried along by the flood," he said without looking up, though he still saw that Bel wore a pair of pajama bottoms, which he must have already had here, because they'd both been living out of their emergency kits from their trunks, which did not include PJs. "Following events, reacting instead of getting out in front of this."

"It's different from what we usually do. We're not often worried about keeping somebody alive—" Though that's what they had done with Jamie. "—but figuring out why someone's dead. We're splitting our focus between security for Ally and looking back to Chad. Natural we're not as on top of this as usual."

"Natural or not, it's not good. We need to get a handle on how this started."

"Right. Because something started the dominoes toppling," Bel said.

Landis looked at him for a long moment. "Think you'll make a detective someday, Belichek. Chad's shooting—No. Before that. He'd been doing what he'd been doing for a while. Why shoot him then? Something triggered it. Someone."

Bel turned to him and stated, "You've got an idea what."

Landis didn't return the look. "This is between us. Nobody else. Not Palery. Not Maggie." Now he did return the other man's gaze. "Not Jamie."

One beat. Two beats. "Okay."

"She was leaving him. Ally. That day. Had it all—" He stumbled over that as a possible implication hit him. Where the hell was his head that he hadn't seen that right away? "—planned."

"Planned."

"Yeah. Okay. She'd been doing things. Preparing. Someone could have caught wind of it."

Another interpretation, by someone who didn't know Ally, could be that she made up the story about planning to leave Chad that day. That, instead, she opted for what she'd expected to be a more permanent solution.

He pushed that aside and kept talking, "But *why* did that push them to act? And what pushed them? Why would Ally leaving Northcutt make them shoot him? It's not likely he'd suddenly tell her what he'd been doing because he figured out she planned to leave. It would be stupid telling a woman getting ready to walk out the door and he wasn't brilliant, but he wasn't stupid, either. Besides, why? Try to win her back with the news that he was in some deep shit? It makes no sense. Gets us nowhere. No. Don't say it. I'm warning you, Belichek. You know how many times I've heard that pebble starts the mountain crap?"

"It's not crap. It's how it works. You keep picking up pebbles until you have a mountain."

He groaned.

Belichek had his pebbles, Landis had his own way of thinking of investigations.

He groaned. Only partially at Belichek.

Pebbles or tree rings, this was even more complicated because the person who'd died was Chad Northcutt, the man Ally Lindell married.

"You've got a connection to her—" At that start from Belichek, Landis sent him a warning glare. But his partner kept the rest uninflected. "—so talk to her more. Go get us some pebbles."

✦ ✦ ✦ ✦

THE CHANCELLORS WERE interviewed first. Dana, Wes, and Jamie in separate interview rooms at the Fairlington County Police Department.

That left the rest of them to wait their turns in a less than inspiring break room.

J.D. soon left the group, having gone off somewhere with a murmur about a phone call. Ally would have passed it off as involving his job as a partner in a law firm in the mountain town of Bedhurst, Virginia, except for a quick look between him and Maggie.

Maggie's assistant, the formidable Nancy Quinn, had taken advantage of Maggie being nearby and otherwise unoccupied to walk over from the Commonwealth Attorney's office, bringing matters to inform, discuss, and dispose of with Maggie.

Ally sat at a table in the far corner, writing responses to a few of the messages of condolence she'd received.

"I've got a call in to the doctor about that matter you asked me to check," Nancy said to Maggie.

"Good. I might want to talk to him, too."

Ally wondered for a moment why she'd tuned in to that exchange among all the others, then realized it was the word *doctor*. A word she had alerted to ever since Chad was shot.

She consciously refocused her attention on her responses.

These messages were personal, from college friends, former neighbors, a few former art teachers, and fellow students.

Responding to the mass of other messages would come later. After the ceremonies, after … after things were settled.

She pushed aside that thought and applied herself to her task, appreciating the concern expressed in the messages, but not letting herself feel their impact.

✧ ✧ ✧ ✧

"NOT MUCH TO tell you," Danolin said when Bel and Landis asked for an update on the investigation into the courthouse shooting.

"Bullets are common as dirt. No prints in the room the shooter used and nothing stands out."

Terrington, eavesdropping from nearby, snorted. "No rare fibers from ancient Peru or something useful like that."

"What about witnesses?" Bel asked Danolin.

"Witnesses? How about witless?" Terrington inserted. "For every hundred we talk to, they've got two-hundred-and-fifty descriptions of suspicious people."

"Yeah? Well, you're going to take another description because I want you to talk to that homeless woman again."

Terrington groaned. "Like I'll ever find her again. I can't exactly knock on her door."

"Use your detective skills."

"I have to finish the report on that domestic. I'll look for her to-morrow." He got up and walked toward the elevator.

"You really want him to follow up with a homeless woman or was that a ploy to get him gone for a while?" Landis asked.

"No idea what you could mean. Detective Terrington is a dedicat-ed and valued colleague I will greatly miss when I retire in seven years, five months, and twenty-three days."

"What's the homeless woman say?" Bel asked.

"That she saw somebody come out of the back of the Edisto Building at the right time."

They both waited, curbing the desire to say something smart-ass.

"Someone she says dressed like a homeless person, but wasn't. Our recently departed friend failed to ask her what she based that assess-ment on. Navy blue hoodie was what he got. Best we can do on the video we've seen to date is a blur at the right time and place. I want to talk to the woman myself to decide about making finding more a priority. Terrington says she's batty. I say who's more of an expert on homeless people than homeless people?"

"And what better way to torment Terrington?"

"Definitely a bonus."

ALLY LEFT THE interview room feeling as if she'd been relieved of every memory of Tuesday's events.

No less tired, yet somehow lighter for having expressed them.

Captain Palery had done the questioning, with the man he'd introduced only as Detective Jenkins, remaining silent yet observant throughout.

Palery had taken her over Tuesday's events multiple times from multiple angles.

The only time she felt uneasy was when he ventured away from Tuesday into the past. That focused on the period of the task force. Unlike Tanner and Bel, he did not delve into what she might have known or suspected about Chad's activities, though he explored possible connections between that and Tuesday's events.

Clearly, he ran into the same wall—how to connect the shooting of Chad with the shooting at her across the chasm of more than four years. She certainly couldn't explain it. But as long as it remained, it might provide a measure of cover, if…

She shied away from that thought, as if the law enforcement officers across from her might read it.

Palery barely brushed on the period before she married Chad Northcutt—the period when she had known Tanner.

Perhaps that added to her feeling of lightness.

Maggie, on her device, and Nancy on her phone, awaited her in the break room.

"Oh, good, you're done," Maggie said, while Nancy nodded to her, as she left the break room, still on the phone. "How'd it go?"

"Fine."

"Any breakthroughs?"

"No."

Maggie's eyes narrowed at her. "You almost sound relieved. I'd think you'd want to know who tried to shoot you."

"Of *course* I do. You're imagining things, Maggie. Where's everybody else?"

"Bel is off conducting an interview. Landis went home for fresh clothes. J.D. went to find a private corner to talk to his law office. Jamie went for coffee with her parents before they head home, because they needed reassuring that all will be well if they leave the three of us without their supervision, because in their eyes we're all still about twelve years old."

Ally almost grinned at that last part. "Dear Aunt Dana and Uncle Wes."

"Yeah. I love them, too, but—"

Nancy Quinn's return stopped Maggie's words.

"I have that meeting you wanted. Ten minutes open, if we can get there now."

"But Ally—If you stay with her—"

"I don't need anyone to stay with me. I could use some coffee, too, so I'll go—"

"You are not going outside this building without security and—"

Nancy interrupted. "She will be best off coming with us. We'll check her in to the connector through security."

Ally suspected she meant a passageway that connected the police department and the building that included the Commonwealth's Attorney's office.

The other two women exchanged a look that appeared charged with messages Ally couldn't intercept.

"Fine." Maggie closed her device and picked up her phone. "Let me message the others we'll meet them back here."

✧ ✧ ✧ ✧

THE CONNECTOR THEY took—after security examined her ID and the credentials of Maggie and Nancy, despite calling them by name—did not take them to the CA's office, but, instead, into a back hallway of the courthouse.

Each of the three buildings—the courthouse, the police department, and the building with the CA's office—faced a different city street, but these secured passageways connected them for those allowed through.

Ally trailed along as they twisted through courthouse hallways until they stopped at a closed doorway with a judge's name on the door. Ally caught only DaSilva before Nancy knocked, then opened the door to an outer office, with a woman sitting at a desk.

Without a word, she rose and went to an inner door.

"Judge, Margaret Frye is here."

"Please, come in, Maggie. You, too, Ms. Northcutt."

Surprised that the attractive woman coming around the corner of a large desk with her hand extended knew her, Ally hesitated.

"I'm Angela DaSilva."

Automatically, she met the woman's hand, and felt herself drawn into the room and directed to a loveseat on the right-hand wall.

A judge. She heard Jamie's disbelieving voice in her head again. If she could see this woman she wouldn't disbelieve.

She also was aware of an exchange of looks between Maggie and Nancy before Maggie took a seat on the loveseat and the door closed with Nancy in the outer office.

The judge sat across from them. She smiled a moment longer at Ally—a smile that did not completely hide an examination of her—then addressed Maggie.

"I suppose you're here to look into that horrible shooting on Tuesday."

"As you'll understand, Judge, we're—"

"Checking alibis."

Alibis.

Tanner's women. The judge . . .

"I have one, as you surely know, Maggie. In court. You would not have waited this long to confirm that."

But it was only yesterday Bel brought up this possibility… Ally didn't interrupt to point that out. In this world, clearly, that would qualify as *this long.*

"There was an old prosecutor who told me something in my first internship that applies here." Maggie's voice had changed. Not to her full court voice, the way she'd sounded when Ally and Jamie had listened to her try a couple cases. Not the clipped, almost telegraphic exchanges with Nancy. But also not the protective tone she took with her two younger cousins. And certainly not the tone Ally had marveled at when she'd overheard it with J.D. This was a layer of diplomacy overlaying a bedrock of business. "In all the courses, textbooks, internships, part-time jobs, seminars, and full-time experience, I've never learned anything I've used as often as his one sentence:

"Alibis were meant to be broken."

The woman across from them smiled slightly. "A wise prosecutor. However, you will not break this one, for it has the benefit of being the truth, Maggie, you are welcome to look into my schedule, short of infringing on defendants' legal rights. I will inform my clerk. Would you like me to have her coordinate with Nancy?"

Ally didn't know the ins and outs of the courthouse, but it struck her that a woman with anything to hide or even to be slightly embarrassed about would have insisted none of this go beyond her and Maggie. Certainly wouldn't have involved two assistants.

"Yes, please. Thank you, Judge."

"Good. That should take care of the official aspect of this. There is, however, one thing I would like to straighten out amongst us. And that's my attitude toward Tanner Landis.

"Do you wonder if I'm bitter? I'm not. I wanted more from Tanner. Of course I did. But I am not naïve. Not only was he honest in our dealings, but I recognized how he was from the start. He was unattainable. The core of him, I mean. I've come to realize that was a great deal of his appeal to me. Not all of it," she said with a self-deprecating smile, "but a great deal of it.

"I did not want a deep relationship at the start. I did not want him to be attainable. I wanted what he gave me. A chance to be a woman—

a desirable woman—again. It was only when I regained my feet in that arena that I toyed with the idea of more. But then I had to accept that his unattainability had not changed regardless of any changes in my feelings."

She turned to Ally. "And when I saw him looking at you Tuesday morning before you were in court for the plea deal, I understood."

"Me? No. You're mistaken. We hadn't seen each other for—we didn't see each other until the shots."

"I am not mistaken. Tanner had a view of you all entering the courthouse elevator Tuesday morning."

"But—"

Clearly feeling her verdict had been rendered on the matter and that was the end of it, the judge broadened her next words to include Maggie.

"He gave me a gift. To have no games, to know where you stand. Even if you come to want to stand somewhere else entirely, you have to appreciate it. And to acknowledge… It was what I needed. It was what I wanted."

She looked at Ally again, and the thought bubbled up that this woman would understand recognizing Tanner's scent after so many years. She felt an odd almost kinship with her.

"Do I envy you? Yes. Perhaps more than a little. And you're a fool if you shut the door on him. Do I regret opening my door to him? No."

She rose.

"Now, if you'll excuse me, I have a full schedule. But if there is any way I can help with this investigation, do please let me know. And, Maggie, I would appreciate an update when it is resolved."

CHAPTER THIRTY-ONE

BELICHEK WATCHED RHONDA Quesey frown at the business card he'd sent in to her, as her assistant ushered him and Danolin into her office.

"I only have a few minutes, but since you told my assistant this is urgent—"

"Thank you, Ms. Quesey. It is." He pronounced it *QUE-see* after checking with the assistant.

"*Dr.* Quesey," she corrected sharply.

He knew a lot of PhDs who did not insist on the honorific and some who did under only some circumstances. Like when they felt at a disadvantage.

"I don't believe I know you—" She looked at the business card again. "—Detective Belichek." She pronounced it *Bel-CHIK*.

"Belichek, yes. And this is Detective Danolin. We're investigating shots being fired near the courthouse on Tuesday that you've probably heard about."

Her eyebrows rose quickly, the inner corners higher than the centers, which tipped her expression toward anxiety rather than confusion or surprise. But that could have been a fluke.

"I did hear about it, but what could it possibly have to do with me—"

"We're asking many people about their whereabouts at the time of the shots."

"Well, really—"

"If you need to know the precise time…"

"I can tell you that Tuesday is regularly one of my heaviest patient days, with one appointment after the other. I certainly don't recall any cancellation or breaks of any kind on that day. Nor—"

"We can confirm that with your assistant."

"—did I hear the shots, nor know anything about that event."

"Are you familiar with any of the potential targets? Jamison Chancellor or Margaret Frye or Allison Northcutt or Dana and Wes Chancellor or—?"

"None of them. I had not so much as heard any of those names before the news reports about the shooting."

"That's quite comprehensive, Ms.—*Dr.* Quesey." It was also inaccurate. He remembered her mentioning Maggie one of times he'd taken one of her irate calls meant for Landis. The context had led him to think she considered Maggie a rival for Landis' attentions. She'd sounded jealous then. She looked jealous now.

If she'd somehow gotten wind of the connection between Landis and Ally…

"It's comprehensive because I had absolutely nothing to do with it."

"In that case…" He stood, nodding to Danolin, who went out the door, leaving it open, and could be heard asking the assistant to confirm Dr. Quesey's schedule for Tuesday.

Bel moved with far more deliberation.

Two feet from the chair he'd left, he turned back to her.

"You and I have never met, Dr. Quesey, but we have talked on the telephone at times. Especially late last summer."

She didn't change color under her makeup, but he spotted stiffening in her shoulders and jaw.

"I'm afraid I don't recall…"

"When you called Detective Tanner Landis at his office. Numerous times."

The jaw stiffening harshened her voice. "I have severed my consultation association with your department, Detective Belichek. You will find that there is nothing you—or that emotionally stunted, sex-crazed teenager trying to pass for a human being who doesn't know when to let go—"

Bel would have far preferred not to know the details and Landis never discussed it besides saying once that he was trying to extricate himself from the woman, but he'd unwillingly heard and witnessed enough to know who hadn't let go of whom.

"—can do to me. So your threats, whether they're made at the behest of Tanner Landis or—"

"Not here on the behest of Landis. Nothing he'd like better than for me to not be here, believe me." Those last two words were muttered under his breath. He returned to his neutral delivery. "Nor am I making threats. We're conducting an investigation. Your name came up in connection with it. We're pursuing that connection. We'll continue to pursue it until we prove it or disprove it."

✧ ✧ ✧ ✧

BACK IN THE break room, Ally, Maggie, and Nancy found the rest of them except for Bel.

Maggie immediately said to Tanner, "I talked to that Dr. Sala we saw the day Chad died."

"What? You talked to Dr. Sala? Why?" Ally asked.

"Double-checking. Always double-checking. Also heard back from another doctor who'd cared for Chad for several years. Apparently quite a high turnover in that duty because of Iris—either she fired them or they went screaming into the night. Even better, talked to that nurse—Judith—and a few more who have been around the whole time. They're unanimous that not only was this abrupt decline predictable, but also that they would have expected it to happen years ago.

"They begrudgingly say one reason it didn't was Iris Northcutt and then they happily say the other reason was Ally. Don't give me that cynical look, Landis. That's accurate reporting, not bias. They also said it would be darned hard to purposefully cause what happened to Chad over the past month in any circumstances and almost impossible to do it without a conspiracy, because of the number of people involved in his care. They said that many people would act as an informal check and balance against an angel of death type scenario."

"Angel of death? Not usually a favorite target of medical professionals."

"Fine. They didn't say that last part, but that was what they meant. But the important part is they were adamant his demise was not hastened. So, with that out of the way, now we can take advantage of Landis' one true talent," Maggie said.

"Talent?" Ally asked, then seemed to regret it.

He studied her, making sure it wasn't obvious to anyone else that he was. She'd seemed a bit shell-shocked since she'd returned with Maggie and Nancy … from somewhere none of them had specified.

But the most surprising thing was that Maggie betrayed no sign of picking up on Ally's regret. "Finding great little restaurants. We could go out for lunch and take a break from the funereal casseroles."

Nancy Quinn pursed her lips. "You have to also give him clothes as a talent, although a superficial one."

"Picking a partner," Jamie added.

"Thanks for all your kind words of praise," he said dryly. "But no restaurant visits."

Everyone sobered immediately at the reminder of potential danger for Ally in public appearances.

With that victory, he continued, "I'd vote no on the visitation and funeral, too, but—"

"I have to," she protested.

"—at least there will be enough law enforcement to deter anyone halfway sane." His conclusion further dampened spirits, since they might be dealing with someone *not* halfway sane.

Jamie perked up. "We can still do takeout. Tanner tells us which restaurant to go to, he takes Ally back to my place where it's safe, we go get lunch, and by that time Bel should be able to join us. It's all set."

✧ ✧ ✧ ✧

HE WAS WRONG about Ally being shell-shocked, but there was

something different about her, he decided as he watched her take a stack of dishes out of Jamie's kitchen cabinet in anticipation of the arrival of the lunch-shoppers.

Her hair swung with the movement, revealing the line of her throat.

She still looked tired—exhausted—but it was the exhaustion of a real person.

How much of this real person was the Ally he'd known—or thought he'd known—that was anybody's guess. But a real person for sure.

"What I never explained to you back—" She stopped as abruptly as she'd started, then tried again. "What I never explained to you at Mikey's because I wasn't brave enough to, was that I fell in love."

He remained still. Knowing how to not react outwardly.

"Not with Chad. I fell in love with his family—with the idea of his family. Though I didn't realize that part until much, much later. Much too much later."

"His family," he said flatly.

She grimaced. "I know. It seems crazy now, especially after his mother…. But, in fairness, she is a champion of the name. Protective. She wants the Northcutts to have their due—No. That isn't it. Iris wasn't—*isn't*—after what the Northcutts *deserved*. Because she doesn't require anything from the Northcutts to earn respect, simply being a Northcutt is sufficient."

"And it all reflected on her."

Ally's head came up. "Yes. It was—it is—the blood in her veins." She exhaled. "But I didn't see any of that to start. What I saw was a close-knit family, devoted to a tradition of law enforcement—serving and protecting. Generations and branches. And the connections so strong they lived near each other—most of them—and gathered together and supported each other and were deeply involved in each other's lives."

"Unlike your immediate family."

"The exact opposite of the homelife I had growing up."

"You had your cousins—"

"Yes. And Aunt Vivian. Especially Aunt Vivian. She understood things that Maggie and Jamie hadn't. Not then. Those summers were my oasis. And that summer, the last one, was like an idyll. Everything right. Vivian was happy, really happy. In love and sure she was loved back. And we felt like the love she'd always given us was doubled with him there. Like we were a real family."

She fell silent.

"Until your aunt was murdered."

"Before. When that monster tried to grab Jamie. Maggie… Maggie knew it beforehand. I heard her talking to Aunt Vivian, trying to protect Jamie. She and Aunt Vivian always had such a strong bond and Maggie said those things, even with Vivian getting angry at her. Doing what was right. While I was entirely selfish. Because I was angry at Maggie. *Angry* at her for trying to break up what we had, what *I* wanted…"

Her first taste of family.

"You were a kid."

"Not such a kid that I didn't comprehend what Maggie was saying, that he really was after Jamie. I did. I've thought about this a lot and I definitely did. I was still angry at her for threatening what I saw as the family group. And then, when he tried to grab Jamie, it was Maggie who saved her. I did nothing."

"You called 911."

"Anybody could do that."

"You did it. You got help there fast."

"It wouldn't have mattered if Maggie hadn't saved her."

"They wouldn't have found him as fast if law enforcement hadn't gotten there when they did and that wouldn't have happened if you hadn't called."

"I suppose."

The quiet settled around them. She opened the utensil drawer, took out forks and knives with unnecessary clatter pushing it away.

"You know it's bullshit."

Her gaze came up. "What is?"

"You thinking that because you wanted things to be the way you hoped they'd be, with that guy not a pervert, not a killer, that you somehow made it happen that he was one."

"I don't think—"

"Maybe you don't think it when you look at the logic of it, but you feel it. It's called magical thinking. Kids do it a lot. I wished for snow so I didn't have to go to school, it snowed, my parents had a car wreck that totaled the car, it's my fault."

"Magical thinking?"

"Yeah. And that time it worked. Didn't have to go to school the next day."

"Your parents must be very forgiving. To love you despite causing their car to wreck." Her smile slipped toward quizzical, but she went on. "I know you have a good relationship with them. Yet you wouldn't talk about them when… Before."

Possibly to rescue her from that awkward ending, he asked, "How could you possibly know what kind of relationship I have with them?"

"By the way you reacted to my parents. I learned that as a kid. They're a litmus test for revealing someone's expectations of family."

He met her look long enough to think that what he'd likened to an avatar of her face had given way completely to true flesh and blood.

Or was he seeing more clearly?

Either way, her thoughtful expression slid wariness into him.

"So, back to your cousins." His heartiness didn't ring quite true. "You had each other as kids and now…?"

"Ah. Now Maggie is a respected prosecutor, putting all her intelligence and strength into serving justice and—"

"*Feared* prosecutor. Makes her happiest to be feared."

She ignored his interruption, but a smile tugged at her mouth. Still, she continued in the same unemotional way, "And Jamie is the revered leader of the Sunshine Foundation, as well as a talented author, who pours her heart and her determination into making people's lives better."

He considered her for two, three beats after she finished, feeling impatience rise.

"Christ, Ally," he finally snapped.

"What?"

"You know what. You want me say it? I will. Maggie's a prosecutor. Jamie's behind the Sunshine Foundation. And you are—?"

"That's inconsequential."

"Bullshit."

"Tanner, I hold my cousins in very high regard and I'm very proud of them, of what they've accomplished. I won't ever not praise them for who they are and what they've done."

"Good. They deserve it. So do you."

She didn't argue. She might as well have.

"You're an artist," he said. "You're talented and—"

"I gave that up—gave up who I was—to try to have a family."

"No, you didn't."

She frowned a how-can-you-say that question at him. "I did. I haven't painted in years."

"Did that about as good as you have at blocking out your cousins. Taking workshops when you couldn't take classes, keeping a pad under your bed, sketching at the Chate. As for the painting. Maybe. But you didn't give it up, either. You said you have a storage unit. Said that's where you locked up your art. If it's locked up there, it can be unlocked."

She stared at him for an uncomfortably long time. When she spoke, she didn't say the *You're right* he might have been hoping for. She said, "That's an interesting take on it."

Heat rose up in him.

Anger. At her. At himself. At the years that had passed.

"Why didn't you leave? Before he was shot. After he was shot. Why the hell didn't you get out of it? Did you care that much about what other people thought of you? I never—"

"No. I cared about what *I* thought of me. I cared about living up to my promises. I cared about seeing things through when I'd made a commitment to other people."

He studied her for a long moment.

"Your parents."

She jolted at that. "What?"

"You didn't want to be your parents. You made a commitment to—Not just Chad. The damned Northcutt name and the family and you wouldn't walk away from it. You thought if you'd left after he was shot, you'd have tarnished the name. I suppose it's a damned miracle you were willing to leave at all."

"I'm sorry I didn't, Tanner. If that's—" She turned to the sound of the others arriving through the back gate. The motion of facing him again set her hair swinging the way he remembered. "I'm sorry, Tanner."

CHAPTER THIRTY-TWO

OVER LUNCH FROM the best Lebanese deli on the Eastern Seaboard, Maggie reported her conversation with Judge DaSilva, which seemed to incline her, J.D., and Bel toward faint amusement, while doing nothing for Landis' appetite.

That had to be what bugged him now. Not that *I'm sorry, Tanner.*

What about that bugged him?

Sorry she hadn't left Chad early, yeah. That made sense. But that last one seemed … *off.* What was going on in her head? What was she still keeping from them?

"…which makes me wonder about her judgment," Maggie concluded, "except Nancy also looked into her movements and at the time of the shooting at the courthouse, she was presiding in court. That doesn't mean she couldn't have paid somebody, but Nancy's convinced she hasn't been hiring hitmen or even breaking and entering specialists."

Nancy Quinn's opinion clearly was good enough for Maggie.

For that matter, it was good enough for him, too. The woman had a network of connections that put spy agencies to shame and knew her stuff, having started as a cop before switching to the CA's office nearly two decades ago.

But his discomfort wasn't over.

"I talked to Rhonda Quesey," Bel said. "Remember what Maggie said about the judge and looking at Landis more in sorrow than in anger? Flip it for Rhonda. Can't clear her."

"That's the one who was so angry at Tanner for breaking up with her?" Jamie asked.

"One of them," his supposed always-had-his-back partner said. "Among the more recent. She's definitely pissed enough to take a shot at him. Though I don't know about shooting at Ally. Thought she was telling the truth when she didn't seem to know anything about a connection between them."

Landis dipped a grilled shrimp in eggplant-pomegranate chutney, his favorite.

It was tasteless.

I'm sorry, Tanner.

He should be glad Ally was sorry for not leaving Chad North-cutt—at any time.

But was that what she meant?

If it wasn't… It had to mean she was sorry for ever marrying him in the first place. For choosing Chad, the damned Northcutts.

J.D. said his contacts indicated no red flags raised with or around the Piscattoway County Police Department of awareness of their ad hoc probe into a possible connection between the shooting of Chad Northcutt and the attempt at the courthouse.

Despite himself, Landis cut a look at Ally at that. For once she didn't argue against the possibility.

It didn't help his gut any, but it was interesting.

"Have you talked to your contact from the task force, Landis? See if there's anything more you didn't know about?" Bel asked, pulling his attention back.

"No. I have a call into him. Asshole's on vacation on some house-boat in the Keys with his wife. You'd think a guy who'd been married as long as they have would be past that sort of thing."

"Ever the romantic, Landis. No access from this houseboat?"

"He's got it. He's turned it off."

Bel grinned at his partner's bitterness. "Keep trying. Felicia Ewer had better luck finding Willow Spencer."

"Who?" Jamie asked.

"I haven't told them yet," Ally said. "Please, Bel, will you?"

He explained Willow's relationship with Chad to the rest of them, along with his bankrolling her and his mother.

At the end, he said to Landis, "Thought we'd go see her this afternoon. Schmidt, can you find the address?"

Ally leaned forward. "I want to go."

"No," Landis said immediately.

"Okay," Bel said at the same time.

✦ ✦ ✦ ✦

OUT THE BACK door, Landis demanded, "Are you on something, Belichek? *Not* a good idea. Under any possible scenario."

"You're protecting her. She doesn't want to be protected. Willow Spencer's been questioned before and gave up nothing that wasn't already known from Chad's records and his big mouth. Ally being there might throw her off. Give us more. Worth a try."

"This might not lead anywhere—"

"The mountain of evidence we need starts with a single pebble—" Tanner growled.

"—then adding to it, pebble by pebble. So shaking her up with Ally's presence might get us more pebbles."

"That's a risk—"

"She wants to."

"I want to, Landis. I want to know…" Whatever she'd started to say from behind him fell apart when he faced her. She repeated only, "I want to know."

Schmidt appeared behind her in the open doorway, holding up Ally's cell. "Your mother's on your phone for you, Ally. And I've got the address, sir. Seventeen-nineteen Narragansett, here in Fairlington. But she's not off work for another two hours."

"I'll be ready," Ally said firmly.

That firmness didn't carry over to responding to her mother.

They could hear Greta's complaints about how much time she was missing at this vital moment for the gardens by coming to her daughter and now her daughter wasn't even here … only her father and that horrible woman across the street.

✧ ✧ ✧ ✧

THEY WERE LUCKY to find a parking spot almost directly across the street from the apartment building that Willow Spencer's current address came back to.

The building was nobody's idea of luxury, but still solid after decades of use. The stairs barely creaked as they climbed three floors because the elevator was out, a fact advertised by a sign that had been there months, if not longer.

Willow Spencer answered the door with impatience that turned to curiosity when Bel showed his ID, then morphed to something far less benign when recognition of Ally dawned, once they sat at the small table beside the kitchen.

She had been cute in the photos in the record. It was hard to tell if the passage of time or her reaction to Ally bore more responsibility for the erosion of that cuteness.

"Willow, we're hoping you can provide us additional background as we look into what might have led to the shooting of Chad Northcutt."

"Now? Now, you want more *background?* Now that he's dead?"

"Yes," Bel said evenly.

She kept her protuberant blue eyes pinned on Ally.

"Can you tell us how you met?"

"At a bar. He bought me a drink and we got talking. That's all it took with us. Chad never dragged his feet when it came to being with me."

Steady and thorough, Bel took them through their association and Chad's financial support.

"He spent more time here than he did at home, it was only right he helped me out," she said defensively. "Promised I'd be taken care of, too."

"Did he express any concerns in the time leading up to when he was shot?"

"Like he expected to be shot in the head at his own house? No. Besides, he didn't spend his time with me whining about *concerns.*"

"Who did he talk about from the job?"

"I don't remember any names."

Not only a lie, but surly.

"Not even Northcutt?"

"Are you trying to be funny?"

"He had cousins and other relatives in the department. He must have talked about them."

"Suppose he mentioned them. But we didn't spend a lot of our time on that. We had other things to do, fun things."

Bel continued patiently. "Did he talk about anyone he was having trouble with at work?"

"Nah."

"Or in his life?"

"Other than her, you mean?" She leaned forward toward Ally. "I know who you are."

"I'm Allison Lindell Northcutt."

"Yeah. Lindell, sliding that in like Chad's name hardly counts. He knew you did that on purpose. You weren't slipping anything by him."

Bel tried to recapture her attention. "Willow—"

"He talked about you. Not any way you'd like."

"What did he say?" Ally asked.

Landis suppressed the urge to intervene, stop the other woman from taking up Ally's invitation to repeat—or make up—possible cruelties.

"Said he was sick to death of you. Said he couldn't stand you always being around like a ghost. Said his mother had told him from the start you weren't strong enough to be a cop's wife and she was right. Takes a woman with balls so-to-speak to be with a cop. *Really* with a cop. To be there *with* him every step of the way."

Clearly, she saw herself in that role.

"He said he was supposed to love you. That's how he said it—he was *supposed* to love you, but he never did, as much as he tried."

"Did he say, then, why he refused to divorce me? Did he say why he threatened me and my family if I ever tried to leave him?"

Spoken with almost light curiosity, it took Willow a couple seconds to absorb the import of the words.

"He wanted a divorce. He wanted to get rid of you. You wouldn't go. Hung on like a vampire bat, sucking him dry."

She faltered, possibly hearing the hollowness of the words, recognizing the lies Chad had told her as she repeated them.

But Willow wasn't about to be defeated.

She leaned farther forward. Triumph pulled her lips back from her teeth. "And he always said you killed his father. Wouldn't put it past you to have had him shot, too, then stuck around to make sure you got all the money."

CHAPTER THIRTY-THREE

BEL CROSSED THE street first.

Landis hung back, behind Ally, who seemed distracted. Not as upset as he might have expected from what Willow Spencer said, but definitely distracted.

There was something about all this he wasn't seeing. Him or Bel.

Ally's reactions—

The sound alerted him first.

Pedal to the floor acceleration on a narrow street.

He didn't look—wasn't wasting the time. He lunged, grabbed Ally around the waist and spun them both into the gap between the back of Bel's vehicle and the truck behind it.

If the truck hadn't been wider, providing shelter faster …

Landis automatically noted make and color. And that the tag number was covered by what looked like a strip of tape.

That was all he had time for as he surveyed the area—no other dangers apparent—hustled Ally around to the back passenger side, half shoved her in that door, then got to the front seat in record time.

"Ally?"

"Okay. I'm okay."

"Deliberate?" Bel had the engine started. "Won't catch up."

"Deliberate. Silver Camry, Virginia tags. That'll only get us a million to go through."

"See the driver?"

Which meant Bel hadn't. Damn. "Too much sun glare."

"We weren't followed here. Fluke?"

"Not worth the risk of thinking it was. Let's move. I'll call it in."

"If we leave—"

Calling in wouldn't do much good. "Better than sitting here waiting for proof it wasn't a fluke while he or she tries a different weapon on the next pass."

Bel cranked the wheel to pull out of the parking spot.

✧ ✧ ✧ ✧

ALLY WAS UNNATURALLY quiet.

"Don't let it spook you." He heard his own gruffness. That should make her feel all warm and cozy.

Oh, hell. Maybe warm and cozy was the worst thing for her. Scared and alert was a hell of a lot better.

"What?" she responded belatedly, seeming to return from somewhere far away. "Oh. You mean the car? You and Bel are on that. If it is anything. I was thinking about what Willow said toward the end."

He was supposed to love you. That's what he said. He was supposed to love you, but he never did, as much as he tried.

It bothered her that much that Chad said he hadn't loved her? Hell, not even that. That an ex-girlfriend of Chad's said he'd said it.

The accusation against Ally? That seemed unlikely to bother her. She must have known she was looked at early-on. But he was keeping this open-ended.

"What struck you about what she said?"

Immediately she said, "It doesn't make sense."

"Agreed. I saw him around you at the start. He loved you. He was telling the girlfriend what she wanted to hear."

"Not that. I mean about Chad saying I killed his father. I didn't even know him when his father died."

"She made it up to rile you."

"I don't think so. I think she believed it. I wonder…"

"What?"

She didn't answer for a mile, maybe more. He didn't push.

There was a bozo in the right lane—not a silver Camry with Virginia plates—who seemed to think this was a fine time to practice his bumper car skills.

Her voice came from the back seat. "You have to understand, Chad would say things. If he felt trapped or pressured, it would build up and he'd … say things."

"Lashing out." He'd witnessed that in action at the academy.

"Maybe. Or…" She nodded slightly to herself. "More like redirecting. Taking the focus off what was making him uncomfortable, shifting it to something else."

"Yeah. I can see that. You're right."

He felt a shift in her expression, but with the bozo in the right lane now trying to move into the space occupied by the back seat of this vehicle, he didn't check it out.

"I got him," Bel muttered.

He knew that. He did.

And as soon as they were clear of the bozo…

Bel smoothly pulled in a gap in the left lane to pull around the vehicle in front of them, leaving the bozo behind. Landis looked toward her, but she was back to neutral except for the tuck between her brows.

"You've laid it out that Chad might have been redirecting, now tell me what he said."

"It was crazy, really, but he was so angry at her for leaving and taking the kids…"

He sorted through the cast of characters… "Natalie? David's widow?"

"Yes. He was ranting that the family was breaking up and it was all her fault. Taking the kids to Illinois. *Keeping them from their family*, he said. And then he started going back, back to when they were just engaged, and something happened, some big blowup between David and his parents, and then he said, *She killed him*. And I asked, who? And he said his father. He said his sister-in-law Natalie killed his father."

❖ ❖ ❖ ❖

WHEN THEY CALLED Natalie Northcutt, she first reacted with warmth to Ally. She said she'd just sent a note after hearing about Chad's death and then—to her shock—that Ally had been shot at on the same day.

Caution overrode the warmth and concern as he and Bel—mostly—explained that they'd like to talk to her as part of their investigation, without specifying too closely what their investigation entailed.

If she was coming to the funeral…

She wasn't. She didn't elaborate.

They'd come to Illinois then.

"When?"

"Tomorrow," Ally said, as they'd primed her to. "With the visitation the day after tomorrow and the funeral the day after that, I have to be here and…"

"We need to get answers for Ally's safety," Landis said when she didn't.

Natalie agreed to meet them, but specified it would be at the police department. And, greatly to her regret, she would not let Ally see the kids because it would be such a brief visit and they wouldn't understand why Aunt Ally wasn't spending time with them.

As deep as Ally's disappointment was, she said she understood, and thanked the other woman for agreeing to talk to them.

They would let her know as soon as they made the arrangements to fly to Illinois.

❖ ❖ ❖ ❖

BEL WENT UPSTAIRS to the tiny second-floor room he used as an office at Jamie's house to figure out how to get them to Illinois the next day without bankrupting the Fairlington County Police Department.

Maggie and J.D. left on some unspecified errand. Possibly to have time to breathe together, the two of them.

Landis sat on the loveseat in the living room across from Ally and Jamie.

Both looked tired. He probably did, too. They could take these few minutes. Recharge.

Ally had her eyes closed. Her eyelids no longer looked translucent, but darkened circles showed underneath. No woman would want to hear that she had more color in her face because of dark eye circles, but on her it looked … more alive.

"Oh."

Jamie's soft voice brought his attention to her. She stared at her cousin's face as if she'd spotted the answers of the universe.

Ally's eyes blinked open. "Jamie?"

Still staring in that unnerving way, she said, "I got Tanner pretty quickly. Even before, when he was investigating me. The women, the clothes, the food. Not that he doesn't like them, but they're also—"

He waited for her to say compensation. She wouldn't be the first, including that department consulting psychologist he'd gotten involved with last year who threw in some ad hoc analysis as a parting shot. She hadn't been nice about it, either.

"—protection. Like bird feathers letting them hide in trees."

"Armor," Ally murmured.

Startled that she remembered or—more likely—stumbled on the same word she used that night she'd sketched him at Mikey's, he still pulled off amusement, saying, "I am sitting here, you know."

His words didn't appear to reach either of them.

"Armor," Jamie agreed. "So that made sense with him and your history together. But you … I didn't get it. I mean, some of it, yeah, of course, because you've had your own armor, not letting feelings show, trying not to feel them. You're coming out of that, thank goodness, but then there'd be moments when it was like you were caught in a flashback of fear and—"

"Jamie—"

"—that didn't make sense." Jamie's soft voice did not relent. "Because you're not afraid of Tanner. But—Oh. Oh, Ally. Afraid *for*

Tanner."

Ally stared at her cousin, her lips parted.

He went for amusement again. "You have got the wrong end of this stick, Jamie. Hell, you've got the wrong tree."

It didn't work.

He felt his face stiffening as she slowly turned to him.

"It's really very simple, Tanner. Ally never had a family, a real family, like mine. For a while, with Vivian and Maggie and me she had it, but that ended." Her voice cracked. "She tried so hard with Chad and the Northcutts... But she learned how wrong she was. She was ready to leave him. Maybe you were in her thoughts then, the connection you had."

"Me? If she wasn't going to contact you or Maggie, no way would she—"

"Exactly. *Because* she loves us. She'd protect us no matter what."

She watched him expectantly.

He said nothing.

She exhaled. "Tanner, Ally's been protecting you. In case you shot Chad."

CHAPTER THIRTY-FOUR

"I SAW YOU," Ally said from behind him.

He stood at the fireplace, facing the painting she'd done of a spot by the river that Aunt Vivian had loved.

Jamie had left. It was just the two of them.

"You saw me? What does that mean? When? Where?" He didn't turn around.

"It was while I was preparing to leave Chad. Suddenly, after years, there you were. The middle of the night, sitting in a car a couple houses down, staring. I knew it was you. No question at all. And then, two days later, I was following Chad, making sure he was at a bar with his friends before I went to the library to work on my plan and I saw you at a café across the street. I knew it was you, yet it was like it wasn't you at all.

"After that, I saw you more. I know you were watching the house, investigating Chad. And me. But I didn't know it then."

"You think I shot Chad?" Now he did turn. He spaced each word with precision and impact. "Do you think I shot Chad Northcutt in the head four years and six months ago in your driveway?"

"No."

He stared at her as if that would untwist truth and lie from the syllable.

"Did you ever?"

She glanced away, but almost immediately came back to him. She stood to own these words. "I was afraid."

"Afraid of me."

"Afraid for you." She didn't move toward him, but in the small room they were close enough that she saw the pain she'd caused him, pain he contained everywhere except deep in his eyes.

"Because you thought—what?—I was stalking you? Chad? That I tried to kill him to get you? I'd have to be an idiot or a psychopath or both to kill to try to get you, then never contact you."

"I knew you weren't an idiot or a psychopath. But I didn't know you weren't going to try to contact me until you didn't. It wasn't until time passed…"

"Shit. You must have been relieved as hell never to hear from me."

"No," she said simply. "It's not logical, but it's how I felt. The shock of Chad and—I was terrified you'd come around and someone would notice, get suspicious, start looking at you… I wanted you to stay away. Far away. But I also wanted… I wanted so desperately to tell you everything I was thinking and feeling, to get it all out to someone I knew would listen to the bad with the good. Who wouldn't blame me like the Northcutts or even try to comfort me, like my cousins. Who'd just let me talk, just let me be.

"It didn't last, that fear, that crazy thought. I *knew* you wouldn't have—*couldn't* have done that. But then all this and you're suddenly there and Chad dying and the talk about his shooting. Jamie was right, it's been like flashbacks. Flashbacks to that fear. Or like—" She shook her head, the words not coming. "—like lightning striking. I can't predict or control it, I can only feel it strike. I learned to go numb to fear, to pain, to everything. For a long time. Only I can't stay numb anymore. And it hurts, Tanner, it hurts losing the numbness, coming back to life. Like when you've been frozen and the blood starts to move again." She looked down at her hands, flexing them slowly.

"It burns. The good floods back in, but so does that fear and confusion and realizing how what you've done ripples out, crossing ripples with other people and you've hurt those people. The last ones you'd ever want to hurt."

"No one can take on the responsibility for every ripple that crosses any other ripple out there in the world, Ally."

He took her face between his palms. She believed he intended comfort.

Didn't matter what he'd intended.

She looked up at him. She reached up to him.

His mouth came down on hers. A decade. An instant. Forever.

She wrapped her hands around his wrists holding him holding her. They tilted their heads, finding entry to each other.

The sensation, the connection, the intensity—

"You think this is a good idea?"

Bel's voice jerked Landis away from her so fast she stumbled. He caught her arm, half pushed her into the chair, then released her as if burnt by that contact.

"No. It's a fucking bad idea considering Ally thought I tried to murder her husband."

Tanner had retreated behind sharp, would-be humor.

"That's not—"

"And then locked herself up for four and half years out of guilt because if I shot him, it was *her* fault. Christ, Ally—"

"Yes, I felt guilty, but it wasn't only—"

"*Only*—"

Bel shoved Tanner's shoulder, knocking him off balance enough that he took a step backward to keep from going down. He didn't resist when Bel pushed him toward the door.

"Excuse us, Ally," Bel said, "I need to talk to my partner."

ALL THE WAY through the kitchen and out on the back patio, Bel herded him like he was a damned sheep.

Once there, though, Bel didn't talk.

In the face of another of his silences, Landis paced, turned and paced the other way. But he forced himself to stillness before he could start another pass.

It required enough concentration that he shut out Ally's voice in his head and barely heard Bel when he finally spoke.

"Explains why she didn't want us investigating Chad's shooting."

It took a couple beats for him to take in the full meaning of the words.

Landis stared at his partner over his shoulder then jerked around. "Great. She still thought *now* that I shot him. Not only when the shock and stress of it first happening provided some excuse, but—"

"You want to talk about shock and stress? After years of day in and day out being at his bedside and dealing with that mother of his, she's shot at, Chad dies, and Iris tosses verbal hand grenades at her in public—oh, yeah, and you show up out of nowhere. You had warning. She didn't. So, yeah, she's had a little shock and stress these past days."

Landis shoved his hand through his hair.

"Yeah, that's right. Start using your brain again," Bel said, not kindly. "You think you're angry because she doubted you, but somewhere down where you try to hide everything, it's the possibility that she locked herself up for four and a half years on your behalf that gets you."

"Fuck you, Belichek."

"One last thing. With all these flaming curveballs coming at her these past days, what was her instinct? To protect *you*. To try to steer everyone away from connecting Chad's shooting to the attempt on her, because some part of her flashed back to that fear that you might have been the one who shot Chad and she wanted to save your worthless hide."

CHAPTER THIRTY-FIVE

LANDIS GOT OUT of his vehicle in the parking garage for his condo and strode to the one that had pulled into the next empty parking space.

"You followed me home? If you think I'm going to ask if I can keep you, forget it."

He addressed Ford Belichek as the other man emerged from his vehicle with exactly the right twist of humor. He couldn't do that if he wasn't in control. He couldn't do that if he wasn't using his brain.

He added, "What are you doing here? You were supposed to stay at Jamie's tonight."

Bel had said he was staying with them when he ordered Landis to leave.

"Take the night. We're going to Illinois tomorrow and you need to have your head back on straight by then. You two need some space."

"After that car tried to run her over, I'm not—"

"I'm staying here. Go. Or I'm calling Palery and dumping the whole history in his lap."

And he'd meant it.

But now Bel's being here meant Ally was in the house with only Jamie—

"J.D. and Maggie got back right after you left. They're staying until I get back. No, no they don't know what happened. At least they didn't when I left. Though they sure as heck sensed the atmosphere. Don't know if Ally or Jamie will tell them. I just said I wanted a drink with my partner. *From* my partner. Since you've always got the good stuff."

With effort, Landis produced a passable grunt. "You could buy the good stuff, too, if you didn't save every penny like it's your last."

"Not much of a consumer."

"Except for the good stuff I buy."

"Except for that," Bel agreed.

Neither said anything more until they were in his condo, holding glasses of whiskey, and looking out toward the Potomac River from the balcony.

"You could have bought a swimming pool's worth of the good stuff—" Bel hoisted his glass. "—which is very, very good, by the way—if you hadn't sprung for the balcony and this river view."

"I have an image to uphold." He'd actually selected the place because of the in-unit washer and dryer.

"For whom? You never let anybody come here. Certainly not your women. Am I the only one who's ever been invited in?"

"You weren't invited. Not by me. You invited yourself."

Bel grunted. "Remember me saying I originally thought you were thinking of Maggie when you mashed that pen. There was also something you said that I've been thinking about."

Abrupt changes of subject were part of Bel's style, meant to knock those he was questioning off stride. To prove he wasn't knocked—not by anything—he came at it head-first. "Back to your crazy theory about a broken pen? But at least, you're finally coming to your senses and recognizing the brilliance of my words."

"You could say that. What you said was, *You're caught this time, my friend. And not even your career's going to save you. Take it from an expert.* I thought you were talking solely about me. I got that one wrong. You were talking about yourself—how did I miss that?"

He'd expected this to go personal from the moment he'd spotted Bel behind him. "You got it wrong, all right. Now. Totally wrong. I was talking about you and falling for Jamie."

"You were also talking about you. *Take it from an expert.* Should've known you were talking about yourself then. All the women who've rolled through your life like they were on an assembly line? Not one of them caught you. Didn't come close. Yet you were claiming to be the expert in getting caught. So that happened before we started working together. And not even your career saved you. Meaning you were still caught."

"You don't know what you're—"

"Ally. That's what I'm talking about. You were—you are—caught by Ally. And your career didn't save you. Even when you first tried to hide behind your career by investigating her. And then used the excuse of career to get away from her. Far away, where you thought you'd never see her again."

He said nothing.

"Must have been one hell of a shock to realize she was Maggie's cousin."

He said nothing. Again.

"You do know the Northcutts did a number on her," Bel said. "To the point that, in the car, after leaving Willow Spencer's, your saying she was right knocked her completely sideways."

"You were watching the rear-view mirror instead of the bozo."

"Screw you, Landis. Don't talk to me about her, about you, but don't feed me bullshit." Bel turned and went inside.

He followed more slowly.

"Mind if I—?"

Before Landis recognized Bel's intent, much less reacted to it, the other man had gone into the bedroom.

For a slice of a second, he thought Bel was checking if he had a woman here. But Bel knew him better than that. He never brought women here.

"Sure, go ahead."

But Belichek didn't move toward the bathroom, on the right. He turned left inside the door, toward the dresser and bed.

It wasn't like his partner hadn't been in his place before. Not necessarily in the bedroom except to pass through to use the bathroom, but enough to not be curious. So, what the hell?

He followed and found Belichek standing in front of the dresser, staring at the painting hanging above it.

The hairs on the back of Landis' neck stood up.

He already knew before Bel said, "She hadn't settled into her full, personal style yet with this one, had she?"

Saying nothing wasn't much, but it was all he had.

"Hadn't settled into her signature, Theodora Lindell, either," Bel added. "But the foundation's there."

It was almost tone on tone. The blacks, whites, and grays, though, shifted depending on where you stood and how the light touched it. On some days, at some times, parts seemed to almost shimmer, especially in the corner of it where a light showed a shabby sign that read "Mikey's."

"Were you stalking her?"

"Nice to know what my partner really thinks of me. No, I wasn't stalking her. I didn't shoot Chad Northcutt, either."

Bel looked over his shoulder. "I'm not saying that Ally thinking— worrying—you might have shot Chad is easy to swallow. I'm still coming to terms with it, too, but there are angles to it. Interesting angles."

"Surprised Jamie didn't tell you a long time ago."

"Don't think she knew until she was saying it to you. Besides—" One corner of his mouth lifted. "Haven't had a lot of alone time. Might surprise you to know we don't spend what we do have talking about you."

He *huh'd.*

Bel studied him another beat, then, apparently satisfied, turned back to the artwork on the bedroom wall.

"How'd you get this?"

"Are we now past attempted murder and onto the lesser of my supposed offenses, stealing?"

"Cut it, Landis. You said you weren't stalking her. How'd you get this without her knowing you—" He turned. "Or *does* she know you have it?"

"It's just a painting for Christ's sake."

"So she *doesn't* know you have it. How'd you get it?"

"It's no big deal. There was a student art sale at the place she'd told me she was studying. I went. Stayed out of her sight—only to avoid anything awkward. When she went to lunch, I bought it."

"Why this one?"

He didn't answer.

"Ah. Significance to the two of you."

"To me."

"Only you, that's what you mean." Bel clapped him on the back, combining in that one contact a direction to turn and leave, an announcement that he'd stop probing—for now—and a message of consolation.

"I do finally understand why you never brought a woman back here. One look at you looking at that painting… You wouldn't be getting any that night, that's for sure. Not unless it was the kind who didn't mind you being in love with someone else."

—DAY 5—

SATURDAY

CHAPTER THIRTY-SIX

WES CHANCELLOR'S CONNECTIONS got them on a flight to Chicago for a price that fit into even the Fairlington County Police Department budget, though Captain Palery muttered about billing Piscattoway if it ended up helping clear one of their cases.

Chancellor didn't even ask too many questions about what they were after in Illinois.

Unlike Maggie.

Bel put the brakes on that by saying they wouldn't risk any potential damage to the investigation by sharing anything. If something came out of it, they'd assess if anything could be shared. If nothing came out of it, Ally could decide if she wanted to tell anybody anything when they got back.

Maggie had been so big on Ally's autonomy, she couldn't very well try to steamroll it now. And her professionalism wouldn't let her argue with his other reasons. Even though she wanted to.

She was reconciled to the situation—as reconciled as Maggie got to things she didn't like—when they said good-bye before Jamie drove them to the airport.

Jamie and Bel's good-bye at the airport trounced all over the man's previous-to-Jamie's objections to public displays of affection.

Landis considered calling him on it for the half second before he realized it would make the situation even more awkward for Ally. And him.

He and Ally didn't address each other. Didn't look at each other.

It was like the first day after you'd had the flu and it felt like any wrong move or hearing the wrong word would set it all off again, so you went through space like you were spun glass. Or this ... *truce?* ... was.

They untwisted already straight shoulder straps, rearranged zippers, and smoothed pockets on their overnight bags. Not looking at Jamie and Bel.

Focusing away from Ally brought a kid of about seventeen or so into his peripheral vision. A kid staring at them—at Ally?—with an intensity that brought Landis around to face him fully.

The kid startled and ducked behind a bulky business man fast-walking a rollaboard.

"What is it?" Bel asked, having finally disengaged from Jamie, who waved to them all before getting in the driver's seat to pull away.

"A kid." Scanning the crowd, he saw no sign of that kid. "Nothing."

Waiting at the gate was no place to discuss what was on their minds. And idle conversation didn't appeal. The three of them remained mostly silent.

His phone going off came as a welcome break.

Checking the incoming number, he gave Bel a significant look, then strode to another gate area that was deserted.

He answered with, "A houseboat in the Keys? Totally out of contact?"

The man on the other end chuckled. "As patient as ever, huh, Landis?"

He didn't mind proving the guy's point by asking, "Did you ever get anything on who might have wanted Chad Northcutt out of the picture?"

"Only speculation, based on logic. Someone who wanted to cut off a loose end who was being too noticeable. If that was the reason, they did a great job of it. Someone who wanted to take over the operation. If that was the reason, they've stayed so low to the ground there hasn't been a whiff, and we've been paying attention all along—not investigating, because there wasn't anything to investigate, but ear to the ground. I kept coming back to something … personal."

Landis waited.

The other man's voice changed. "I wondered some about the wife, but I gotta say never picked up anything there we could use. And most everybody sings her praises. Sure can't fault her for the way she's stuck by him, no matter whether he was worth it or not."

"*Most everybody*," he repeated.

"Hell, Landis, when you left the task force, you said you knew her and Chad some. You also must have known Iris Northcutt's a piece of work."

"Ah. Anybody else?"

"Not that I ever heard."

"In other words, you've got bubkes for me."

"Pretty much," he said cheerfully. "Sort of like that damned task force. You were probably smart to get out when you did. Good thing you ended up in homicide. Never were a great fit for corruption."

That jolted "The hell I wasn't" out of him.

"You weren't. You're better off where it's more black and white to go after every murderer."

He thought of conversations with Bel on the topic and grunted a passable concession.

"Anyway," the voice on the other end said, "For anything deeper, I'd have to check my old files—though I don't think there's much of anything there. This is all from dredging my memory because I thought I might hear from you when I heard about the shots fired at your courthouse. Didn't know you were right in the thick of it until I got into where there's connection and caught the video from the news. Allison Northcutt, huh? Think she was the target?"

"We're a long way from sorting that out. Have to look at the possibility. Strongly look at it."

"Of course. Especially with Chad Northcutt dying the same damned day. That's gotta make your nose twitch."

"It does. Which is why—"

"You called me. Figured. I'll tell you right off, for all intents and purposes the investigation died with Chad Northcutt getting shot down in his driveway. Well, good as. We poked around for a while. Seeing if anybody surfaced to take his role. Nada."

"Any whispers on who might have shot him?"

"Nothing. Quiet as the grave—no pun intended. Which was a pretty damned appropriate way for that investigation to end. I had high hopes for when it started. Thought it could get some rat bastards out of law enforcement for good and pin a few gold stars on some of the good guys. But it was one frustration after another."

"No sign of activity since Chad was shot?"

"None."

"Could he have been the leader and that's why it died with him?"

"No." No hesitation there. "Not smart enough to keep the operation hidden as well as it was … except for where his actions exposed it to the air."

"What about possible confederates?"

"The buddies, Paulz and Selton. Paulz suddenly has a cabin he says some distant relative left him out of the blue. Selton says nothing about his new, flashy boat."

"What about Northcutt's cousin?"

"Mark Junior? Possibility. Stunted career, possibly frustrated. Didn't see any blips up in his spending, unlike those other two with the boat and cabin. Which would make him smarter than the rest of them…"

"Which didn't seem to fit," Landis filled in.

They kicked that around for a couple minutes until the boarding call came.

His caller signed off with, "Bottom line is, Chad Northcutt's death cut the legs out from under that task force. And after that we never got anything more."

✧　✧　✧　✧

WHEN THEY BOARDED—late—Ally had the window seat. Bel said his ticket was for the aisle, but Landis overruled him, saying he needed more leg room than his shorter partner. Bel gave him a I-know-what's-up-with-you look.

The flight landed late.

With Landis behind the wheel, they drove west from the airport, through packed suburbs to more open ones, then angled southwest, with the land gradually overwhelming the houses and spreading out to farms.

It was hard to tell if it was as spacious as it felt or if some of it was illusion from the straight line of the road vanishing only at the horizon, the three-sixty view of the sky, and the flashing-by perspective lines of already lush crop rows.

"Some of the most fertile soil on earth," Bel said.

"It's… It's awe-inspiring," Ally said from the back seat. "Like the ocean. The vastness and the motion and the timelessness."

Landis, behind the wheel, didn't disagree with their observations, but was more interested in the flat, straight road with decreasing traffic letting them make up time.

Drago was a small town that appeared to be undergoing a major revitalization of buildings from the past century or more. The sign outside town directing visitors to facilities belonging to the Zeke Tech corporation explained the revitalization. He remembered articles about Zeke Tech, a leader in the Northern Virginia tech surge, opening an operation in Illinois and offering employees the option to move to the quieter, cheaper, and less-busy area. Apparently, a good number took them up on the offer.

Instead of following signs toward Zeke Tech, they took the route through town to the town hall building, which housed the police department in the basement.

Not only were they meeting at the police station, but as it turned out, in the presence of a Drago police officer.

Natalie reached out to Ally and she reciprocated, bringing them into a teary-eyed hug.

They squeezed hard then released each other. As she wiped at her eyes, Natalie said, "This is my sister-in-law, Ally Northcutt. Ally, I'd like you to meet Darcie—" She hesitated.

"Barrett." The officer accompanied the fill-in by extending her hand to Ally, then Bel, then him.

The hesitation and the fill-in said Darcie Barrett was married, but used her maiden name professionally.

She had intelligent eyes and a tendency to smile.

"You come well-recommended," she said to Bel and him. "What, you don't think we have connections out here in the heartland? What do you think we do all winter? Anyway, we have a number of two- and three-degrees of separation connections. Plus, my husband has, uh, business in the Washington metro area and we have some connections that way, too. Talked to several.

"They say you're good detectives and essentially—" Her direct gaze came to Landis for the caveat. "—good guys. That's why I recommended Natalie talk to you. Though I encouraged her to have a lawyer here. She said she'd rather try it this way, with me. But if I think it's heading anywhere near where she should get a lawyer, I'm saying so."

"Of course," Ally said. "This is for information and Natalie's insight into family matters that I simply don't have."

It was about more than that, but Landis felt no obligation to say so, since Darcie clearly already knew that and had her friend's back.

He smiled smoothly and said, "Let's sit down and get comfortable."

He deliberately took a chair at the end of the rectangular table so there couldn't be a complete breakdown along East Coast/Midwest or—more important—questioners/answerer lines.

That became moot when Ally and Natalie sat next to each other on one side, while Bel and Darcie sat across from them.

"How are you, really, Ally?" Natalie rested her hand on Ally's arm as she asked that.

"I'm okay. Truly. It's ... I can see it's going to be okay. How are the kids?"

"Thriving and they'd love to see you sometime, so—"

"Sorry," Darcie said. "Hate to stop you two, hope you'll come back to visit for real sometime, Ally, but I know there's a tight timeline today. What do you need to ask Natalie, Ally?"

He appreciated Darcie moving this along. Her putting this solely on the basis of Ally asking the questions, not so much. But not enough to stop things before they started. See how it played.

"We—I was wondering about some of the dynamic in the family, before I came into it. What you recall of how David and Chad and their parents interacted."

The other woman subtly rolled her eyes. "Fraught. Always. They were all … touchy, especially about each other. It probably sounds like a typical outsider in-law, but it's the honest truth that David was a different man away from his family. Even he realized it. He chose to be the different man. It's why we weren't around the last year or so before he was killed. The happiest year of our marriage."

The same period when Ally had been realizing her marriage was not going to be what she had hoped for.

Ally made eye contact with him for an instant.

"Natalie, I hadn't met Chad yet when his father died and he would never talk about it. None of them—the Northcutts—would talk about it. Can you tell us about what happened?"

A sort of low current charge went through him. Had she read his mind? No. Stupid. Of course not. She knew what Willow said. It was the reason they'd come to Illinois. She'd followed the logic. Had nothing to do with any supposed connection between them.

There wasn't one.

If there ever had been it was long gone and buried.

"A heart attack."

"Was there anything … strange?"

"He didn't have any history and seemed very fit. I might not be a neutral party." Natalie exhaled slowly. "You know David's father was totally against his marrying me?"

"I heard that."

"Why?" Bel asked.

She glanced at him. "I wasn't police wife material. I came from the wrong stock. That's what he said. Not only no law enforcement background in my family, but a few lawyers. David said that's what really got his goat. And David would use it as a weapon against him. He'd goad him. I begged him not to, but… He and his father were always at knives drawn. As horrible as it is to say, I wondered if the interactions with the rest of his family would get better after he died."

"It didn't?" Bel asked.

"No. It was like… It was like his mother stepped up her game. Like she'd been restricted somehow with her husband around, but with him gone she could do whatever she wanted. And what she wanted was to be in every nook and cranny of David's life. Preferably—" Her mouth twisted. "—with me out of it. I was the fly in her ointment. Although that makes it sound more benign than it felt, than it was. The woman hated me."

"What about Chad?"

"He didn't deserve what happened to him."

"Nobody does," Ally said.

Natalie breathed out a sigh. "No."

They waited.

"Chad was a good kid. He was always a good kid at the core. Even when he wasn't a kid anymore."

Or good anymore?

"David always said Chad didn't get a square deal growing up. And things he did do weren't all his fault.

"He said they watched their father beat Iris about every week. Chad didn't remember any other sort of life at home before that. He thought it was normal. Until…" Natalie's head jerked slightly, as if an electrical impulse tweaked her neck. "Until their father was gone. But as far as Chad was concerned, that was marriage. Not the physical abuse, but—Unless—Ally, he didn't—?"

"He didn't," Ally confirmed. "Punches were not his weapon."

"David said he wouldn't. Still… Chad was baffled by David and me. Our marriage. To him, marriage was about distance. Not *giving himself away*. Maybe a power struggle, the way his parents' was.

"He never understood that toeing the line because you think you won't be loved if you don't isn't love at all, and not much of a life."

The tuck returned between Ally's brows.

"Yet for all that, he never had a problem with me. Chad adored David, David loved me, so I was okay with Chad. Until the kids and I were leaving. He did come the night before we left. He'd been drinking." She cut a look toward Ally. "You never knew, did you?"

"No."

"He called me every name under the sun. I don't know what might have happened if my uncle wasn't there. He's about six-five and burly. He came out to the driveway, where I was trying to talk Chad down, trying to keep him away from the house so the kids couldn't hear him, see him like that, and Uncle Olaf put me behind him, then he just stood there. Chad kept on for a while, but it must not have been satisfying to shout these things basically to Uncle Olaf's hairy arms crossed over his chest, getting no reaction at all."

"I'm so sorry he did that, Natalie."

"Nothing you could do about it."

"I married him." She closed her mouth tight. Breathed through her nose, then looked up to the other woman. "Did you know he cheated on me? No, no, don't feel sorry for me. In a way I'm grateful to him. It makes things so much tidier, clear-cut, provides an understandable reason for why I didn't love him, why I was going to—"

She cut it off, but neither Natalie nor Darcie had any trouble putting it together.

"We're holding on to that for our investigation," he said to the two Illinois women. "Please don't mention it outside this room."

"I won't," Natalie pledged. Darcie declined her head in a gesture of professional acknowledgment.

Bel took on the task of filling in the two women from Illinois. He even expanded his frequently telegraphic style to make it less staccato, while leaving enough out to draw a thoughtful look from Darcie Barrett.

In an almost detached voice, Ally said, "Chad might have cheated on me a lot, but for certain he had an ongoing girlfriend. She said Chad told her that he thought I had killed his father."

"*What?*"

Landis would stake his reputation that Natalie's shock was genuine.

He found himself liking her for her unmistakable disbelief that Ally could be guilty of such a thing.

"That's ridiculous. Not only does it make no sense because you would never—I can't even say it, it's so stupid. But there's also the fact that you didn't meet Chad until after David Senior died. Not to mention, Chad wouldn't ever say that, because—"

Her vehemence abruptly ran out of steam and, for the first time, Natalie Northcutt looked at the local police officer.

Without turning his head, his eyes went to the Drago officer. Darcie Barrett gave a small nod.

Natalie drew in another long breath.

"There was a night, maybe six months after their father died when Chad came over as we were about to go to bed. He'd been drinking. A lot. He was … agitated. David took him out on the patio and said I should go ahead and go to bed.

"They'd been talking a while, when Chad's voice rose. Not shouting, but the window was open some and it pulled me awake from a doze. I couldn't *not* listen.

"Chad told David he thought Iris might have killed their father.

"I remember sitting up in the bed, hugging my knees and holding my breath to hear what David would say. He didn't say Chad was crazy or anything else to show he didn't believe him. It was almost like he'd expected it. But he'd never said anything to me. Not a word, ever, and I couldn't believe…" She sucked in oxygen like a dry sob. Her voice dropped. "David told him to keep his mouth shut. That what mattered now was what it would do to all of them. If he wanted a career, he'd keep his mouth shut, because if he didn't, the shit would splash all over them.

"The next day, I asked David what Chad wanted to talk about. He said he was just drunk and rambling. David never said anything more about it to me and I didn't ask again.

"Then, when David died… He'd always been the center of their mother's world. As far as she was concerned when he died, he ascended into heaven and became the center of the universe. Yeah. I see that look. You're thinking it's the bitter daughter-in-law talking.

Maybe so. But it's also a mother who watched her mother-in-law trying to co-opt her children and subject them to the same indoctrination their father worked so hard to escape.

"If she'd been more subtle… But she wasn't and I'm grateful, because it pushed me out of the family, out of its shadow. All the way out of its shadow, here, halfway across the country. It's worked well for us, the kids and me."

"But Iris—" Ally bit it off.

"You think because I'm the closest thing to a child she has left that I have to be her mainstay? Not going to happen. I admit I thought about going and saying goodbye to Chad—to the kid I remember. Iris? I said goodbye to her a long time ago. And that's all I'm saying to her." Chin down, she peered at Ally from under her eyebrows. "Should be all you say to her, either.

"You did more than right by Chad. You can't help him anymore. Get away. Get out."

Would Chad's sister-in-law be so concerned about her welfare if she knew she'd been ready to walk out that day?

CHAPTER THIRTY-SEVEN

LANDIS FELT THE shift in Natalie Northcutt, the need to move away from that revelation, its possible implications, the worry that if she had asked the right question in the right way something might have been different somehow.

He doubted it. Certainly couldn't have changed her husband being hit by a drunk driver while he was on the side of the road giving a ticket to another drunk. And that his last act had been to push the drunk he'd stopped out of the way of the out-of-control car.

"But, really, it had to be Chad's grief and the alcohol talking. Chad was their father's golden boy. While it was the opposite with Iris. David hung the moon as far as she was concerned. Although—" She gave Ally a sympathetic look, "I heard that changed after we moved away."

"Not after David's death?" he asked.

"No," she said. "Initially it was like she transferred all she felt for David onto her grandchildren, especially our son. They'd always talked about him becoming law enforcement, being a *true* Northcutt, but after David died, it became … obsessive. That's why I took the kids and came here, where I have family."

Ally nodded. "That's when she concentrated on Chad."

"How did David and Chad get along?" Bel asked.

"Surprisingly well considering how their parents pitted them against each other. Chad adored David and David accepted it as his due." A fleeting smile crossed her face. "Though that was changing, don't you think, Ally?"

"Yes. David changed under your influence. He orbited around you and the kids instead of the Northcutt … cult."

Natalie pulled in a breath. "I thought of it that way, too, but never wanted to say it aloud."

"What about your interactions with and what do you know about the others in the Northcutt clan, beyond Iris and David Senior and their family?"

"There were a lot of them I never met. You must know the stories that Northcutts had been in law enforcement for generations." After Ally's confirming nod, a nod that swung her hair, Natalie said, "From the first, there were lots of brothers and cousins who went into the *family business.* They have annual family picnics. Big, sprawling gatherings at parks around the area."

"I never knew that," Ally said.

"No, because David's family—David's and Chad's—stopped going. They didn't interact socially with many of the ones they weren't as closely related to. I know it might sound silly, but there seemed to be a feeling that others were less Northcutts—*wanna-be Northcutts,* Iris called them—because they had different last names, because their mother or grandmother or however many times great had been a Northcutt.

"Iris was as rabid as David Senior, maybe more so, despite—as he reminded her—not being a blood Northcutt. I got the impression— this might be gossip…"

"Go ahead, Natalie," Ally urged her. Landis thought that for the moment she'd forgotten the investigation and, instead, was intent on filling in gaps from the years she'd been in a family she hadn't truly known.

"Well, the *impression* was that David Senior had a bad relationship with one of his more distant relations because the man advanced much more quickly than David Senior did. It was… silly, really, but he'd almost make it sound like he should have been promoted faster because he had the *purer* Northcutt bloodline. He became quite bitter about it."

"But Mark Senior and Preston?" Ally offered.

"Yes, they interacted with them." Enough wryness came through

Natalie's otherwise plain words to point out that they both had the surname Northcutt. "They're closely related, of course."

"What sort of careers did they have?" Landis asked.

"I don't know if he's retired yet, but Preston—"

Ally shook her head that he hadn't retired.

"—had done quite well by the time we left. But he was younger than David Senior. He wasn't direct competition. And Mark Senior never was direct competition because he wasn't in the game. He always seemed fine with wherever he was at the moment. When he retired and did some other jobs, he was fine with those, too, even when David Senior needled him about the jobs being beneath him."

"Their kids?"

"Mark's younger brother went west to school and has stayed out there." She gave a dry chuckle. "Became a lawyer, actually. Can you imagine? A Northcutt being a lawyer. And a sister in between is married and living in the Boston area. Seems nice. No involvement with law enforcement for her or her husband. Rachel is an only child. The apple of her father's eye. And vice versa, if that makes sense."

"So Mark Junior and Rachel are the only ones to go into the family business from those two branches of the family?" he asked. "What about their ambitions?"

"Right, the only two. Rachel is far, far more ambitious. As far as I know, also more capable. You know she was promoted—?" Their nods relieved her of further explanations. "Mark seems much more like his father. Easy going. From what David said, from earliest childhood Mark was always trying to catch up with David and Chad— both older than him. Never could. They'd leave him in the dust, is how David described it. But he'd pick himself up, smile, and keep plugging.

"I think… I hope David was becoming a kinder person than that. He'd watch our kids, who scrap like all kids, but are basically kind to each other, and he'd talk about how he and Chad were to each other, how they treated Mark, how they didn't even acknowledge Rachel, basically, and he had regrets. He said the best thing in his life was becoming independent from his parents."

"Because of you," Ally murmured.

"I hope so. Chad was becoming more independent, too," Natalie said.

"No." Ally's negative surprised Natalie and—he suspected—the three law enforcement representatives at the table, definitely including him, though none of them showed it. "He was… It was like he was trying to win over Iris. And criticizing David for not being around as much that year before David died won her favor."

As she spoke, Natalie started to nod. "I can see that happening. I can."

✧   ✧   ✧   ✧

THEY WERE WELL out of Drago on their way back to the airport when Bel spoke from the back seat.

"Convenient that she turned Willow's suspicion of her to her suspicion of Iris."

He recognized Bel's probing for pebbles in that comment.

"I believe her," Ally said.

"More reason than that you like her?" Landis asked.

"Yes." She paused. "Not that you—either of you—will like it much better."

"Don't let that stop you."

"I won't."

Bel gave her an approving look for her strong and fast response, though she couldn't see it with him seated behind her.

"It was another time Chad had been drinking." After the briefest hesitation, she said, "More than that. He was drunk. We'd been married less than a year. We were talking about having kids. This one night, he suddenly said, maybe we shouldn't because we'd be risking a kid getting some of his family genes.

"At first, I thought he was kidding and laughed about it. But he wasn't kidding and he wasn't laughing. He started muttering phrases, including getting away with murder and his mother. His *mother.* And he kept a distance from her—an emotional distance.

"But after David died and Natalie left with the kids, it was very different between him and his mother... I tried to ask about what he'd said about genes. Once. He talked about how he'd been wrong, totally wrong and if ever I had an idea to repeat what he'd said before I better get over it or he'd make my life miserable." She ducked her head. "Tuning into other people's feelings was never his strong suit. He didn't realize I already was miserable.

"Even without that, I believe Natalie."

He didn't question that this time, but waited.

"I painted her with the kids." Ally sounded almost dreamy. "When someone sits for you like that, you see—you can see what most don't."

He cut a look toward her. Her thoughts were elsewhere. Not thinking of sketching him in charcoal.

One side of her mouth lifted in a half grin. "Especially with two rambunctious toddlers."

They drove through the warm sunshine for several more miles.

He checked the rear-view mirror and saw Bel staring out the passenger window as if searching for mountains made of pebbles in the plains landscape.

"Natalie was right about Iris hating her," Ally said abruptly. "She still does. Possibly even more than she hates me, because Natalie took the kids away. Though it evens out, because I've been right there in front of her, reminding her that I was alive and healthy, while her son was ... was not."

She slid her hand up, then down the diagonal of her shoulder seatbelt.

"What else?" Bel's question came evenly, unrushed from the back seat.

She breathed out. When she started talking, though, she didn't hesitate. "There was a time after Natalie and the kids moved away when I heard Chad and his mother talking about going after them, about taking the kids. Rachel was there, too, and I think Iris saw our reactions and she shut him up fast.

"There was coolness between them and Rachel for a while."

"That's what was going on when he was shot?" he asked.

"No, that was different. A captain in Rachel's division died suddenly. They shuffled things, moved people up, and the upshot was Rachel got a promotion. Chad hated that she outranked him.

"She never said a word about it, but he was jealous. At the second-to-last family Sunday brunch, he basically accused her of sleeping her way up the ladder. Then the fight the next week was even more out in the open. That's why they weren't talking at the time he was shot. But they did before that and then they'd get past it. Like when Chad and Iris talked about taking the kids.

"I couldn't believe they were serious at first, but I saw that Rachel did believe they were. She tried to josh him out of it, but he didn't listen.

"When we were alone, I told Chad he couldn't do that. He started ranting at me, but when I said if he was really concerned about the Northcutt name, he wouldn't do something that would surely connect it to crimes, that he couldn't possibly think that they could steal a boy from his mother—because they weren't interested in his niece—then raise him openly to be a Northcutt and *not* get caught and arrested. And if the idea was to take his nephew and hide away somewhere and change their name from Northcutt, what was the point? And if he didn't believe me, he should check the laws and the consequences.

"I talked and talked and talked. I had no idea if I'd made any impression on him. Not until a few days later when Iris started railing about the criminal justice system giving all the rights to mothers and punishing grandmothers and uncles. The only reason she'd do that is if Chad told her they couldn't kidnap her grandson with impunity."

"They had to know—" Landis started to protest.

"Not when they got lost inside the Northcutt cocoon. You have no idea. Did you notice when Natalie hesitated? It wasn't about David's father beating their mother. It was *after* she told us that."

She stalled. She shifted, adjusting the seatbelt again.

"She hesitated when she talked about David Senior's death. And... And Chad saying his mother might have done it."

"Did he ever say that to you?"

"No." She glanced toward him, then away. "In his sleep he said things a couple times that... But he was asleep. Dreaming. And I might have misunderstood."

They drove a couple more miles, into heavier traffic now, before Bel said. "You're right, Ally. Can't take any of that for gospel. Still, interesting it was on his mind."

AT THE AIRPORT, they picked up a quick meal. Boarding, he again played the longer legs card to get the aisle seat.

He congratulated himself for the forethought when Ally fell asleep and her head tipped onto Bel's shoulder.

CHAPTER THIRTY-EIGHT

"**WHAT ARE YOU** doing?"

Ally's words didn't surprise him, because he'd heard her soft foot-steps coming down the stairs. He had more warning than he'd had with Belichek this morning, but more at stake, too.

He'd breathed out when his peripheral vision registered that she wore a zipped-up hoodie over a t-shirt and lounging pants.

A negligee would not have done this tentative truce any good.

He'd brought his copy of the file Schmidt gave them and a large paper map he'd had an aide find for him, spreading them over the desk in the little office off Jamie's living room.

Looking for inspiration, but not waiting for it.

Thinking.

"Going back over the case," he said.

She looked at the map, clearly identifying what area it covered. "Chad's shooting."

"Right." It was the moment he would say something sharp, some-thing about now that she'd stopped stonewalling because she'd gotten over thinking he shot her husband they could get on with trying to solve it. He didn't. "It's still what we can look into best. Fairlington's occupied with the courthouse shooting. Piscattoway has this way in its rear-view mirror. Leaves us room."

"Even with the break-in at the house Tuesday?"

He huffed. "Maybe that perked up Piscattoway's interest. On the other hand, they haven't followed up on it, come back to talk to you or any of the rest of us."

"No, they haven't." She looked down at the map "Any insights?"

"Not blinding, but yeah. Had to be somebody who knew the area."

"Why?"

"Working backward, because of where the car was found. Someone knew the perfect spot for it to burn in peace. And not many people would have reason to know about the spot. The few locals all checked out with PCPD and they were double-checked by the state police. J.D. found that out for us."

He saw her quick uptake of what that doublechecking meant.

Her gaze came up to his. "You're thinking it might have been someone in law enforcement."

"Or a forest ranger."

Her mouth shifted in a grimace. "Chad might have known a forest ranger or two, but the odds…"

"Yeah. Weighted toward law enforcement. Someone who knew when and where Chad would be. Someone who knew how to find a car with deeply tinted windows. Someone who didn't take the risk of involving anyone else. The driver was the killer. No distribution of duties. Someone who drove from where the car was stolen to your house, then your house to the burn site without more than a few blurs showing up on any camera. And then, *poof.* Nothing caught on cameras anywhere around the burn site, just like there hadn't been when the car was stolen."

She frowned. "But how did the killer get to the car to steal it, then away after setting it on fire. He or she had to have transportation."

"Ah. Now you're thinking like a detective."

"Or a criminal," she shot back. He liked it. "Were the two locations near each other?"

"Twenty-, twenty-five-minute drive."

"As the crow flies?"

He shifted the map.

After he'd pointed out the spots, she said, "Not as long a drive from the house to either of those spots as from where it was stolen to where it was burned. Like the driver was trying to keep the time to a minimum."

"That's right."

"But nothing on any cameras? The routes go past areas with lots of shops, places I'd expect security."

"The direct routes would go places like that."

"You think he—"

"Or she. Your neighbor couldn't tell if it was a man or a woman. Dressed to obscure, head and face covered, and too fast."

"I know. She must have apologized to me every time I've seen her since. It was amazing she saw anything. And to remember that partial plate…"

"Good witness," Tanner agreed.

"Got it." Ally looked up with her eyes aglow with intensity. "Each spot's within a couple miles of a Metro station, but neither's a direct route. Zigzagging through apartment complexes to get to the car to steal it. Then, from the burn site, going through that wooded area and across the highway."

"Well-spotted. Though there's a deep culvert between the far side of the wooded area and the highway."

"How do you know that?"

He shrugged.

She answered herself. "Because you've tried it." Then she tacked on a question. "Anything someone in good shape couldn't do?"

"No."

"Uh-huh. And the person could look like a casual jogger or walker for most of the trip?"

"Yep. As long as he or she wasn't carrying a lot of bulky stuff."

"Like what?"

He shrugged "Tools. Accelerant."

"The car had its own accelerant, didn't it? Gas tank."

"Yeah. Can't be sure if anything else was used because it burned so thoroughly. A car fire you catch fast—But that one burned through everything. They tried afterward. State police even disassembled the car to see if there was anything, anything at all. A fiber caught, maybe. Nothing."

"So the car doesn't tell us anything."

"Wouldn't say that. It told us this wasn't spur of the moment. Those locations don't leap right out at you, especially the burn site. So, this is a planner. A thorough, careful planner. Even if the car hadn't burned out, I don't see this guy leaving any trace." He tipped his head to the map, her gaze following. "Also someone who knew the area well. Two dissimilar parts of the county. Known intimately."

"True."

He waited.

She lifted her head. "Like the shooter in Fairlington?"

"The indicators aren't as strong. Could be someone who did careful reconnoitering."

"Same sort of slipping in and out, apparently without being seen."

"Yes."

She frowned. "But why come after me in Fairlington?"

"Interesting question."

"And, especially, now? If they thought I knew something—and if they did, they didn't know Chad well or the dynamics of our marriage. But anyway, if this person did mistakenly think I knew something, or thought I was a danger to them, or even wanted revenge because they held me responsible for Chad being shot, why not right after Chad was shot?"

He said nothing as she considered her own words. Her head jerked up.

"Someone knew Chad's condition had taken a turn for the worse? His dying was going to change things? That's why you wanted to know about the will. But it was what we expected, so how does his dying change things? *How?*"

"Don't know. Don't know if that's the answer, either. It's a possibility. That's all."

She dropped back against the chair back, rubbing her eyes. "Too many possibilities. How do you ever sort them all out?"

"Keep moving forward. Eliminating some, reinforcing a few, adding new ones."

"God, maybe Chad was right about me."

Tanner clenched his jaw to keep from saying he didn't believe

Chad Northcutt had been right about her or for her or to her.

"I don't have a mind for police work. He always said I was too arty. Too unconnected to reality."

"Bullshit. It's not that I'm pushing you about continuing art—"

"You are." She softened it with half a smile. "But why? Why would you care that I gave up a hobby and—"

"That was no hobby."

"You can't know—"

"I know. From seeing your painting at Jamie's. From hearing you talk about it. Not a hobby. Put away—some of it—because you thought you had to in order to make a go of your marriage, but no damned hobby."

Toeing the line because you think you won't be loved if you don't isn't love at all, and not much of a life.

He heard Natalie's voice saying the words. He thought Ally might be hearing them again, too.

She pushed into a spate of words.

"Well, that's kind, but if that's why you're pushing me, you can let it go, Landis. Even if Chad wasn't a fan of me painting, I made the decision. He didn't like the mess and the smell and my distraction when I was painting, but it was my choice to pack it up and put it in storage. And it felt good. He was happy about it. Felt it showed I was truly committed to him and the marriage and for a while, things were … better. Besides, if I'd truly wanted to paint, I could have taken those things out of storage years ago and set up the spare room the way it was before there was any thought it might be a nursery someday. But I haven't."

She had her wall up and fortified. He went another direction.

"Get back to your arrangements to leave Chad. Give me the details."

That surprised her. "Why?"

"As Bel puts it, that's when the dominos started to fall."

She considered that for a long moment.

"I researched leaving. Basic things. I—"

"How'd you keep him from knowing what you were planning?"

Her eyes widened slightly.

He didn't wait for her to ask how he knew. "He was a controller. Isolated you from your family, friends. No way he wouldn't track your phone, email, Internet usage, including searches."

She didn't confirm it. But he saw what it had done to her.

"He did it, Ally. You didn't. Do not take on guilt for what he did."

"I let him."

"No, you didn't. Not anymore than someone *lets* a thief take their car. He was a thief, too. An accomplished one."

"Of my self-respect? My independence? My backbone? Is that what you're saying?"

"No. You have all those things. What were you getting ready to do that day? Leave. Because he hadn't succeeded in taking those away. So how did you keep him from knowing what you were planning?"

"I went to the library. Different libraries so nobody got used to seeing me. Had real errands nearby, then I'd go in a side or a back door to the library. Never more than half an hour. I'd finish up with other searches. And when I was leaving I looked for people to offer my seat to. Another layer of covering my tracks. People doing genealogy were the best. They never cared what someone else had been searching for. They wanted to get right to their searches."

"Smart. All of it."

"I wouldn't have thought of the things in the articles, on the websites, though. About if the person was in law enforcement and all the tools he had. The searches he could do. That he would know the addresses of the women's shelters, even though they're kept secret from the public.

"I considered one in D.C. or Virginia, but he'd still have connections with law enforcement anywhere in the region, farther. And going to one in Virginia… If he'd thought Jamie or Maggie helped me… I planned to text them both when I was a mile from the house, tell them I was okay, tell them I was going to be out of touch for a while, but not to worry."

"Yeah, that would have worked. Neither of them would've given it a second thought," he said dryly.

That left corner of her mouth quirked. "They would have been pissed as hell at me for not going to them, but neither would have tried to find me because they've both dealt with it in their professions and they'd know how Chad could have ridden on the coattails of any search they did."

"If you were going to text them right after leaving, he wouldn't have had to. You don't think he knew about your phone usage in real time? Probably had a handful of tracking apps on your phone in case you found one, in case others stopped working."

"Not from my regular phone. That would've stayed at the house. I'd already figured that. But there were a lot of things I didn't figure out on my own. About getting a couple burner phones, bought at different times, different places. But still using my regular phone enough to not arouse his suspicions."

He didn't raise an eyebrow or add a question to his look.

Still, she said, "Yeah, I'm sure he was keeping track of me through my phone. And I also called a few new people to give him something to do. To not suspect…"

As she let the word slide away, he watched her remembering, perhaps reliving the moments of deciding to go, learning how, putting the plan into action. And having it end.

She cleared her voice. "I also learned about setting up a new identity beforehand and not doing everything on the same day or even in the same month so pieces of the new identity wouldn't be easy for him to string together. After I researched, it took me more than six months to put things together. A new name. A bank account in that name. Small deposits. Building it up, giving it a real history. Different kinds of clothes and shoes. Even a different voice. A driver's license. I was only going to stay there a few days, but I wanted that transition place to be a dead end. In case…"

"In case he picked up your trail."

That she didn't respond to. Not directly. "I don't remember anything else."

"We'll work on that."

He took her back to the start. Took her through one by one. When she said that was all, he asked questions, starting runs of memories. Short ones. One or two longer ones.

He didn't know if it got them anywhere. Never did until an investigation is over.

It did impress him with her preparations.

"That's it, Tanner. I swear that's it. You've pulled every single thing out of me—"

"Except where you were going."

"—that I did."

"You really weren't going to go to your cousins."

"No." Her voice dropped at that.

"Thought you'd disappear from their lives, too?"

Her silence said yes.

"Thought you'd keep them safer that way."

More *yes* in this silence.

"You were wrong, because they would have kept trying to find you. And the more worried they got the less cautious they'd be. Maggie alone would have had Chad Northcutt by the throat in no time flat. And that was before Carson was around to exercise his calming effect on her."

"Jamie—"

"Jamie would have told Maggie not to kill him—until after they had the information they needed from him."

She opened her mouth to refute what he'd said.

She closed it.

Satisfied, he prepared to ask more.

Until she proved she wasn't cowed, after all.

"You've been asking all the questions, now it's my turn."

Half amused, he said, "Have at it."

SHE DIDN'T NEED a second invitation. As a matter of fact, she wouldn't have waited even if he hadn't offered the first one.

"The judge—Judge DaSilva—likes you."

He regarded her warily.

"Would the other woman, the one Bel talked to, say nice things like the judge did?"

"No."

"Why?"

"Hell, Ally."

"I'm serious. Why?"

"I was an asshole. Is that what you wanted to hear?"

"No. I want to know the truth."

"We saw each other, started talking. I knew she was married, no kids, not her first time at this. Said she just wanted a change from her marriage. No strings. Then she wanted strings. All kinds of strings. Talking about leaving her husband, us moving in together, more."

"What did you do?"

"I said hell no."

She stared at him.

"I pulled back. She swore I lied, led her on. When I said she knew I didn't she swore she loved me. Going back and forth, back and forth from one swearing to another. I told her it was over. She wouldn't … It was like one second she hadn't heard me, the next she was angry. Beyond angry. I said she needed to talk to somebody. That really set her off. I cut it off hard. Even then, she didn't let go."

"Sounds like she was indulging in magical thinking." She saw that knocked him off his stride, which pleased her. "When you said you wished for snow so you didn't have to go to school, then your parents had a car wreck, it was more than totaling the car, wasn't it?"

"What? You're thinking childhood trauma? That's going to put all the pieces together of the Tanner Landis puzzle?"

Acid edged his words. Did he know how much of his smooth he'd lost?

"It's not like they died. Dad only missed a couple days of work. Mom was laid up longer, but got out of the hospital after a few days and then she was home—some PT, eventually, so—"

"Who took care of you while she was recovering enough to start physical therapy?"

"Aunt Erica."

"How old were you?"

"Eight."

"Do you have siblings?"

"Yes."

Even as he clipped the word, she saw he regretted it. He recognized it sounded like he was avoiding talking about this, which he thought made a lot bigger deal out of it than he meant to.

He was right.

Voluntarily, he added, "One older sister and younger brother."

"Must have been difficult for you all … and for your aunt?"

"We barely made a dent at Aunt Erica's. She had her two and her husband's one from previous marriages, then twins together."

And he was there, amid all of them, thinking it was his fault his parents were hurt. Safe, fed, loved, but his magical thinking—his guilt—invisible to all. "How long before you were all back home?"

"No idea. Couple weeks maybe. Kids don't track stuff like that."

"Tanner, something like that for a kid, taking on the responsibility for what wasn't his fault, that can be traumatic."

"Bull. It happened, it passed. Mom's still around, doing great. Her and dad. I've seen kids with trauma—real trauma—from what happens in their families. A car accident and a few months of routine being shifted around during recovery is not it."

"You won't talk to me—I understand that—but you need to talk to somebody about closing people out. Bel, another friend, a priest, a professional. Somebody."

"Did I hear my name?" Belichek asked from the bottom of the stairs. "Do you two realize it will be morning soon? And Ally has a couple long, hard days ahead of her."

—DAY 6—

SUNDAY

CHAPTER THIRTY-NINE

TODAY'S VISITATION WAS officially an evening event, followed the next day—taking up most of the day—by the procession from the funeral home, the funeral, procession to the graveside, the graveside service, and then a reception.

But the visitation actually started in the mid-afternoon.

They returned to the house in Piscattoway County in the morning to give Ally a chance to prepare, with Jamie's parents planning to join them in time for the visitation.

Her day included final consultations with the police department officials in charge of the funeral events. Jamie accompanied her to Iris' house for the meeting.

He and Bel were out back, in that one spot not visible to observers. This time they'd dragged over a bench from the patio while they read reports Palery had forwarded them.

They could be summed up as *Still nothing.*

Nothing on the forensics, nothing from video, nothing from witnesses, including the homeless woman Terrington hadn't found. Make that nothing useable from witnesses. A number of called-in tips had highlighted suspicious characters lurking around. Each was reviewed through video.

At least one bit of comic relief came from that—one of the suspicious characters turned out to be a Fairlington County Board member, a renowned grandstander.

"Wish I'd been in the office to hear the lines about that," Landis said, closing the last report.

Bel had finished a minute before him and was staring at a tuft of grass at his feet.

"Yeah. Ally looked sad."

Another of Belichek's changes of topic.

Landis knew what he was in for. But maybe this time, he directed the conversation instead of playing defense. Especially since he was damned sure his partner had heard Ally's words.

You need to talk to somebody. Bel, another friend, a priest, a professional.

Wasn't talking to a professional. Nor a priest. Didn't have *another* friend. That left Bel.

Supposed it made sense, since his partner had been trying to psychoanalyze and exorcise him since this thing started.

"She's got this idea I had a screw loose."

"Had?"

"Hah."

"About women?"

"No," he said harshly. He deliberately lightened the next words. "That accident my folks were in when I was a kid, for Pete's sake. I told you about staying with my aunt while Mom recovered. Ally thinks that was a hardship for me, which is crazy. Mom was back to a hundred percent and my aunt's a champ."

"Uh-huh."

"Trauma for God's sake. You know my family…"

"I do. Good people. Like them a lot."

"Even though Mom teases you about your dimples?"

"Even though. Never understood why you hold them at a distance."

Tanner jerked. "I don't hold them at a distance. I get along with them fine."

"When was the last time you visited them?"

"Last year. You've forgotten going out to dinner with them?"

"That was them visiting you, not you visiting them. You haven't gone home as long as I've known you. Your siblings do. Whole family together—except you."

"We don't have exactly a nine to five job."

"Other people in homicide manage visits home. Not every holiday, but some. And you made time to see my Gran before she passed. One of the few people you didn't hold at a distance, including your family."

"I don't—"

"You do. Not as bad with them, maybe, as you do with most people."

He chuckled. "Oh, c'mon, this from the guy who's been after me about getting too close to too many women? What—"

"Sex. Totally different. In fact, you use sex to keep them at a distance." He cocked his head. "Except Mags. Maybe because you had no choice there. I'd've killed you if you went after Mags. Not to mention she's as good at the distance-holding as you are—she *was* as good. Until her stint in the mountains, J.D., and getting involved more with her cousins.

"Only person I ever saw cut through it with you was my Gran. She wouldn't let you pull any of your stiff-arm tricks. Had the advantage that you were nosy about me. I wore you down for her by not satisfying your curiosity."

"You're saying your silences have been a plot all along to get me to reveal myself?"

"No. A beneficial side effect."

"Didn't think you were that clever."

"Wasn't that interested," Bel shot back.

He laughed. At ease now.

Then Bel pulled the rug out from under him. "She's right you know. Ally. Should've put it together myself. Don't let anybody too close, then you can't get too hurt if something happens to them. Maybe it's not all self-centered, either. Maybe you're concerned you'll hurt them. Don't let them in and everybody rolls along. Safe. But not happy. Is that what happened with Ally when you two met?"

"I told you. Nothing happened. She was involved—engaged. I moved on."

Bel studied him.

"Uh-huh."

He would not ask uh-huh what. He knew better.

What he should do was walk away.

He didn't implement that plan in time.

"She went away, too. You shut down more, shut out more. Sex, yeah, but nothing permanent. Intended it to be nobody who could expect anything like commitment from you—more important, anybody you could ever expect or hope would commit to you. You slipped up some lately. Judge DaSilva in one direction—a good person, who accepted your limits, but far more dangerous professionally. But Rhonda Quesey, now that was a major mistake. You're definitely slipping, Landis."

"This is all—"

"Bullshit. Yeah, I've heard that opinion from you before. Ally, me, we're totally wrong about you. Okay, Tanner, but what if we're not?"

"You are. Enough of this crap. Let's get to something worthwhile. Our jobs. Like always. When there's not a next step, we go back to the beginning. That's those dominos starting to fall, that's Chad getting shot. The task force not finding anything after that doesn't mean there wasn't anything there. The consensus was Chad wasn't smart enough to stay invisible. That's one possible reason for him to be shot. Getting rid of the loose lips, tightening up the operation."

For half a beat, he wondered if Bel would revert to the previous topic.

Then his partner offered, "Straight falling out among thieves or taking out Chad was the goal and they didn't care about picking up the activity."

"Possible. But why take out Chad?"

"Need to know more about him to see if there's an answer there. Partners."

Landis rolled his eyes. "You're going to say nobody knew him better than his partner. That's your misguided ego talking."

Bel didn't rise to that bait. "No ego about it. Partners don't know everything. They do know stuff no one else does. Amount of time spent together. High pressure. Way minds work. Happens whether the partners want it to or not," he said telegraphically and edging too close to the previous topic. "But there's another kind of knowing. When you let someone else know you. Choose it. Participate in it. Reciprocate."

After a beat of silence, he added, "Jamie," as if Landis needed that clarification for where this had come from.

"You have to choose," Bel added.

Landis hadn't needed that clarification, either.

"So, in addition to talking to the various partners, we work Ally to get what she might have held back. You this time, for a different angle."

"Tanner—"

"But we start with the partners, because we'll have them all available at the visitation today and the funeral tomorrow."

Bel's protest stopped dead. "Fine. We talk to the partners."

▬▬▬▬▬▬

PISCATTOWAY COUNTY POLICE DEPARTMENT

ADDRESS: 1567 Gardington Rd.
REASON FOR CALL: Report of officer shot
RESPONDING OFFICER: Det. T. Wamdler

EVENTS:
At approximately 6 hours 57 minutes on November 4th, the PCPD received a call reporting a shooting had occurred in the driveway of 1567 Gardington Rd., the home of PCPD Officer Chad Northcutt. The caller said the victim was Officer Northcutt.

PCPD uniformed officers were dispatched. Upon their arrival, the officers secured the scene. Among the initial arriving officers were F. Brentford and T. Nevens. They confirmed the identity of the victim. They received an explanation from witnesses that a dark-colored sedan driving northbound on Gardington Rd. had driven across the lawn and intercepted Chad Northcutt as he approached his own vehicle in the driveway. The driver shot Chad Northcutt twice, then the sedan returned to the street, continuing northbound.

Officers Brentford and Nevens briefed their supervisor Sgt. Tucker. Sgt. Tucker contacted Sgt. Roming of Major Crimes Bureau and requested the detectives respond. The shooting was reported under PCPD Event #PC180605-1243.

At approximately 8 hours 14 minutes, I, Det. Wamdler, and Det. Vanderoff arrived at Piscattoway County Hospital to which Chad Northcutt had been transported. We were informed his condition was critical.

We were escorted to a private waiting room where Allison Northcutt, wife of Chad Northcutt, and Iris Northcutt, mother of Chad Northcutt, were with Officer Nevens. We asked the officer to take Iris Northcutt out of the room so we could interview Allison Northcutt. Iris Northcutt refused to leave, saying this was where the doctors would come first with information on Chad Northcutt's condition. Det. Vanderoff and I escorted Allison Northcutt to a private office nearby.

Det. Vanderoff and I sat down with Allison Northcutt and recorded her statement. Below is a summation of her statement and not verbatim.

She said Chad Northcutt had not awakened her that morning. She heard him leaving the house at approximately 6 hours 45 minutes or 6 hours 50 minutes, his usual time for the shift he was scheduled for that day. She said she heard a vehicle accelerating, then the sound of two shots. She ran toward the front door. She heard Iris Northcutt, who lives across the street at 1560 Gardington Rd., screaming, as Allison Northcutt opened the front door. She saw Chad Northcutt on the driveway of 1567 Gardington Rd., bleeding from the head. She said he was not moving. She called 911 to report the shooting.

She said she had not spoken with her husband since the previous morning (November 3rd) when he left for work at approximately 6 hours 45 minutes. She said she was in bed when she heard him arrive home at approximately 1 hour 30 minutes of November 4th.

She said she had no idea who could have shot her husband. She could not think of any enemies that he might have. He had not spoken to her of difficulties or conflict on-duty or off-duty.

She provided no additional information.

Det. Vanderoff and I left Allison Northcutt in the office with Officer Nevens and interviewed Iris Northcutt in the waiting room. She consented to have her statement digitally recorded. Below is a summation of her statement and not verbatim.

Iris Northcutt said she was in the kitchen of her residence at 6 hours 40 minutes. The kitchen window looks out on the street and across the street to 1567 Gardington Rd. She said she frequently sees Chad Northcutt departing for work and they wave to each other on those occasions. Today, she had not yet seen him exit 1567 Gardington Rd., when she turned away to make coffee. She needed additional coffee and went to her pantry for it. While there, she added to her shopping list for that day. She approximated five or six minutes passed in these activities. As she left the pantry, she heard the sound of a vehicle accelerating, but "did not think anything of it." She began to prepare the coffee. She heard the vehicle slam on its brakes, then two shots, slightly spaced. She ran to the kitchen window and saw a person lying on the driveway.

She ran outside and across the street. She recognized her son. She provided a general description of the vehicle as a dark-colored sedan with Maryland plates.

Evidence Techs who had reported to the hospital, removed the blood-stained clothing of each witness and gave them scrubs to wear. Allison Northcutt cooperated. Iris Northcutt objected strenuously. She complied only when retired Sgt. Orlington (former partner of deceased officer David Northcutt Sr., who was married to Iris Northcutt) arrived and persuaded her.

Informed that Chad Northcutt had gone into surgery, which was expected to last for several hours, I instructed the Evidence Techs to secure all of his clothing and possessions for processing. Det. Wamdler and I left for the scene.

At 1567 Gardington Rd., we observed additional Evidence Techs processing the scene, including taking impressions of tire tracks. We issued a BOLO for the vehicle as described by Iris Northcutt.

The neighborhood canvass produced one neighbor who claimed to see the car from three houses away. She claims the driver was muffled in a scarf and jacket, preventing her from identifying gender or other details. She claims she did see the driver lean over Chad Northcutt after the second shot and appear to take something from inside his jacket.

Iris Northcutt, shown an inventory of Chad Northcutt's possessions, said nothing was missing. Allison Northcutt concurred.

The statement by the neighbor and others is included in the canvass results below.

ADDENDUM November 7th.
Interviews of Chad Northcutt's fellow officers reveal no motive for his shooting.
BOLO added detail, per witness statement.

ADDITIONAL UNITS ON SCENE:
Asst. Chief A. Paglia #
District Cmndr S. Longe #
Det. Sgt. C. King
Det. D. Rodgers
Det. R. Sanders
Det. V. Ludlow
Lt. P. Northcutt
Sgt. R. Northcutt

Officers:
M. Northcutt Senior
F. Brentford
E. Paulz
D. Selton
E. Tancroft
S. Wuertl
PIO Officer E. Anderson

CHAPTER FORTY

"**NOT MUCH TIME** before the visitation. We'll need to change and get going," Jamie said.

In other words, not much time for repairs to the damage done by their time spent with Iris, Ally thought.

Jamie had run her hands through her hair several times. Ally felt as if she had taken a couple steps back toward numb.

That didn't improve when Greta emerged from the house as they walked up the sidewalk. She waved to the photographers behind the police tape and turned Ally toward them by the arm.

"Mother—"

"Did you talk to that nice young man earlier?"

"Tanner?"

"Not him. I mean the *nice* young man who came looking for you."

"What nice young man?"

"You know. I'm sure he caught up with you or he'd have come back. He said he would, and then I could have given him the brochures on the garden he forgot to take with."

"When was this?"

"Yesterday. No, the day before. Just after I called you and you said you had a meeting to go to, while I stayed over here with nothing to do and no company except—"

"Jamie, go get Tanner and Bel," she said in an undertone. "Mom, let's go inside now. Wouldn't you like a drink of water? I would."

✧ ✧ ✧ ✧

"… **AND SO** interested in what we're doing to reclaim the land. The younger generation cares about these things. If only the so-called adults would."

"Who was this, Mrs. Lindell?" Bel asked.

"I said already," Greta said. "He was asking about the garden. Very well informed and so interested—"

"A member of the media?"

"I wouldn't think so. Far too young. Although he showed more wherewithal and enterprise than any number of so-called journalists who have come to do interviews or photo shoots at the gardens entirely unprepared. All they want is to get in and out in the shortest amount of time possible, instead of doing a thorough job of understanding so they can educate the masses."

"The poor, unwashed masses," Maggie said under her breath.

"But this guy had done his homework?" Bel's persistence could be annoying. It also could be prescient. Landis listened more closely.

"Yes, he had. And he had genuine interest. Whenever the conversation drifted toward other things, he brought it back to the gardens."

Ally shook her head. Short and quick, an apparently involuntary reaction to her mother's words. The reaction matched Landis' impression that Greta Frye Moban Lindell was the one who always brought the conversation back to her gardens.

"That can happen with conversations, can't it?" Bel said. "What sort of drifts did it follow, before he brought it back to the gardens?"

"Unimportant things. Trivialities."

"Such as?" Bel's insistence was mild, but solid enough that Greta seemed to recognize she wasn't going to get around it.

"Unreliable computers. Traffic. Navigation software that insisted you remember the precise address, when getting in the vicinity that should be good enough. Like what hundred block of a street."

Landis slowly, slowly turned toward the woman. He didn't want to spook her.

He didn't need to ask the question. Bel did, in the same unhurried, lulling voice. "Must have used an example to explain that. Like Main or Maple or—"

"Narragansett."

Behind him, Landis was aware of small movements, like jerks of muscles as others squelched reactions.

"Why Narragansett?" Bel asked, smooth as ever.

"It just came to me. Seventeen hundred block of Narragansett. Odd I remember that. Of course there's the *malus Narragansett*. A crab apple. Though I don't believe I saw it when I was at the Arboretum."

"He was interested in crab apples?"

"No." She clicked her tongue. "We did not discuss crab apples. Particularly that hybridization, because I don't believe it would be hardy for my gardens' location. The combination of the overall elevation, yet sitting in a natural bowl formation can allow more extreme frost than one would expect."

"I'll bet," he said with convincing sympathy. "What was he interested in, in addition to your gardens?"

She looked blank.

Ally had partially turned toward her. Landis was aware of her sharply breathing in through her nose.

Bel remained as patient as ever. "Did he ask you about the gardens right off?"

"Oh, that. No. He approached Allison's father first, who was, as always, in far too much of a hurry to concern himself about anyone else on the planet and their interests. I had heard him tell Allison's father that he must have just missed you—you and Detective Landis. That he'd been sent after you, but only had the address here to meet you. And he didn't know what would happen to him if he had to go all the way back to the police station and admit he'd missed you. Allison's father couldn't be bothered, of course, but I called him over because I felt sorry for the young man—boy, really. I even said something about that, how he seemed far, far too young to me to be a police officer and he got red and sort of laughed and said he was merely part of an auxiliary unit that supported the detectives and he hated to have missed you and fail in his mission.

"Allison's father rudely tried to interrupt, but I told the young man the seventeen hundred block of Narragansett was where you were and he had plenty of time to catch up with you there because the person you were meeting wasn't going to be there for two hours. And when I told him about *malus Narragansett* that, naturally, led to a wider discussion of plants and my gardens. He asked excellent questions. Really, quite intelligent. And when he left, he asked for all the contact information for the gardens, as well as my phone number because he said—" She preened a bit. "—he couldn't imagine seeing them without the benefit of my insight."

Jamie exchanged a look with Bel, then sat beside Greta on the upholstered chairs that faced the front window, tossing her questions about the gardens, distracting her.

Bel jerked his head toward the back of the house. The others followed.

"He could have hacked her phone."

Ally closed her eyes. "He socially engineered her. No need to hack. No one could be easier to socially engineer. Just listen to her talk about gardens and she's putty."

"He knows how to play women. Mother figures," J.D. said thoughtfully.

"Crap." Landis spun around, heading back to the living room.

He interrupted Greta's monologue about Japanese beetles.

"Mrs. Lindell, what did this kid—young man—look like?"

"Well, really, I didn't pay att—"

"Aunt Greta, you're so observant and you talked to this nice young man for a while. I know you remember," Jamie said. "Did he have dark hair or light hair?"

"Closer to dark. Definitely not blonde. With some auburn in it."

"That's great. His eyes?"

"Brown. Definitely brown. Not that flat all-dark brown, but with some variation in it like the trunk of the—"

"And how tall was he?"

"Really, Jamie, how could I—?"

"Was he eye-level with you when you talked?" Landis inserted.

"Oh, that's interesting. Somewhat taller than me, I think, though I didn't need to crane my neck to converse with him."

"What kind of build, Aunt Greta? Chubby or—"

"Skinny but soft." Landis turned for the back of the house again. "I saw him. Bel, he was at the airport when we were leaving. He was watching Ally."

"But why would a kid—?"

Bel, with his phone out, had already reached the back door to outside and the rest followed.

Ally's eyes widened. "How did he know we were going to the airport? Mother didn't. Did he hack—?"

"No need. He could have followed you to the airport," Maggie said.

Landis was grim. "To do that he had to know where we started from."

"Or followed you from Willow Spencer's."

"He didn't," Bel said. "But I wasn't looking for a tail on the way to the airport. Yeah," he said into his phone. "Eddy? What are you working on? ... Drop it. That call from the seventeen hundred block of Narragansett we made Friday? We've got more on it. Landis will give you a description."

ALLY, YOU NEED to get changed." Jamie, having left Greta in the living room, nudged her cousin toward the bedroom hall. "Bel and Landis can be late, but you can't."

Ally took a step in the right direction while asking, "But why would a kid come after me? I don't recognize anyone from that description. Certainly not anyone connected to Chad."

"If we can track him through the security cameras around Willow Spencer's building, we'll worry about why later," Landis said.

"But you said the license plate number was covered."

"Eddy Knarr and Felicia Ewer are tracking both forward and back. Forward to see where he went after trying to run you down and back to see where he came from. They already know both the front and back plates were covered, so that was no accident. At some point, he had to stop to take the covering off or put it on. If they can find that, we're that much closer to the plate number and an ID."

"Go, Ally," Maggie said. "J.D. and I will take you. If Jamie needs to come later—"

"No, I'll make it. C'mon." Jamie latched onto Ally's arm as they started down the hallway.

Greta's voice followed them. "I don't know why you want to find this young man right away when he'll contact me soon about seeing the garden, but you *could* thank me for helping."

CHAPTER FORTY-ONE

A POLICE CRUISER draped in black bunting, with its blue and white lights going, sat outside the funeral home. Funeral wreaths flanked it, with sprays of flowers on the hood.

A large U.S. flag raised high by a fire truck flapped over the entryway.

In procession, the Piscattoway Police and Rock Creek Police departments had accompanied Chad Northcutt's body here days ago.

Now law enforcement from the entire metro area on both sides of the Potomac River, from across Maryland and every Mid-Atlantic state, and even farther, from Illinois, Ohio, Georgia, and more, dwarfed the locals. They lined up in neat, patient ranks to enter the funeral home to pay their respects to the family. The double line extended out the door, to the sidewalk, then down the street, and around the block.

Civilians headed the lines with more blocks of them interspersed between law enforcement units, police departments, sheriff departments, state troopers.

Landis and Bel would be part of the formal honors tomorrow, but for now they continued with their other duty.

They passed the line and went along the side of the building.

"Going to be a long day," he said.

"Hard. But she'll have Jamie and Mags with her."

Landis cut a look toward his partner, but did not call out how he'd shifted a general observation to specific concern for Ally. "Long day for us, too. Watching all these people pass by in case one loses his or her mind, jumps up on a chair and proclaims guilt. Though which guilt we'd still have to sort out—shooting Chad, taking a shot at Ally, breaking into the house."

"Still, it would be a big step forward," Bel said evenly.

He snorted, gesturing Bel ahead as they reached a narrow passageway to a back entrance. Not the working entrance—that was masked by a wall.

An officer at the door checked their credentials against a list and let them in.

"Mags," Bel said.

Surely wasn't the doing of Iris getting them on the admittance list and unlikely the Piscattoway County Police Department organizer would have thought of it.

The Northcutt funeral occupied double rooms opened up to each other across one side of the building. Another room across the entrance hall offered light refreshments.

The lines from outside and through the front doors proceeded into the double rooms, down the near side, where the lines paused at the corner where Mark Northcutt and his mother stood, then turned to where Ally stood, then passed the closed casket with flower wreaths, arrangements, and plants extending to either side, before coming to Iris.

There, the head of the line, populated with dignitaries, stalled while Iris held court. Rachel remained at her elbow. Preston stood farther back, looking uncomfortable.

That stall left those farther back to extend their chats with Mark and his mother or Ally to awkward lengths. Jamie moved forward to Ally's side, clearly pitching in to help carry that load. Maggie said a few words to the people caught between those two groups.

Landis and Bel took up a spot in the opposite corner, not quite hiding behind the green plants there, but certainly welcoming the shadows.

"Don't envy them," Bel murmured.

No. "Let's get coffee."

"You go. I'll keep an eye out here."

After the eventual release of the dignitaries—Archie, of course, the county chief executive, the governor of Maryland, county commissioners—the line moved better, though snagging consistently when it reached Iris.

When Landis returned, handing Bel a cup, the double rooms had pockets of those who'd come through the line and didn't want to be seen as making a quick exit.

As time wore on, those pockets of chatters spread into the hallway and the refreshment room.

The highlight of the first hour was Captain Palery walking past them as if they had, indeed, become potted plants. Danolin made no eye contact, but winked.

About half an hour after that, he nudged Bel as a figure entered from the center door. That was a first. The line of those paying their respects came in from the door by the front and left by the rear or the center door. Staff entered and left by the rear door.

It was Willow Spencer coming in that center door.

She didn't make a scene of it, while also bypassing Ally at one side and Iris at the other end of the receiving line.

"Tact?" Bel asked under his breath.

"Or easier on herself. Watch Mark. I'll catch Iris and Rachel."

And they'd both cover Willow Spencer in the middle.

She walked three-quarters of the way into the room, sparing a long look for the blown-up photo of Chad in uniform by the head of the casket. Then she advanced again, slid into a gap between people, put a hand on the polished surface of the casket for a moment.

Rachel turned her head, surveying the room as she did regularly, as any cop would. She spotted the woman. With an air of casualness, she shifted her weight by rocking forward, which blocked Iris' view.

Interesting. Did Iris know Willow Spencer? At least by sight?

Rachel did.

In another beat, Willow turned and left by the door she'd entered. Not fast enough to draw attention, but wasting no time.

Rachel eased back to being at Iris' elbow instead of even with her.

Landis glanced toward Ally.

She showed no sign of having seen the other woman. She did look tired.

At that moment, Jamie handed her a cup of water and Ally smiled briefly before drinking all of it.

"Anything?" he asked Bel.

"Mark never saw her. Didn't look that direction at all. Ally did."

He shifted his gaze toward his partner.

"She didn't miss a beat," Bel said. "Unfazed."

"Rachel recognized her immediately. Blocked Iris' view."

"And why do that if Iris didn't know her, too?"

"SUSANNA WUERTL," LANDIS muttered to Bel as a woman turned away from Iris with a released breath that eased taut shoulders. "Middle partner of the three after Ortiz."

They casually moved to intersect her path.

A vein in his head ticked like a clock. Like he needed any reminder of the passage of time and how damned slow this whole thing was going.

He hoped to God the Fairlington team searching for that kid and, more widely, investigating the shots at Ally broke the whole thing open fast, because at the rate he and Bel were going with this background approach, Ally could be—

No. She wouldn't be.

"Hello, Susanna Wuertl, right? Ally Northcutt pointed you out the other day." It was almost half true. With forced ease, he introduced himself and Bel.

She looked them over quickly but closely. "Looking for connections on this side of the river to shots at the courthouse." She did not make it a question.

"Got to consider it," he said without confirming or denying.

In this short exchange, they'd shifted around a few feet, which put them out of the line of traffic, back toward the corner, with a console table to either side of them, so nobody could sidle up and overhear.

"I can see someone shooting Chad, but his wife? Why?"

He didn't waste time saying that was the question they needed to answer to figure out who and stop another attempt. God, he hoped Knarr and Ewer came up with something fast.

With no evidence of urgency—unless she could see the vein in his head ticking—he asked, with mild interest, "You didn't like Chad Northcutt?"

"Liking or not liking is immaterial to doing the job well, cooperating to bring about the right outcome, and having each other's back."

Landis tipped his head in acknowledgement. "All true. And admirable. Still, can't help but like some people you work with and not especially like others. It's human. Some people connect better than others. That's what I've been telling our boss for years. Please get me somebody other than Belichek."

The object of that gibe grunted. "Mutual."

The ramrod in her back eased ever so slightly.

He pushed that progress, gambling she'd respond to straightforward. "Did he sexually harass you?"

"No." After half a beat she added, "Not really. Nothing I couldn't handle."

"Jackass."

She switched her gaze to Belichek's unyielding face, which matched his tone.

"Yes," she said simply. "But not alone in being a jackass. Don't get me wrong. Most of the guys are good people. It's a few. Between them and some citizens who get rubbed raw by having a female officer telling them what they did wrong, it can get old fast."

"Think we're getting a picture here," Landis said. "Northcutt was a jackass to you because you're female, but didn't reach standout status in that category because he had company and some of them were worse."

Her mouth didn't change, but the corners of her eyes crinkled. "That's an accurate summation."

"Good. Now, in addition to sexist crap, did you witness him breaking regulations, crossing lines?"

"Not really."

Timing is everything.

If she'd said it immediately and casually, it would have meant one thing. The extra beat between the question and the slightly strained answer, turned it into something else entirely.

Landis looked toward Belichek with one eyebrow up.

Her gaze followed.

"Yeah," his partner said, introducing his next line in a sequence they'd followed before. Call it good cop, better cop, which Bel had earned in her view with the *jackass* judgment on Northcutt. "Gotta work on your delivery, Susanna. What happened?"

She tried the ramrod back again. "Nothing. Really."

They looked at her. Landis aimed for the more in sympathy than in anger expression he'd found useful with many female witnesses, but he suspected Bel did it better this time. It didn't help that Susanna Wuertl was a cop and thus less susceptible.

For a flash, he wondered if that was why he'd never dated any women in law enforcement, rather than from the shred of good sense Bel credited to him.

It didn't help that he wanted answers from her *now*. If he had to shake them out of her.

"What did Chad Northcutt say that made you think he wasn't on the straight?"

Bel's word choice switched from what happened—what Northcutt did—to what he said. It softened what they'd get out of Wuertl, making it practically mush. It would take even longer to lever her up to actions.

Time. This was all taking too much time.

"He... He used to make jokes. It was the same thing with the sexual innuendo. Say it as a joke. If anyone called him on it, he acted shocked they were so stupid and uptight they couldn't see he was kidding. Except I don't think he was kidding. Not about the sexual stuff and not about..." She shot a look from Bel to him, then landed in a neutral space between them. "About how an officer could supplement his salary without working overtime. That's what he called it. Supplementing his salary."

"How?"

"Stopping bad guys—that's what he called them—and taking drugs and money from their cars. Getting it off the street was how he termed it. A civic service. Our duty, in fact.

"I… I thought he might be sort of feeling me out, seeing if I'd be interested. I made it real clear I wasn't. And was told I had no sense of humor. Became a whole shtick for him and some of the others. Called me DGTK for Doesn't Get The Joke.

"But I have to say, I never saw him take anything from anybody. Ever. I never saw anybody do that. And I never heard anybody else say they saw it. So I never said anything, either. I mean, what could I say? Chad Northcutt makes jokes about stealing from citizens he stops? You know how some law enforcement are with the jokes. It lets off steam. To take them at literal face value…"

"You were between a rock and hard place." Landis gave it a bit more empathy than he felt. Another time he would empathize. Right now he wanted answers. "Did he ever say anything on the radio?"

"No, never. Not when I was around and I can't imagine he'd make a mistake like that, even though he wasn't the best with technology. Oh." Her eyes glinted with what might have been a bit of malice—but toward them or the man going past she reached out to? "Brent, come here. Detectives Landis and Belichek, let me introduce you to Franklin Brentford, who was partners with Chad before I was. Almost two years, wasn't it, Brent?"

CHAPTER FORTY-TWO

FRANKLIN WAS THE officer with the F. Brentford nametag Landis had spotted Tuesday night at the Chate Center.

Today he was just as tall, just as thin, and just as worried.

Possible that was how he expressed sorrow or sympathy, considering he just left the deceased's mother.

That possibility faded when Susanna performed the introductions and left. Brentford's worry deepened toward fear.

"Sorry for your loss," Landis said.

Brentford stared at him, apparently not comprehending the words.

"Chad Northcutt's death. That's tough. Real tough to lose someone you partnered with. Two years, Susanna said?"

"A—" He cleared his throat. "About that. But it was a while ago. Years." Apparently remembering it had been years since Chad Northcutt had done most things, he added, "Years even before he was shot."

"Still, a partner. That's a bond."

"We weren't really close."

Landis raised one brow. "Two years?"

"I was new. Young. They wanted … consistency."

"Did you not like Chad?"

"I… I… Didn't say that. I barely knew him really. Of course any loss in the department is devastating, but I … I didn't know him."

He wasn't going to let the guy slide away from this. "Sitting in a patrol car with him for two years, day in, day out, watching how he operated, what he did, having him give you the benefit of his experience, you must have formed some opinions."

"Not really."

"Was he a by-the-book kind of guy? Measure up to everything you'd learned at the academy?"

"I… I never saw anything that would, you know, lead to somebody thinking otherwise."

"What do you do for PCPD, Brent?" Landis hoped that might put him at ease enough to help get back to the tougher questions Brentford had totally bailed on.

"I'm the assistant Public Information Officer. And I see my boss over there, wondering why I'm not doing my job. I've gotta go, get some stuff to the media about tomorrow's schedule. They need it. Right now."

✧ ✧ ✧ ✧

"HE SHOULD HAVE had that role on the old *Hogan's Heroes* show. The one where the character kept saying *I know nothing*," Bel said when they were alone in their corner.

Landis acknowledged that with a grunt. But the ticking was in his head, louder than ever.

"If he was part of whatever Chad was into, he would have been the weak link and the one the task force spotted first," he said. Could he have gotten something out of the guy if he'd taken a different approach?

"He'd never have spent any of the money," Bel protested.

"No, but fear rolling off him like sweat would've given him away."

"It was rolling off him like that anyway and I seriously doubt he did a damned thing. Now, could we use that to our advantage? Especially if we find a lever that moves him and—"

"With all the time in the world and nobody shooting at Ally or breaking into her house, we probably could. Might even get enough from him to figure out what the task force was after. But—"

"We don't have all the time the world, somebody did shoot at Ally, and that's what matters now, not PCPD corruption. Agreed."

Landis shifted back to an earlier possibility. "We haven't looked much at if Chad took drugs and money from the wrong person."

"Wouldn't have taken it all."

"Right. Too many stops of people involved in the drug trade with nothing showing for them would raise eyebrows. But he could have reported some, while keeping a good chunk."

"True."

"And not likely someone like that would come after Ally. Not after all this time. If they'd been after cash or drugs, the break-ins would have happened right away, not years later."

Which would be great news, except it would still leave the question of who the hell had shot at Ally on Tuesday? Until they knew that…

He watched a man who blended African-American and Latino heritage into flat-out handsome approach Ally, his arms opened wide. She stepped into the embrace, his arms wrapping her tight, her face into his chest.

"Shindell Ortiz. We'll catch him when he leaves Iris," Bel said to himself. Then he addressed Landis. "By the way, I'm touched you recognize the bond of our partnership."

"Knew I'd pay for that. It was a ploy, Belichek, purely a ploy. Sure wasn't talking about us."

✧　✧　✧　✧

"I'VE BEEN THINKING," Maggie said abruptly.

The line had backed up at Mark and his mother this time, which cleared the clot in front of Ally and gave them a short breather. Shindell had already moved on to Iris, or they could have had more time together.

Even from their brief visit, she felt less drained than she had before his hug. He was a great hugger.

"About?" Ally provided Maggie the obligatory question. The answer surprised her.

"What Judge DaSilva said. It got me thinking about knowing somebody, but not being as much a help to them as you could be. Like following another car with a brake light out."

Ally's gaze met Jamie's for an instant. Her cousin didn't know where this was going, either.

"You can see their brake light's out. But they can't. No matter how hard they try, no matter how smart they are, no matter how careful they're trying to be, as long as they keep driving, they can't see that brake light's out. But to you, behind them in traffic, it's glaringly obvious. If only there were a way to tell them.

"You follow along, thinking if they get in the other lane and you're both stopped at a red light… But they turn right and you're going straight and you never have the chance to tell them. And maybe you send up a little prayer that nothing happens to them because of that brake light being out."

"Brake lights, Maggie?" Jamie asked.

"Yes. Or another way to look at it is that sometimes you know things without really knowing them. Then something jolts you into realizing what you know when you could have sworn you had no clue at all."

Ally smiled slightly, having followed the drift of Maggie's gaze. "What jolted you about J.D., Maggie?"

"A lot. But the specific I'm thinking about was the first time he laughed—that I heard him laugh. It definitely jolted me and he—of course—caught it. Later, he said something about being sorry he scared me—"

"Ah. Deliberate provocation."

"Yes, it was. I wasn't *scared*. No reason I would be scared. He doesn't have a scary laugh. Just a laugh. Deep and resonant, but just a laugh. But it did startle me."

"Why?"

Maggie nodded. "That's the point. Why hadn't I expected him to laugh? And the reason was because he'd never before laughed around me."

"Well, you *did* prosecute him for murder."

"Right. And nobody'd recommend prosecuting a guy for murder as a matchmaking service, although you do learn a lot about somebody.

You just don't hear them laugh. In court, I'd seen him give slow, warm smiles to a few of the witnesses. He'd grinned a time or two at his defense attorney's comments. But he had never laughed. Because he hadn't had any reason to. That's the point," Maggie finished.

Ally stared at her.

"Don't you get it?" Maggie asked, impatient as usual. "If Judge DaSilva's take on him is right, it could be it's the same situation with Tanner. Nobody expects him to have a real relationship with a woman. Flirtation, short fling, then move onto the next, sure. A real relationship, though? No way. But what if it's because he hasn't had any reason to."

✧ ✧ ✧ ✧

"ALLY SAID YOU'D probably want to talk to me. Nice place you've got here," Shindell Ortiz said with what might have been a genuine twinkle in his eyes.

He'd cordially met their introductions when they intercepted him after he'd left Iris and Rachel, willingly stepping into their conversation corner.

His comment let it be known it was cooperation on his part, not manipulation on theirs that had him in the perfect spot for a private chat amid the crowd.

"Serves the purpose," Bel said mildly.

"Saw you talking to Susanna, so I suppose you're hitting the former partners lineup. Any leads at this point?" Almost immediately, he added. "Sorry. Force of habit. I'm used to being the one asking the questions. What do you want to know that I could tell you when I haven't been around much and wasn't Chad's partner for years even before he was shot?"

"You can tell us what you knew of or suspected about wrongdoing by Chad Northcutt before, after, or during your partnership."

Landis might have rushed it, but for all Ortiz' air of cooperation, he didn't like the guy's not-so-subtle distancing himself from Chad Northcutt. Washing his hands of any association ... the same hands that had spread across Ally's back like they knew they'd be welcomed.

"That's comprehensive. Never saw any evidence at all of him doing anything wrong. Or I would have reported it."

"No evidence," Bel repeated thoughtfully.

That could draw a defense similar to Susanna Wuertl's *not really*. Or one that underlined he'd never seen anything wrong.

The man's response, though, went a different direction. "I want to help. Told Ally I would, one hundred percent. And if the bureau's resources can be of assistance, I'll do my best to connect you with the right people. On the other hand, this doesn't seem like the place or the time for these questions, what with him being buried tomorrow."

With would-be casualness, Landis said, "Wouldn't be my top choice, either, if it weren't the best we've got, what with someone shooting at Ally Northcutt and breaking into her house. Not to mention—"

"Breaking in—? For what?"

"—that questioning you here and now serves our top priority, which is keeping Ally Northcutt safe."

Bel's slow voice took the tension down a couple notches while keeping on the pressure. "Look at it this way, we'd rather ask questions at a funeral than let there be cause for another one."

Ortiz' deep brown eyes rested on Landis' face.

"Damn." He dropped his head. No longer Shindell Ortiz of the FBI, but just a guy. Which, as a matter of fact, could be a downright useful guise for Shindell Ortiz of the FBI. "You're right. You're right.

"Ally's safety is top priority for all of us. Ask what you want. But I never did see any evidence of anything wrong. Chad gave me a lot of shit because I'm strictly inside the lines and he considered the lines impediments. Got in the way of serving the good people fast, he said. Griped about that. A lot. But I never saw him go over the line. Never."

"Or you'd have turned him in."

Ortiz pushed past the edge in Landis' words with earnestness. "Yeah, I would have."

Could be the truth. Certainly was the obligatory response.

"Know anything about Ethan Paulz or Dewey Selton?"

He snorted. "Heard they'd become Chad's playmates. His and Mark Junior's. That wouldn't have happened if David, Chad's older brother—" A lift of his eyebrow asked if they knew that history. They nodded they did. "—was still around."

The subtle implication was it also wouldn't have happened if Chad had still been in Shindell Ortiz' orbit.

"Didn't overlap with them much so take this with a grain of salt, but I wouldn't want to rely on either one of them when my ass hung in the balance." He grimaced. "A pretty broad indictment and definitely no evidence. Impression, only. Selton keeps his mouth shut, while Paulz runs his, but don't let that fool you. Of the two of them, Paulz is sharper. Not the sharpest, but definitely sharper than Selton.

"You think they and Chad were up to—? Sorry, there I go again, asking the questions." He smiled self-deprecatingly.

"You said if you'd been aware of Chad going over the lines you'd have turned him in. Wouldn't you have been gambling your career by going against a Northcutt, even in those circumstances?" Bel asked.

Shindell's exhale edged toward a snort. "The myth of the Northcutts was just that, a myth. David used to laugh about it. Especially since there were a fair number in the department with Northcutt in their family line, but they don't all get along, much less work in unison to—what?—wield power? Run the department?" This sound was all snort.

"Did Chad laugh about it?"

"No. He took it seriously. He took himself seriously."

"David Northcutt didn't?"

"More down to earth."

"How well did you know them?"

He lifted one shoulder. "Knew David from the time I joined PCPD. Got along with him well. Thought enough of him to volunteer to partner with his brother when Chad joined."

"How was that partnership?"

"Fine." No edge in the answer, but also not a whole-hearted endorsement. A solid B-minus. "He was eager to be the senior guy, but, with some encouragement, he accepted he had to get more experience.

And my connection with David helped."

"What about your contacts with the rest of the Northcutts?"

"You mean the far-flung relatives? Good as far as I knew. Can't rule out I didn't run up against somebody I didn't realize was part of the clan. Hard to be okay every second with every person in a department."

Especially for someone clearly on his way up, as Shindell Ortiz must have been. That sometimes irked the lifers.

"How about the Northcutts closer to Chad and David? Mark Junior?"

"I got along fine with him. Some got frustrated with him, but I kept my expectations in line with what he was going to deliver, was never disappointed, and we got along fine."

Ortiz had just described some officers Landis had encountered in his career, who had rubbed him the wrong way so hard he'd been raw. But he wasn't stupid enough to miss that Ortiz' approach was smarter.

"How'd he interact with David and Chad?"

This answer didn't come as fast, for whatever reason, and Landis reminded himself there could be several, including legitimately doing his best to recall any useful information.

"Good overall. Better with David than Chad. There was some friction there, mostly over Mark Junior, carried over from childhood. Chad razzed Mark Junior pretty good. I tried steering Chad toward letting go of how they'd been as kids. He said it was all in fun, just ask his cousin. But, about nine months before I left, he got called in, told to knock it off. It was a step short of going on his permanent record, but he finally stopped. Though he was pretty hot about someone *snitching* on him."

"He thought it was Mark Junior?"

"I don't think so. General opinion was it was Mark Senior. He never rose up the ranks, but built a lot of long-time friendships."

"What about Mark Junior?"

"Ah. That's interesting.

"More ambitious than his father, partly from always trying to play catch-up to Chad and even David. Wasn't naturally on a par with either of them, but trying elevated him. Sports, policing, women, all of it. Hard to read on the razzing issue. Never got angry, never got rattled. Which served him well with his colleagues."

He tipped his head, appearing to consider.

"It also indicated to me a stronger personality and determination than he's often credited with. It'd be interesting to get a sharper take on how he's fared these past years without either of his role models.

"And if you're going to continue with the closer cousins, Rachel's sharper than any of them, except maybe David, and way more ambitious. Mark stands in awe of her. David never had a problem with her ambition—might have been because she wasn't a direct contemporary—but Chad competed all the time and usually lost. He hated that. Definitely caused friction with him, feeling it was history repeating itself."

He looked from Landis to Bel.

"Preston got promoted right when David Senior didn't, which was why he retired. Chad felt that shortened his father's life and those two were real close, so Preston and, by extension Rachel, doing well got under his skin."

"What about David Senior? How'd you get along with him."

"Only met him in passing. He was getting set to retire as I came in. Didn't cross paths with him after and then he died suddenly a couple years after retirement."

"Iris?"

"Stayed as far away as I could get." Ortiz continued without showing if he recognized that his vehemence and honesty took his listeners aback. "Told Ally before the wedding that she should bail as long as Iris was around. Unfortunately, she didn't listen to me. Worse, she didn't believe me until she had the scars to prove me right.

"Also told her to get out after Chad was shot. Didn't listen to me then, either."

CHAPTER FORTY-THREE

LANDIS WATCHED SHINDELL Ortiz make his way toward the exit. It was slow going as other attendees stopped him for hand-shaking, back-thumping, shoulder-patting, and talking.

"Chad Northcutt doesn't like the lines. Chafes under them. But he's got a partner who sticks to them," he mused.

"Who would have turned him in," Bel added to the recap as they also watched the flow of people still coming in.

"Yeah. That message came through clear. So, presumably, Chad's restrained. But David dies, then Shindell leaves, taking his moral compass with him. Northcutt gets a series of less experienced partners. Makes some of them uncomfortable for reasons involving varied ethical issues. And then the department changes to roving. Where backup on calls can be potluck. Sometimes nobody you know particularly well. So, you play it by the book."

"But sometimes a crony's there," Bel added. "Like Selton and Paulz. Maybe Mark, with Chad being the stronger cousin calling the shots."

"Opening the door to all sorts of things. And the change to roving coincides with Northcutt giving money to his mother and girlfriend."

"Also with Ethan Paulz getting a cabin and Dewey Selton buying a boat."

"That's interesting," Landis said. "More misbehaving above the water line so to speak. If someone else ran the show, their visible spending could have been another knock against Chad."

"Existing leader clamping down or possibly a leadership takeover,"

Bel offered.

"Either way, no sign anyone picked up the reins and took over the operation. If killing Chad was to take his place, why let the operation atrophy?"

"Sure it atrophied?"

"That's what—Hey, Rachel. How are you holding up? Tough duty over there."

She smiled as she joined them in their corner, but lines at the corners of her eyes looked deeper than they had Tuesday.

"Not so bad. Smile and shake. Shake and smile. Iris does most of the talking. Seems like you two are working today, too. Looking for more background from the partners?" she asked, not really expecting an answer. "Makes sense."

Landis raised an eyebrow at her.

"Saw you talking to Susanna earlier, then Brent—Franklin Brentford. So, after Shindell, you've now got the complete set of Chad's partners who are still walking around. First one died a while back."

"Still missing one," Bel said.

She looked up, surprised. "No, you're not. Ted. Well, Edward officially, but everybody calls him Ted."

"Okay." Bel drew out the second syllable, making it clear he didn't follow.

"You met him. Absolutely. Both of you."

"There've been a lot of people here and—"

"Not today. After the break-in at the house—Chad and Ally's—the day Chad died. He was the property crimes detective at the scene. Ted Tancroft."

Landis knew Bel had the same reaction he did, which was a mental litany of words and phrases that did not shed approbation on Tancroft's character or morals.

Neither of them showed it.

"Feels like a hundred years ago with all that's involved with this funeral. We'll have to circle back to him." He said it smoothly, not like a detective whose internal monologue threatened the bounds of his cop vocabulary. "Can't help thinking you got short-changed in all that happened."

"Me?"

"The timing, I mean. With your promotion happening right before Chad was shot. Must have felt like it got lost in the tide of events. And this one's following the same pattern. Making sergeant's a big deal."

"It is. But neither promotion was important by comparison. It wasn't any time to be celebrating then and it isn't now."

"You've had opportunities to celebrate in between and you'll have more, won't you? You've got one hell of a career going."

She grinned. "Nice of you to notice."

"Couldn't miss it. Aiming to outrank your father in the end?"

"That's the goal. And nobody would love it more than him. Which reminds me, I've been sent to get more water for him and Iris. See you later."

✦ ✦ ✦ ✦

LANDIS WASN'T PARTICULARLY subtle when he hooked Edward "Ted" Tancroft, said they needed to talk to him, and led him back to their semi-private corner.

"What's this abo—?"

"You were Chad Northcutt's partner."

"Yeah. For a few months."

"Interesting you were so fast to arrive at his house Tuesday night after the break-in call."

"I was next up and don't live far from Gardington Road."

"You didn't mention you'd been his partner, nor knowing Ally Northcutt. Would've been natural."

"I don't know her—didn't. Met her for the first time that night. As for mentioning I'd been his partner for a brief time several years ago, why should I? PCPD knows. You two? You're nothing to me except a couple of out-of-town cops who seem to have their noses deep in another jurisdiction for no good reason, unless you're trying to distract from civilians becoming target practice in front of your courthouse with a Fairlington County Police Department security detail, including the two of you, right there."

"Feel better getting that off your chest? Must have had those words stored up the past five days waiting to spill out. But here's the thing, Tancroft. They're not worth the spit you used to form them."

"Posturing," Bel inserted. "Distraction."

"Exactly. Unless, of course, you've got some reason to hide your association with Chad Northcutt or you're the kind of small-minded cop who puts jurisdiction first and little things like keeping a citizen alive and figuring out why another one—a *cop* and one from your department—died. Is that you, Tancroft?"

"Go to hell."

"Not outside the realm of possibility. But before I do, we're going to get you in an interview room."

"Fuck you."

"Now that *is* outside the realm of possibility."

Tancroft strode away.

"Good line." Bel took his phone out.

"You're not going to say I cut off any chance of cajoling him by indulging in my good line—multiple good lines?"

"No chance from the start. Or he'd have told us Tuesday night. Might as well get the satisfaction of the good li—Captain?" he said into the phone. He moved toward the exit for more privacy in outlining the situation to Wilson Palery.

Landis stayed put, watching Tancroft edge through the crowd. He had maybe an eighth of the interactions Shindell Ortiz did, and all limited to handshakes and hellos.

Bel returned with a two-word result. "Their place."

"We need him in Fairlington. Get him off-balance—"

"We're lucky we're getting to talk to him at all. Yeah, it's home court for him, but it's more convenient for us, too. And Palery pulled it off that it's in an hour. Gives us some time to grab Schmidt and do homework beforehand. No interview room, but we record. I'm there as referee."

"Don't need a referee, and if those are the restrictions—"

"They are. And I wasn't asking you, Landis. I was telling you."

✦   ✦   ✦   ✦

"OFFICER TANCROFT, DO you mind if I call you Ted?" Landis asked with practiced neutrality.

When they'd told the others they were leaving, didn't know for how long, and would meet them back at the house if it was after the hours of the visitation, Maggie practically vibrated with curiosity, Jamie bestowed a glowing look of confidence on Bel, and Ally's gaze went from Bel to him with that tuck between her brows.

The Piscattoway County Police Department building was a wide, low-slung building with a two-story glass entry that looked as if it had been added. There'd be little chance of getting lost here. One main hallway went to the left, another to the right.

They were in a small, square conference room off the right-hand corridor, with two recorders running—theirs and Tancroft's.

"No." Tancroft didn't grit his teeth, nor did he overflow with friendliness.

"Good. Let's start by going back to Tuesday night, when we met at the home of Allison Lindell Northcutt at 1567 Gardington Road in Piscattoway County, and we conducted ourselves as cordial colleagues. You listened to the background information provided by me and my partner, Rutherford Belichek, and you ran that preliminary scene professionally."

Tancroft glanced at the recorders as if he wanted to be sure they picked up the positive review.

"Then let's go farther back to when you were partners with Chad Northcutt in the Piscattoway County Police Department. How long a period was that?"

"Four months."

"How long from the time you were no longer partners and when he was shot in his driveway?"

"Eight months."

"Why did your partnership end?"

"Department-wide shift to a closest-responder system for backup. Allowed for better coverage than keeping the same two people close enough to be consistent backup."

"Did you ever share a car with Officer Northcutt?"

"Not after the first two weeks."

"Why only two weeks?"

"Break-in period. I'd moved to Piscattoway from another jurisdiction in northwest Maryland."

"How long were you there?" he asked, as if he didn't already know. Including why Tancroft left.

"Two years."

"How did you feel about the departmental change away from tethered partners?"

"Made sense. Allowed for better coverage."

"Some members of the department complained about losing the continuity of having someone they knew well being backup. Were you one?"

"No."

Landis interlocked his fingers, put them behind his head, then leaned back into them, studying the other man.

"Why'd you leave your first department, Ted?"

"My wife got a job down here."

"Did that happen before or after you reported a fellow officer for misconduct during a traffic stop?"

Tancroft said nothing.

Landis sighed, remaining tilted back. "Took a lot of guts to do that. Him a veteran of the department, you barely on the job for eighteen months when it happened. Between the lines, it reads like the higher-ups backed you, but that doesn't tell what it was like on the ground. Rough?"

"I survived."

"You were smart to leave."

Tancroft blinked, but didn't make eye conduct.

"You gave yourself a fighting chance to not be the oddball. And then you got assigned Chad Northcutt. A dirty cop. Did he try to recruit you?"

"No."

"Did you witness any illegal—"

"No."

"Did he say or do anything that could be used in court or disciplinary action or—?"

"No."

"What made you think he was dirty?"

His mouth twisted. "I know you think you're luring me into making a disclosure against my interests, but I have done absolutely nothing wrong. That's why I'll answer your question. Yes, I did suspect Chad Northcutt could be breaking regulations—laws—in such a way that he justifiably could be termed *dirty*. I also state that I had no factual evidence to support that suspicion. To put it succinctly, I had no evidence, just experience."

Landis unlocked his fingers and came forward, resting his forearms on the table. "Look, Ted, we're not investigating corruption. We do need to know everything we can about what was going on to try to figure out who shot Northcutt back then, killing him now, because there's a good chance that's behind the attempt on Allison Lindell Northcutt, too. She could have been shot Tuesday on our courthouse plaza. She wasn't. She's still alive. We need to keep it that way.

"You say you have no evidence, okay. But you saw or heard or put together something to make you think he was dirty. We need to hear that. I can't guarantee it won't lead to you having to testify against somebody or—more likely—having it get around Piscattoway PD. We'll do the best we can to prevent that, but you know we can't guarantee it. You'll have to do it anyway. And I know it could be tougher this time. You have kids in school, your wife has a good job, you're settled in Piscattoway, not starting out."

"I can't help you. I've got nothing concrete that will help you."

"Tell me what you do have."

"Impressions. Jokes that weren't jokes about how I must be looking to pad my salary with a wife and a kid on the way. He said he sure needed to because he had a ... *babe*. He'd visit her, talk to her during shift. Didn't try to hide it."

"Know her name?"

"Willow. Never heard the last name and I didn't ask."

"He said he needed money to give to her?"

"He did. Not that it proves anything."

"Did he treat some stops differently from others?"

One side of his mouth lifted, saying without words, *They're all differ-ent*. Then it dropped as a brighter light came on in his eyes.

"There was one. He called in the stop. I radioed I was stuck behind a truck that just broke down. Was going to put out flares. He said don't bother, he'd handle it alone. Turned out the guy got the truck re-started and I followed him to a service station, so I went straight to Northcutt's stop to back him up. He was searching the car. It had South Carolina plates. He was not happy to see me—that's subjective. Objectively, I can say he abruptly let the guy go. He did not thank me for backing him up," he finished dryly.

"Could you pin down when that stop was?"

"Maybe. Probably. You're thinking cross-referencing with his call-in and see if the citizen—"

"Possible." Landis dampened his enthusiasm. As he'd said, catch-ing Chad Northcutt for corruption now not only lost out to keeping Ally safe, but it seemed way beside the point with the guy dead.

On the other hand, his confederates remained a top interest.

"How did he express that he wasn't happy you backed him up?"

"It was one of several times he let me know he had other people he wanted as partner. They *understood*. His cronies, those guys he'd go fishing with, went to games with, other stuff."

"Who specifically?"

"Ethan Paulz, Dewey Selton. His cousin."

"Was there anyone outside of the usual chain of command Chad seemed to defer to, treat differently from his other colleagues?"

That intrigued Tancroft. But, after a pause while he apparently scoured his memory, he shook his head.

"Anything else you can tell us that might be helpful?"

He paused long enough for Landis to doubt he'd give them any-thing more.

But then he looked up, assessing them. First Belichek, then him.

When he spoke, he went back to Bel.

"Maybe. Or it might be a big fat nothing. We were breaking in new body cameras the last week we were assigned together. He was really crappy at any new tech. Not that good with old tech, either. He kept hitting where the old button used to be when he meant to turn it off, but it didn't turn it off on the new set. I never heard anything, but if he slipped up… That button turned audio on, too."

Which might have caught Chad Northcutt saying something he wouldn't have intended to be saved on his body camera.

"The thing is, most of the department kept making the same mistake, especially the ones who'd been around awhile. I heard they had so much from the first month that they had to go out and get a contract for off-site storage."

"They didn't dump it?" Landis asked.

"They hadn't the last I heard. They'd set an official start date, so they covered their asses by keeping from that date forward, but with that first month segregated and parked." He looked from one to the other of them again. "Nobody's ever gone through any of what was recorded that first month."

"What about after that?"

"Spot-checked and searched for specific instances."

✧ ✧ ✧ ✧

"BODY CAM FOOTAGE," Bel said after they left Tancroft.

It was a slim hope. Chasing it could take days—weeks—of slogging through footage. And that was if they got approval—approval from Fairlington to ask for it and approval from Piscattoway to look through it. And, of course, if it existed at all.

Time.

That damned ticking clock.

"Schmidt," Belichek said.

Landis snorted out his pessimism. "If we're okay with not seeing him for the next several months. Christ, can you imagine how long it would take to comb through all that? Even sorting by division or officer. It's not like we could tell him to look for a date or time. Best-case scenario, with it accurately sorted by badge number, he'd have to listen to every word Northcutt said on every shift for the whole month."

Belichek's responding grunt was equally pessimistic. "That's best-case scenario *and* the tech works. If nothing shows up the first month, we couldn't just drop it. We'd have to cover it all. And if he implicated anyone…"

"Yeah, them, too."

"CA's office," Bel said as shorthand.

The Commonwealth's Attorney's office could apply its resources to that sort of research. The catch was they'd do it for someone they were prosecuting to trial. Not on the off-chance a guy now dead might have said something that might have implicated someone still alive and chargeable in another state.

"Or a new hobby for us through our golden years after we've run out of every other lead."

"Or that."

It sure wasn't going to save Ally if someone was after her now.

CHAPTER FORTY-FOUR

ALLY SAT AT the dining room table, her mind a blank, her mouth twitching as muscles responsible for solemn smiles and appreciative thanks cramped.

Her father slid into the chair at right angles to her, at the head of the table.

"That was quite a turnout," he said.

"Yes."

"All the leaders of the community."

"Yes."

"I imagine it will be the same tomorrow at the funeral."

"Yes."

Through her exhaustion, she recognized the familiar path of where this was going. Her mother had been front and center at the visitation. He wanted equal time.

"For tomorrow, I'll be sure to be at your side. Just don't forget to tell those officers that I am your father. They wouldn't let me through to you for the longest time."

He prepared to rise.

"Dad, did you fight for me?"

He looked at her, not comprehending.

"When you and Mom divorced, did you fight for custody of me? You didn't, did you?"

"A girl should be with her mother, especially at that age, a girl wants—"

"I didn't. You knew—I begged you ..." Her clasped hands slid forward, bending her over the table toward him. Too much like begging. She opened her hands, pushed her palms against that surface to straighten her back. "Mother and I never got along. We don't … think alike."

A tolerable difference when he'd buffered them, it degraded in his absence. With the first sign of friction, Greta withdrew. Unruffled to all appearances, but absent, even when she was in the same room.

"Living with her made it worse. Far worse."

"I'm sorry to hear that," he said formally. "But you could not have lived with me. I worked so much. It would have been impossible to try." He slanted a look toward the other room. "You and your mother still don't get on well?"

Their competition never ended.

He wanted her to say yes. He wanted to beat Greta at this, to win where the prize was something neither of them wanted—a relationship with their daughter.

Being a family.

"I'm surprised you had her beside you today, then, Allison. Especially after her giving away information that could have—"

She stood, unable to listen to his eagerness to put his ex-wife in the wrong.

"Dad, Mom," she added, pitching her voice to the living room. "It's time for you both to leave."

"I am rather tired. Such an exhausting day for me—" Greta Frye Moban Lindell directed a disapproving look at Landis and Belichek. "—with the uproar earlier. Though, I will say, Allison that you should have smiled more today. You appeared quite grim at times. And when I was telling people about my garden, it was a dissonance that distracted from what I was saying."

From the corner of her eye, Ally saw Jamie puff up in her chair, like an irate bird spreading its feathers in preparation for attack.

Kurt patted Allison's hand. "Thoughtful of you to be concerned about me. I'll be fine for tomorrow. Plenty of energy."

"Oh, energy," Greta said to the room. "I have ceaseless energy. There is nothing to keep one young like gardening. The exercise, of course, but also the contact with the earth and—"

"Yes, and I won't deny you those benefits any longer. Go back to your garden, Mother. Go home. You too, Dad. It's time for you to go."

Both of them frowned at her. Kurt said, "The funeral's tomorrow. After that—"

After that, he thought the score would be even.

"No. Go to the hotel tonight, now. And go home in the morning. I don't want either of you here any longer."

Landis stood.

He and Bel arrived about ten minutes ago, looking grim.

For a second, she thought he was going to say something to her parents. She didn't want him to. She didn't want anyone to say anything.

He went to the front door and put his hand on the knob.

"Allison, really." Her mother looked around, as if expecting others to support her.

"I'm going to bed now. Good night and good-bye, Mother, Dad."

From the bedroom, she heard no sound until the front door closed. A moment later, a light knock sounded at the bedroom door.

"All clear," Jamie called. "Way to go, Tiger."

Ally, having changed to a hoodie and leggings, wasn't far behind as Jamie returned to living room.

"The nerve of that woman criticizing her for not smiling when she's never done a thing Ally's whole life to protect her. You know why she doesn't smile in public? Because a follow-up report on Chad a year after the shooting—"

"Ally." Tanner had spotted her. "You should get some sleep."

Jamie spun around. "You should. But I'm not sorry you heard me and I'm going to tell them," she said defiantly.

Ally took her usual chair. "I don't suppose it can make things worse."

"It might make them better," Jamie, ever the optimist, said. Though she sounded more outraged than optimistic as she turned to the others, focusing on Maggie. "One of those follow-up TV stories caught Ally in the background while Iris took center stage—of course—and for an instant it looked like Ally was *almost* smiling and Iris got the screen grab, printed it out, came in here—into *Ally's* house—and plastered it all over the place with comments scrawled on them like, *Why are you laughing over your husband being shot?*"

"She did that?" Maggie demanded. "I never heard this before. I hope you—"

"We know what you hope Ally did," Jamie interrupted, "but you can tell she didn't, because she's still being kind to Iris."

"And Iris is still alive," muttered J.D. Other than that, the men in the room left the floor to the cousins.

"I changed the locks. And didn't give her a key."

"That's a start," Maggie approved. "That woman deserves to be told—"

"Which is why Ally made me swear to never tell you, because you'd plow in and only make it worse, when that woman already acted as if Ally weren't at his bedside all the time, acted as if Ally ran away from him or—"

"I did." She locked her gaze on her hands so it didn't go to Tanner. In the sudden, complete silence, the hum of the refrigerator swelled like a jet taking off. "I would have."

When no one else spoke, she slowly continued. "I planned to leave Chad that day, the day of the shooting."

She told them the same account she'd given him.

At the end, Jamie expelled a breath. "Thank God."

Ally's head jerked to her in surprise.

"No, she didn't miss the part about you not planning to tell us." Maggie's sharpness softened some as she continued. "She's thanking God because it means you don't love Chad now, you haven't loved Chad for these years since he was shot—"

"Or before," Jamie slipped in.

"—or before. And that means you have been distant to us because you sensed we didn't like the guy—"

"At all."

"—at all—I was *trying* to be tactful, Jamie. And in a choice between loyalty to him or staying close to us, you chose to be loyal to him, which we can respect. As long as you don't or didn't love him and aren't heartbroken."

Jamie nodded. "That's it exactly. Though we—Maggie and I—haven't talked about it ever. Because—"

"That would have been a betrayal of you, to gang up on you behind your back."

"Right."

Ally looked from cousin to cousin, saw their younger faces, when they'd been together for the happiest times of her life and the worst. "I... I don't know what to say."

"Say that now you're going to start a new life. You're going to stop thinking you still owe him or any of them anything. You're going to put Chad, Iris, the Northcutts, and all this behind you and do what *you* want."

—DAY 7—

MONDAY

CHAPTER FORTY-FIVE

THE PALLBEARERS SLID the flag-draped casket out of the back of the hearse with deliberate dignity.

Mark and Rachel Northcutt were pallbearers, along with Ethan Paulz and Dewey Selton. Landis didn't recognize the other two, neither in uniform.

Bagpipers played something familiar he couldn't name.

Probably didn't matter. It was the sound of it.

The casket came to rest on a wheeled carrier, the pallbearers lined up on either side as it moved forward between parallel ranks of law enforcement at attention. They all saluted.

The family followed.

Iris released her brother-in-law's arm and edged ahead of Ally, who walked on at her same pace, looking straight ahead.

Mark Northcutt's mother, Rachel's father came next, Aunt Dawn, then a cluster of other relations.

Behind them walked Piscattoway County Police Department and political dignitaries.

The Fairlington County Police Department contingent stood on the right side, beside a group from Baltimore. Looking straight ahead and saluting.

Landis breathed out through his nose.

"He wore the uniform," Bel said under his breath from his left. To his right stood Danolin, beginning to stretch his uniform, but hoping retirement came before he needed a new one.

However they might regard the individual, the uniform deserved respect. That was Bel's message.

"Yeah."

It was Chad Northcutt's funeral and his mother had chosen this magnitude of pomp, taking more out of Ally each second, which made Landis angry.

Yet he couldn't hold onto all of the anger against the sound of the bagpipers, the faint rustle of the casket rolling forward, the barely-breathing reality of his fellow officers, the footsteps a low drumbeat under the bagpipes.

It was beyond Chad Northcutt, beyond Iris Northcutt.

It was for all who wore the uniform. Who had worn it. Who would wear it.

This ceremony carried continuity. It cemented the officers. It connected law enforcement and the community.

It even reminded Landis of Chad in the academy. Sailing through the physical requirements, but always with a frown in the classroom. Who had he been then? Who had he had a chance to be? Or before that, being brought up in the home Natalie Northcutt described.

The family mourners passed inside the building. The two lines of officers turned in unison and slowly began to file in the same direction, re-forming smoothly into one line.

The family was seated at the front of the large hall, with every seat beyond them filled by dark-clad civilians. Jamie, her parents, Maggie and J.D. were in the fourth row back.

On the right side, the first row held the dignitaries, then a swath of empty rows for the honor guards. Beyond that, uniformed law enforcement filled every row all the way to the back. More uniforms were in the gallery.

Silently, the officers from the saluting lines outside walked across the front to pass in review.

A pair of state troopers stood, one at the foot of the casket, the other at the head, with their white-gloved hands clasped at their waists. Their downcast heads showed only the tops of their hats.

Flowered wreaths and arrangements stretched beyond them in each direction.

Landis had been to other law enforcement funerals. He'd watched officer after officer put a hand to the casket, a contact, a farewell, a comfort.

None he saw made the gesture now, including Susanna Wuertl, who was not that far ahead of them.

Perhaps the pallbearers had earlier.

Landis glanced at the casket.

He couldn't mourn the man's death, but he knew he'd do his damnedest to find out who'd shot him, even if it was separate from Ally's safety.

The victim of a crime could make that crime worse—a kid or another innocent—but the victim, no matter who it was, couldn't make it better. Murder was murder.

He followed the line of officers into the reserved rows, where they stood until their row filled before sitting and baring their heads.

The county's chief executive talked first. Landis tuned out after his careful generalities revealed he hadn't known Chad, didn't know the family.

From his spot closer to the right aisle than the center, with an angled view to the lectern, he saw Iris' profile, the bulk of her brother-in-law next to her, and nothing of Ally, except a slice of her straight back against the top of the seat.

His attention refocused when the politician gave way to the police chief.

Archie acknowledged Iris and Ally—and in that order. Iris' tight jaw eased slightly at that and his aside on the devotion of mothers and how law enforcement couldn't operate without it. That tight jaw eased a bit more as he piled on praise for the history and service of the Northcutts in law enforcement.

Nothing he hadn't heard or read before. No digging beneath the surface for this speech.

The division chief who followed had a major advantage because he was brief. Hard not to be, since he hadn't known Chad.

He ended by dropping his voice a note and saying, "You can rest easy, Chad. Your brothers and sisters in law enforcement will take it from here."

Emotion ramped up when Mark Northcutt rose to speak.

"For those of you who don't know, I'm Chad's cousin, Mark Northcutt. Yes, another Northcutt."

He grinned and a ripple of amused acknowledgment passed through the assembled.

But Mark's hands shook and his voice had a quaver to it as he continued.

"I'm honored the family allowed me to talk. We thank you all for how you've let us know we're in your thoughts, when Chad was ambushed outside his home, through the years while he fought to come back from his injuries, and these past days after his fight ended.

"All the gestures you've all made, some big and some small—though, really, none of them have felt small—mean a lot to all of us."

Landis wondered if Iris would have been half as gracious as Mark Northcutt was being.

"I knew Chad all my life. We were born about a year apart and from photos, we were thrown in cribs together. We sure as heck were thrown in the same play pen, because I remember Chad whapping me in the head with toys."

A flicker of chuckles rose and expired.

"And I wouldn't be the least surprised if some of those toys were stuffed badges or something and we were wearing little outfits with *Police* across the back. That's the way it is for Northcutts. I cut across it some, especially as a teenager. But, Chad... Chad knew who he was and what he wanted to do from when he could first talk.

"Can't tell you how many times I was *arrested* by an Officer Chad missing his two front teeth. He was older and he always claimed the right to be the cop. I was the robber. And let me tell you, this bad guy was the kind we love—dumb. Got caught every darned time."

This time the chuckles ran wider and longer.

"Just like with knowing what he wanted to do, Chad knew he wanted beautiful Ally from as soon as he saw her. Nobody was surprised and everybody—" He put a little emphasis on that, almost rebelliously. "—was delighted when she said yes and joined the Northcutts.

"We all know how she's been at his side every day since the ambush, along with his mother."

Landis saw the back of Iris' jaw tighten, likely at getting such an off-hand mention.

"As for me, I was always following in Chad's footsteps. Going to school, playing sports, going to the academy, and then into the force. Never catching up, because he was always ahead.

"And he rubbed that in. Because that's how guys are. But he also included me when he didn't have to. As kids and right on up to when Chad would gather me and Ethan Paulz and Dewey Selton, and we'd go hunting or fishing or to a ballgame or kicking back. I miss all that. I miss our games of poker, the days out in a boat." The man choked up. "It's end of watch, buddy. End of watch."

Mark half stumbled as he left the lectern, possibly because of tears.

The minister who'd been at the visitation spoke of sorrow, of solace, of salvation.

The pallbearers rose. The family rose. Everyone rose. And the departing procession began.

This time, as Landis stood with the others to honor the flag, the uniform, and maybe even what had been good in the man, he did recognize the haunting music the pipes and drums played and how appropriate it was for the journey to the cemetery. It was called "Going Home."

The detail commander ordered "Present arms" as they slid the casket into the hearse and all saluted.

The hearse eased forward, accompanied by four motorcycles, one at each corner of the vehicle. It was followed by official police department vehicles with their lights flashing.

Two limos slid in under the portico and the family got in. He tried to see which one Ally got in, but couldn't spot her without breaking his stance.

With the limos departed and more official vehicles behind them, they were dismissed.

"Schmidt. Over there," he said to Bel. He'd spotted the young officer by a Fairlington County Police Department vehicle, waiting for them.

Landis, being taller and having longer legs, got the suicide seat. Bel sat behind Schmidt.

As they slid into a spot in the procession, Schmidt said, "That was… very… Is that what they're all like?"

Remembering his first police funeral, Landis skipped any hazing comments and said, "Yeah."

Into a protracted lull, Bel said a single word. "Genuine?"

"Could be and still could've shot Chad. Genuinely misses the fun times together, regrets the *necessity* of shooting him, but believed it *was* a necessity."

"Mark Northcutt, the cousin," Schmidt muttered, possibly to himself.

Landis said, "We haven't tested his alibi for the time of the shooting at the courthouse, if you're thinking—"

"Evidence first, then thinking," Bel said.

Landis told Schmidt, "And now he talks about picking up pebbles that, eventually, created a mountain."

"The pebbles build—"

"The mountain. Got it. What does he say he was doing at the time of the shooting?"

"Lunch. Same as Rachel, though hers was later. His was earlier— way earlier than usual."

HOW MUCH LONGER did this crap go on? Plant the corpse in the dirt already.

The only good thing about this interminable day was being able to know exactly where Landis was at all times. They printed the schedule online for Chrissake.

They'd been at it since early this morning, including being holed up in some old building, where the boys in blue marched and saluted and all that claptrap.

Now, the schedule of events he'd saved from online said they were going to the cemetery, probably for more of the useless ceremonies they'd been posturing through all day.

Then came a reception.

Time to take advantage of that freedom of knowing where Landis was.

CHAPTER FORTY-SIX

ALLY HAD HER cousins at either side of her, Jamie's parents behind her and Bel and J.D. on the flanks.

Her mother-in-law had Rachel on one side, the chief on the other, then a phalanx of department brass ranged around them.

Anyone looking at the scene would think she was the widow, not Ally.

The flag honor detail moved into place. In unison they raised the flag, holding it taut above the casket.

New orders cut through the still air, followed by the gun salute.

A bugler sounded *Taps*.

The detail commander pivoted and walked slowly and solemnly to the mourners, presenting the folded flag to the chief of the Piscattoway County Police Department. He accepted it with dignity, then turned and ceremonially handed it to Iris Northcutt. He said a word to Ally, then returned to his spot.

Landis saw a few looks exchanged, especially among the visiting law enforcement.

The flag should go to the widow. Hell, all the honors should go to the widow.

A lone bagpipe began the familiar haunting of *Amazing Grace*. The bagpiper came into view across from them, and slowly walked diagonally up a rise.

After one refrain, a band of pipes and drums picked up the melody. Only then did Landis realize the solitary piper had been heading toward the band. Twice more they played the aching song.

A figure in uniform appeared, the face obscured, all identifying marks covered in black, so it became not one police officer, but all officers.

The lone bagpiper split away from the group and the figure followed. The band completed a refrain. The drums silenced. The other pipes quieted. Until it was only that one bagpiper, resuming a curved path higher up the rise, the figure following him at a distance.

Until first one, then the other, crested the rise and disappeared on its far side.

The sound of the bagpipe faded away to nothing.

After a long moment, the minister recalled their attention for a final prayer. It felt like an afterthought.

The true farewell to a police officer had ended with that figure disappearing on the other side of the hill.

✧ ✧ ✧ ✧

AT THE RECEPTION afterward, Iris held court, absorbing the condolences and ceremony as her due. They almost seemed to swell the woman.

In contrast, Ally sat still and mostly quiet.

Bel considered her.

Still and quiet, but not shrinking, even in comparison to Iris.

A good number of people beyond her own family had spent time with her, too.

Without moving his head, his peripheral vision picked up the direction of Tanner's focus. As he'd expected, Ally.

Understanding more about his partner didn't feel like much of a gain at the moment.

But he couldn't do anything about what happened between him and Ally.

"Let's talk to some people," he said.

Answers wouldn't cure Landis. No guarantee they wouldn't bring more pain. But they were answers. And in their business that was the bottom line.

✧ ✧ ✧ ✧

SHINDELL ORTIZ FROWNED at them. "Chad's shooting and an attempt on his wife, especially with the timing of his dying, I get. Answered your questions willingly. But David's death? Why are you asking about a closed case?"

"Why aren't you answering?" Landis shot back.

Bel said quietly, "A Northcutt death. Natural connection."

He shot Landis an unfriendly look before saying to Belichek, "Fine. But there was no sign of anything beyond another over-the-limit driver killing another member of law enforcement. Happens too many damned times a year."

"Agreed. How did Chad take it?"

"Hard. Shut off. Except to Iris. And they fed the worst in each other.

"How did you react?"

"That was the night—seeing David Northcutt out there on the road, knowing he'd saved one drunk's life from another drunk, but died himself—I decided to leave PCPD. I'd always planned a shift to a federal agency, but let time roll on with PCPD. Put in my FBI app the next day. Looking for something safer."

"Safer?"

"And faster than trying to work up to detective like you guys." His eyes crinkled. "Better hours, too."

"Understand Preston Northcutt showed up to the scene when David died."

"Most of the department did."

"Same with Chad Northcutt's shooting. Cast of thousands."

A crease marked Ortiz' forehead. "That's normal. You think there's something—?"

"Were you surprised Preston Northcutt notified Iris Northcutt of her son's death before notifying his widow?"

"No. Preston and Rachel were tight with them despite…"

"Despite what?"

Impatience came through Ortiz' answer. "I told you. Iris was difficult. It came out in different ways. Especially with Preston and Rachel advancing."

A potential area of conflict surfaced in Landis' memory.

"But they had to stay in good with Iris, since she ran the family trust, and that's how Rachel could get her townhouse."

Ortiz lifted a shoulder. "Don't know anything about that. You should ask Rachel."

✧ ✧ ✧ ✧

LANDIS WATCHED MARK Northcutt Junior return to the reception room.

"How long has he been AWOL?"

"Last I saw him was when the chief was talking to Iris at the start. Have focused on her since."

"Yeah, it was all hands-on-deck then for the Northcutts. That's, what a couple hours ago, though. Let's go talk to him."

✧ ✧ ✧ ✧

"ALLY?"

She blinked up to Chad's cousin.

"Hi, Mark."

"Hi. I, uh, wanted to ask… I mean, I know you're going to get everything of Chad's now, but there was one thing I wondered if I could have. It's not valuable or anything. It's just the old-fashioned photo album he had. It's got old family pictures in it and stuff. Not the official one Iris keeps, but nice anyway."

"Of course, Mark. Just give me a call to be sure I'm home and you can come get it any time."

"Thanks. I also wanted to say—" His finish came in a gulp. "—I'm sorry if I ever made you uncomfortable."

"Uncomfortable?" she repeated, then fought not to look in the direction of her mother-in-law. Was Mark Junior apologizing for not standing up to Iris? Of all of them, he'd be the last she'd expect to—

"At Mikey's. When you used to go there, before you and Chad got married. You got, uh, razzed a lot and I know I joined in and I'm sorry if that made you feel, uh, not welcomed or… anything."

Razzed. Not welcomed. Or anything.

Oh, yeah, all of the above. Mark Northcutt Junior had participated, but he'd certainly not been the worst. That honor went to Chad. Mark had—as always—followed along.

There'd been a time when all that had hurt her a lot.

It sank into oblivion under later, greater pains.

And then those pains, too, went numb. Because she deliberately went numb.

But she wasn't numb now.

She put her hand on his arm. "It means a lot to me you saying that, Mark. Thank you. But it's time now for all of us to put those things behind us." She softened that by adding, "Don't you think?"

"Yeah, yeah, I do. Put all of it behind us and move forward."

Move forward.

That's what she'd intended to do the day Chad was shot.

Horrifyingly, thrillingly forward.

She couldn't. Then. Caught by her own sense of duty or maybe it wasn't as noble as that. Maybe it had been caught by her inability to imagine being a person who walked away from Chad under those circumstances.

Move forward.

Her heart lurched, pulling her stomach up into her throat.

How had she not recognized it until this moment that now she could move forward.

That now she had to.

"Mark, I have a question for you."

❖ ❖ ❖ ❖

LANDIS AND BELICHEK intercepted Mark Northcutt Junior as he walked away from Ally.

Her first expression had Landis lengthening his stride, intending to latch on to whatever body part of Mark Junior he got first and not letting go.

But that expression evaporated under the heat of something that made her appear almost … joyful.

"Hey, Mark," Bel said. "Got a minute?"

Landis checked Ally again. She looked fine. And Maggie and J.D. had just joined her with drinks and plates of food from the buffet.

"Sure."

"How was Ally?" Bel asked, proving he hadn't missed her expression either. Probably had been prepared to grab hold of Landis to keep him from committing any crimes on Mark Junior.

"She, uh, she seemed okay." He stiffened his back. "I wanted to tell her I was sorry if I'd ever been, you know, not as welcoming as I should have been."

"You didn't want her to join the family?"

"What? No. That isn't what I meant. She's nice. Always has been, since the first time Chad brought her around. It was—" His glance toward Landis bounced off before reaching the destination. "—other places. I guess Chad wanted, you know, to keep family separate from the guys and I sort of went along. More than I should have."

More heartily, he added, "Hell, at family gatherings Ally's always the bright spot. Made some of those Sunday brunches almost tolerable."

"Guess some got tense, especially that last one, the one before Chad was shot. Him and Rachel? Then you went to Chad and Ally's to smooth things out."

"Me? Smooth things out between Chad and Rachel? No way. They were always at it. Chad had trouble adjusting to her not being the skinny girl he could boss around from when we were kids. But if you're thinking that was the last Northcutt family Sunday brunch, you're wrong. I wish. Had one yesterday. Command appearance."

To which Ally hadn't been invited. Already out of the Northcutt family. Did she know? Did she care?

"Who all was there?" Bel asked.

"Me, Dad, Mom, Aunt Dawn, Uncle Preston, and, of course, Rachel."

Circling back to his question to Shindell, Landis said, "Guess you've all got to stay in Iris' good graces if you want to buy a place, since she runs the family trust."

"Which means I'll probably never have a chance," he said morosely. "She's said no to winter places for my folks and Preston, even though they were paying for most of it themselves. Last one she approved was Chad and Ally."

"What about Rachel?"

"She didn't use the family trust. Paid for her own place. She's always on me about how I could do it, too, if I watched my expenses and invested.

"Yeah," he added with an air of grievance, "and in the meantime, the trust grows and grows with nothing coming out of it that could help any of us now."

❖　❖　❖　❖

"POSSIBILITY?" BEL PROPOSED.

"Following the money rarely goes wrong. But how Iris sitting on the trust could have gotten Chad killed or endangered Ally... Something with the house? Yeah, you're right. We need to look into that. But right now, this thing looks like it might be finally wrapping up."

PISCATTOWAY COUNTY POLICE DEPARTMENT

ADDRESS: 1567 Gardington Rd.
REASON FOR CALL: Report of breaking and entering
RESPONDING OFFICER: Elijah Garrid (Rock Creek County deputy sheriff, covering shift for Piscattoway PD during funeral for PCPD officer Chad Northcutt)

I responded at 20 hours 35 minutes to a 911 report of a breaking and entering at 1567 Gardington Rd. the residence of Allison Lindell Northcutt. Dispatch informed me that her husband was the officer buried today. Dispatch also reported this was the second breaking and entering at the address in a week.

A patrol vehicle was in place in front of the residence with police tape marking off 1567 Gardington as well as the house directly across Gardington (1570).

Patrol Officer C. Nashua from Monacan Police Department was on duty. He was talking to two men when I arrived. Det. F. Belichek and Det. T. Landis identified themselves as Fairlington County (Va.) Police Department officers.

I called for an additional unit.

I ordered Officer Nashua to go into 1567 Gardington, gather all persons there into one room and remain with them, noting anything they said.

Belichek and Landis said homeowner Allison Lindell Northcutt and her party returned to the residence at 20 hours 25 minutes. after leaving the post-funeral reception at approximately 20 hours 10 minutes. They described the previous break-in. Report No. 051728. The house had been ransacked.

I contacted Piscattoway County Police Department Detective E. Tancroft, who had written Report No. 050921. He arrived on scene at 21 hours 05 minutes.

Officer Nashua's report follows.

Patrol Officer Chandler Nashua (Monacan PD, substituting for Piscattoway PD)

I reported to 1567 Gardington to maintain a presence between it and 1570 Gardington while the residents were attending the funeral, with instructions to remain by the patrol vehicle parked in the street. I noted no activity inside or outside either house from my position. No noise came from either house.

The resident—Allison Northcutt—and her party returned at 20 hours 25 minutes. They had not all entered the front door of 1567

Gardington when they abruptly stopped and those who had entered exited the front door. Detective T. Landis of Fairlington County Police Department (Va.) came to my vehicle, identified himself, reported there had been a break-in at the residence, asked that I call it in.

Elijah Garrid, Rock Creek County, Md., deputy sheriff arrived at 20 hours 36 minutes. I reported to him there had been no indication of disturbance at 1567 Gardington during the time I was stationed in front of it. However, the back door could be accessed without being observed from my location.

Deputy Garrid instructed me to stay with the group that included the homeowner gathered by the front door until relieved. None of them spoke during that time.

CHAPTER FORTY-SEVEN

"**NOT CAREFUL THIS** time," Belichek said under his breath.

"Rushed," Landis agreed at the same volume, which was low enough that none of the law enforcement representatives from the various Maryland departments could hear them.

After hearing their accounts, the responding officer dismissed them. Tried to send them back to the family group by the front door. They'd moved off a few feet, but stayed within earshot of those not talking under their breath.

They'd heard the Rock Creek Sheriff's Deputy report, accurately relaying what the young—very young—Monacan officer said. He hadn't included that Chandler Nashua was stricken that he'd missed a break-in.

Before the others arrived, Belichek had offered the solace that it could have happened before the kid came on duty.

Ted Tancroft, looking weary, arrived fifteen minutes ago. He sent word to the Rock Creek deputy, but stayed behind the police tape.

Landis went to him.

"Answer any lingering doubts? The first one was unlikely enough—she'd've had to stage it before she left for court in Fairlington early in the morning. Well before the long-term care facility called and said her husband was dying.

"But this? She'd have to be Houdini reincarnated. She's been visible to you and the rest of the Piscattoway PD, departments from all over the region and far-flung states, and TV cameras every moment."

With more than a little satisfaction, he walked back to his partner.

Now they considered other possibilities.

"Desperate," Belichek proposed.

"Going in with a patrol car out front? Hell, yeah, he's desperate. Question is if it's a different person, this one more desperate than the first break-in joker. Or if it's the same person getting more desperate. Either way, what's making him desperate? Time? Something else?"

"Go back to the people."

"Paulz or Selton are possibilities. Ortiz? But after this time away? Wuertl would be playing one hell of a dangerous game telling us anything if it's her. Brentford would have to be the best actor, ever. And I might be wrong, but, like Wuertl, why volunteer anything?"

"Keep going," Bel said.

"Could Mark Junior really be as easygoing as he seems, as Natalie described? Especially considering what she said about how David Junior and Chad treated him?"

"Her and Shindell. But some people are that easygoing. Although that doesn't mean he is."

"Well, that covered it," Landis drawled sarcastically.

Unmoved, Bel said, "Pretty much. Same goes with what he knew. Possible Mark didn't know what Chad was doing because his cousin didn't confide in him. Or he's pretended ignorance to try to distance himself from Chad. Or—What are you thinking? You've got that look."

"I'm thinking about the shooter. I'm thinking *like* the shooter. You need to kill a cop badly enough that you shoot him outside his house on a weekday morning."

"Yeah."

"And when he doesn't die, and Iris Northcutt is telling every camera, every microphone, every reporter that Chad—the cop you so badly needed to kill—will be back on his feet any day, what do you do?"

Bel twisted his neck to face him. "You wait."

"You wait," he agreed. "For four years and six months, you wait. Instead of making sure the job was done. Because suddenly it wasn't as vital that he be dead. Or—" He drew it out while Bel rotated his wrist, telling him to hurry things up. "—you knew he wasn't going to get better. Because you knew the truth from the start. Because you were inside."

"Mark."

"Yeah. Junior and senior, though why senior would…"

"Paulz and Selton?"

"Don't know. But Ally will."

✧ ✧ ✧ ✧

"ALLY, WE HAVE a question if—Are you okay?"

She sat on a bench in the middle of the front yard, the others standing nearby. Her eyes opened at Tanner's voice.

"Yes. I am."

He thought that would be the end of it. But after a couple breaths, she started talking again.

"I didn't want all of the ceremony, but maybe Iris was right in a way. The sense of community is palpable. I think… I think it was good for the department. They needed this."

"What about you?"

"Not the same way. And yet… That figure following the bagpiper over the hill… It felt to me like Chad, the good in him, found peace. I thought—*felt*—he's let go now. I have let go."

"Ally," Bel said gently, "we need your help."

"Of course. Your question. Sorry."

"After Chad was shot, who knew how bad his condition was?"

"The doctors were very honest with us—Iris and me—from the start. She wouldn't accept it."

"When that article came out, the one that made Iris so angry, was that when it became known beyond a few people?"

"I don't know."

"It was," Maggie said. "We—Jamie and I—didn't even tell her parents. That's how tight we kept it about his condition."

"Right. And who else knew that was the situation? The Mark Northcutt family?"

Ally looked at Bel, then back at him. "I think so."

"Anyone else?"

"Preston and, I suppose, Rachel. Preston was with us when the doctors tried to tell Iris the first time."

"What about Ethan Paulz and Dewey Selton?"

"I assumed they did. From Mark Junior. But I can't say for sure. I don't know. I just don't know. I'm sure Iris wouldn't have told anyone because she refused to believe it."

"What about who you told—beyond Jamie and Maggie?" Bel asked.

"I didn't tell anyone else except…"

"Shindell Ortiz," Landis said into her pause.

J.D. commented, "Wouldn't take an FBI agent to figure out this was the best time to break in. Anybody who can use a search engine could find out when the reception was scheduled."

"Cop car out front didn't deter them. Didn't bother to keep the disarray down this time. Someone in a hurry," Landis said. "Because he had to get back to the reception before being missed."

Showing no sign of reacting to that implication, Ally said, "If it was somebody different, how did they know that whatever they were after hadn't already been found?"

No one else said anything for an instant.

"Great, Ally," Landis said.

"There's something else. I was thinking about someone searching for something—it's not that big a house and I'm not a pack rat. If they didn't get it this time … and going through the whole house like that, it doesn't look like they did unless it was the last place they looked, but I *know* what's in that house. I've sorted and straightened out and—"

Maggie interrupted. "You don't have to talk us into listening to you. Say what you're thinking."

Ally's gaze flashed from her to Landis.

"It's a long shot, but … My art supplies are in a storage unit. I told you that." He was aware of both her cousins looking toward him, but kept his focus on her. "A storage unit in Fairlington, actually. I wanted it away from the house. I went there one last time before I was going to leave. I couldn't take it with me, there was too much. And I knew I had to travel light. But I thought maybe someday… It's not likely Chad would have put anything in with my art things, but it's the only place I can think of that we haven't looked. That the person or people who have broken in haven't looked."

"Did you use one of your new identities for it?"

"No, but…"

"Chad didn't find it?"

She licked her lips. "No."

✧　✧　✧　✧

"I WASN'T GOING to put the locker under Northcutt in case he did look for it. And then the guy at the storage place was creepy. I thought when the typo happened that it was just as well, so even if Chad looked for it… Heck, if *I* were looking for it by name only, *I'd* have a hard time finding it. That's—"

"Back up. What name is it under?"

"Lindell Theodore."

He frowned. "Your maiden name as a first name?"

"Yes. I did that on purpose. But I meant to fill out the form Lindell Theodora. That's my real first name—Theodora, not Ally or even Allison, which is legally my middle name. But then the guy misread my handwriting and made it Theodore instead of Theodora. I saw what he'd done, but, to be honest, I wanted to get away from that guy. I sure didn't want to tell him he'd made a mistake. And maybe I was a little relieved he didn't have my right name. As it was, he hung around the whole time I loaded my canvases and supplies in. Didn't offer to help, just watched."

"What did you use for an address?"

"Not the house. I told you, I wanted to keep it away from Chad. I used the address of my art school."

Not bad. An address she'd remember, but not one Chad would. He'd pick up the connection if he looked up the address. But first he'd have to have a reason to focus on that address among all those listed and that would be after finding that specific storage facility.

"How'd you pay?"

"Cash. I still pay for the year ahead. After that first time, I've only gone in the morning. Haven't seen the creepy guy again."

"Have you gone through everything there?"

"No. I've barely gone at all."

After a moment, Landis said to Bel, "It won't be open now."

"We could get a warrant."

"That would call attention to what we're doing."

Without any of them looking, they all acknowledged the presence of local law enforcement around them.

"I don't want to raise hopes," Ally started. "I don't have any reason to think there *is* anything there. It's my stuff, not Chad's. It's only that it's the one place…"

"We haven't checked," he finished. "Which is the reason we're going to check it."

Bel said, "We can't stay here anyway tonight, they'll be processing this scene a lot longer than the first one."

"Because it's so messy," Jamie said wisely.

"And because they can't dismiss it as Ally's imagination," Maggie added grimly.

"Back to Jamie's," Bel said.

"Maybe some diversions tomorrow, in case anybody's watching," J.D. added.

"But sleep first," Jamie concluded.

—DAY 8—

TUESDAY

CHAPTER FORTY-EIGHT

JAMIE AND BEL went out the front door first.

The drizzle cooperated. Jamie wore a rain hat and Ally's coat on the off chance someone would recognize it, and Bel held an umbrella over her head as they got in her car.

At the same time, Ally's car, with the windshield wipers going fast, left from the garage with Maggie in it, wearing Ally's clothes and with her dark hair in a scarf.

J.D., already in place a block away with a view of the path of both cars, called as promised. He wasted no words.

"Nothing."

"Was worth a try," Landis said.

"Yeah. I'll keep an eye out at Maggie's."

That's where she was headed now, with J.D. following.

Bel was taking Jamie to the Fairlington PD, with Danolin watching their backs at the building.

Landis and Ally got in his car twenty minutes later, knowing the others were at their destinations.

They drove to a parking deck with exits on two different streets. On the third level, he pulled in to a spot on the far side of a panel truck, but not all the way in.

"Come around the front," he told her. "Quick."

He hit a button on a key fob and a side door of the truck opened.

Wet tires climbing the parking deck's ramp reached them.

Landis pushed her inside with a good shove to her back. Not enough to hurt, but plenty to hurry her inside. He came in right behind her, closing the door as he did, dropping dark all around them. He crowded against her back.

"Tanner—"

"Quiet."

The sound of a vehicle approaching reached them. It passed the truck then stopped sharply.

After seven breaths, it drove on. She knew it was seven breaths because she felt them on her neck.

Seven of his breaths, anyway.

The movement of his breaths set up a slight friction with her blouse. She'd searched for something white to wear today. It was the only thing she'd had with her. It was dressier than her jeans, with small pearl buttons all the way from the high neck to the hem.

Her own breaths were coming faster by the time the vehicle moved again.

Still, he remained where he was. At least the inside of the van became clearer as her eyes adjusted.

She hadn't heard anything for another nine of his breaths when he said, "Okay."

He edged her to one side with his hands on her shoulders. She was aware of the weight and the gentleness of the hold before he climbed between the two seats and into the driver's seat. "C'mon."

She clambered into the passenger seat, trying hard not to put her derriere into his face.

To distract—him? herself? both of them?—she said, "Now to the storage unit."

"Yep."

Throughout their rush-hour trip to the storage facility, Eddy Knarr reported that they were clear of a tail.

His last report came with them inside, but before they'd committed to going deeper into the building, much less close to her unit.

"All clear," Knarr said. "See you on the flip side."

✧ ✧ ✧ ✧

THE STORAGE AREA included drop-cloth-covered canvases in holders that kept them upright. Boxes labeled with names of paint, brushes, and other supplies stacked neatly.

A single aisle down the middle allowed access in the narrow unit that ran about twelve feet deep, eight feet wide.

Ally walked that aisle like she'd entered a church.

"Oh, a full box of vellum paper. I always liked vellum paper for charcoal."

"Because smooth doesn't work as well because charcoal doesn't stick to it," he said.

"Yes."

"So, you don't like smooth."

She turned and eyed him. "It depends on what it interacts with."

They were close in the small area. He heard her breathing. Saw it, under that white blouse. The movement glinted lights off the small white globes of buttons.

She licked her lips again, then moved down the aisle, her hand touching boxes. "Bel said you took classes…"

"No drawing or painting. No talent. I've picked up some about the art world, art theft. Knowing the basics has come in handy."

"Ah. Solely for career advancement."

"Exactly."

"Interesting."

"I'm supposed to ask what's interesting?"

"You are," she said solemnly. "Though if you don't, I'm not going to let it stop me from saying I heard otherwise."

"Bel again. You shouldn't listen to that philistine. So, what's interesting?"

"Last night, at the reception, I was remembering that Sunday brunch before Chad was shot and asked Mark Junior what he remembered. With the break-in, the mess, and everything else it sort of faded out of my mind.

"Mark said he heard Chad accuse Rachel of sleeping her way to the top. When she didn't rise to that bait, he said she must have a sugar daddy, too. That's when she got angry.

"I do remember even Iris saying he needed to apologize for the *good of the family*. He blew her off. I'd never seen him do that before. Just walk out while she was telling him to do something."

"Rachel got angry about him saying she had a sugar daddy, huh? That is interesting. Could he and Rachel have been having an affair?"

Her mouth dropped open. "*Rachel?* I can't imagine... She saw him as a brother. No. No, I'm sure not."

"You can't imagine it of Rachel, but you could of Chad?"

"Well, Willow is certain proof that he could—" She broke off and pulled the cover off a line of canvases.

"It could explain the tension between them before he was shot."

"That was Chad's jealousy over her promotion, I told you. Oh. *Oh...*"

"What?"

She'd pulled one canvas free. He saw only the back of it, but she was looking at the front. "Something wrong with it?"

"No." She made a strangled sound. "I shouldn't cry. I'm happy, really."

He reached over and pulled her into him, not caring that the corner of the frame dug into his thigh.

"I'm lucky... I'm so lucky... After what could have happened Tuesday—"

"It shouldn't qualify as good luck to keep on breathing."

She shook her head, the movement a friction against his shirt that instantly brought his body to arousal. He lost her next few words.

"...moving forward and now here are the things that open my heart. They're still here."

The things that open my heart...

"This is the portrait of David's family I told you about."

His phone rang.

He cursed. "It's Bel. I've got to get this." He answered with, "What?"

"Get back here. Now."

"Why—?"

"We've caught the kid, the one in the car that tried to run you down outside Willow Spencer's building. He was trying to get into Jamie's house. He's Rhonda Quesey's son."

CHAPTER FORTY-NINE

HE JOINED BEL to watch the interview.

"He was never after Ally," Bel said.

Landis had figured that out on the way to Fairlington County Police Department.

The son of Rhonda Quesey had no reason on earth to harm Ally.

The kid shot at him.

Not Ally.

On the drive back, he'd run his mental tape of the shooting through again and again. Fast-forwarding through all the moments except after he'd come out of that door onto the plaza. Then he slowed it down, examining it frame by frame.

Had he started to make his move toward her before the shot? Had he brought the kid's aim toward her. Not saving her, not protecting her at all, but endangering her by his presence, by his damned existence.

Why the hell hadn't he stayed away from her? Completely away, as he had for years.

True, he'd done that for his own sake, to avoid seeing her married to another man. Why hadn't he stuck with that, no matter what excuses he needed to tell himself.

So he didn't bring a bullet to her.

"I have to tell Ally."

"After. Danolin's about to start."

That familiar voice came through to the small office used for observing interviews. "You're entitled to legal representation—"

"That's for guilty people."

"—or for your parents to be—"

"That's for babies. I'm eighteen."

"—here while we talk."

"Talk. Right. Just a couple of buddies having a chat."

"You're not taking this serious, Simon."

"No kidding."

"It's very serious. Shooting at someone always is."

"Shooting? You're crazy, buddy."

"…and breaking into Ms. Northcutt's home—"

"I didn't break into anyplace."

"Let's start with easier questions. How do you know Allison Northcutt?"

"Don't."

"You recognize the name. That's clear."

"Big deal. She's all over the news. Never heard of her before that. She's the one who got shot at by the courthouse. Everybody knows her now."

Danolin opened a folder, placed three photos face down on the table. The kid stared at their plain backs.

Danolin flipped over one.

Ally. From a newspaper shot.

"Recognize her?"

"All over the news, like I said."

Slowly, Danolin's hand went to the next photo. The kid breathed faster.

He turned over Belichek's picture.

"Not who you were expecting, huh?" Danolin said easily.

He flipped over the last one. Landis.

The kid's lips drew back from his teeth. For a second it reminded Landis of Iris Northcutt.

"He knows your mom, huh?"

"That's funny. That's real funny. Yeah, he knows her. And I knew about him. Knew it for ages. She thought she was so smart. Sneaky. Like she even had to be for Dad. Oblivious. Trusted her, he said. *Trust.*

He's an idiot. Trusting her."

"Why was that?"

"This guy wasn't the first." His dismissive world-weary tone conflicted with the fisting of his hands on the table. "Except it's different, totally different. They're getting divorced. Because of him. She dumped my dad, left him, left *me*, all so she could go after this asshole. It's funny."

His throat went taut with dry hacks that were supposed to be laughs.

"He doesn't even want her. He broke it off. That didn't stop her. She kept after him. Kept calling him and calling him. I heard her. I even heard him tell her it was over. Forever. But she still can't let go. Dad would take her back. He would. He's that pathetic. It wouldn't be like before, but it would be a hell of a lot better than it's been and it would all be worth it. If that bastard Landis was gone. If he was dead, she'd come back. She'd have to.

"When I heard that shot and saw him going down, I thought… I thought…" His voice broke. Spittle flecked the corners of his mouth. "I thought he was shot. I thought he was dead. *Dead.* God, I hoped he was dead. I wanted to see him dead, right there in front of me. Blood and brains and all of it. But the bastard didn't even get hit."

Sobs overtook words, his head dropped to his arms on the table's surface, as his narrow back shook.

"He heard the shot and saw you going down," Bel muttered.

Landis turned away. "He wasn't the shooter."

CHAPTER FIFTY

THEY SAT ON a bench near the back elevator. Even at this time of day, this hallway was deserted as he told Ally all of it.

"He's not the one who broke in?"

"He said he didn't. And it fits."

"So he didn't shoot, not at me, not at you. He didn't hurt either one of us."

"Not for lack of trying. I'd only have gotten you run down instead of shot. And we still don't know who fired at you."

"What happens now?"

"We go back to square one."

"I meant for the boy."

"Danolin will work on that. The kid's a mess, but he's not a master criminal. There are programs."

"Tanner, this wasn't your fault," Ally said.

"The hell it's not."

"You mean not yet finding the shooter from the courthouse, but I meant the boy."

"So did I."

"We do things. We let situations that aren't good go on … go on too long even when we know we shouldn't. And then they affect other people—people we might not even know exist—and in ways we can't possibly imagine. But we can't take on the responsibility for every ripple that crosses any other ripple out there in the world. Someone told me that."

"I wanted her to go away. When she finally did, I was relieved." He dropped his forearms to his thighs, bent his head. "A kid. Just a damned kid."

She reached toward him, hesitated, then curved her hand over his arm. The shirt was warmed by the muscle and sinew beneath it, reminding her of his strength, but it wasn't his strength she was talking to now.

"You didn't know. She made sure you didn't know."

"I should've—"

"You should've ended the relationship and encouraged her to get help when you recognized her instability. And you did."

"I should've seen it before—"

"We all can torture ourselves with should'ves, Tanner. You think I don't have a pile of them? But this past week I've learned to ask *How do they help?*

"Look, if you're going to take on complete responsibility for this kid's problems—forgetting nature and nurture and all the years of his messed up homelife that came before you ever crossed paths with his mother—then you also have to take what Judge DaSilva said. That's the other side of the coin and both are real.

"I realized that about Chad."

Still leaning forward, he turned his head toward her. "When?"

"I can't tell you a precise moment. I know I was sitting with him at the Chate center. It must have been around a year after he was shot. I knew there was no chance he was going to get better. I also knew that I'd stayed—"

"Because you thought I'd shot him—might have shot him."

"No. It was because of my fear. That was my sin. In—"

"*Your* sin? Bull—"

"Yes. Yes, *my* sin. Like with Vivian. My fear of having things change from what I *wanted* them to be, so I tried to hold on even when it was all a lie."

"You were a kid."

"I let myself be used so long by my parents out of fear. And then I did the same damned thing with Chad, when I was no longer a kid. That day, sitting with him in the Chate Center, I think that was the first step of coming to terms with myself."

"Then why stay?"

"I think… I think I was completing my promise. You could say I was completing my shift. Waiting for my End of Duty call. You don't get that by closing up shop and going home when you feel like it. You go when the job's done."

"Christ, Ally…"

He put his hand over hers, still on his arm.

They sat like that, how long didn't matter.

"Tanner?"

"Hmm."

"Will you take me home now? Your home."

HE WATCHED HER taking in his place. Slowly pivoting from her spot four feet inside the door.

"It's very like you."

He didn't know what to do with that statement.

He liked his place. He'd picked each piece carefully, on its own and how it worked with the rest. He'd lived with only the sofa for a year before adding the end table. The walnut coffee table came quickly, spotted in the workshop of a furniture rehabber who'd been a witness in a case. But the lamp behind the sofa took two false tries before he got it right.

He tried to see it through her eyes.

Two images flashed through his mind.

That godawful living room on Gardington Road where she'd immured herself.

And the painting—her painting—over the mantel at Jamie's.

Guess it could use some artwork.

He felt the inane words working their way up his throat and swallowed hard to send them to perdition.

"Wow. That's quite the view."

She went to the balcony doors, but made no move to open them, to step onto the balcony and really take in the sky, or the river glinting between jumbled blocks of buildings.

She turned her back on the balcony to face him. "Where's the bedroom?"

She headed straight toward it.

"Doesn't matter, because we're not going there."

He stepped in front of her, blocking. She came up against him and stayed, but her eyes, startled wide, came to his face. "We're not?"

He pulled out his best grin. "No. I couldn't take the payback after all the shit I gave Belichek for getting, uh, *involved* with Jamie during a case."

She was supposed to smile at that.

She didn't. She said, solemnly, "I see."

He felt the necessity of emphasizing, "This is not heading to that bedroom, Ally."

She sighed, the breath against his throat tautening every bit of his body. Some bits more than others.

"Tanner, we've been heading there since the night at Mikey's. Don't you think it's about time we arrived?"

"Time is the problem. This investigation, what's been happening to you, around you, it distorts your view of time, makes some things look more important, bigger than they really are—like mirrors. *Warning: Images in this mirror may appear distorted.* This is a chunk of time torn out of your real life. And when you get back to that real life, you'll— What?"

"That's what you do, isn't it, Tanner?"

"What?"

"With the women. You give them a chunk of time torn out of their real lives and then you send them back. Are most of them better off, like the judge? A little healed, a little stronger? But what about *your* real life?"

She couldn't have expected an answer. Not when she put her mouth at the base of his throat and gently sucked there.

This was wrong.

He should be seducing her. He should be...

She nudged him backward a step. A second. A third.

"Ally, we don't have to do anything."

"I think we do." She circled him, continued toward her destination. "Is this the bedroom through here? Ah, yes... *Oh.*"

He trailed her into the bedroom. She stood in front of her drawing.

"That night at Mikey's. It became a study for a painting I did. Working with dark to create light."

From behind, he rested his hands on her hips, his head beside hers, looking at what she'd created, at what he'd had of her for these years.

She put her hands over his a moment, then moved them to her throat.

She was unbuttoning her blouse.

He turned her, giving him her mouth to kiss, her lips to stroke.

Her hands kept moving.

When they had to breathe, she used some of her oxygen to say, "These damned buttons."

He kissed her again for cursing them. His tongue stroking into her mouth.

Then he was helping her with the buttons. Trying to. They were small, slippery, and so damned many of them.

They pulled his shirt off. She stepped out of her pants. He chucked off his. And still there were buttons.

But he had the blouse open enough to bare her shoulders.

His hold gapped the neckline's V deep and wide. He could smell the warmth between her breasts. Then he tasted it.

He pushed the bra aside, bunching the material against her to put his tongue on her nipple. He felt it changing. He opened his mouth over her.

"Tear it, Tanner. Just tear it."

He wouldn't. Couldn't. Not to her.

"Ally."

Christ, it sounded like begging. It was.

She rocked against him.

"Ally." This was a warning. A final caution to her. To get out. Now.

"You want me, Tanner. I want you. If that's all you can give me, I'll take it. It's like you said, it's time out of time, not part of the calendar of our lives."

He'd give her now. He'd give her this time out of time.

The last buttons tore loose, pinging against the wall, the dresser, his skin.

She shrugged the blouse off, the bra going with it.

He twisted them down to the bed, finding his way inside her.

As HIS CHEST heaved, her hand rode up, then down, the motion dragging her fingers gently across his skin.

His breathing slowed, steadied. But her hand's motion continued. Her fingers drawing over him.

His eyes drifted closed, seeing her fingertip smoothing the charcoal on her sketch, feeling it across his flesh.

"You like my place?" *God, Landis, more begging?*

But he didn't even feel bad enough about it to open his eyes.

"I like this bed. A lot."

"You said this place is like me. What did that mean?"

"Gorgeous. Stylish. Smooth. Needs some messing up. To show it's being lived in, not just visited, but—" That neared what she'd said before about women. He tensed. "—most of all to be loved."

She shifted, leaning over him, opening her mouth over his ribs, stroking now with her tongue.

He lasted longer than he expected. Maybe twenty, thirty seconds before he yanked her on top of him.

"Open."

She did.

"Your eyes."

That, too.

"If you have to come…"

"Oh, I'm coming all right."

CHAPTER FIFTY-ONE

His phone rang.

"Bel," he predicted.

Her phone rang.

"You answer."

"Afraid your caller is Maggie?" he teased her.

"No. No more being afraid. Besides, Maggie would pound on your door."

She had a point.

He answered.

"If you haven't resigned from this case, you better get dressed, Landis. We're downstairs. All of us. With food. We need to go back to square one."

✧　✧　✧　✧

The food was good.

The knowing looks at her wearing his t-shirt in hasty decency under a blouse missing half its buttons were unexpectedly tolerable.

Square one wasn't.

The third time Belichek came back to saying they needed to stop going over the same ideas and take a fresh approach, Landis said, "You're the one who thinks outside of the damned box. Who communes with the victim and the killer even before we know who it is. So commune.

"I'm the one who keeps track of the mundane details like physical evidence. I don't turn things upside down and backwards, which this sure as hell calls for, since we've gotten nowhere the straightforward way, going through the logical steps of cause and effect. Go ahead, be brilliant. Turn those upside down."

"Tanner." Bel's single word, especially using his first name was an appeal to calm.

He was breathing hard.

Frustration, he told himself. He'd been here before on cases…

He'd been here before.

The hell he had. This wasn't just a case. This was Ally.

Frustration was way down the list.

Fear—terror—that not figuring this out left Ally in danger. That's what this was about.

This wasn't a murder case where the victim couldn't get any deader than they already were, so police work—his kind of police work— could sift through possibilities, take the time to let the right solution develop.

They didn't have time.

Not with Ally in danger. Which meant it needed to be his partner, because he was no damned good now that they'd run through the logical, now that they'd looked at cause and effect—

"What is it, Tanner?"

He was still breathing hard but it was different now.

"Cause and effect. What if we've been looking at them backward? Or in the wrong combination? We've always been thinking the timing of Chad going downhill caused the break-ins and the shooting. All of them together, in a clump. What if the timing of Chad going downhill caused *one* event, but then that event caused the others?"

"Separate them?"

"Maybe. Yeah. In fact… There could be two actors. One triggered by Chad's imminent death, another triggered by the first."

Bel frowned ferociously. "Okay. Let's talk about that."

CHAPTER FIFTY-TWO

"**S**EE?" V**INDICATION IN** her voice, Ally held the canvas up to him in the scant light in her storage locker.

They'd returned to the storage area less than an hour before it was to close at ten.

The creepy guy was not there.

Tanner wouldn't have minded if he was. No dragons around to slay for Ally, but he could have dealt with one creepy guy.

"Yes. I see."

She tried to look around the edge to see what she'd painted while keeping it visible to him. She shifted to get more light on it through the open door to the hallway.

"Doesn't it show you just what I said about Natalie?"

"It shows a lot. Difference is, you're talking about seeing Natalie. I see *you*. In this painting, in all of them. That night at Mikey's, the night we sat at the picnic table while you drew and I talked—"

"I talked, too. About art."

"Yeah. You said it made sense of what you see around you."

She blinked at him. "It does. It always did. I wonder if that's why when Chad insisted I give it up, I sort of went off the rails of myself for a while. I was trying so hard to be what he wanted. To have the family—I know. My cousins would say that family didn't exist. That I made it up in my head. You don't need to say it."

"Wasn't what I was going to say. I thought that night that you didn't see what other people saw and that was because it was you seeing it. You put yourself into your art. I told myself then that I didn't say it because it would make you uncomfortable.

"Truth is, it would've made me uncomfortable. I wasn't the man you drew. I'm even less that man now."

She stared at him. "You're wrong. You were and you are."

"Well, isn't this touching."

Rachel Northcutt.

Before her first word was out, he'd pushed Ally behind the crate, out of Rachel's sight and the aim of the gun she held.

"And isn't that even more touching? Proving Ally right that you're some kind of hero, huh? Not that it's going to make any difference. You'll notice I'm at the doorway. With my weapon drawn, while yours—which I'm quite sure you have—is not. You can't get it out, you can't get past me. I shoot you, then I shoot her, one-two.

"You might as well come out, Ally."

Ally hadn't learned much from Chad about guns, but enough to recognize a substantial handgun with a suppressor on it.

Rachel sighed as if in deep disappointment. "This has been a long time coming, I'm afraid."

Ally inhaled sharply. "You only volunteered to help after Chad was shot to go through his things. What were you looking for?"

"Records. At least that tells me you never found them. I wondered about that."

"That's what you fought with Chad about at the Sunday brunch."

"Very good. I realized you wouldn't defy Iris. I relaxed and took it slow. Got through a lot of stuff over the years. Eliminated all the best possibilities. But you were coming out of it, whether you knew it or not. The stuff with your cousins the past year and a half was pulling you more and more out of the Northcutt Triangle. Iris saw it. Drove her mad. I saw it. And I prepared."

"Wait a minute. How did you get in? I changed the locks."

She scoffed. "And left the keys on the counter when I *helped* you the next weekend. Said I was going out for takeout, took the keys and detoured to duplicate the keys. You never even knew they were gone."

Why was Rachel talking like this? Putting off what she intended to do?

"But why shoot him? You and Chad were always close."

"Close? He tormented me as a kid. I used him as an adult. Then he thought he could start ordering me around. Killing him was the only reasonable solution to protect my position." She looked away from her.

Rachel didn't want to do this—she seemed to genuinely like Ally—but she would.

And she didn't have any trouble looking at Landis.

"Protect your position how? If you were both doing the same thing?"

"We were *not* doing the same thing. I selected a few spread-out targets for a specific goal."

"The townhouse."

She didn't bother to confirm. "Chad, undisciplined as always, scattered-gunned, involved more idiots, and then thought he was going to tell me we weren't stopping when I said we were. He thought he could dictate to *me*. I only took him in because I needed a short-term boost."

"How did his taking people's money give you a boost?"

"Consider it a franchise fee."

"What do you think, Bel?" Landis asked loudly, focusing over Rachel's shoulder to the hallway.

She sneered at him. "Right. Like I'm supposed to turn around to see if your partner's behind me."

Ally looked from him back to Rachel. Her voice shook with the same vibration as her accelerated heartbeat. "But... how did you have time? If you did the break-in at the house looking for Chad's notebook, how could you have been at the Fairlington Courthouse trying to kill me? Because you were on-duty later, when the department learned about Chad's condition deteriorating."

"You think I shot at you at the courthouse? I'll shoot you now, but I didn't shoot at you there."

"But—"

"I did."

Iris Northcutt held a large, old-fashioned handgun, pointed at Ally. It shook, even in her two-handed hold.

Rachel moved over, making room for the older woman, whose focus never left her daughter-in-law.

"*You* said he was dead. You told 911 he was *dead*. You—"

"I thought he was. All that… damage."

The older woman hadn't heard. "—*wanted* him to be dead. And I vowed that day that when you got your wish and my son truly was dead, that I would kill you."

"I never wanted him dead and I'm sorry I said that. But what I said didn't change anything. They did everything they could. You know they did. Just as he fought as hard as he could to keep living.

"He did and you did and, whether you believe it or not, I fought, too. Hoping he would recover. Because if he did, I could leave him. I could start a new life. Otherwise, I was tied to him in ways I could never escape."

"*Escape? You?*" Her voice shook with venom. "*Escape.* You were never good enough for him. Never deserved him or to be a North-cutt."

She raised the gun again.

CHAPTER FIFTY-THREE

"**OH, FOR GOD'S** sake," Rachel snapped.

She wrenched the gun from Iris with a one-handed hold on her wrist that made the older woman howl with pain.

Landis' muscles tightened, but he didn't lunge. There wasn't time before Rachel dropped Iris' gun in her pocket and was focused on him again. Her aim at him had never wavered.

"Why did you do that?" Iris held her right wrist in her left palm. "I told you I'm going to shoot her."

"Not with that thing you're not. We'd have everybody in a square mile here in seconds with the noise that thing would make."

"You knew Iris planned to shoot Ally," Landis said.

"Now or at the courthouse?" She smirked. "I knew she *said* she meant to shoot at her. Never thought the crazy old lady would actually try, and if she did try, there was no reason on earth to think she'd hit her. Uncle David taught her to shoot back in the dark ages and she hasn't practiced since. Ally wasn't in any danger. Then."

"Yet you chose *that* day to go into Ally's house and check for the records. Like there was urgency, which there would have been if Iris killed Ally, because then other people—especially Iris, assuming she got away with it, but alternatively Ally's family—would have access to the house and potentially go through the few things you hadn't yet checked. All this time after shooting Chad, you'd finally know for sure."

"After shooting... You? *You* shot my Chad?" Iris screeched.

"Be quiet. He's trying to confuse you. We'll talk about this later,

Iris."

"She did, Iris," Ally said. "She shot Chad, then drove away and left him bleeding on the driveway."

"I don't know," Landis said, "that sounds a lot like cause and effect to me."

"Cause and eff—? Stop that, Iris. *Stop.*"

But Iris continued to claw at Rachel's gun-holding hand, distracting her as Rutherford Belichek came around her other side and neatly disarmed her.

He also snapped the handcuffs around her wrists.

Tanner Landis put the cuffs on Iris Northcutt.

"I cooperated," Rachel shouted as she was led out. "Remember that. You wouldn't have flushed out Iris without me. And I never shot at Ally."

"Yeah," Bel said under his breath, "thanks a lot for that."

✧   ✧   ✧   ✧

"THE RIGHT MURDER suspect is like the perfect utility knife—it solves all your problems, answers all your needs. That's what Rachel did," Landis said, answering a question from Jamie.

They were all in the break room at Fairlington PD, with Ally and Tanner enjoying the freedom of being out of their body armor, while waiting for the tech to set up so they could listen to Danolin's just concluded interview of Rachel Northcutt.

Nobody had questions about Iris Northcutt's actions or motivations.

"Solves all your problems. Might use that line someday," Maggie said.

"As long as I get credit," Landis said. "Rachel answered the need for someone who knew the routine on Gardington Road. Who knew the areas of the county to jack a tinted-window car and dispose of it, who knew the routes to avoid security cameras and the perfect spot to dispose of it.

"She also answered the major question of why do nothing for four and a half years, then begin to act. Because she had been acting all along by searching all along."

Bel picked it up. "At first, she'd thought she had what she needed—Chad's little black book of crime. Except what she took off him after shooting him was a new book after he thought he lost the old one."

"Thought? Didn't he lose it?"

"Misplaced it. He put it under the bed, tucked into a strap under the mattress. That was his line about keeping it close to his heart—that's where his heart was when he slept. Except Ally had been stowing her sketch book under the bed, too. He unknowingly slid his book into the sketch book.

"Ally took that sketchbook to the storage locker during her preparations to leave him, not knowing his notebook was jammed inside. She found it on our first trip to the locker today."

"Okay, and I get that Chad wouldn't quit, but shooting him?"

"She ran the group, taking a cut, using Chad as her visible lieutenant—no one else knew who the leader was. She had a specific goal—to get her own place without the Northcutt family trust, because Iris was holding tight to those funds. When Rachel achieved that, then got first one promotion, then more, she had a lot to lose. And—unlike the others—she'd used the money carefully, so she didn't need more.

"Chad wasn't about to stop with his mother and girlfriend to support. Plus, he'd pulled his buddies in."

"And Mark Junior? Was he in it? Is that why he came over that Sunday? To try to make peace between his cousins?" Jamie asked.

"We don't think so. His finances show no sign of other income."

"If he was stealing," Landis added, "he's the worst thief ever, because he has nothing to show for it. Neither Rachel nor Chad thought he was smart enough to include. They also might not have been sure he'd go along."

"But she said she was at the dentist, how did she break in to Ally's house Tuesday?" Jamie objected.

"She lied," Landis said. "Never thought anybody would check. We checked. What we didn't expect was Iris showing up."

"That's why Rachel kept talking. She expected Iris. I had no idea, but you saw her, didn't you, Tanner?" Ally asked.

"I saw a shadow in the hallway that wasn't Belichek."

"Because I wouldn't have been sloppy enough to let you see my shadow."

"Because you would've had to shrink. A bunch."

"And then he used the *cause-and-effect* line to really get Bel to move, reminding him of Tanner's insight about there being two actors," Ally said.

She saw a few grins at her praise, but didn't mind, because he winked at her.

"Here we go," the tech said. "Missed the beginning, unless you want me to rewind."

"We'll rewind if we need to."

Rachel's voice came.

"...and he was out of control. Plus, I knew Ally was getting ready to leave. Chad didn't see the signs—too caught up in the wonderfulness of Chad to ever think she'd actually do it. When she finally got up the gumption, I was ready, because he would have lost his mind, along with every bit of self-preservation or protection of the operation. He'd have bulldozed and blundered, gouging and crashing through my careful wall of protection. Might have killed her, too. And then the investigative spotlight would have been turned on him full-force. Couldn't have that.

"Better, far, far better to kill him. Sure, they looked into some of his cases looking for suspects. But I'd covered my tracks. And a word here and there pushed Wamdler farther off."

Rachel looked no different. She seemed at ease.

"What were you searching for?"

"Don't ask stupid questions. You know what. Or if you don't, Landis and Belichek do. If they didn't tell you, I don't hold out much hope for your career." Her sneer faded. "I couldn't find his damned records. Only knew he'd kept any after he got drunk and started threatening me—as if *he* were in charge. I thought I had them when I took the notebook from his pocket, but it was almost new, just a few days' worth. He'd had another one somewhere. I had to find that."

Jamie whispered, "Why is she talking now?"

"Common trait with Chad—ego," Bel said.

"Iris bought you time with her refusal to let anything change in the house."

"Fat lot of good it did me. All that work for nothing. I should have known Chad wouldn't have hidden anything that well. The first search should have turned up anything he stashed. But I couldn't count on that. I kept thinking maybe the next time, the next thing I checked, I'd find it."

"Until Tuesday."

"Yeah. When the news came about Chad finally getting ready to die, which meant Iris was going to be otherwise occupied—"

"Trying to kill Ally," Maggie growled.

"—and you'd all be frantic in Fairlington, then converging on Chad, giving me time to search again. He said he kept it close to his heart. I figured his house or that other woman's place. Willow's was a breeze. Had it covered the first week after he died. In and out whenever I wanted. Found stuff I can't unsee, but nothing of his.

"Worked through the house methodically. But with Chad failing… Then I thought about that line about his heart again. The jewelry box, in case he was being sentimental. Literal with the underwear drawer— undershirts for covering his heart and shorts because from the time he hit puberty that was the closest thing to his heart. All that crap still there because of Aunt Iris."

"Why under the bed, Rachel?" Danolin asked.

"*Hah,*" Maggie said.

"Because I thought Ally might be like a normal person and have shit under the bed, but of course she didn't. Nothing. I got damned *nothing.*"

"Wouldn't say nothing," Danolin said. "Conspiracy to attempt murder for starters."

"You're nuts. You think I put that crazy bitch up to shooting at Ally, setting off mortar rounds left and right. I wanted to kill the woman myself. Not the first time."

"You were ready to shoot Ally today."

She lifted one shoulder.

EPILOGUE

THE SEARCH THROUGH Chad Northcutt's body cam footage proved frustrating and worthwhile. Frustrating because it was incomplete. Worthwhile because it twice caught incriminating statements, apparently when he thought it was off.

Better, he implicated Dewey Selton in both statements, so he was in custody. It was less clear if Ethan Paulz was involved, although it turned out he had inherited the cabin from a great-uncle. More investigative work to be done there.

Word did trickle out in the Piscattoway County Police Department about the roles played by Susanna Wuertl and Ted Tancroft.

Landis and Belichek talked to each of them. Neither showed any sign of leaving.

It wasn't all rose petals thrown at their feet, but they had support from enough colleagues and superiors. Mark Northcutt Junior made public gestures of support.

He and his parents cut off contact with Iris, while reestablishing connections to other branches of the family.

Rachel's father moved. Not very far, because he continued to support her through the legal process, but no longer in the Northcutt neighborhood.

Iris, of course, had an entirely new address.

Her house, and the one across the street from it, sold to people who didn't know each other.

The homeless woman Danolin forced Terrington to track down identified Iris as the figure in the hoodie after Danolin won her over with a homey interview room none of the rest of homicide recognized.

Iris and Rachel continued to process through the justice system. All concerned expected its apparatus would eventually wrap them up and deliver them to where they belonged.

Any hastening of David Senior's death by his wife, Landis and Belichek gladly left to Piscattoway to sort out.

Ally's mother and father returned to Pittsburgh—separately— where they pursued their individual interests and kept abreast of what the other was doing. They had limited contact with their daughter.

Tanner took her home to meet his family three weeks ago. If there was ever love at first sight, that was it.

And there was no question of him holding them at arm's length. Not if he wanted to be with her.

Ally walked away from the house on Gardington Road, signing it over to the Northcutt family trust, which now meant Mark Junior and his parents. He took the TV and a photo album. The rest was sold, proceeds going to a fund for the children of slain law enforcement.

Ally took only her clothes and the jewelry box. And, of course, the contents of her storage unit.

Jamie insisted Ally move into her house in Fairlington. She said it was a win-win. Her spending a lot of time at Bel's house left her house empty. She got security for the house, Ally got a change of scenery.

ALLY HAD FINISHED a new painting.

Against a green hill, a lone bagpiper just showed over the top of the ridge, the next step of his descent to take him out of view. A less defined figure—yet recognizable as wearing a police uniform—stood at the crest, prepared to follow the piper over.

Every person who first saw it said nothing for the longest time, simply looking.

Ally gave it to an auction to benefit that same charity for the children of law enforcement.

She immediately began another project. It was early. She wasn't talking about it yet, much less showing him.

That was fine. She was painting.

She had rented a studio space a couple miles from Jamie's house—a couple miles toward the more run-down part of Fairlington.

Tanner Landis knocked on the studio door.

"Come in! It's open," she called.

"It shouldn't be." As he entered, he pulled in a deep breath with satisfaction.

She had the tuck between her brows. But from concentration now. He liked it and half wished he hadn't interrupted her.

He loved to watch that tuck when she studied a scene she hoped to capture on a canvas. She'd have wrinkles there someday. They'd be deep and distinctive. He would love them. Because they came when she created. They came from who she was.

The other half of him had no regrets about interrupting and fully appreciated the way her attention came to him.

She chuckled. "I've never known anyone other than a painter to enjoy the smell of a studio the way you do."

"What makes you think I enjoy it?"

"You breathe it in every time you come in here the way some people breathe in the ocean."

He did love it.

It meant she was working.

It meant she was happy.

"I'm almost ready," she told him.

They were driving up to Bedhurst in the Virginia mountains for a weekend celebration of the wedding of J.D.'s law partner to his long-time love. Two people they'd all become almost as attached to as Maggie and J.D. were.

"Uh-huh," he said.

"I am. I just stopped for a moment, because I left my wedding present for Dallas and Evelyn here to finish drying. I'll have to wrap it at J.D.'s when we get there. What do you think?"

It was about a foot square frame with a mist of mountains piling blues and greens on each other under a sky that deepened its blues by contrast to white clouds.

"I love it. They'll love it."

"You always say that."

"They'll smell the mountains."

She turned to him, the painting forgotten.

This man…

Her man.

Since he first sat across from her at a picnic table outside a dive bar? She didn't know, couldn't know. But from here forward, she did know. Absolutely.

"Oh, Tanner. That is wonderful." She kissed him.

He pulled her onto his lap and stroked the inside of her thigh the way that always made her shiver.

"If we're going to make it up there for tonight's events…" he warned.

"Yes, yes. I'm ready. Just let me get my bag."

"I've got it."

In his car, her bag having joined his in the trunk, she caught his thoughtful expression.

"What is it, Tanner?"

"I know we're taking it slow, but Dallas and Evelyn got me thinking. You know, about vows and things. Someday."

Her heart caught.

Someday…

She had a way to go. He had a way to go. They had a way to go.

But they were getting there.

"What about them?" she asked.

"I want you to swear to me that if something happens to me, you won't stick around. You'll get the hell away and live your life."

"In sickness—"

"You've done your time in purgatory and I won't be responsible for more."

"It wouldn't be purgatory staying with you."

"That's what you say now, but you'll get pissed at me again and—"

"That's for sure."

"I want you to swear."

"I swear. If you're incapacitated and I have the first twinge of purgatory, I'll skedaddle."

"I mean this, Theodora Allison. And I'd know. Brain dead or otherwise, I'd know."

"Okay. We'll put it in the vows when we get to that point, just the way you said it. As long as you vow not to let anything happen to you."

The End

To get briefed on upcoming books, as well as other titles and developments, join Patricia McLinn's Readers List and receive her twice monthly free newsletter.

patriciamclinn.com/readers-list

Thank you for reading Tanner and Ally's story in **PREMISE OF INNOCENCE**, *the conclusion of Patricia McLinn's* **Innocence Trilogy** *mystery series. If you like mystery with romance, try Patricia's two cozy mystery series,* **Caught Dead in Wyoming** *and* **Secret Sleuth.** *The former finds a big-city TV reporter recovering from a betrayal that disrupts her career and lands her in a rough western ranching town. Her investigative skills and the talents of a widening circle of friends—and more than friends—are tested with each murder they solve.* **Secret Sleuth** *follows an "author" starting a new life in small-town Kentucky who bonds with fellow rescue dog owners, particularly after they help her get to the bottom of a killing at the local dog park. She has secrets, and that complicates a blossoming relationship with one of the dog owners, an observant ex-cop.*

THE INNOCENCE TRILOGY

PROOF OF INNOCENCE (Book 1)

She's a prosecutor chasing demons. He's wrestling them. Will they find proof of innocence? Or will the demons win?

PRICE OF INNOCENCE (Book 2)

She runs a foundation dedicated to forgiveness. He's a cop running down the guilty to make them pay. If they don't work together, people will die.

You can buy this book and all my others, including print editions and audiobooks, from my online store. I've added direct-to-you buying options to better control how my books reach you, while giving you special bundles, early offers, and exclusive bonuses.

Patricia's Bookstore

shop.patriciamclinn.com

Tanner, Ally, Maggie and Jamie ask if you'll help spread the word about them and The Innocence Trilogy. You have the power to do that in two quick ways:

Recommend the book and the series to your friends and/or the whole wide world on social media. Shouting from rooftops is particu-larly appreciated.

Review the book. Take a few minutes to write an honest review and it can make a huge difference. As you likely know, it's the single best way for your fellow readers to find books they'll enjoy, too.

To me—as an author and a reader—the goal is always to find a good author-reader match. By sharing your reading experience through recommendations and reviews, you become a vital matchmaker. ☺

More mystery from Patricia McLinn

Caught Dead in Wyoming series

SIGN OFF

Divorce a husband, lose a career … grapple with a murder.

LEFT HANGING

Trampled by bulls—an accident? Elizabeth, Mike and friends dig into the world of rodeo.

SHOOT FIRST

For Elizabeth, death hits close to home. She and friends delve into old Wyoming treasures and secrets to save lives.

LAST DITCH

Elizabeth and Mike search after a man in a wheelchair goes missing in dangerous, desolate country.

LOOK LIVE

Elizabeth and friends take on misleading murder with help—and hindrance—from intriguing out-of-towners.

BACK STORY

Murder never dies, but comes back to threaten Elizabeth and team of investigators.

COLD OPEN

Elizabeth's search for a place of her own becomes an open house for murder.

HOT ROLL

One of their own becomes a target—and time is running out.

REACTION SHOT

Sometimes cattle rustlers still get a death sentence.

BODY BRACE

Everything can change … except murder.

CROSS TALK

Prime suspect: The most annoying man in Sherman.

AIR READY

Love and death decisions.

HOLIDAY BULLETS

A Christmas wish with Elizabeth's name on it.

CUE UP

On the trail of murder.

"Colorful characters, intriguing, intelligent mystery, plus the state of Wyoming leaping off every page."

—*Emilie Richards, USA Today bestselling author*

Secret Sleuth series

DEATH ON THE DIVERSION
Final resting place? Deck chair.

DEATH ON TORRID AVENUE
A new love (canine), an ex-cop and a dog park discovery.

DEATH ON BEGUILING WAY
No zen in sight as Sheila untangles a yoga instructor's murder.

DEATH ON COVERT CIRCLE
A supermarket CEO meets his expiration date.

DEATH ON SHADY BRIDGE
A homicide cold case heats up.

DEATH ON CARRION LANE
A reunion for murder in Haines Tavern.

DEATH ON ZIGZAG TRAIL
A spooky legend twists grave matters.

DEATH ON PUZZLE PLACE
Season's greetings: Whodunit?

If you like romantic suspense, you might also try:

Ride the River: Rodeo Knights

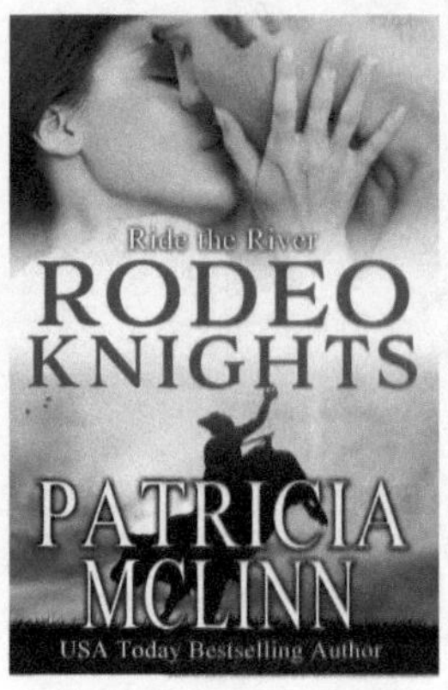

Her rodeo cowboy ex is back … as her prime suspect.

Bardville, Wyoming series

A Stranger in the Family

A Stranger to Love

The Rancher Meets His Match

Explore a complete list of all Patricia's books

patriciamclinn.com/patricias-books

Or get a printable booklist

patriciamclinn.com/patricias-books/printable-booklist

Patricia's Bookstore (buy online directly from Patricia)

shop.patriciamclinn.com

About the author

Patricia McLinn is the USA Today bestselling author of more than 60 published novels cited by readers and reviewers for their wit and vivid characterization. Her books include mysteries, romantic suspense, contemporary romance, historical romance and women's fiction. They have topped bestseller lists and won numerous awards.

She has spoken about writing from London to Melbourne, Australia, to Washington, D.C., including being a guest speaker at the Smithsonian Institution.

McLinn spent more than 20 years as an editor at The Washington Post after stints as a sports writer (Rockford, Ill.) and assistant sports editor (Charlotte, N.C.). She received BA and MSJ degrees from Northwestern University.

Now living in northern Kentucky, McLinn loves to hear from readers through her website and social media.

Visit with Patricia:

Website: patriciamclinn.com

Facebook: facebook.com/PatriciaMcLinn

Pinterest: pinterest.com/patriciamclinn

Instagram: instagram.com/patriciamclinnauthor

Copyright © 2022 Patricia McLinn

Paperback ISBN: 978-1-944126-89-6

Ebook ISBN: 978-1-944126-88-9

www.ingramcontent.com/pod-product-compliance
Lightning Source LLC
Chambersburg PA
CBHW031002190726
48285CB00004BB/1428